PASSION PLAY

"Do you remember the first time we kissed?" Doris said softly to her husband of less than one hour.

The thought of their first passionate embrace brought forth overwhelming desire in him now. Logan took her in his arms and found her warm and enticing.

"Get undressed," she whispered.

With trembling fingers he quickly complied; when he glanced around she was naked. She slid into his arms, soft and beautiful, and in a moment he rolled her back onto the bed. The surge of desire was more than he could control. He gathered her up as his heart pounded like the rush of waves to a stormy shore.

Her sighs were deep and he knew, feeling the warmth of her body, that he would never be lonely again—as long as he could keep the vicious and destructive Lily Berlanger out of their lives . . .

SENSATIONAL MISSISSIPPI SAGA

RIVER OF FORTUNE: THE PASSION   (561, $2.50)
by Arthur Moore

When the beautiful Andrea Berlanger and her beloved Logan leave
their homes to begin a new life together, they discover the true
meaning of life and desire on a Mississippi riverboat and the
great . . . RIVER OF FORTUNE.

RIVER OF FORTUNE: THE PAGANS   (608, $2.50)
by Arthur Moore

When Andrea's life is threatened by her mean and evil stepmother,
Lily Berlanger, Logan realizes that nothing is worth the gamble of
losing the woman he loves and the life of passion and adventure
they share on the great Mississippi River.

RIVER OF FORTUNE: THE PROUD   (665, $2.50)
by Arthur Moore

Logan's dream finally comes true when he becomes the owner of a
magnificent fleet of Mississippi steamers. He hopes for life-long
happiness with the woman he loves, but soon realizes that Lily
Berlanger—his ruthless and scheming rival—will stop at nothing to
see him destroyed!

*Available wherever paperbacks are sold, or order direct from the
Publisher. Send cover price plus 50¢ per copy for mailing and
handling to Zebra Books, 21 East 40th Street, New York, NY
10016. DO NOT SEND CASH!*

RIVER OF FORTUNE
THE PROUD

BY ARTHUR MOORE

ZEBRA BOOKS

KENSINGTON PUBLISHING CORP.

ZEBRA BOOKS

are published by

KENSINGTON PUBLISHING CORP.
21 East 40th Street
New York, N.Y. 10016

Printed in the United States of America

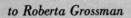

to Roberta Grossman

The devil can cite Scripture for his purpose.
                              Shakespeare

They love truth when it reveals itself,
and they hate it when it reveals themselves.
                              St. Augustine

CHAPTER ONE

It was a misty June morning, and the watery sun touched the smoky brown river with glimmers of gold. Amos Fowler stood in the pilothouse of the *Jewel*, both side windows open despite the chilling wind. He brushed the steamboat past a row of drowned cottonwoods and whistled a lilting tune, one he'd heard in a coffeehouse in New Orleans two nights past. The boat's twin paddle-wheels churned the water to lacy foam, and far off to the right, behind the willows of the bank, a fox barked.

Amos sighted on a huge white stump and when the boat was abreast of it swung the wheel over and made his crossing against the current. He glanced up at the eight-day clock above the fore windows; in five hours they'd nudge into the levee at Vicksburg, the largest town between Natchez and Memphis. They were making good time. Kenneth Fraser had been insistent about time and keeping to the schedules. The new Jeffries-Fraser Line had to keep schedules in order to entice business away from Berlanger-Bryant.

The relief pilot, Ben Townsend, came into the pilot-house three minutes before he was due and lighted a cigar. He was a tall, elegant man in neatly pressed broadcloth, high silk hat, and polished patent-leather boots. A diamond stickpin glittered in his silky cravat.

"The captain tells me we're following a boat—"

Amos nodded. "Yes. She's about ten minutes ahead. You can see her smoke now'n then."

"Ten minutes? Where'd she come from then?" Townsend pulled on calfskin gloves. As he stepped to the wheel, Amos turned it over to him.

"I think she's the *Locust*. She left Natchez before us."

"It must have been a half-hour before."

"Yes. She's dropping back."

"Slowing up? What in the world for? *Locust* is a Berlanger-Bryant boat, isn't she?"

Amos nodded again. He peered ahead. A light rain flurry ruffled the surface of the water and swept on across the woods to larboard; a covey of birds whirled and flitted off into the trees. He was a shorter man than Ben, but just as elegant. A Mississippi River pilot had a certain style to keep up. No river packet company worth its salt would hire a shabby pilot.

"Maybe she's having engine trouble," Ben said and reached to slam down one of the windows. He leaned far to the right, and as they slowly rounded a bend he could make out the smudge of black, drifting smoke. The *Locust* was somewhere under the dark haze, though he couldn't yet see her.

Amos went out and down to the cabin deck, where he found a table and ordered food and coffee, ignoring the glances of the passengers. He was used to being pointed out and stared at.

Capt. Ralph McDade came in from the deck rubbing his sleeves. He pulled out the chair opposite Amos. "With your permission, Mr. Fowler?"

"Yes—please sit down, Captain."

McDade sat and crooked a finger to a steward and

ordered coffee. He combed his dark beard with clawlike fingers. He was dressed in a gray coat with black velvet lapels and silver buttons, not half as fine as Amos' clothes, but then a captain did not earn nearly as much as a pilot. "You figure Frank Pierce will be reelected?"

Amos shrugged. "I don't figure there'll be fewer snags either way. The river don't care."

"Been quiet all morning, seems like."

Amos smiled. "The quieter the better, Ralph, makes less bother all round. How's the missus?"

"She fine, sir. That's the *Locust* up ahead of us, ain't it?"

"I reckon it is." His food came on a tray, and the steward served it deftly and departed.

"Don't care much for him slowin' down like he is. *Locust*'s a B an' B boat and I wouldn't put nothing past 'em."

Amos ate busily, eggs and ham, and shrugged neat shoulders. "There's not a thing they can do t'us, Ralph, except maybe open fire with rifles. You don't look for that, hey?"

The captain grunted. "Maybe not—maybe not. Just the same I'd rather *Jewel* was leadin' them."

Amos nodded, knowing what McDade meant. There were more than whispers about B & B toughs and unexplained damage done to Jeffries-Fraser boats. So far Lily Berlanger hadn't been hauled into court, and Amos suspected the question of jurisdiction had something to do with it. Which court or set of lawmen, along both sides of the long, winding river, could enforce rules—or wanted to? It was a problem most sheriffs and judges turned away from. Others on the river took the law into their own hands.

11

Amos finished the last bite, drank his coffee, and pushed the cup away. "Got to catch forty winks, Ralph." He rose. "See you in a couple hours." He slapped the other's shoulder and went out to climb the steps to his cabin in the texas. Pilots were on duty four hours and off four, around the clock. He glanced upriver once more, saw only a patch of drifting smoke, and unlatched the cabin door. It was Ben Townsend's problem now—if it ever became a problem.

He doffed his clothes and lay on the bunk, closing his eyes. What could one steamboat do to another on the river? Tied up at a landing was another matter; a stationary boat could be a sitting duck, especially at night, if determined men wanted to damage her or set her afire. But they were in midstream, perfectly safe.

He drifted off to sleep, and it seemed the watchman shook him awake a moment later. "It's time, sir—"

Amos looked at his watch. More than three hours had passed. He thanked the man and sat up, running hands through his hair and yawning. He pulled on his pants and looked out. Black as the inside of a stove. He washed, dressed carefully, and entered the pilothouse fifteen minutes later to find Peter Bowmer chatting with Townsend. Bowmer was a pilot, unemployed at the moment, making the trip north to "look at the river." All pilots on the loose customarily rode free, keeping their hands in, always eager to help out should it become necessary. Bowmer was a thick-set, nattily dressed man who greeted Amos toothily and shook hands.

Ben Townsend said, "We're just coming out of Hog Bend, Amos. River's rising a bit. It's more noticeable now—more stuff drifting." He nodded toward the clumps of brush and branches that swept past. Captain

12

McDade had lanterns out, strung along the sides.

Amos peered ahead; the lights of the *Locust* were plainly visible, half a mile or more away. Ben said, "She's been losing speed steadily but holding on like that for an hour."

"Meet any other boats?"

"Two. One was away over, hugging the bank, and I couldn't make her out. T'other was the *Maura*."

Bowmer said, "You figger *Locust*'s in trouble? A floating log could have wrecked one of her buckets."

"Might have," Ben replied, "but she's not acting crippled worth a damn. If a paddlewheel was busted on one side she'd slew around some."

"And she'd have tied up at Somer's place too," Amos said. Somer's was a woodyard just south of Hog Bend, an ideal spot to repair broken paddle buckets. He stared at the distant boat, wondering.

"Well, she hasn't made a signal to us," Ben Townsend said. "And she damn well knows we're following." He struck a match to a cigar and blew smoke. "We'll pass her just above the next island if I'm any judge."

Amos had formed the same opinion. He glanced at the clock and took over the wheel when the hand indicated the time. Bowmer said he was hungry and went down to the boiler deck, but Ben stayed in the pilothouse, curious about *Locust*. As a rule, all the Berlanger-Bryant boats were pushed to the limit because the company was constantly printing notices in the press about speed. Speed was important to some shippers, and they claimed to hold records. The B & B steamboats bragged about being the fastest on the river, and yet here was *Locust* dawdling along like a child on his way to school.

Amos was busy his entire watch, avoiding drifting

13

debris, brush, logs, and an occasional tree, though now and again a log struck the hull a glancing blow and swirled off sluggishly. It was impossible to see every dark log in the black water, despite the lanterns. But there were stretches with no driftwood at all, and he could drink the coffee one of the stewards brought up steaming hot. Ben Townsend went below after an hour, to catch a bit of sleep. *Locust* remained in the same position, neither losing nor gaining.

Soon after Ben came up to take over the wheel again, they ran into several miles of floating brush, and he swore terrible oaths. The danger was that a big log would come booming along under water and hit the boat square and tear out the threshing paddle buckets as Bowmer had suggested. A rising river always set driftwood to floating, and the only cure was to clear it from the banks along the entire length of the Mississippi. But, of course, such a thing was impossible.

Amos slept again, and when he once more took the wheel it was only a short time till dawn. The *Locust* was holding steady, Ben said, but had dropped back a bit. Her lights seemed much brighter, Amos thought.

Ben stayed in the pilothouse again and, as it began to get light, went out to the deck and bawled down for a spyglass. In several moments a steward climbed up with one, and shortly thereafter Captain McDade appeared.

Ben studied the *Locust* through the glass and shook his head. "Nothing untoward about her, Amos. She's just plain slowin' down." He passed the glass to McDade. "See if you can find anything, Ralph."

McDade refocused the glass, chewed his lower lip, and rested the spyglass against the side of the window. "They're lookin' at us, sir," he said after a minute. "Fella

14

in the pilothouse with a glass." He passed the 'scope back to Townsend.

"I see 'im," Townsend grunted.

McDade said, "Less smoke from her stacks. Maybe they short of wood."

Amos shook his head. They'd passed plenty of woodyards. He rang down for reduced speed. It was obvious that *Locust* wasn't going to tie up. Despite her slow speed she had managed to stay ahead of *Jewel*, and she was going to pass the island, less than half a mile ahead.

"If she goes into the channel, she going to be a goddam bottleneck," Captain McDade said. "You think they doing that deliberate?"

"Hard to tell," Ben said. "But if you make a crossing, it might take more time than to foller her through."

Amos nodded and swung the wheel slightly. He still had the option to make a crossing, and it was entirely up to him to do it or not. He was the pilot on duty. But Ben was right. It would probably take more bother to go around than to follow the slow-moving *Locust*.

He glanced at the sky; hardly any overcast, and it was rapidly getting light. Townsend had the glass to his eye. "She's entered the slack water, Amos, and she's slowin' down even more, I think."

In a moment they were in slack water also, and the two boats were hardly a pistol shot apart; the *Locust* was making thin gray smoke and occupying the exact center of the narrow channel. They were close enough to see several dozen people lining the cabin deck guardrails; a few waved, and a handful of rousters were gathering at the stern on the main deck.

"Grin and bear it," McDade said.

15

Ben Townsend folded up the spyglass with a click. "Well, soon's we pass 'em we'll show 'em our heels."

They swung inshore; the *Jewel* was only a pebble's toss from the starboard bank, and there were reefs to larboard and the hind side of the long island that was choked with stunted growth and weeds. Amos knew there was no turning back. He held the wheel tightly, wondering at the action of *Locust*'s pilot. Even if he had orders from Lily Berlanger to slow them up—what in hell would that accomplish?

Then he saw the deckhands remove the aft guards on the *Locust*'s main deck. Ben Townsend saw it too and swore, yanking out the spyglass again.

McDade said, "What the hell're they doing?"

Amos watched in consternation. The deckhands were rapidly shoving logs overboard! They had piled a huge stack there, and, as he stared, they tumbled them over, three, four, five at a time, a lethal logjam that splashed and tumbled, bearing down upon the *Jewel* with the rapid speed of the current.

There was no way to avoid them!

Townsend shouted, and Amos grabbed the bell rope to stop the engines—but too late. The heavy logs hit the turning paddle buckets, thudding and smashing, and the *Jewel* shuddered. Her speed was suddenly cut in half, and the boat slewed; steam whistled through the gauge cocks, and people yelled and screamed on the main deck, not knowing what had happened.

"Sonofabitch!" Townsend yelled, "Sonofabitch! They scuppered us, the bastards! Where the hell is a gun?" He rushed out onto the texas, shouting for someone to fire at the *Locust*.

The engines stopped, but the damage was done. Amos

16

spun the wheel as the *Jewel* drifted. She was helpless, with both paddle wheels out of service. Logs hit the yawing side of the boat with thundering noise and heavy thuds; they scraped along the side and rolled past.

The *Locust*'s chimneys belched black smoke, and she began to draw away as the deckhands put up the stern guards again. Someone on the hurricane deck waved as Ben Townsend swore and shook his fists.

It had taken only a few moments, and the *Jewel* was wrecked, drifting to run aground. She struck in another minute, slamming stern first into the mud, shuddering with the blow. Amos was thrown from the wheel as it spun. He wound up on hands and knees by the rear bench, Captain McDade was also on his stomach on the deck.

Amos sat up and held his head. He should have known *Locust* was up to no good. He should have gone round the island.

He should have.

In her office in St. Louis, Lily Berlanger received a notice stating that the B & B steamboat *Locust* had disabled a Jeffries-Fraser steamboat. It was a brief report containing only three lines of scrawled writing. She went to the door and called for Udell Winter.

Udell was a tall, dry man with gray hair and spectacles. He came into the office, closing the door behind him. "Yes, Lily?"

She waved the paper. "Have you seen this?"

He took it from her and looked at it. "Yes. One of Captain Haynes' clerks brought it not long ago. I believe *Locust* is tied up in front of—"

"Is the clerk still in the building?"

17

He shrugged.

"Go and find him. I want to talk to him."

"But Lily—"

She shouted. "Go and find him!"

Udell hurried out. Lily paced the room. She was a lithe and beautiful woman, dressed in dark blue with a froth of lace at throat and wrists, her dark hair carefully curled and held in place with a jeweled ribbon.

With mounting anger she read the note again. Disabled a Jeffries-Fraser boat! She crumpled the paper and flung it from her. What in the world was Haynes thinking of? He was an idiot!

She turned at the knock, and Udell entered, pushing a thin, mousy-looking man before him. The man had a very pink face with squinty eyes and a wide mouth. He held a wool hat in both hands and stared at her with something like fear in his eyes.

"This is the clerk, Lily. Name of Palmer."

She faced him. "Were you on the *Locust* this trip?"

He nodded, "Yes mum."

"Tell me how the Jeffries boat was disabled."

"Well, we were coming upstream—"

"I know that, you imbecile!" Lily shouted, turned away, and got her breath. "I'm sorry, Mr. Palmer. Start again."

Palmer seemed about to faint. Udell put out an arm and touched his back, and Palmer took a long breath. "We left Natchez about a half-hour before *Jewel*, Mum. When we got to the channel by Royer's Island the cap'n had the men throw over a lot of logs. They smashed the *Jewel*'s paddles, Mum."

Lily stared at him. "Smashed the paddles. Is that all?"

"Yes, Mum. But *Jewel*'s stuck onto the bank."

She looked at Udell. "For how long, a few days?"

He nodded.

She turned away and went to her desk. "Thank you, Mr. Palmer."

Udell opened the door, and Palmer scuttled out. He closed it and leaned against it. "Haynes is an eager captain, Lily."

"He's a fool!" She sat and slapped the desk. "This is the biggest piece of stupidity I've seen in weeks. They'll have that boat repaired in no time. Haynes has accomplished nothing." She swore under her breath. "Not only that, but Jeffries and Fraser will bring a suit against us. They've probably got a hundred witnesses. Get rid of Haynes, Udell. I don't need fools for captains."

"All right. Do you want to see him?"

"Of course not."

"He'll request a hearing—"

"I don't care what he requests. Get rid of him—and his entire crew if they're loyal to him."

"Yes, Lily." He opened the door.

"And Udell—"

He paused.

"Tell Mr. Paddock I want to see him."

He nodded and went out.

CHAPTER TWO

Doris Aiken held fast to the cabin-deck guardrail, her heart pounding as she gazed down at the New Orleans levee. In another few moments she would leave her solitary days behind and enter a new life, an enormously exciting thought! Inside the hour she would be married to Logan Jeffries.

The steamboat *Carrie* had been burning rosin and pitch pine for an hour, darkening the sky with coal-black smoke. The outward-bound flag hung at the jack staff and another on the verge staff astern. Doris watched the procession of barrels and boxes, carried on the sweaty shoulders of a hundred rousters, come to an end as the mate shouted orders. A last hurrying group of passengers streamed across the stageplanks, men with carpet sacks and women with reticules and bandboxes; they rushed up the forecastle companionway as the clattering windlasses ceased and the hatches were slammed down.

The boat trembled like a live thing. Half-naked Negroes hauled in the planks, roaring songs and shouting to others on the levee. Doris looked around as Logan came up beside her, sliding an arm about her waist. He was dressed in gray with a ruffled shirt and snowy cravat, a gray beaver hat on his head at a jaunty angle.

"They'll fire the cannon in a moment," he said. "If

20

you've any parting words for New Orleans, you'd best say them now."

She laughed, clinging to him. It was easily the most wonderful day of her life. She was aboard a Jeffries-Fraser boat with the man she loved, about to start a journey up the river to St. Louis. "I want to say to New Orleans that I expect to be back one day—"

"You will be, many times."

"With you."

His arm pulled her closer, and only the throngs crowding the deck kept him from kissing her. She felt the boat move, and people on either side along the rails began to cheer. The *Carrie* backed into the stream as cannons boomed. Doris put both hands over her ears and leaned against Logan. The crew massed on the forecastle yelled, and backing bells clanged. The boat slowed and paused; it shuddered, then surged forward as the paddle buckets reversed and beat the brown Mississippi to foam. Black smoke roiled, curling out behind them like a huge live snake, its teeth firmly clamped about the two chimneys. The flags snapped, and Doris found herself shouting good-byes to nameless faces on the levee as Logan grinned at her. They were off!

The crowd milled about the deck, cheering and laughing; women waved parasols and handkerchiefs, and Doris stood with misting eyes as the city receded. More than a year had passed since she'd gone out of the little house in Defiance and found Logan badly shot, lying on the wet ground. So much had happened in that time. How incredible that nothing in her life had been the same since she'd stepped from that house.

The ponderous wheel beat of the *Carrie* hurled billows of mud-yellow water, wildly rocking the small boats nearby as the steamboat glided majestically past. It was a fine spring day with hardly a cloud in the sky, and Doris wanted it never to end. She took Logan's arm, and they went along the deck and inside to the main saloon, the resplendent long tunnel, the social hall and dining room of every steamboat.

Kenneth Fraser, correct and proper in a black frock coat, pale yellow shirt, and gray trousers, met them at the door. "There you are! I was about to have you sent for. It's not the best luck for bride and groom to be parading together just before the ceremony, you know."

"We wanted to see the boat off," Doris said.

"Lady Luck will make an exception in this case," Logan promised.

Fraser nodded. "Yes, perhaps she was busy at the tables and didn't notice. I've known her to be remiss before." He glanced around the busy saloon. "Ira Heinz got us a preacher all right, and I've engaged him. He turned out to be a Baptist."

"No objections," Logan said, "so long as he's ordained and legal."

"Oh, he's legal all right. I've seen his credentials. And I've warned him we want no sermon, just the service. Some of these traveling jacklegs are windbags."

"I think I'd like to change," Doris said.

The saloon was rapidly filling with hungry passengers. Waiters scurried from table to table, bringing chairs and seating the ladies. Logan asked, "Where will the ceremony be held?"

"In Ira's cabin." Fraser smiled at them. "Is anyone nervous?"

Logan extended a shaking hand. "Not at all."

They laughed, and Fraser said, "It'll soon be over—

the wedding, I mean." He patted Doris' hand. "Are you certain, my dear, that you want to subject yourself to this man for all eternity?"

"More than anything."

Fraser pretended to sigh deeply. He shook his head as if unable to comprehend and then took her hand and placed it firmly on his arm. "If that's the case, Miss Aiken, I will escort you to your stateroom for your last-minute preparations. Logan, we'll meet you presently on the upper deck."

Logan went outside to the promenade and walked the deck, hands in his pockets. He was a big, broad-shouldered man, with the catlike grace of the natural athlete. His hair was brown, worn long so that it touched his collar, and his eyes had the direct gaze of one very sure of himself. He and Kenneth Fraser owned six steamboats and vied very strongly with Berlanger-Bryant for the trade of the three mighty rivers.

Berlanger-Bryant.

He had a terrible score to settle with Lily Berlanger. Doris had once saved his life when a killer, hired by Lily, had come after him with several others.

But he could not allow himself to dwell upon that this day. He must banish Lily and all thoughts of her—until tomorrow. This was his wedding day, and all else must take a back seat.

Gripping the guardrail, he stared down into the saffron water and looked across to the far shore, lined by chinaberry trees; he could see men and wagons moving along the distant road of some quiet sugar plantation. Once he finished the business with Lily, then he and Doris would settle down to a peaceful— He caught himself up short. He *must* put Lily behind him.

Turning resolutely, he ran up the ladder to the hurricane deck and strolled along the texas cabin. Lily Berlanger tended to solve her problems with violence. He had bought a house in St. Louis and hired two men, butler and driver, both experts with weapons. Lily would not catch him asleep—

He swore and turned about, slapping the rail. Forget Lily! Capt. Ira Heinz waved to him, and he walked to the front of the texas. Ira's was the large fore cabin, directly beneath the two tall chimneys. Ira, a big, jovial man, held the door for him and clapped his back. "The lamb has arrived for the slaughter."

"Some lamb," Fraser said.

It was a square and very spartan room with few decorations. A thin carpet covered part of the plank floor; a few framed pictures graced the walls alongside a pair of crossed flags. He saw that Doris had changed her gown. It was light blue with false sleeves that narrowed at the shoulders and had ruffles at the knees. She looked positively radiant. She had purchased the gown in New Orleans especially for the occasion, and he'd never seen her wearing it. She was beautiful, and as he stared at her he became conscious that Ira Heinz was nudging him.

"What?"

Ira said, "I want you t'meet the preacher. This here's Reverend Hugo Grumsky."

Logan moved the beaver hat and nodded. "Hello, Mr. Grumsky." Grumsky was a tall, skinny man with gray sideburns and a long, red nose. A pair of gold-rimmed glasses perched halfway along his nose and the man ducked his head to see over them.

24

"Pleased to meet you, sir," Grumsky said in a reedy voice.

Ira asked in a hoarse whisper, "Have you got the ring?"

Logan nodded, patting his waistcoat pocket. He had purchased the ring the day Doris' divorce had become final—the day she'd received the letter of notification. He moved near the window at Grumsky's request.

"Just stand there if you will, Mr. Jeffries," Grumsky beckoned. "If the bride'll come over here. You just stand there, please. Now, who's the best man?"

"I have that title," Fraser said.

Grumsky placed him, took a black-bound, well-worn Bible from under his arm and opened it to a mark. He cleared his throat, gave them both a look, and began to read.

Logan gazed at Doris' profile and clasped her hand tightly. Her eyes were closed as she listened intently, and it was all he could do to keep from sliding an arm about her and pulling her close. Gravely he placed the ring upon her finger at Grumsky's direction and kissed her as the brief ceremony came to an end. She clung to him, and he breathed in the perfume of her and felt at peace. This was the woman he wanted.

Reluctantly he stepped back as Fraser and Ira pulled at him, shook his hand, and wished Doris every happiness. Grumsky had papers for them to sign; then Fraser poured the preacher a drink, handed him an envelope, and rushed him to the door.

Ira Heinz opened a cabinet and took out bottles and glasses, pushing aside the bottle Fraser had used. "We never give preachers good whiskey." He pressed a glass

25

into each hand, went around filling them, and proposed a toast to the new bride and groom. "May you never have a sad day, and may the good Lord bless all your dreams."

"And the devil take Lily Berlanger," Fraser added.

Ira shook his head. "No talk of Lily here on this day. This here's a blessed occasion and she's a blasphemy." He filled Fraser's glass again, glaring at him. "You want to spoil it all?"

Fraser ignored him. "Surely the groom has something to say?"

Logan smiled and touched his glass to hers. "If I knew how to express myself properly maybe I would—" He looked round at them. "All I can say is that I'm damned lucky to be here with a beautiful wife and good friends."

"I thought you couldn't talk," Ira said. "That sounded just fine, for a tongue-tied man."

Doris gazed at him over the rim of her glass. Of all the men she had ever known, Logan was the only one in command of himself—even when she'd found him lying in the rain, bleeding from a wound, and brought him inside the house, he'd understood instantly and though in terrible pain had tried to do something about his state. Looking at him now it was hard to recall how he'd seemed that night—a stranger, hurt and in deadly danger. She moved close and took his arm, handing the empty glass to Fraser.

Fraser said, "I promised you two supper—"

"They don't want no supper," Ira protested.

"They're civilized," Fraser said. "Come along. I've spoken to the cook, and he has a surprise for you."

Doris tightened her arm about his. Logan said, "Very well, let's have supper."

Fraser had indeed spoken to the cook, and to the

stewards. There was iced champagne waiting in silver buckets at the table, and a beautiful display of roses. Doris was astonished, as Logan seated her, for she had expected nothing at all. A steward hurried to fill her glass and went round to fill them all as they gathered about the table. Then Fraser gave them another toast, "To happiness, forever and forever and forever—"

They sat, and Logan pressed her hand. Fraser said, "The cook has prepared a Creole gumbo—chopped onions, tomatoes, crabs, oysters, shrimp, served with rice. He assures me it will be perfect, because I've promised to throw him overboard if it isn't."

Doris found herself laughing. What a perfect day!

They retired to the stateroom reserved as a bridal suite. It was a fine, nearly square room with a turkey carpet, a large double bed, and furniture stained and varnished almost black. There were floral pictures on the walls and life preservers under the bed. There was also a large basket of fruit on the dresser, along with two bottles of French wine.

She exclaimed over the basket and examined the wine labels, trying to read the fancy script, and Logan gazed at her with a feeling of joy, realizing that he'd not known such an affection for years. When she turned to him, her face was alive, eyes shining, and he took her in his arms, enfolding her, and everything was blotted out. Her flesh was warm, enticing, and his hands moved over her shoulders as their lips met. He felt her body against his, taut and expectant. For a moment he felt he could not breathe for love of her.

Doris turned in his arms, whispering for him to undo the hooks. He found them somehow and pushed the dress

27

off her pale shoulders, running his hands into the folds. It had a silky feel, like her skin, and she moved so that one hand captured a warm breast.

She said softly, "Do you remember the first time you kissed me?"

"Of course. It was in the Seven Oaks."

"No."

He turned her about and kissed her again. "Where was it?"

"While we were leaving Defiance in the old buggy."

"Oh yes, now I remember." He dropped the dress onto a chair, and she sat on the bed. He turned the lamp very low and sat beside her; the light flickered in her dark eyes, and his fingers traced the curve of her cheek. The room was still, and he could hear his own heartbeat.

She said very softly, "Get undressed—"

He slid out of the coat and tossed it to the chair. He pulled off his boots with fingers that trembled. When he glanced around she was naked. She slid into his arms, silken and delightful, and in a moment he rolled her back onto the bed, the surge of desire more than he could control. He gathered her up as his heart pounded, like the rush of waves to a stormy shore.

Her sighs were of deep content as they came together, and he knew, feeling the warmth of her arms, that he would never be lonely again.

CHAPTER THREE

Ben Townsend stumbled into the pilothouse without his fine hat. He moaned and leaned on the window sill. "We're damned well aground, Amos. What the hell d'we do now?"

Amos got up wearily and sat on the bench. "I was a stupid fool, Ben—"

Captain McDade brushed himself off. "No you wasn't, sir."

"For crissakes!" Ben said. "No you weren't. I would have gone up the channel same as you did—anybody would have. You're not a damned mind reader!"

"Well, I should have guessed."

"Hellsfire! I bet that's never happened on the river before." Ben leaned out the window. "Charlie's got them pulling out the logs already. He don't waste no time."

Charlie was the mate. McDade hurried down the ladder to the main deck, and Amos watched him go, glum and defeated. For a pilot to sit in a wrecked steamboat was almost worse than a soul expelled from heaven. Especially if he had wrecked the boat. Of course an inquiry wouldn't blame him—as Ben said. It wasn't really his fault; only he should have been suspicious.

He gazed upriver. The *Locust*'s smoke had almost disappeared, and the boat had rounded the next bend.

Somebody had planned this carefully to arrive at the slack-water channel close ahead of time. A frustrated rage ate at his insides, but he kept it in check. There was nothing to be gained by shouting and carrying on. Ralph McDade was a capable master. He and the mate would have the damage assessed and begin repairs quickly. Depending on the amount of damage, they'd probably fix the paddles so they could limp to the next boatyard.

With Ben Townsend he went out and down to the main deck. Groups of men were busy on both sides of the boat. He and Ben joined the group clustered about the starboard wheelhouse where Captain McDade was talking with the carpenters. They had opened up the housing and hung several lanterns inside, and Amos saw the destruction caused by the floating logs. At least four buckets were smashed into matchsticks, and the housing at the waterline was ripped and shattered.

Ben muttered and growled, seeming to take the affair personally. Amos waited till Ralph McDade finished with the workmen, then they climbed to the cabin deck together. McDade said, "We'll be here a few days, sir. Can't do 'er any faster."

"Sorry I didn't anticipate it, Ralph."

"Jesus, who the hell would figger them to do a thing like that?" Ralph wadded his big fist and shook it. "We've got them bastards to rights. Mr. Fraser'll sue the goddam britches off that fuckin' Lily Berlanger."

The passengers were gathered in the saloon, and Captain McDade stepped up on a chair, asking them to be quiet. "Sorry about this, ladies and gennelmun, but it weren't nothing we could avoid. That damned Berlanger boat throwed a load of logs in the channel as deliberate as

30

blowin' your nose." He pointed at them. "You all are suffering because of what Berlanger done, and I hope you tell it around to ever'one you see."

Someone asked how long they'd be stranded, and McDade said, "They smashed both our paddlewheels, so it'll be a day'r so. I'm sorry, but we doing the best we can." He stepped down.

Amos went out to the deck, his hands in his pockets. Taking out a thin cigar, he ran a match along the rough painted metal of the guard strap and narrowed his eyes at the sudden burst of flame. He lit the cigar and tossed the match into the murky water overside. A fog was stealing upriver, and long, snaky fingers writhed among the willows of the bank. There had been other incidents against Jeffries-Fraser. Was this the opening act of an offensive by Berlanger?" He hoped not.

In the middle of the afternoon a steamboat came into the channel, and Ben Townsend shouted from the pilothouse. "It's the *Carrie!*"

The *Carrie* was a Jeffries-Fraser boat, as everyone knew; the passengers crowded the rails, shouting and waving as the newcomer slowed and came to a landing alongside *Jewel*. Amos was relieved to see the broad figure of Logan Jeffries on the hurricane deck. Now everything would be all right.

Logan was dismayed at the sight of the wounded *Jewel*. He could see only one side of the boat, and not until he ran down the ladders and went ashore to run along the bank to the *Jewel* did he realize that both paddlewheels were smashed.

He went across the planks and met Captain McDade on

31

the foredeck. "What happened to you?"

McDade explained in terse sentences, and partway along his explanation they were joined by the pilots, Amos Fowler and Ben Townsend, who corroborated the entire story. Ben had the spyglass to his eye, he said, and had a good close-up view of the logs being tumbled over into the stream.

"Absolutely deliberate!" Ben said with heat. "They wanted to wreck us, and they did."

Logan listened to everything that was said. He went to each wheelhouse and watched the men at work; everything that could be done was being hurried along.

They would transfer the passengers and some of the cargo to the *Carrie*, he told the two captains. Captain McDade would then finish the repairs as best he could, resume the journey upriver, and stop at Vicksburg, where the steamboat would be put into first-class shape again.

McDade had a five-page report ready, detailing the outrageous crime and the damage to the *Jewel*. It was signed by himself and the two pilots. Logan took it along with him to give to Fraser. A suit would be filed, he assured them.

The transfer of goods and passengers took several hours, and it was getting dark when the *Carrie* finally backed from the bank with a clanging of bells and headed upriver. Logan stood on the hurricane deck with Doris, waving to the *Jewel*'s crew. At least with the passengers gone McDade's problems were drastically reduced.

The *Carrie* was overcrowded, and it became necessary to separate men and wives, to use the available space more efficiently. He and Doris gave up the large suite and

32

moved into Captain Heinz's cabin in the texas. Heinz moved in with one of the other officers.

Doris was fearful for the future. "I've heard them talking in the saloon. Does this mean the start of something worse?"

"I certainly hope not. What happened to *Jewel* is a damned nuisance, but it's trivial in the long run. I can't imagine Lily actually ordering such a thing."

"There have been other incidents—"

He smiled at her. "Yes, that's right. I think the enmity of the higher-ups must filter down to the rank and file. Kenneth and I have talked about it several times. We think Lily would cheerfully blow up one of our steamboats, but she'd hesitate merely to scratch one. And *Jewel*'s problem is really only a scratch."

She looked at him with apprehension. "Then you think—what?"

"I think that Lily may well be planning something sinister against us, and I wish to hell I knew what it was."

On the journey to St. Louis, Logan spent several hours each day in the pilothouse, the privilege of an owner. The pilots, lords of the river, could extend invitations as they pleased, and an invitation to mount to the pilothouse was considered an honor. Logan was as good a pilot as most, though without a license, and since he could hire and fire—at the journey's end—no pilot was foolish enough to exclude him.

He and Doris had planned to take a ship to Europe for their honeymoon, but Kenneth Fraser had prevailed upon them to come north to St. Louis instead. Logan was needed as a troubleshooter. In Fraser's opinion critical times were ahead.

In the privacy of their stateroom, Doris had misgivings. "The closer we get to St. Louis, the more I worry—"

"You know I can't run away from this fight with Lily." He sat her on the bed, and she bowed her shoulders, looking down at her hands. She had known of the bitter feud long before she'd hoped to marry Logan, and she knew he would never give it up till Lily was destroyed. But all the same she dreaded the time when he'd go off to battle—and she knew it would come, and probably very soon.

She said, "You've told me that Lily is a killer." The words came haltingly as she recalled that Lily had ordered the death of Logan's first wife, Andrea. Logan believed that, at any rate.

He sat beside her, sliding arms about her shoulders. "Yes, she's dangerous, but so am I. It's not all on her side."

She fought back her feelings, trying to make her voice sound natural. "It's not Lily I fear, it's the men she'll hire. You won't know who they are."

That was damnably true, of course. She had a way of putting her finger on the exact spot; it was the thing that had been in the back of his mind for days, like an old shoe worried by a dog, left to moulder. It was impossible for Lily, in her lofty position of power, to kill with her own hands. She had to hire her assassins, maybe by the dozen. He would never know if the man who carried his baggage off the steamboat at the St. Louis levee was not a killer hired by her. But the thought made him wary. He'd look at everyone more carefully, and it might be sound policy to hire a bodyguard. Certainly Doris would approve.

He said, "Several men have tried to kill me and not succeeded, as you well know."

She forced a smile and kissed his cheek. "I know you're bulletproof, up to a point. But I'd really like you to wear plate armor like the old knights used to do."

He laughed at the mental picture. "If I fell overboard I'd sink to the bottom!"

"I'd rescue you."

He hugged her. "Let's go for a turn about the deck."

When they reached St. Louis and tied up late in the day, Neil Barnes, the Jeffries-Fraser manager, was waiting on the levee. He came aboard as soon as the stageplanks were put down, two husky men at his back. He was overweight and nearsighted; his coat strained to hold him in, and his pink face was round as a moon. When he took off his hat, white hair blew about his face.

He embraced Doris at once, "I wish you happiness—" He shook hands with Logan. "Congratulations, you don't deserve her, of course."

They gathered in the main saloon as the other passengers hurried out, and Ira Heinz ordered a table cleared for them. The two husky men took up stations nearby, staring at everyone, hands in their pockets. Barnes leaned toward Fraser. "I never go anywhere without them. I advise you to do the same. Tell me about *Jewel.*"

He had heard the news on the telegraph. Logan related the details quickly, and Fraser offered comments; Barnes sipped coffee and nodded, then glanced through Ira's report.

35

"*Locust* is captained by a man named Dan Haynes," Barnes said. "I hear he's over-eager, and I'll lay you any odds that Lily gives him the sack. That's not her way."

"Not her way!" Ira said in surprise. "Of course it's her way. She'd smash every one of our boats!"

Barnes shrugged. "I mean she wouldn't wreck paddle-wheels—she'd kill everyone on the damned boat."

Fraser agreed, and Doris gazed at them all with a heavy heart. They were not men to exaggerate, and what she knew of Lily was fearsome. The immediate future promised to be very cloudy.

Neil Barnes rose, saying he wanted to hear about the cargo Ira Heinz had brought upriver, and he and the captain went to the boat's office. Doris sipped coffee and listened patiently as Fraser and Logan discussed business at the table. The boat was nearly deserted, save for the crew and the rousters who were busy unloading the decks and holds. The late, slanting sunlight came filtering in the skylights, and there were a half-dozen large lanterns still lighted along the tables. She was facing Fraser, and she thought he had aged a good deal in the year she'd known him. His hair was more gray and his face more lined. He had retired completely from the gambling trade, and she'd heard him say that it was as well since his eyes were beginning to lose their sharpness and his fingers their skill. He was not up to the constant and eternal practice. Now he was happy to devote his time to administrative details, and their company was doing well. Not as well by far as Berlanger-Bryant, but making profits.

When they had finished talking, Logan suggested Fraser come along with them to the new house.

36

"No, I'll go back to the hotel. Newlyweds shouldn't be intruded upon. Don't you know any of the rules?" He rose and took his hat.

Logan laughed, and she smiled at him, thinking how young he looked beside Fraser. Logan got to his feet, pushing the chair back. "I'll go find a carriage—"

Neil Barnes came in the door, hearing Logan's remark, and said, "Wait a moment, Logan." He beckoned one of the two husky bodyguards. "This is Tom Houdek. Tom, I want you to find a carriage for Mr. and Mrs. Jeffries, then go along with them to—"

"That's not necessary, Neil!"

Fraser asked, "Are you armed, Logan?"

"No, of course not."

Barnes moved his head toward the door, and Houdek strode away at once. Fraser shook his head at Logan. "You know Lily better than any of us. Why is it you have less respect for her claws?"

Logan shrugged. "She doesn't know we're in town."

"She might. This is her town and you're her number-one enemy."

Logan said, "I'm not careless. I know what Lily is capable of. I'll walk on eggshells, believe me."

"Then you'd best get yourself a pistol."

"I will. I hear she's leaving, is that true?"

Barnes said, "She's going to Washington, according to the papers."

"That makes it worse," Fraser said ominously. "She can plead innocence when her paid killers gun you down."

Logan made a face. "When you two get through shooting me, can we get along home?"

37

"I hate funerals," Fraser remarked. "From now on I want you to go armed, and I'd prefer you get a bodyguard." He tapped Logan's broad chest. "And don't form any habits."

"You're a mother hen," Logan said.

Houdek was back in ten minutes with a closed carriage. He supervised the loading of the luggage and nodded to Logan that all was ready. They said brief farewells, and Logan handed Doris into the coach. Houdek climbed up beside the driver, and they clattered off across the cobblestones of the levee to the street.

Fraser and Barnes were right, of course. He must take no chances at all; Lily would do away with him with no more compunction than she'd feel stepping on an ant. He saw Doris watching him and took her hand. Her fingers curled about his, and she said, "Why did you decide for us to live here in St. Louis?"

"Because it's the center of our business."

"Kenneth is afraid of Lily, isn't he?"

"He knows how ruthless she is, and so do I. But Lily cannot break all the rules without paying some price. It's not at all her way. One day I'll bring her to justice."

"I think I'm afraid of her too—"

"I don't want you to be. I'll take every precaution for you and for myself. Would you rather live in New Orleans?"

"I'll live anywhere you want to be."

He kissed her. "Then we'll stay here, and Lily will never touch us—" He did not tell her that geography had little to do with it. Lily could attack them anywhere if she wanted to pay enough. He thought it very unlikely, however, that Lily would ever attack Doris, no matter the

38

opportunity. Not after Andrea's death. Lily was not that stupid.

But she well might send men after him.

CHAPTER FOUR

When Howard Paddock arrived, Lily locked the door of her office, and they took chairs by one of the windows. Paddock was a big man, slightly gray and paunchy, but well dressed in a brown suit and flowered waistcoat, across which was draped a gold watch chain. He fiddled with the chain and watched her with bright eyes. His big nose turned this way and that as if sniffing the air; he was a man always on the lookout for advantage.

"I want to talk about Logan Jeffries," Lily said, with an eye to his expression. She had learned that frequently Paddock's quick eyes manifested more clearly stated opinions that did his words.

She could see that she had startled him, though he only nodded. The fingers at his watch chain were still for a moment. He said, "You mean Logan or his company?"

"I mean Logan. If Logan is—somehow disposed of—then Fraser will retire. I'm sure of it. He's getting on. At any rate we could deal with him alone easily."

"I see." There was curiosity in his eyes. "I've always wondered about your hate for him. What is it, Lily?"

Her eyes veiled. "I don't hate him. I dislike him for a great many things, but mostly in a business sense. I don't allow my emotions to guide me."

Paddock kept himself from smiling. To his mind no

40

one in the world could say a thing like that, least of all Lily Berlanger. "No, of course not," he said, "God willing. But Jeffries-Fraser is no more account to us than a dozen others. By the way, I heard about what happened to *Jewel*. Rather stupid, wasn't it?"

"Exactly. And I've sacked the captain. Fraser will retaliate with a lawsuit, of course—"

"And we'll be able to blame the event on Captain Haynes."

"Yes, of course. The suit will go nowhere." Lily drummed her fingers on the chair arm. "I'm going east to Washington very soon. I received a letter only today from Sam Beckhart. I wish you could come along with me—"

Paddock nodded. Such a thing was impossible, of course. His presence in Lily's entourage would insure defeat for all their hopes. He was a silent and limited partner in Berlanger-Bryant for that reason. It was a source of great frustration to him that it was necessary for him to remain in the background, but the rewards would be great, and he was a man who revered and respected gold.

He said, "What about Logan? What did you have in mind for him?"

Lily smiled. She was a beautiful woman, and her words, coupled with the smile, chilled his blood for an instant. "Oblivion," she said. "It would give me the greatest pleasure when I return from the East to hear that he had been laid to rest. Whatever it costs."

"That's very definite, Lily. Very definite indeed."

"You and I don't have to mince words, Howard."

He sniffed and gazed at her with one brow raised. "But it's up to me, is that it?"

41

She rose from the chair, went across the room, and returned with a bottle and two glasses. It was a bottle of red wine, he saw with surprise. The cork had already been pulled, and she twisted it out with two fingers, put the glasses on a side table, and poured. She handed him one with a smile. He looked at it, red as blood. She raised her glass to him and sipped. Paddock drank; it had an odd, rather dusty taste, and he smiled and sipped again.

She sat and balanced the glass on the chair arm. "Logan is not an easy man to deal with. You know that as well as I do, but I have great faith in you, Howard."

"Something occurs to me, of course."

"Yes?" Her brows climbed.

"He'll know, if we make an attempt on him, who it comes from." He drank more of the wine and looked at the bottle.

"Not necessarily."

He sniffed. "Oh yes, I think so. Logan is not stupid, you know. He wasn't stupid as a boy, and I'm sure he's learned a thing or two along the way. It will take a crew to handle him."

"Then get a crew."

Paddock finished his glass and sighed. "You make it sound easy, Lily, my dear. It won't be easy, and it could very likely be damned dangerous and costly."

She frowned. "Don't try my patience, Howard. You can manage this very well, danger or no danger. As you said, if Logan suspects anyone it will be me, not you." She reached for his empty glass and refilled it."

He took it solemnly. What she said was mostly true. Logan could have no good reason to suspect him. He'd made no move against Logan since the day Logan had come to his office in Cairo many years ago. But that was all forgotten, he was sure. He'd made a move against Dutch, Logan's father, but even Dutch didn't realize who had attacked him—or he'd have shown up to do something about it long ago.

Of course, Lily would be away in the East, safe and sound. He asked, "How long will you be gone?"

"I have no idea. As long as it takes, I'm sure. Maybe a few weeks, more likely a month."

"What about Fraser?"

She shrugged. "I don't care about Fraser. He'll fold up when Logan's gone."

"Have you heard that Logan's married again?"

"It was in the papers." She tipped up her glass and rose, looking at him. "I depend on you, Howard—"

He nodded, finished the second glass, and stood, still wondering why she wanted Logan dead. There was something she was not telling, he was positive. Maybe something that had to do with Andrea. A long time ago. Lily could hold a grudge forever.

He took his leave and went down the steps to the street in deep thought. As he'd said, it might take a crew to dispose of Logan Jeffries. Logan was quick as a cat, a dead shot, and even bigger than his father. Dutch Jeffries was still a legend along the river, the most feared brawler of them all.

He hated the idea that Logan might discover who had sent a killer after him. Paddock considered himself a careful man, not a particularly brave one.

Where in hell would he find such a crew?

He got into his carriage and drove to his home, a fine brick house with a view of the river; he had bought it when he had divested himself of his properties in Cairo and come to St. Louis to live. His connections with the

43

shady characters who traded at night along the rivers were raveling. He no longer bought and sold clandestine cargoes, but there were a few old friends. One of them should be able to help.

But he would have to travel to Cairo.

It was an annoyance, of course, to be doing Lily's dirty laundry, but it was part of the price he paid for being an underling. It was not a position he had intended, not one he had anticipated in any way, but he had discovered that when one worked in Lily's firm one worked for Lily, no matter what one's title. He had thought himself an equal partner, at least in the matter of the contracts to be gotten through Sen. Sam Beckhart, but even that was not so.

It rankled him a very great deal. But he could see no way to change it. If he went to Lily and made an issue of the matter, he would probably lose. She was in the catbird seat, a ruthless and jealous woman. He would have to discover a way through guile to get what he wanted. He wanted money and power. He wanted the things Lily had.

And he would have to be very goddamned careful how he went about it. Lily tended to kill off her opposition.

She had had Hiram Bryant killed, for instance, and gathered up the reins of the company as she stepped over his body. She had tried to have Logan Jeffries killed once before, and the hired killer had not succeeded—had been killed by Jeffries, in fact.

Why was she so insistent about him?

It occurred to Paddock, as he neared the house, that perhaps it had to do with something in Logan's early life, before Andrea. Certainly Lily had no idea of eliminating all business opposition! That was unthinkable.

It also occurred to him that whatever it was in Logan's past that made Lily take such a deadly step might be something useful to himself. Paddock smiled at the thought. An advantage, a lever to use against Lily might be the most important thing in his life!

Who was close to Lily—close enough to know?

Only two men: Paige Robinson and Udell Winter.

And of the two, he doubted that Paige Robinson was the one. Robinson lived in New Orleans, and he and Lily met only at intervals. She saw Udell every day and had for a great many years, since she had lived in Chadwick with old Jacob Berlanger.

Paddock thought about Udell. It would probably not be possible to subvert him from Lily by piecemeal methods. It would have to be all or nothing. He sighed. That probably meant a great deal of money. Udell would have to move from St. Louis—if he divulged Lily's secrets—and take up residence in another state, with enough money to see him through the rest of his life. Unless Udell had a great weakness. Maybe there was something. Paddock scratched his chin.

But maybe he would spend a fortune and get nothing. What if Udell knew nothing? Was that likely?

Nothing was easy. He swore and looked up as the carriage wheels grated on crushed rock as it went up the drive. It stopped before the house, and the driver jumped down and lowered the iron steps and opened the carriage door. Paddock got out slowly, nodded absently to the driver, and went up the steps. The door opened, and Josine Pike smiled at him.

She was a girl from a touring show company that had played St. Louis the year before. She was blond and round-faced and had a bosomy figure, and though she

45

claimed to have gone through five grades in elementary school, he doubted it. She could add and subtract well enough, but could barely read and write—not that he cared a fig. Her education was not his interest. He had met her through the local theater manager and had made her a sound business proposition. "Leave the touring company and keep house for me. I will pay you double what you earn in the company, and buy you clothes besides."

It was the best offer Josine had received that winter. She was already aware that her future in the theater was very limited and would end when she lost her looks. She thought it over for several hours and accepted. With any luck at all Paddock would marry her.

He did not tell her that she was the fifth such girl to have come to his home in the same way.

She was wearing a pale green dress, one of a half-dozen he had bought for her recently; he grunted as she kissed his cheek and closed the door. "I'm glad you're home, honey," she told him. "I was lonesome. You want a drink?"

He shook his head, heading for the study. She followed, relating the problem she'd been having with the cook, a woman who absolutely refused to change her mind about anything, no matter how ridiculous her stand. She sat in a chair opposite Paddock, still talking, until he growled at her.

He changed his mind. "Bring me a drink—anything, it doesn't matter."

Surely Udell had a weakness; he gazed at the retreating figure of Josine, admiring the swing of her backside. He had met Udell's wife once or twice, a scrawny, bitter-looking woman, if he recalled her correctly. With a

46

woman like that as wife, Udell might very well be interested in something willowy and lovely. . . .

The more he thought about it, the more positive he felt.

But how to broach the subject? He'd have to get Udell aside—after Lily left for the East. That would do it. He'd take Udell to the most private club in the city, feed him a fine dinner, and have a nice chat about the future. He'd feel Udell out. Maybe it wouldn't even be necessary to invest in a girl. You could never be sure about a man like Udell Winter. He might jump at the idea of a cash settlement in exchange for information, and he might jump up and stalk out.

Paddock accepted the glass Josine handed him and leaned back to sip it. Whiskey. He'd really be taking very few risks with Udell, even doing as he planned. He could always swear to Lily—if it came to that—that Udell had completely misunderstood him.

Josine said, "D'you like my hair this way, dearie?"

He glanced at her and nodded. "It's fine." What the hell had she done, cut it short? He watched as she turned this way and that. She had all the taste of a coal heaver. It was much too short and done up with funny little ringlets. He smiled. "Yes, it's very nice."

He wondered where Logan was. Somewhere on the river, probably. One of his first moves would be to find out. And probably the best way would be to hire a detective to track him down and make a several-week surveillance report. He'd need the information sooner or later.

Josine crowded up against him on the settee. He noticed then that she'd unfastened her bodice and was half hanging out of the dress. Paddock put the drink

47

down and pulled her onto his lap as she giggled. She wanted attention. All right, he'd give her attention. With a quick deft move he slid one hand under her nearly bare breasts and pushed the dress down with the other. In seconds she was naked to the waist, and he was kissing the bare nipples as she laughed, kicking her feet in the air.

His hand swept up between her legs, and he rolled her onto her back and pushed between her knees.

From the doorway behind them, cook's voice began, "Supper's ready—" She gasped and fled.

Paddock said, "Shit."

CHAPTER FIVE

Lily made elaborate preparations for her train trip to Washington City. She would leave Udell Winter in charge, with full powers to execute most business—there was the telegraph to connect them in cases of absolute necessity. Over the years she had learned to trust him; he had a good grasp of what his province was and what must be discussed with her. There was little, she thought, that would arise during her absence of such import it could not wait.

She decided to take with her three people: Dennis Foran, a secretary; Tony Burke, a bodyguard; and Pauline Behr, a copyist. Foran was well recommended by his superior. Lily called him into her office and looked him over, asking a number of questions. He was married, a not bad-looking man of about thirty-five, she thought, and knew his place, according to the office manager. She was particular about Foran, since she'd be working closely with him. She found him polite and soft-spoken, and he assured her that he could easily handle all problems of reservations, tickets, and so on.

She was less interested in Tony Burke and thought him rather surly. He was a lean, tough-looking man of about twenty-five who stood with hands in his pockets while she regarded him in Udell's presence. He had a very direct, hard stare but answered her questions easily and without emotion. He was a Virginian, he said, and had spent five years with an express company, two of them as an armed messenger. No, he had never been in jail.

Udell assured her, when Burke had gone, that he had worked for Berlanger-Bryant for a year and a half without trouble and was a loyal employee.

"He looks like a ruffian," she commented.

"It will encourage others to give you a wide berth," he said. "I will be easier in my mind about you with Burke along."

She nodded. "Very well."

The girl, Pauline, was twenty-three and had had some education in a girls' academy. She had been married, but her husband had died of sickness two years past; they had no children. Her work had been very good, Udell said; she was diligent and trustworthy—if a little flighty at times. A strong word would settle her, he told Lily.

She left it to Udell to see that each of them was outfitted with the proper clothes and suitcases and admonished to shake the hay from their ears, since they would be going into the nation's capital, into a fine hotel, and they must not embarrass Mrs. Berlanger.

For her part, Lily summoned dressmakers from the most fashionable store in the city and spent hours with them, ordering a number of gowns for evening wear in the capital. She also ordered several traveling outfits and gowns for day wear. Her wardrobe, when finally completed, filled two large trunks. She also took along three suitcases of accessories and assorted articles.

She did not look forward to the long, tiring train ride, but she was philosophic; what had to be, had to be. It was

50

better than going in a coach and six. She would stop along the way and recuperate in hotels to break up the monotony of the journey, since it was impossible, Udell reported to her, to engage an entire railroad car for the trip. There were no boudoir cars, he said, although several had been tried out—according to the railroad officials he talked to. It would be necessary to sleep sitting up, if one spent a night on the way, a most uncomfortable predicament but one with no solution except getting off the cars to spend nights in hotels.

And if she did that, Lily mused, it would add days to the trip. There were also no facilities for dining on the railroad cars. She would have to depend on Dennis Foran's agility in getting off the train to buy food at the various stops. She would see that food was carried along with them, but it would probably be dry and tasteless after several hours. Udell was sure that men hawking food would come aboard the trains whenever possible, but she could not depend on that.

There were no toilet conveniences on board the trains either, Udell tactfully informed her. That fact alone very nearly caused her to cancel the entire idea of going to Washington. The trains, she thought, were very much more primitive than the steamboats she was used to.

She set a day for their departure and wound up such business as possible; then she sat down for half a day with Udell and went over the rest. In all probability Jeffries-Fraser would file a suit against them, but she expected to be back in St. Louis long before it came to trial. B & B lawyers would get to work on a defense in the meanwhile. Howard Paddock, she insisted, was not to interfere or attempt to influence any part of the business, and Udell

51

was to keep a detailed day-by-day log. It was not her first time away from the office for a long period, but it was a time when several matters seemed to be coming to a head.

However, the matter of government contracts was paramount and could not be left to a subordinate; Sam Beckhart would not stand for it anyway. And even if he could have accompanied her, she did not fully trust Howard Paddock.

They went across the Mississippi on a huge ferry—cars, locomotive, and all—and connected two more passenger cars to make a brigade. Lily was assured a measure of privacy by payment of a generous *douceur* to the conductor and was allowed to appropriate one end of the car for herself and her three assistants.

The seats were reversible, made of a very firm and only slightly-giving cushion covered by a shiny cloth material dull brown in color. Lily had brought along a number of pillows, and these, judiciously placed, made the hard seats bearable for long periods of time. But the cars swayed and jounced, and the eternal clickety-clack of steel wheels on steel rails got on her nerves in the beginning. She told herself it was probably the strong resentment of a steamboat owner to this obviously ill-developed method of transportation that caused her the annoyance. The men who ran railroads had much to learn.

She was delighted to see that Udell had been wrong about toilet facilities; there was a special compartment for men and one for women. It was a blessing.

Both Dennis Foran and the lean bodyguard, Tony Burke, had traveled on trains before. But Pauline, she discovered, was terrified of them. The girl huddled in her seat, scarcely daring to look out, especially on the ferry trip across the river. She was white-faced and resisted being comforted, apparently believing they were all doomed. Lily finally spoke sharply to her, and the girl burst into tears. Foran then led her away, walked her up and down the car, and somehow brought her out of the fear.

When later she saw Foran and the girl cosily seated together, whispering like a couple of lovers, she was briefly annoyed that a married man would carry on so, but decided it was to her benefit in the long run not to be bothered by the girl's fears. It was nothing to her how foolish Pauline became.

The third night she spent in a hotel; she put Pauline in a separate room, not wishing to be bothered with the girl's company, and put the two men together. Late that evening she saw Foran come from Pauline's room in a furtive manner. It was shocking how the fact of being in a strange city, in a hotel, eroded one's morals. Lily smoked a cigar before going to bed and debated with herself whether or not to fire them both. She decided finally to take Foran aside and warn him that in Washington she would stand for no scandal. She had a reputation to maintain, after all.

She was tired and irritable when they finally reached Washington, and assembled the luggage, loaded it into a coach, and drove to the Packer Hotel. The hotel provided a boy, and she sent a message at once to Sam Beckhart that she had arrived.

Her three assistants were put into rooms on a lower

floor, and she took a suite, sitting room, bedchamber, and dressing room. It was done in yellow and powder blue, with accents of white, and provided a view of the Potomac River. Hot water was carried up immediately, and she luxuriated in a bath within the hour. Soon after she emerged a note arrived from Sam saying he was delighted she'd come and was impatient to see her, suggesting dinner that evening. She sent the boy back to say she accepted happily.

She dressed carefully; her gowns had traveled better than she'd expected, and only a slight sponging was necessary on the cambric basque to take out wrinkles. It was made with shirrs on the shoulders and corresponding ones near the belt and was of a pale blue color that contrasted ideally with the dark blue, almost black, ornamented skirt.

A boy knocked on the door to say that Senator Beckhart was downstairs, and she paused before the mirror, inspecting herself critically; every hair was in place, and she went out and down to the crowded lobby.

Sam came to meet her at the bottom of the stairs, both arms extended. "My, how lovely you look!" He kissed her hand, and several near them turned to watch; she thought they recognized him, from the sudden buzz of hushed whispers. Sam looked wonderful, she thought, handsome as an actor, dressed in the height of fashion with a snowy cravat that he had probably donned within the hour.

"It's wonderful to see you again, Sam." She took his arm, and they went toward the dining room. "I missed you terribly when you left St. Louis—"

"And I you! My goodness, what a wrench I felt the day

54

I boarded that train."

"How is Miles?" Miles Broder was his assistant.

"Fine, fine, excellent. Miles never changes. But you do! You are more beautiful every time I see you!"

"Sam! What a flatterer!"

"It's not flattery. I assure you it's true, every word. I will be the envy of the entire city tonight, sitting with you." He nodded to the captain, who showed them to a table immediately. Obviously Sam had already seen him and made the arrangements. He had remembered to ask for a table away from the music. He ordered wine, still pressing her hand as if afraid she'd disappear.

"And how is Howard?"

She shrugged. "Howard never changes either. He sends you his best. I'm alarmed at all the talk of slavery, Sam. I heard nothing else on the train, and the newspapers are full of it."

He smiled. "It's fashionable just now. It sells newspapers, and people love to gossip about it. If we had several lurid murders this week you'd see it all banished to the back pages."

"Will it affect us?"

"No, of course not." He glanced up as the wine arrived. The waiter pulled the cork, poured into their glasses, and departed. Sam touched his glass to hers. "Here's to us, Lily. We deserve it—whatever it is."

She laughed and sipped. It was fun being with Sam again. He was exciting for a time—a week or two—but then he would begin to tell on her as he had in St. Louis the year before. She put that thought behind her for the moment. Sam was very necessary for the immediate future. And she thought he dismissed the slavery question too easily; it went deeper than that, and Sam was from Missouri, a slave state. It would be very sensible to conclude their business in Washington as quickly as possible. Many people were talking ominously about a schism of the states, a frightening subject to her, for if the South left the Union, Sam would go with it.

Sam ordered for them, brook trout broiled in butter. "Make sure they're not curled up," he said to the waiter, "and let's have them with a bit of lemon."

"We have some fish sauce, sir."

"No, nothing else to detract from the flavor." Sam waved the man away. "My mother used to fix catfish," he said to Lily. "She'd make a batter of some kind first. I've tried to find a cook here in Washington who could do it the way she did." He shook his head.

"It may be your memory, Sam."

He laughed. "Yes, it could be. How was your childhood, Lily? Pleasant?"

"Oh yes, very much so. My father was a lawyer, a wonderful man. He would read to me for hours, and my mother took me everywhere—"

"Where was that?"

"In New Orleans. I had a very sheltered early life, I'm afraid."

"Well, you've certainly grown up to be a beautiful, intelligent women because of it." He patted her hand warmly. "No man could ask for more in a woman." He raised his glass again. "Here's to a long and cherished life!" He touched her glass lightly.

"For both of us," she added.

He drank. "Tomorrow I want you to meet Billy Turnbull. Besides myself he's the most influential man in

56

the Senate. With him on our side everything is possible. I've already spoken to him, of course, and he's receptive. He sees the possibilities and the need."

She nodded. She knew of Senator Turnbull; he was much in the news. His name was Danford Turnbull, from Mississippi, and there had been a breath of scandal connected with his name only a few years past. Something about a woman—she couldn't remember the details. But possibly that kind of scandal only enhanced his image in certain quarters. She said, "I'd love to meet him."

"Believe nothing of what he says. I don't think Billy has told the truth to a woman in all his days. Brags about it, you know."

"Does he?" She smiled. "You senators are a race apart, Sam."

"I suppose so."

"Will he tell *you* the truth?"

"Oh yes, certainly. Business is different. But to Billy every woman is a likely conquest. I won't leave you alone for an instant."

The waiter brought the trout, served it quickly, and left, as a small orchestra struck up a tune at the far end of the room. Lily winced—she hated music and tried to ignore it. Sam talked of politics, inside stories that amused her, about how certain deals were made, an account of a bumbling duel between two congressmen in which one was wounded in the buttocks with a sword, and a long, rambling tale about the Democratic party.

They finished the trout and were served ices and coffee; then he brought the conversation around to them again. "How did you find the trip?"

"Miserable," she said. "Trains will never catch on as passenger movers, unless they improve a very great deal."

"I believe they prefer freight. How many people did you bring with you?"

"Three." She gave him a brief listing of their qualities but left out the fact that she knew Foran was bedding Pauline.

"You might have saved yourself the trouble. There are secretaries in plenty here, though I suppose it's better that you didn't travel alone. These are strange times."

"Will there be serious trouble, Sam?"

"You mean about the Union?"

"Yes."

"No, of course not. It's all bluster and hysteria. It'll blow away as soon as we sit down in Congress and straighten it all out. We've been dealing with a few belligerent and stubborn men, but they'll have to give way. Slavery is slowly passing anyhow, and most realize it. Even in the deep South they know it's coming. As an economic fact slavery is gradually becoming too expensive. In my own state most farmers can't afford slaves. What happens when a man pays fifteen hundred dollars for a slave and the damned nigger runs off to the North?" Sam shrugged. "That's too much money to lose."

"There're laws about returning slaves."

He smiled. "Of course there are. If they're enforced. I doubt if there are any figures on how many slaves were returned to their original masters last year, but if there were I'd be willing to bet the figure is damned low. You can't carve your initials on a slave, you know—and branding is unpopular. How the hell can you tell after a year or so if a slave is yours or not?" He shook his head.

58

"In a year or two, bills will be introduced for the government to buy the freedom of slaves—set them free in wholesale lots. Mark my words."

"An interesting idea, Sam. Why don't you do it?"

He grinned. "I just may. I just may. Why don't you show me your suite?"

"I'd love to, Sam." She rose at once.

CHAPTER SIX

Logan went each day to the main office of Jeffries-Fraser, located on Third Street. The firm occupied the entire floor of a new brick building; Kenneth Fraser and Neil Barnes had adjoining offices. Logan had no office at all, since he was usually on the river.

But things were quiet. For the time being there were no more reports of vandalism or damage caused by Berlanger-Bryant hirelings. Apparently the word had gone out.

Fraser had consulted with the firm's attorneys, and a lawsuit had duly been filed against B & B, but the courts were clogged with back cases, and it would take time. Time was on Lily's side, since witnesses might easily disappear.

Doris did not mention it again, but he knew she was gravely concerned for his safety. Logan went as soon as possible to see his old friend detective Clarence Yates. Yates, a short, rumpled-looking man with deep-set eyes that were never still, was delighted to see him and produced a bottle from a bottom drawer of his desk.

"I hear you got married, Logan—it was in the paper."

"Yes." He accepted a glass. "But that's not why I'm here."

Yates laughed. "I don't do divorce work anyway—too

messy. Is it something about Lily Berlanger?"

"In a way. My friends tell me I need a bodyguard. I thought you might know someone—"

Yates made a face. "A bodyguard! You *are* expecting trouble!"

"I'm afraid so." He glanced at the office. Yates had spent nothing at all on it; it was the same spare, undecorated room he recalled from his last visit, and smelly with cigar smoke.

Yates said, "You want this someone as a permanent employee?"

"Well, permanent until I won't need him any longer."

"He can only do so much, you know. He can't protect you from a sniper, for instance."

"Yes, I know."

"And his presence will tell Lily's men that you're aware of the danger. So they'll come after you with five or six—"

Logan sighed. "You're being a cheerful heart today, Clarence. D'you think it's a bad idea?"

"Oh no, no. I just wanted to tell you—" His voice trailed off. "I guess you know the problem as well as I do."

"That's better. Now how about a name?"

Yates dug into a desk drawer and came up with a notebook, which he opened. He leaned back in his chair and frowned, leafing through the pages. He paused, seemed to consider, then shook his head slightly and went on. Halfway through the book he stopped. "Here— this is the man for you."

"Tell me about him."

"His name is Louis Gualco. He's part French, part Indian, and the rest Irish, and I doubt if he's afraid of

61

anything on this planet. You want me to arrange a meeting?"

"Yes. Right away." He gave Yates a slip of paper. "This's where I live."

"My advice is to go there and stay till I bring Gualco to see you."

He brought Gualco in two days. They met in the study of Logan's house, a room paneled in wood with a rifle, several framed pictures, and a deer-head trophy on the walls.

Gualco was not a big man; he was almost of a size with Yates, a dark, well-dressed man who looked much too peaceful to do the job Logan wished. Yates introduced them, and Logan shook hands, asked them to be seated, and brought a bottle and three glasses. Gualco declined with thanks, saying he never touched liquor.

Logan said, "Clarence has told you what we discussed?"

"Yes." Gualco took out a cheroot. "I've never been a bodyguard before, Mr. Jeffries—"

"Logan."

Gualco smiled. "But I was a soldier once, and I've been a train guard and a deputy sheriff."

"Are you armed?"

Gualco nodded, made a quick movement, and suddenly had a Colt revolver in his hand.

"That takes practice!" Yates said admiringly.

Gualco put the pistol back into a shoulder holster and lit the cheroot. Logan looked at Yates, who nodded and poured himself a drink.

Logan made up his mind. Gualco did not look to be his idea of a bodyguard, but that might be to the good. He was

62

recommended by Yates, and Yates was a man who would know. He had trusted Yates in the past and would do so now. They quickly settled on terms, and when he mentioned that Gualco was expected to live in the house, Gualco smiled and said he had a suitcase outside in the carriage.

When Clarence Yates had gone, Gualco said, "I think you ought to give out that I'm a cousin who's come to stay for a visit. It could be that one of your servants is bein' paid by Lily Berlanger."

"I'd hate to think so—"

"Folks do a lot of things for money. They might not think giving out information is of much account. It's not like shovin' a knife in somebody's back."

Doris was surprised at Gualco's appearance. When they were alone she said to Logan, "He doesn't seem like a ruffian—"

"He comes very well recommended, and I've seen how fast he is with a gun."

"Well," she said doubtfully, "I hope Clarence is right."

Louis Gualco settled in very quickly. He was given a room off the kitchen, a large bedchamber with an outside door, and was treated as one of the family. The servants were told he was a cousin from Ohio who would stay for a month or so and might go to work in the Jeffries-Fraser steamboat firm.

The butler—and jack-of-all-trades—was Baxter Ross, an ex-roustabout and brawler, who was capable of wearing a suit of clothes without looking ridiculous and who could handle weapons expertly. He was a big man, as large as Logan, with a square face and sparce black hair. His primary task was to guard Doris Jeffries—with the help of the driver-gardener, Chris Murphy. Murphy was also an ex-brawler and pugilist, who had been a policeman and had learned trick shooting in a carnival. Murphy was not as big, but he was fast, had a bland face and red hair, and read his Bible daily.

The cook was Mrs. Benson, a stubborn woman with no sense of humor but with an ability in the kitchen that made up for all her shortcomings. She frowned at all of Murphy's jokes and frequently confided to Doris that he was daft and ought to be put away. She and the two men had separate rooms over the stable house.

Louis Gualco quickly became acquainted with the men, flattered Mrs. Benson, and accompanied Logan everywhere.

A month passed in almost monotonous quiet.

Howard Paddock carried through on his idea to subvert Udell Winter. Using the excuse of shipping business, he made an appointment with Udell for an evening. He took the dry-as-dust office manager to the Bluebird Club as his guest.

"We'll be able to talk there without interruption, Udell."

"Why can't we talk in the office?"

Paddock smiled. "I thought you'd want to get away from the office! You're there all the time."

"But I've heard the Bluebird Club is a very immoral place."

"Don't believe all you've heard. There are bluenoses everywhere. The Bluebird is supported by many of the finest professional and business men in the city." Paddock chuckled. "And if you don't care to dance with the girls, no one will force you to." He laughed inwardly

64

at the expression on Udell's long face. Did the mention of girls startle him?

Udell had been very surprised at Howard Paddock's invitation, and he accepted reluctantly. He was positive Paddock had something on his mind—Paddock was not noted as a generous man, and he knew the Bluebird was an expensive place.

He was being softened up for something, Udell thought, and he guessed it had to do with Berlanger-Bryant, since he and Paddock had no other worldly connection. With Lily's admonitions fresh in his mind, he was curious. It was obvious to him that Lily did not trust her partner; he knew Lily well enough by now to know she trusted almost no one and, in view of her special instructions regarding Paddock, him least of all. He knew, too, that Lily was in business with Paddock because of circumstances, and he suspected that one day she would find a way to change them.

He could not help wondering if Paddock proposed to make the first move along that line.

With that in mind, he listened carefully to everything Paddock said, but the big man chattered only in generalities as they rode to the club in Paddock's closed carriage. The thought of girls made him stir uncomfortably. He had never been unfaithful to his wife of more than three decades. But he'd thought about it.

When the carriage pulled up in front of the club, the driver swung the door open, and Paddock climbed out briskly; Udell followed more slowly. A uniformed doorman showed them inside, and a young, toothy man took their hats and coats.

Once, many years ago in Natchez, Udell had been in a brothel, and he recalled those feelings as he gazed about.

There was a deep carpet on the floor and the walls were covered with pictures of hunting scenes and barely clothed females and with trophies in brass and silver. There was a hint of perfume in the air, just as there had been in Natchez—well, perhaps more than a hint in Natchez. Here it was laced with tobacco. He could hear music and voices, all muted, and he followed Paddock meekly, gazing about with interest. A middle-aged man in brass buttons showed them to a table, and Udell seated himself in a gingerly fashion and smiled back at Paddock. They were in a wood-paneled booth, with potted plants nearby and tantalizing glimpses of women across the way. Everything was hushed and reeked of good taste. The furnishings were expensive, the lamps were silver, copper, and etched glass, and he felt slightly out of place.

He asked Paddock, "Do you come here often?"

"Now and then." Paddock smiled. "The food's too rich as a daily thing, you know. What will you have, wine or something mixed?"

Udell wanted beer but was afraid to ask. He settled for a glass of wine.

"Did Lily tell you how long she'd be gone?"

Udell shook his head. "She didn't know. I had a wire that she'd arrived safely."

"Ah, that's good."

A waiter came with menus, and Udell studied his, astounded at the prices. A family of six would be able to eat to satiation for a week on what Paddock would pay for their meals. He began to be secretly glad he'd accepted the invitation. Luxury at no cost was very pleasant to contemplate. He was glad also that his wife was not with them to chatter.

Paddock ordered London broil, and Udell decided on

66

the loin of pork with milk. He finished the wine, and his glass was refilled. What a marvelous place, this club. He wondered at the expense of joining; a fortune probably, well out of his reach.

Paddock said, "I'm surprised you've never been here before."

"I don't know any other members. As a matter of fact, I didn't know you were a member."

"It's good for the soul to come now and again. Gives one a lift, eh?" Paddock laughed. "Of course it costs a bit, but there are those who have the necessary." He rubbed his fingers together. "Does Lily pay you well?"

"Well enough," Udell said shortly.

"I'm told she's not a generous woman."

Udell wanted to say, "Neither are you," but he did not. "I've been with her a long time—with old Jacob before they were married, matter of fact. It's only the second job I've had in my life. Not many can say that, I'd guess."

"No, not many," Paddock agreed. "I've never had a job at all, so to speak. Never worked for anyone for wages, I mean."

"Is that so?"

"Yes. Nothing like having money. It eases everything—especially old age."

Udell nodded slowly, sipping the wine. He had mused a good deal about old age in the last few years. He was getting on, and there were times when he thought Lily looked at him with speculation in her eyes, as if she were thinking of replacing him. And the more he knew about Lily the less he really trusted her—down deep. She was a ruthless woman, no question.

Paddock said, "You've really been with the firm that long?"

"Oh yes. I wasn't even married at that time."

"You must know everything about Lily's affairs, then."

Udell shrugged his thin shoulders. "A good bit. Lily's not a woman to tell things, you mind. She keeps everything to herself. Never even writes it down."

The food came, and the waiter served them, refilled Udell's glass, and disappeared.

"What's Logan Jeffries to her?"

Udell stared, then shrugged again. "She hates him—but you know that. She hated his father, Dutch. Lily can hate pretty well."

"Has Logan ever attacked her?"

"No. He came to the office twice—to see her. She wouldn't see him, of course."

"Is it true she had Andrea killed?"

Udell's hand jerked, and he spilled wine on the tablecloth. It was a question he hadn't expected. He glared at Paddock. "How could I know such a thing?"

Paddock smiled and sniffed as he nodded. "Oh, you know, all right. I think she did—a lot of people think she did."

"What!" Udell was horrified that such a notion should be the subject of popular debate.

"You can't hide everything, Udell." Paddock rubbed his nose. "Of course, proving it's a different matter. A far different matter. I'd suspect Lily covers her tracks well. Edward Taylor did it for her, aye?" He cocked an eyebrow.

Udell sighed and sawed with his knife. Edward Taylor was long dead—killed by Logan Jeffries, matter of fact. He glanced at Paddock. "I don't know anything about it. D'you mind if we change the subject?"

"Well, no, of course not. But everyone else talks about it, so I naturally thought—" Paddock let his voice trail off. "But I respect loyalty, Udell. Respect it highly. It's just that I can't figure why Lily hates him so."

"Who?"

"Why—Logan Jeffries." Paddock chewed contentedly for a moment. "It must stem from something back in Chadwick a long time ago."

"I told you she hates Dutch."

"That doesn't explain anything. A thousand people hate Dutch."

Udell narrowed his eyes. "Why do you care about how Lily feels about Logan?"

Paddock sniffed and chuckled. "I've got the curiosity of a dozen cats, that's why. Can't help wondering. Lily is so goddamned logical about some things—and then this crops up." He reached across and refilled Udell's glass. "Do you ever wonder about things?"

Udell shrugged. "Now'n' then." He finished the pork and put his fork down. The meal was delicious, the wine just right; he belched, murmured "sorry," and sipped more wine. Paddock's questions had stirred his brain. He'd wondered many times why Lily had done away with Andrea; he had finally decided it had something to do with the firm. Andrea was her father's heir—along with Lily. He was sure that Lily was simply eliminating that heir.

He wondered that Paddock had never thought of it. Now that Andrea was gone, Logan was the heir.

CHAPTER SEVEN

On the sideboard in the sitting room of Lily's suite there was a double row of glistening stemware and several bottles. Sam Beckhart pulled the cork and poured brandy into two glasses, then looked at the liquor against the light, swirling it gently. He crossed the room and handed her one.

"I never knew what brandy was till I was nearly of age. No one I knew as a kid drank anything but corn squeezin's." He made a face. "Terrible stuff. Kicked like a mule."

"You drank it as a boy?"

He grinned. "I stole a drink now'n' then, yes. Had to see what the grown-ups were getting drunk on."

She pushed off her slippers. "Make a fire, Sam. I love a fire in the bedroom." She sipped the brandy and watched him doff his coat and get down to arrange sticks in a tiny pyramid. "When are you going to marry again?"

"What!" The question surprised him, and he turned with a lighted match in his fingers. "Marry again?"

"A presidential candidate should be married."

The match burned him, and he swore and dropped it. Then he smiled. "Is this a proposal?"

"Oh, goodness no! I don't want to be a first lady!"

"Why not? Think of all the things you could do. I

70

should imagine you'd revel in it!"

"Well, I can do them all now, with less publicity. I'm not made like you, Sam, I don't care for the newspapers poking into my life. But you'll need a wife before you get into campaigning, won't you?"

He sighed deeply, pushed sticks into the growing fire, and nodded. "Miles thinks so. There's never been a bachelor president up to now. Miles says people want a stable man. They think that marriage means stability." He shook his head again. "I don't know. I think it means something else."

She stretched languorously. "You don't want to marry at all? You'd deny some woman the honor?"

"Now who's the tease?"

She laughed. "Be different. Don't marry at all, Sam."

"If I had my druthers, I wouldn't." He grunted, "Not at all." Rising, he swirled the brandy in his glass and sat by her. "But I may have to, for the good of the country."

"For the good of the country." She laughed again, and he looked at her with speculation.

"No one measures up to you, Lily."

"Do you have someone in mind?"

"No. I think Miles does."

"Miles is an ambitious man. What will you do about him when you're elected, make him an advisor?"

"Yes, certainly."

"Who does he want for you?"

"I don't know. I'd rather have you."

She laughed again. "You're the tease now, Sam. You wouldn't marry me if I said yes."

"Oh, yes I would. Try me."

"I think you have someone in the back of your mind; you must meet hundreds of women—thousands!"

71

He chuckled. "You'd be surprised how many of them are dowdy and pockmarked or fat and wheezy. And their daughters are too young for me. I'd have to marry exactly the right one. Someone like you."

She finished the brandy and put the glass aside. "Well, you have almost two years more before election time—"

"No, only one. Not even that, really. It would be best to marry well before the election—for the newspaper coverage, you know. It would evoke a more romantic feeling in the voters."

Lily smiled at his expression. "Men don't care if you're romantic or not."

"Ah, but their wives do. They can't vote, true, but they can tell their husbands how to mark the ballots. Women are becoming more and more interested in politics."

She pursed her lips, wondering where he got his information. Politics, local and national, was such a male-dominated enterprise that she doubted women would ever be allowed to influence it. A woman in office was almost unthinkable. And they might easily tell their husbands how to vote, but there was no way they could go to the polls to make sure their instructions were carried out. Sam was a dreamer.

She got up and pulled the spread off the double bed, folded it neatly, and turned down the two lamps till the room was shadowy. Sam was already getting out of his clothes. She felt almost detached; no sign of excitement moved her pulse. She might be preparing to step into a tub instead of a bed; she must feign the emotion, and she smiled at him as he came to unfasten her hooks and helped her slide out of the dress and petticoats.

How different it all would be if Paige Robinson were

here instead! Smothering a sigh, she hung the dress over the back of a chair.

His face was in shadow when he crawled onto the bed beside her, but she could see the pale sheen of his teeth. "I've waited an eternity for this moment, Lily. You know you've spoiled me completely for other women."

"No, of course not." He gathered her up. Her skin was wonderfully soft under his hands, and she moved sinuously, returning his kisses with burning passion. He was surprised at how ardent she was.

Sam was just as she remembered him, far too hasty when he'd entered her. So much of him was show, so much was pose. When it came down to it he fell short—but never would she breathe a word of her true feelings.

She whispered that he was magnificent, that he pleased her beyond words—and she thought again of Paige when Sam rolled away. How soon could she get back to New Orleans—or he come north? She would never be happy with anyone else.

Sam introduced her to Billy Turnbull the next day.

Sam came to the hotel at midday, and they drove to Genilli's, a small and exclusive restaurant frequented by upper-caste politicians, captains of industry, and military men of star rank. The restaurant occupied the ground floor of a red brick building; there was a garden to one side, not used at the moment, but crowded with tables where guests were served in summer.

They went in through a small foyer, paneled in rosewood, and followed a brass-buttoned personage who showed them to Turnbull's table. The main room was alive with people, eating and laughing, and Lily was not surprised to see the vice-president, Mr. William King;

she recognized him from a picture she'd seen during the last election.

Turnbull had a corner table beneath a row of framed pictures of seascapes and tall ships. A big, well-dressed man with graying hair and a bulbous nose, he was talking earnestly with a young woman when they approached the table. He noticed them and motioned the girl away; she was lithe and hot-eyed, Lily saw with interest. She leaned close to Turnbull when he spoke to her, replied with a few words, gathered up a coat, and disappeared quickly into the crowd without a backward glance.

Billy rose, extending his hands expansively. "So this is the beautiful Mrs. Berlanger! My dear—Sam didn't tell me half enough! Come, sit here, sit here." He held a chair for her, pushing Sam aside.

"I warned you," Sam said. "Be careful of him."

Billy sat and leaned toward her. "Whatever he said— it's a lie. I deny it."

She smiled at him. His brows were thick and drooped over bright, eagle eyes. The white hair about his ears pushed out and fell over his collar. "He told me how gallant you are," she said.

"Bosh." Billy shook his head. "Sam would never say a thing like that. But thank you, my dear. You're very kind."

"Who was the girl who just left?" Sam asked. "I don't think I've seen her before and I thought I knew all your—"

"Enough!" Billy interrupted. He looked at her. "The man makes out that I do nothing but chase about after females! What calumny! Sam, you are the limit."

"Yes? Who was the girl?"

Billy glared at him. "My daughter's music teacher. If

74

you must know. We were discussing her lessons." He signaled a waiter and ordered wine, then turned to Lily. His voice changed instantly. "I know all about this fabulous project, Mrs. Berlanger—"

"Please call me Lily."

He smiled broadly and winked at Sam. "Certainly, and my friends—my close friends, mind—call me Billy." He patted her hand. "As I was saying, I completely support the project, as Sam has surely told you, and I expect great things of you, Lily."

She said, "Great things? This is simply a business proposition."

"Ah, that's a politician's phrase," Sam said. "He means plenty of newspaper space and his name mentioned prominently and spelled right."

"Of course, certainly," Billy agreed, unruffled. He eyed Sam with arched brows. "Many of the voters in *my* state can read."

Sam laughed. "Well, we Missourians aren't entirely bumpkins. We can always find someone to read the papers to us. Even in the Senate." He took a menu from a passing waiter. "The quail and grouse are excellent here, Lily, and the venison too, when they have it."

"Famous for it," Billy said. He beamed at the waiter who poured more wine. "Bring us a blackboard, Jules."

The special menu was on the blackboard, Billy explained, and she gazed at it as the waiter propped it on a chair near them. There was cold trout in jelly, poached whitefish, bouillabaisse, and mousse of lobster. Sam passed her the regular menu, and she finally chose pheasant in a cream sauce with asparagus.

Billy launched into a story concerning one of his committee members, who, he swore, was so stupid—

"You know who I mean, Sam"—that he could barely recall his own name. He was interrupted half a dozen times by men who stopped by the table to shake Sam's hand and wish him well. "Kansas has done for Frank Pierce, Sam, you'll see."

Kansas had long been the scene of lawless violence. Bands of out-of-state, armed men had taken over the polls in many places and controlled elections. People blamed President Pierce for doing too little, or for doing too much. Sam agreed with all that Pierce was a one-term officeholder. It was time that Missouri led the nation.

Lily listened to Billy Turnbull with half an ear and to the government business discussed on every side. She remembered to smile and nod now and then, and Sam pressed her knee under the table.

When Sam got up to talk to a group of cigar-smoking men at another table, Billy quickly leaned toward her. "I'm told you're a single woman, Lily—"

"Yes."

"I've a lovely place just across the river in Virginia. Why don't I send my carriage for you this evening?"

"I thought *you* were married."

"I? Not at all."

"You have a daughter—"

"Ah, that's true. But my wife died years ago. My daughter is nearly thirty."

"And you still pay for her music lessons?"

He burst out laughing. "That's what I tell Sam. What about this evening?"

She looked desolate. "I'm so sorry, Billy. I've an engagement this evening, and the next. Perhaps we can have lunch."

He sighed deeply and cocked his head at her. "You do

believe those ridiculous stories Sam conjures up."

"I'm never influenced by gossip."

He smiled. "Certainly. We must have lunch one day."

The next morning Sam took her on a round of calls. It was vitally necessary, he said, that she be seen in the halls and the meeting rooms and call on those men who swayed committee votes. People in office were jealous of their powers and incredibly envious. She was a rich and powerful steamboat owner from the West, and it did something for their egos to have her rapping on their doors. Nonsense, all nonsense, he said, but necessary.

His presence got her admitted quickly to each office. A procession of faces, thin, fat, and hairy; names that she recalled from the papers, some she'd never heard before; platitudes and promises—it exhausted her.

She had lunch in a huge, noisy, crowded office-building restaurant, with Billy Turnbull suddenly at her side, pushing to sit by her. "Ah, Lily! How you brighten up the drabness—"

"What, no music teacher?" Sam asked.

She drove down a broad avenue in an elegant carriage with Sam and three other senators who asked interminable questions and flirted with her. One slipped her a card with his name and address.

Later she attended a committee meeting and answered more questions, with Sam by her side. In an undertone he said, "You're doing very well. You've got them all eating out of your hand."

"How much more of this?"

"Not much more today. They'll adjourn in a moment—"

Then in the evening there were parties. Sam took her

from one to another; people drank too much; Billy Turnbull appeared and pressed her again to run off with him to his house across the river, but Sam was always close, watching, guiding. He got rid of Billy somehow and maneuvered her into a dining room where she ate boned leg of lamb and a fruit compote Madeira. Did Washingtonians make this dizzy round constantly? She began to long for the quiet of St. Louis.

But Sam had other plans. He steered her into a parlor hung with crystal, lavish with mirrors and oil paintings and deep-pile rugs on the floors. "You must speak to that man there, the one with the goatee. He's Horace Yearsley, a presidential advisor. The woman with him is Edna Something or other, his niece. She keeps house for him—among other things. It'll be a great scandal one day. Come along, I'll introduce you—"

Twice in the first week she slept with Sam. He came to her suite late at night the first, and early the next—and each time left at dawn to return in the middle of the morning for more business rounds.

She had brief discussions with her three assistants; Foran was keeping himself busy, he said, talking with people in various government departments. Pauline went window-shopping often, and Tony Burke brooded. He asked her to send him back to St. Louis, but she refused, saying they would all go home shortly and she would need him on the train.

Things were going well, Sam told her, better than he'd expected. It was desperately hard to move lawmakers from their accustomed ruts or to change their minds—especially where a woman was concerned. It had been necessary, he said apologetically, to tell some of them that Berlanger-Bryant was really run by a council of men, and not by Lily Berlanger at all. It rankled her, but she understood; Sam had to do what he had to do. For every favor, Sam went on, they wanted two in return; he hinted at compromises and settlements, but when she was alone with Miles Broder, he smiled and said: "Leave it all to Sam, Lily. He's in his element, and Sam never loses."

Each day she dictated pages of notes, opinions, and observations to Dennis Foran. She wrote dozens of letters, retaining copies made by Pauline, and shrugged off Tony Burke when he complained that she did not take him with her. Wasn't he a bodyguard?

Sam Beckhart's political advisors, and his central committee, were pressing him to begin a tour of the New England states. His campaign could not be put off much longer. Miles agreed that he must soon make a decision. Lily Berlanger was enormously important to him for financial reasons. The presidency was important for history. Sam knew himself to be a man for the future.

And his supporters were clamoring to see and hear him.

All this was a source of considerable concern for Lily. If Sam went she would have only Billy Turnbull to carry her battle; not that Billy was second rate, but she was not eager to have him claim rewards—to climb into her bed. It seemed to be his life's ambition.

And in the middle of that conflict, Sen. Gilbert Collier rose in the Senate to say that Sam Beckhart was attempting, through his connivance with Mrs. Lily Berlanger, an ill-advised, probably illegal, and certainly self-serving business venture underwritten by the United States government. Collier described Mrs. Berlanger as a

Lorelei of the Mississippi who had beguiled Sam Beckhart and was attempting to loose a flood of dollars into her net.

Sam stormed out of the Senate, furious. When the newspapers picked up the catchphrase Lorelei of the Mississippi, his rage knew no bounds. He declared to a circle of reporters that if he had fallen for a siren's song, then Gilbert Collier was a foolish drunk and ought to be committed and his body soaked in healing waters. "And while he's at it," Sam shouted, "let him soak his head also!"

He had got his temper back when he saw Lily next. Gilbert Collier, he told her, was one of the last of the Whig party, a political group that was fast disappearing in favor of the new arrivals, the Know-Nothings, or American party. Collier had declared for the presidency several times and had not once come close to nomination. He was a rock-faced old curmudgeon with a soul of Alabama mud, Sam said, and how he'd remained in Congress was more than anyone could imagine. The voters in Alabama must be dumb and blind.

"Come to bed," Lily said. Nothing was to be gained by pacing the room railing against Collier. "Can he hurt us?"

"He can damage us severely, yes. Maybe not beyond repair, but he can intervene and delay and lose us half what I'd hoped for. He's a damned gadfly."

"Come to bed and forget him tonight."

Two days later, on an afternoon she'd been testifying before one of Billy Turnbull's committees on the subject of spring floods and river tonnage, Billy brought the hearing to a close and insisted she accompany him to an important gathering just across town. She hesitated, but when he mentioned that Miles Broder would be present, she relented.

She entered Billy's palatial carriage, and they drove to a lovely, old Georgian house near the river. It stood on a rise with a vast reach of greensward before it; the drive was lined with ancient maples, and the fences were painted white. The party, Billy said, was in honor of some obscure admiral of the War of 1812, an ancestor of their host. He couldn't recall the admiral's name but would find out for her if she cared.

It was not a small gathering. The crowds overflowed the house into two gardens, a noisy, chattering throng through which she made slow headway, with Billy pushing a path and introducing her as they went.

Miles found her, said he was delighted she'd come, that Sam was unfortunately unable to attend—the damned committee again—but he would see her home. He captured a chair for her and brought her one of the new mixed drinks, and Billy brought her a small plate of sweets. He also brought two congressmen and a cabinet officer who regaled her with stories, which Billy, to judge from his expression, had heard before.

Miles drifted into conversation with another group, and Billy Turnbull wandered off with a young lady on his arm. Lily found herself talking to a tall, broad, very good-looking man dressed in black and gray with an emerald stickpin in his cravat. He had white sideburns and high cheekbones, and after a bit he dragged up a chair and sat knee to knee with her. The congressmen gave up and the cabinet officer lingered, then followed them. The conversation turned to Mississippi River traffic.

"Your company handles a great deal of it, I understand."

"Only our share," she said, thinking of Paige Robinson all at once. She began to realize this interesting stranger reminded her of him. He had the same soft speech and way of smiling.

He asked, "Is it really credible that one company could dominate river commerce, Mrs. Berlanger? I mean to the extent that Sam Beckhart proposes—"

"He is speaking only of government business."

"Yes, I realize that. But surely the Missouri-Mississippi is one of the world's longest rivers."

"It is, but for hundreds and hundreds of miles, especially on the upper Missouri, the traffic is very little."

"For the moment."

She smiled. "As you say, for the time being."

"I understand you're from New Orleans, originally."

"Yes, I was brought up there."

"A beautiful city. I've been there often and hope to go again soon."

She thought him a man in his forties, despite the gray in his dark hair. He had blue eyes and a slightly aquiline nose, a very patrician face. His smile showed even teeth, and he looked as if he spent much time out of doors. When he asked her to dance, she rose at once and took his arm.

Music caused her discomfort, but if she closed her eyes just a bit he might be Paige, leading her onto the floor. She put the harsh, unintelligible sounds of the small orchestra from her mind and concentrated on stepping in rhythm with him; it was not easy, and she was hard put to keep time and listen to his voice. If only she could understand the meaningless jumble and blur of sounds that others seemed to enjoy.

She caught a glimpse of Billy Turnbull on the sidelines, and the expression on his florid face was curious. There seemed to be astonishment there, and something else.

The music sounds went on and on, but she got the hang of the rhythm soon and was able to reply to his questions. How long did she intend to remain in Washington? Not long, she said; her mission was nearly complete. He was sorry to hear that; it would be the city's loss. . . . But the dance was over at last, and she breathed an inward sigh. He led her to one of the large side doors. "Would you like a bit of fresh air? . . . It's so close in here."

"I would indeed."

"Do you find Washington a surprise?"

She smiled and walked out onto the terrace. "Yes, and no. It's quite different, of course. Everything is business here, even at parties."

"Yes, it never stops, and there may be more activity just now. Many think it certain that Mr. Pierce will not run again, and Sam Beckhart will certainly get his party's nomination. Big changes are in the offing."

"Will Sam be elected?"

He shrugged slightly and smiled. "Barring unforeseen happenings he has the best chance of all."

"What kind of unforeseen happening?"

"War," he said.

She looked at him quickly. "You believe that possible?"

He nodded. "It is possible because there are certain fools in Congress who will let it go that far. I know that Sam is your friend, and I want you to know that I do not consider him one of the fools."

"I don't want to think about war. It means—too many

changes—too much that cannot be planned—" She walked to a low brick wall that surrounded part of the garden. In the west the sky was saffron and flame as the sun left a last residue. The trees about the estate lifted leafless branches, a shadowy filigree, and she was very conscious of his presence, the grave tones of his voice and the way his glances warmed her. It had been so long since she'd been in Paige's arms—months. What was it about this man that so reminded her of him? . . .

She half turned, and he was close, so close her cheek brushed his; she felt his arms slide about her waist, and she let him draw her nearer. He said softly, "You are a beautiful woman, Lily Berlanger—"

"Thank you."

"—and I think you have quite turned my head this evening. I would not have thought it possible in such a short time."

She was about to reply, then his lips closed over hers, and she was breathless, clinging to him. The kiss lasted only a moment, then he stepped away, bowed, and was gone.

She took another moment to get her breath, to tell her racing heart to behave—then Billy Turnbull came out onto the terrace, glaring at her. He stood, hands on hips, shaking his big head. "I wouldn't have thought it of you, Lily."

"What?"

He moved toward her, his face angry. "What in God's name were you doing with that man?"

Lily lifted an eyebrow. "What business of yours, Billy?"

"You—coming out here with *him!*"

"I don't understand. Why are you so upset?"

He threw up his hands. "My God, woman! Don't you know who that was?"

"No—" She stared at him.

"Your archenemy, Gilbert Collier!"

CHAPTER EIGHT

Sam was very annoyed when he heard. He came to her suite and paced up and down, hands behind his back. "Lily—what in the world! Billy says you were actually kissing that man!"

"He kissed me, Sam, before I could stop him!" She was amused at his agitation, but tried not to show it.

"Gil Collier!"

"No one introduced us. How was I to know? He obviously knew who I was, and I assumed he was some congressman friend of yours. He spoke well of you."

He halted in astonishment. "Spoke well of me!"

"I forget his words, but, yes, he did."

"Incredible."

"He was charming, and we got on famously. Are you sure this is the man who—"

"Billy knows who Collier is . . . of course, I'm sure."

"Calm down, Sam. I signed nothing."

He took a long breath and shook his head. "It was a shock to me, Lily. Well, we'll see what he does now on the Hill. His kind of leopard doesn't change spots easily."

She kissed his cheek. "Maybe he's not a leopard at all."

He grunted. "Promise me you'll not see him again."

"Sam! for goodness' sake! I didn't see him at all—he merely spoke to me at a party. Let us please keep things in perspective."

Her tone brought him around. He gazed at her, nodded, and sat, crossing his legs. "Forgive me, Lily, just the thought of Gil Collier can make me upset. He's up to something—"

"Why do you think that?"

"He always is."

"You suspect a rival company?"

He fingered his chin. "No, probably not. Collier is a thoroughgoing politician, not a business brain. As far as I know he doesn't think in those terms. Legislation is his field, but he hasn't much time left, and he may not have the votes." He rose and took his coat.

"Where're you going?"

"I have to meet Miles and the steering committee." He kissed her fondly and went to the door. "I'll see you for dinner."

His election committee claimed much of his time each day. But the hearings on their project were largely over, and when Sam was gone she had many free hours. Billy Turnbull called at the hotel several times, knowing that Sam was away, and each time they went out for a drive or to a gathering she took Tony Burke along, making sure first that he was properly outfitted. He was very careless about dress. Billy growled about the man's presence, but Lily only smiled, saying he was necessary for her.

Three days after she'd met him, Lily received a note from Gilbert Collier. A boy came to the hotel door; she invited him inside while she read the brief lines. He asked her to accompany him for a carriage ride and a lunch in the woods. If she agreed, he would come to the hotel in an hour.

She quickly composed an answer and sent the boy

back. She was delighted to accept.

She laid out her traveling dresses and selected one, a brown and beige basque and skirt with black accents and buttons. As she changed clothes, she thought about Sam, about how angry he would be if he found out. It would be best to avoid notice and sidestep a scene with him. She carefully adjusted a rust-colored scarf about her head and took a parasol. She said nothing to Burke or the others, but hurried down the back stairs. She met two waiters with a napkin-covered serving wagon; they stared at her in astonishment, but she went by them without a word, hearing their chatter as she reached the foot of the steps. She went across the huge dining room and slipped out to the street without going through the lobby.

Gilbert Collier's carriage was just pulling up to the entrance.

The driver jumped down and opened the door for her, and she slid inside and almost fell into his arms. He laughed, helped her turn about, and in half a moment the carriage was moving again.

He said, "How nice to see you again, Mrs. Berlanger."

"Lily." She got her breath and unfastened the head scarf. "May I call you Gilbert?"

"My close friends call me Roy. It's my middle name."

She gazed at him with a half-smile. He was dressed in more casual attire, brown pants thrust into boots and an almost black sack coat. "I had quite a talk about names the last time we met—the first time we met. You neglected to introduce yourself."

"I confess I did it on purpose. I wanted to meet you, and I was afraid my name would cause problems between us." He smiled. "But I see it did not."

"I don't let others do my thinking for me. If you're as

88

big a rascal as they say, I'd like to see it for myself. *Are you all they say, Roy?*"

He laughed. "Probably. It all depends, you know. I'm a hero to some and a scoundrel to others, but so is everyone else in the Senate, Sam Beckhart included. It depends on which side of the aisle you sit and who your friends are, among others."

"Sam says you're a Whig."

He nodded. "So do many others. I've been a Whig, but no longer. The party is dying . . . so I've decided to return to the Democratic fold. My state is largely composed of Democrats."

"Alabama?"

"Yes. We're neighbors, you and I. I come from Montgomery and you from New Orleans."

"Why do you oppose Sam?"

"I only oppose him on some things. I spoke against him recently on the floor because I was assured that he was forming a huge combine to loot the government, but now that I've met you I can see my information was faulty."

"Oh, I might be worse than Sam!"

"Never! Never in this world!" He took her hand and held it. "No one so beautiful could have a heart of straw. God would certainly forbid it."

She smiled and curled her fingers around his, wanting him to kiss her. She hoped he would not notice her flushed appearance nor hear her pounding heart. How attractive he was! She looked away from him, through the side window. "Where are you taking me, sir?"

"Across into Virginia. We'll come to the bridge in a moment. Have you done much sightseeing?"

"Very little, except in offices. I'm sure Washington

has more offices than any city in the world."

"And more officeholders. All blockheads." He laughed and squeezed her hand. "I'm one of them, of course."

"Tell me about you," she said. "All I know is what your enemies have told me."

"I'm a planter's son," he said. He had grown up on a cotton plantation, had gone to school in the East, studied at Harvard, and become a lawyer. But before going into practice he'd gone to Europe and spent a year and a half traveling and enjoying himself. Then back to Montgomery and an office. He had prospered, taken in a partner, and run for public office, because he could speak well. He'd been elected to the state legislature and gone from there to Congress.

"And you never married?"

"Oh yes. I was married fifteen years ago, and my wife left me for a traveling man. They were both drowned at sea, poor souls."

The carriage suddenly became noisy; the horses' hoofs clattered, and the wheels rumbled as if over loose boards. She looked out and saw they were crossing the Potomac. A dozen white-sailed boats were beating upriver, and a paddle steamer trailed black smoke and left a wide, creamy wake. She sighed, following it with her eyes.

"You're homesick," he said, noticing the signs.

She smiled. "I'll be glad to get back."

"Tell me about you. What did you study in school?"

"Whatever they told me to. I was a model child and a dutiful student. I got good grades and plenty of pats on the head. Beyond that there's nothing to tell."

"You've been married, I hear."

She sighed deeply and gazed at him with sadness. "I've been married twice and both times my husbands died of

90

sickness. I've been very unlucky."

"Married twice! I didn't know that."

"I was married very young; my father arranged it with a much older man. But he was kind to me, and I was terribly upset when he died. I married again several years later, after my parents died and I was alone. I didn't want to be so alone."

"No, of course not."

They rolled off the bridge onto dirt, and the noise stopped suddenly. "That's better," he said.

"Does your driver know where to go?"

"Yes. We discussed it at length." He glanced out. "We'll come to a village very soon—ha, there it is now, just ahead." He leaned back and kissed her hand. "I'm going to be very sorry to see you go back to St. Louis."

"You hardly know me."

"I can tell you're an exceptional woman, Lily. How much does one need to know? Have you any bad qualities?"

She laughed. "Very few. I get grumpy now and then, that's the worst thing." She could smell the fragrance of tobacco—the driver must be smoking—and the thought of a cigar made her bite her lip. Apparently Roy did not smoke at all, a very unusual thing. She hoped he didn't take snuff.

They rolled through the village without stopping, and a canopy of green trees seemed to gather them in. How close the country was to the great city! She wondered what Gilbert—Roy—had in mind; if it was a picnic, there seemed to be no food or drink, and he had not stopped in the village to procure any. . . .

Well, she would find out soon enough. The carriage turned off the main road into a one-track path that wound into the woods, and branches scraped the sides of the coach.

"The weather has been marvelous," he said, "probably in your honor. It usually rains this time of year. We'll be there in a moment. I own a farm nearby, and occasionally we come out here to hunt."

"You mean hounds and red coats and all?"

"No, just to shoot birds or small game. I'm a farm boy, as I told you. My father didn't approve of riding to hounds." He leaned toward the window. "Ah, here we are."

The team slowed and turned off the road. The carriage bumped and swayed, as dry leaves crackled under the wheels. When it stopped, Roy opened the door and jumped out quickly, pulled down the iron steps, and helped her to the grass. They were in a charming little glade ringed with trees, and far off to the right she could see the rooftops of a house and barn, from which a column of smoke was rising.

The driver jumped down as Roy took her arm. "Come along—there's a wonderful view just a moment away—"

They walked through the grass, under the trees and up a gentle knoll. At the crest he halted and pointed. Lily brushed a wisp of hair from her face, marveling. Before her, like a huge, living map was the Potomac Valley, the river, shining like beaten silver, wending its way through it. The city was far off to the left, barely visible because of the encroaching trees.

"It's beautiful," she said. She felt his arms slide about her waist and half turned. "The driver?"

"I've sent him to the farmhouse. He's to stay till he hears the horn."

"Horn?"

"There's a hunting horn in the carriage."

She laughed. "You think of everything."

"I try. For instance, I have several bottles of the best light wines—"

Turning in his arms, she touched his cheek with a finger. "I believe you've planned this outing as a campaign, Mr. Collier."

"Why, I believe you're right, Mrs. Berlanger." He kissed her lightly. "And this is the first move."

She moved closer, and his feathery kiss became more engaging. When he released her, Lily took a long breath, bent her head to his, and closed her eyes for a moment. Her heart was racing, and she knew her face must be flushed. He said softly, "Shall we open the wine?"

"Yes, of course."

They went back down the knoll to the carriage. Roy opened a boot in the rear of the coach and took out a basket and a plaid blanket. He spread the blanket on the grass under a gnarled oak. "There you are, my dear—"

She sat, spreading her skirts, and he opened the basket. It contained a square metal box in which were two tall bottles packed in ice, and a second compartment with food. She said, "You *do* think of everything!"

Smiling, he produced two stem glasses as if by magic and set them on a square of board which he extracted from the side of the basket. "I even have a corkscrew." He attacked the first bottle. "This is a young Beaujolais, not too cold, I trust—" He pulled the cork and poured into both glasses. "Now, let's see. We have breast of chicken Parisienne—cold, of course—and a beef strudel, not to mention carrots and leeks with bacon."

Food had been the furthest removed from her thoughts, but seeing and smelling the delicious odors as he opened the basket made her realize she was famished. "I'll have a little of everything."

He served them expertly and smiled at her over the rim of his glass. "I am delighted that you came with me today. You didn't mention it to Sam, did you?"

"No. He wouldn't approve. Or Billy either." She began with the chicken. "Sam is very possessive—but I imagine you know him better than I."

"In a sense. I mean in the Senate, yes. Sam is really several people all rolled into one. He shows one face to the public, another to his friends, and, I suspect, quite another to you. Will your proposed amalgamation make him a rich man?"

"I doubt it," she said. "Unless he has plans I know nothing of. I have no private agreement with him." She gazed at him innocently. Would he believe that? He made no sign that he did not.

He changed the subject completely. "This is my last term in the Senate, I think. My sojourn is up in two years. I want to get back to the country."

"And give up politics?"

"Yes. I've served my stint. How's the chicken?"

"Absolutely delicious."

"It's an old recipe. My mother got it from someone in Mobile—been in our family for years." He poured more wine into her glass. "Have you ever been in Alabama?"

"No, never."

"You'd like it. I'm going back to be a planter again. My father died three years ago and my mother can no longer manage—"

"Sam told me you wanted to be president."

He laughed. "Once I had that notion. But I can't satisfy both ends of the party at the same time. I'm afraid

I speak my mind. To be president these days you must please everyone or fall into enormous luck."

She was curious. "What do you mean by luck?"

"Capture the nomination when the party is at loggerheads over other candidates. I suspect that'll happen soon because of slavery."

"What d'you mean?"

"People are taking sides, even men of the same party. I think the time is coming when the republic must stand wholly free or wholly slave. Have you read the book *Uncle Tom's Cabin?*"

"No . . . only excerpts."

"It had a tremendous effect on ordinary people, I think more than many politicians realize even today. And Henry Clay, Mr. Webster, and Calhoun are no longer with us. New men are taking their places in Congress, lesser men in many ways."

"I don't know that I am encouraged by the gloomy picture you paint—"

He smiled suddenly. "It's a failing of mine. Let's forget it all, the entire world. I'm sorry to cast a pall over—"

"Have some more wine." She poured from the bottle as he held his glass. "What a pleasant place this is. Is that your farm there—where we can see roofs?"

"Yes. I bought it as an investment a dozen years ago from a congressman friend, and it's been rented to the same family all that time. I'm hoping they'll buy it when I pick up sticks."

She settled back, placing her empty plate on the blanket. Birds were flitting in the nearby trees, and toward the farm dogs were barking as if in play; the sounds rose and fell, and suddenly she was thinking of Chadwick. Paige had come to one of their last large gatherings before old Jacob had passed away and they'd gone for walks in the woods. She glanced at Roy and saw that he was watching her. He said, "What is it?"

She shook her head. "A few old memories, that's all. I used to visit a place very much like this when I was a girl. I remember running down a road chasing a hoop."

"Why have you never married again?"

She laughed. "I don't really want to, I suppose. Men have a terrible tendency to take charge of things, you know. I'm sure that would cause trouble now. I've been single too long."

"No, no trouble with the right man."

"You men say that easily."

"You've received dozens of proposals, I'm sure—"

She made a face. "A few, yes. But I should ask you that."

He began to gather up the plates and put things away neatly into the basket. "I haven't remarried for many of the same reasons you haven't, I'm sure. Let's finish this wine, shall we?" He divided it between them.

There was only half a glass, and she drank it off and rose, brushing her skirts. He put the remains of their meal into the basket, closed it, and took it to the carriage boot. She followed him, and when he turned she was in front of him. Her arms went about his neck, and he drew her close, kissing her urgently.

He said, "I don't know how I can let you go—"

She was surprised at the intensity of his voice. She wanted to say, "I am not gone yet," but her lips were pressed against his again, and she lost the inclination to speak. In the next moment he pulled her into the carriage, and they sprawled on the wide, padded seat, arms about each other. She was glad she'd worn a traveling dress and not a stiff and uncompromising crinoline. His lips were on her throat, moving down— down. She lay quiet as he unlaced her bodice and began to kiss her bare breasts. Eyes closed, the blood pounding in her temples, she rose slightly, then turned his face up.

"Roy—"

"Yes, my love?" His restless hands captured her.

"There is something I must know."

He kissed one red nipple. "Cannot it wait?"

"Tell me something."

"What?"

She took his face in both hands and kissed him lightly on the mouth. "Are you going to oppose Sam and me in the Senate?"

He stared at her for what seemed an eternity, then he broke into a laugh. "Lily, my darling, I will oppose you in nothing."

"And Sam?"

"Or Sam." He pushed her back into the seat.

CHAPTER NINE

Logan made a journey to New Orleans and back on the palatial *Monarch*, talked to all their agents and captains—and to everyone else who had an opinion—and learned that though the river was quiet, not all expected it to remain that way. Since the incident of the *Locust* there had been no further trouble; however, a few of the agents talked mysteriously of a "grapevine" that warned of trouble ahead. They urged him to at least arm the officers on each boat. A few went further and thought he should organize a roving strike force capable not only of guarding the boats but of inflicting damage. Lily Berlanger, they said, did not understand kind words.

When he returned to St. Louis, Logan discussed the matter with Fraser, who was against the use of force. "I agree that we should arm the boat's officers, though I imagine most of them are armed by now on their own accord. But I cannot see that a strike force would help matters." He paced his office floor, arms behind him. "Besides, the cost of a platoon of men—" He shook his head.

"If we advertise that our boats are armed, it might do a bit of good," Logan said.

"Let it be known along the levees, you mean?"

"Yes, that might be enough. Has Lily returned

from Washington?"

"Not according to the papers, and her arrival is sure to be duly noted. Thank God that's one thing she can't control." He stopped in front of Logan. "Arming the boats is something I'll leave up to you. Whatever you decide—" He shrugged. "We must remember that men cost money, and we only get money by hauling passengers and cargo. One guard means one less passenger."

"Well, almost."

Fraser looked at him. "You know what I mean." He went behind his desk and sat down. "Speaking of arming boats and of cargoes, I've some news for you. Since you were away we have a new client—or we will have very soon. He comes to us because of difficulties he's had with other shippers. They either charged too much or routed his material to Memphis when it was intended for Cincinnati. I've promised him things will be better with us."

Logan fished for a cigar. "One client more or less has never been news before."

"Well, yes. But this one ships only special cargo."

"Special cargo? What does that mean exactly?" He struck a match.

Fraser leaned back. "Munitions of war." He rose at Logan's silence. "Other shippers charged exorbitant rates, because they loaded gunpowder barrels along with passengers. I propose to haul no passengers with such munitions, so the risk is cut in half or more."

"Who needs that much gunpowder?"

"Well, it isn't all gunpowder, of course. There're caps and fuses and all kinds of equipment. The client is a munitions maker. We'll have a meeting in a day or two with Mr. William Stivers, their representative. You ought to be present."

"We'd be hauling for the military?"

"Not entirely. Much of the material goes to consignees in New Orleans. I suppose they sell abroad and to South and Central America. But that's not our problem. All we have to do is get it to the warehouse."

Logan smiled. "Munitions of war. That's a likely target. I wonder how soon Lily will hear about it."

"She'll know soon enough. There aren't many secrets along the river, especially about cargo." He tapped Logan's chest. "We're talking about special rates, you know."

"Due to the dangers involved."

"Yes, certainly. Barring emergencies it should be a lucrative contract for us."

Logan went to the winow and stared out. "You mentioned hauling freight only. That's using half a steamboat, which is—"

"Which is foolish," Fraser said. "I had in mind buying boats just for this particular trade. There are any number of small sternwheelers available that can be remodeled to do the job."

Logan puffed the cigar and nodded. Smaller boats would mean smaller crews, and none of the outlay for crews and supplies needed for passengers; it would be simpler all around.

Fraser got a bottle from his desk. "Let's have a drink on it."

The meeting with Mr. William Stivers took place three days later in Fraser's office. Logan, Neil Barnes, and Fraser were present, along with a secretary, Lester

Dunlap, who took notes.

Stivers was a large, expansive man in a perfectly tailored dark suit and figured waistcoat. Draped across his middle was a shining gold watch chain, from which dangled an ivory tooth set in tooled gold. His pink face was round, edged with curly white hair, and he wore a small, white moustache. There was a diamond stickpin in his snowy cravat and gold rings on plump fingers. He appeared delighted to meet Logan. "Kenneth has told me so many fine things about you, sir."

"Kenneth has an active imagination, Mr. Stivers."

"I agree, and a colorful one, and he is a good judge of whiskey."

"Mr. Stivers and I were at the Bluebird Club," Fraser said. He passed around coffee and offered cigars. "Help yourselves, gentlemen."

"I've heard of that place," Neil Barnes said with a touch of envy. "Never been there. I understand the girls are—" He wriggled his fingers.

"Yes, they are," Fraser smiled. "Yes, they certainly are."

"Too much for me." Stivers grinned amiably and pulled at his moustache.

They seated themselves, except for Stivers, who faced them with a cigar in hand. "Let me tell you a bit about my company, Maxwell and Coles—" He had been representing them for some thirty years, he said, and had traveled to every part of the nation and to Canada. Maxwell & Coles had started out as a purveyor of women's ready-to-wear, and at present the company was still in that field, though now ready-to-wear, both women's and men's, was a small part of the whole. The main thrust of the firm was in equipment, supplies, and munitions. They made

101

military uniforms for the United States Army, Navy, and Marines, and for the armed forces of several other nations. They manufactured accouterments and every sort of military goods, not including small arms or artillery. They held a number of government contracts requiring them to ship these supplies and equipment to both army and navy depots such as those in Louisville, Memphis, and New Orleans. They also supplied private firms.

"We buy small arms and resell them," Stivers said, "but we have not yet decided to go into that field. Perhaps later. We will ship on your boats every kind of powder, blasting powder as well as gunpowder, fuses, caps, cartridges, portfires, slow match, sponges, and rammers—a thousand and one items, packed and boxed to insure the utmost safety during transit."

"A great deal of gunpowder?" Barnes asked.

"Yes, but I assure you it is safe from most problems." Stivers puffed smoke and smiled expansively. "For instance, a bullet fired from pistol or rifle into a keg of powder will not set it off. Some are not aware of that."

"What about fire?"

Stivers' brows rose. "I fear that fire is our enemy, gentlemen. Let us try not to set fire to the cargoes."

Fraser laughed at his expression. "Yes, we will all try. But the best insurance is secrecy."

"Ah yes," Stivers agreed. "In the long run secrecy is better than a company of armed men." He raised a finger. "However, there must be guards."

"There will be guards," Logan promised.

Neil Barnes asked, "Where will the cargoes be loaded?"

"At our own docks on the Illinois River at La Salle,"

Stivers said. "Our factories and shops are in Chicago, and the material is sent by wagon to La Salle. There we can control everything and use as few people in the warehouses as possible. Also only one or two key persons will know about shipments. They will be loaded at the last minute, so nothing can be learned ahead of time. Our people are accustomed to this kind of secrecy, because of the goods we deal in."

"Excellent," Fraser said. "More coffee, anyone?"

Stivers showed them papers of the projected shipping schedules worked out by his company officials. Jeffries-Fraser steamboats would be required at La Salle twice a month to start with, and occasionally there would be special shipments in between the regular ones.

When the meeting was concluded, Stivers shook hands all round and went downstairs with Fraser to take his leave.

Neil Barnes said to Logan, "I've located two stern-wheelers, across the river. Kenneth says we'll need two to begin with."

"Yes, two or three, depending on size. But I think we ought to do the remodeling out of town."

"How does Pittsburgh suit you?"

"Pittsburgh? Isn't that too far?"

Barnes shrugged. "Kenneth says he has an old friend there, somebody named Ritter, who owns a boatyard."

"Well, that's out of town all right. What about those boats?"

"We can see them anytime you wish."

Logan looked at the clock on the wall. "What about right now?"

They drove to the levee, Barnes, Louis Gualco, and

103

himself, and Barnes arranged for a squat steam tug to carry them across the river. The day was misty and cool, cold when they got to midstream, chugging across roiling brown waters. The stern-wheelers were tied to the bank in a small inlet and were owned, Barnes said, by a produce company that had used them in part to haul vegetables to market.

"They're a little smelly now, but we can have them swabbed out before you take them to Pittsburgh."

They were the *Ionia* and the *Freedom*, both nearly the same length, and both looked small to his eye. They were about the size of a ferry steamer, and *Ionia* was a good five years older than the other. But they were ideal, he thought, for the Maxwell & Coles project.

Neither had a texas; the pilothouses were on the hurricane decks, but they would save half a dozen cabins on each for the crews and tear out the rest.

With Neil Barnes at his elbow with a notebook, Logan went over each steamer from fireboxes to pilothouses, and Barnes noted deficiencies. A hog chain required adjustment here, a paddle bucket needed replacing, the steam steering apparatus was long overdue for maintenance. . . . But nothing was seriously wrong with either. *Freedom*, being newer, had few problems and could probably be taken to Pittsburgh with no repairs. She could use a paint job, he said to Barnes; the wheelhouses were garish with someone's idea of a partly draped woman and a flag with the boat's name in red.

They went back across the river, and Logan reported to Fraser, who immediately sent a message to the boats' agent. They would purchase.

Fraser also had a list of crewmen, which he gave Logan for approval. Barnes sent a crew of roustabouts across

104

the river with a foreman who had orders to clean the boats out thoroughly. The engineers and carpenters followed. In five days all was finished.

Doris was very satisfied with her house, but after a short while she found herself pacing the rooms when Logan was gone, looking for things to do, thinking about the job she'd left. It had not been much as a job, but it had kept her occupied. Logan had provided her with a butler, cook, and driver-gardener, and she felt she was spending her days at unimportant tasks as she waited for him to return.

He discussed with her the problem in setting up a guard system for the steamboats, but those times were all too few. And he was about to take the two new purchases off to Pittsburgh.

She picked what she thought was the opportune time to broach her idea. He had arrived home late and was standing with his back to the fire in the study, when she brought him a sizzling hot toddy and kissed his cheek.

"Darling, there's something I'd like to do."

"In what way—about the house?"

"Nothing to do with the house at all."

He looked at her sidelong and sipped the toddy. "I believe I have a suspicion—"

"Not what you think."

He smiled. "What do I think?" His brows lifted. "You want to go along to Pittsburgh, of course."

"No, not that."

"Well, I'm glad. It'll be an uncomfortable trip, I'm afraid. But what is it?"

She hesitated. She had always found Logan understanding. Why should she doubt him now? "I want—to

105

go to work in the office." It came out with a rush that surprised her.

He stared in astonishment.

She said, "Not that I wouldn't like to go to Pittsburgh, mind."

"Well, of course, you may if you wish, though it'll be—" He took a breath. "Why do you want to work in the office?"

He knew, as he asked the question, what the answer was. She had not enough to do in the house, and he should have seen it before. Doris was not a hothouse flower as some women were.

"The house is lovely, dear, but it's confining. Surely there's something I can do there."

He sat and sipped the toddy. Fraser would be off to the Maxwell & Coles plant in Chicago, and might be gone several weeks. Neil Barnes had several times complained about inadequate help. . . .

She said, "I've had office experience, sir."

Logan laughed. "You're sure it won't prove just as confining as the house?"

"At least there'll be life there and things going on. If all else fails I can look out the window to the street."

He rose and embraced her. "I can think of no sensible reason why you should not go if it's your earnest desire. When would you like to start?"

"At once," she said, pleased.

"Neil will be astonished, you know." He sat and took up the cup.

"Let me handle Mr. Barnes. After all, I'm the boss's wife. What can he say?"

He laughed again. "I believe you will manage him. Very well, tomorrow then. But you'll have to obey Kenneth."

She slid onto his lap. "Kenneth will have no objections at all."

In that he knew she was absolutely right.

That evening after supper she spent an hour going through her clothes to select the right dress to wear in the morning. Since her marriage she had acquired a small wardrobe and was adding to it; it was important that she dress in a manner becoming to her new station. But there had been a time, not to very long ago, when she'd had no more than two simple, patched, very worn dresses to her name. Logan might forget that, but she never would.

She finally decided on a severely cut, black and dark blue top and skirt with shirrs near the narrow belt. She looked good in dark colors. The skirt allowed a simple bustle instead of a cumbersome crinoline, which would not be suitable for office wear.

She'd expected more opposition from Logan and was very gratified that he understood her feelings so promptly. Over supper they'd discussed his coming trip to Pittsburgh; he'd be away at least a month, he thought, depending on the refitting of the two boats. He stressed that she must exercise extreme caution when traveling to and from the city and listen to Chris Murphy and Baxter Ross. She promised.

Privately she thought it would be stupid of Lily Berlanger to attack her. Lily would gain nothing but revenge, and it would cause a storm that might overwhelm her; it might even set some smug police official to thinking.

It was exciting to dress in the morning in preparation for the adventure. She imagined Neil Barnes' face when he learned she would be a permanent addition to the staff. He would be astonished, taken aback—and maybe annoyed. The men in the office where she'd worked before marrying Logan had reacted in various ways to her, but most, she thought, disliked the idea of a woman's invading their sacred precincts.

They had breakfast together as usual, and Logan was very matter-of-fact, but Mrs. Benson put on a face like a thundercloud as she served them. Though she said nothing it was obvious she disapproved strongly. But, of course, Mrs. Benson disapproved of most things.

She arrived at the office and met Neil Barnes; when he understood that she had come to work, he accepted the decision with a calm that surprised her. "Welcome, Mrs. Jeffries," he said gravely. "What position did you have in mind to fill?"

"I leave that to you and Kenneth."

Logan said, "You're both being very formal—"

Barnes adjusted his glasses and squinted. "One is formal when the wife of one's employer comes to require employment for herself. Have you worked in an office before, Mrs. Jeffries?"

"Yes, I have. And you may call me Doris."

"Make up your mind to it, Neil," Logan said. "She's very determined." He took his hat. "I'm going to the levee." He went out, with Louis Gualco at his heels.

Kenneth Fraser was also surprised to see her, having had no warning. He came in, hung his hat and coat on hooks in the outer office, and warmed his hands at the small stove. "You've come to work here, my dear?"

"Yes, certainly—"

"Well, I'd thought you would have your fill of offices by now." He smiled at her expression. "Then we must find something for you to do. Let me think—"

108

"We have three clerks," Barnes said, letting his voice trail off.

Doris said, "Let me look about and see where I can make myself useful. I hope you won't mind if I ask a great many foolish questions?"

"Ask away," Fraser said. He went into his office, leaving the door open.

The clerks were in a room by themselves, Lester Dunlap, Mr. Muchem, and Mr. Silva. Dunlap was a tall, skinny man with a sad face; Muchem was middle-aged, short, and stout and had hardly any hair; Silva was about the same age, spare, and gray and had round, protuberant eyes. All were astonished to learn that she was to be one of them, and more astonished to learn who she was. One of their main jobs, they told her, was billing. They showed her how forms came from the offices downstairs, how they were translated into monthly or daily statements, how they were sent out to customers, and how bank drafts were received. It was not complicated, but tedious. At her question Dunlap told her that ordinary shippers paid in cash at the counters downstairs.

In the middle of the morning she went down the steps to the ground floor in company with Fraser. He showed her how shipments were received, how they were tagged, listed, and routed to the proper conveyance for delivery—wagon, cart, train, or steamboat. There were various kinds of goods requiring special handling; there were insured goods and even mail. The handling of shipments could become very complicated, he said, especially as cargoes were also received from incoming wagons or boats and redistributed. Many cargoes were stored until called for by draying firms or customers or reshippers, and many were picked up by consignees in their own wagons.

A battery of clerks in the shipping office kept the records, filed them, and sent the proper papers to the different departments. Copyists were busy making duplicates; other clerks took in cash, weighed merchandise, and tagged it; baggage handlers made a stir with their short, iron-tired carts; and teamsters shouted from the loading docks.

At first visit all was a blur of noise and bustle, and she could see only hurry and confusion. But Fraser was patient, and the workings of the depot began to come clear. In a very few days she understood how the interlocking pieces fitted, and she suggested to Fraser that certain of the tags be printed in colors for instant identification, so that handlers did not have to stop and read each tag separately.

Fraser was delighted. "My dear, you will revolutionize us within the week!" He gave orders to a printer for colored tags to be made up. The idea was then extended to differentiate cash from credit clips and certain other forms. Fraser declared that she had more than earned her keep for the year by one simple idea.

Neil Barnes spent much of his time in the ground-floor shipping and receiving offices; Fraser spent the bulk of his upstairs, interviewing prospective shippers, settling complaints, and discussing insurance. Fraser's abilities at judging people, gained during his years at gambling tables, stood him in good stead when people claimed more than they had shipped or exaggerated the worth.

But Fraser was preparing to go to Chicago, to the main plant of Maxwell & Coles, to complete the agreements

110

they had talked about with William Stivers. Neil Barnes would have to assume many of his duties. Could Doris take over others?

She was determined to try.

She saw Logan off to Pittsburgh with the two small stern-wheelers, and three days later Fraser left as well. Both office and home seemed empty, and she did her best to plunge into work to make the time go faster.

A week after Logan had departed, she went downstairs one afternoon to discuss an insurance problem with Neil Barnes and was told by a clerk that he had stepped out to the tobacconist's on the corner.

When she went to the wide side door that gave onto the street, she saw Barnes getting out of a carriage a hundred yards down. As the carriage came toward her and passed, she saw Howard Paddock inside!

Paddock had been pointed out to her by Logan and was one of Lily Berlanger's partners. Doris moved back from the door, turned, and half ran up the steps to the offices, a cold hand clutching her heart.

What was Neil Barnes doing with Howard Paddock?

CHAPTER TEN

She hurried into Fraser's office, where she had a small desk, and closed the door. Neil Barnes had not seen her and probably would not come upstairs immediately—but she must compose herself before she saw him again. She must not let him know what she had seen! She had no idea what he would do if he found out, but it was something she did not care to think about.

What should she do? Or should she do nothing until Logan or Fraser returned?

She thought about it all afternoon as she forced herself to go about the ordinary tasks she'd assumed, but the picture never left her mind. Neil came upstairs shortly before he went home, said a few words to her perfunctorily, drew on a topcoat, and went out.

Doris breathed a sigh of relief. Even after hours had gone by, she feared her face would give her away. She put on her own coat and went downstairs to the rear and waited several minutes till Chris Murphy showed up with the carriage.

At home she went through Logan's desk for the name of the steamboat yard and found it at last—John Ritter. There was no building name, but a wire would doubtless reach Logan there, addressed to the boatyard in Pittsburgh.

112

What Neil Barnes was doing was not obvious, and maybe it was no more than keeping Paddock informed of what went on, but it alarmed her that Barnes would be able to tell Paddock exactly where Logan could be found in Pittsburgh.

Mrs. Benson had supper ready, and Doris ate it more quickly than usual, informed Chris Murphy that she wanted the coach brought around—to his astonishment—and put on a heavy coat.

When it pulled up to the steps, she hurried out, and Murphy opened the door. "Where you going this time o'night, Mum?"

"To find a telegraph office."

"Telegraph?"

"Yes. Let's hurry." She climbed in and he slammed the door.

She had the wire composed in her head. "Neil B. conferring in secret with H. Paddock. Send instructions." She could imagine Logan's feelings when he read it. He would probably wonder, as she did, who else had accepted Paddock's money to spy on them.

They found a telegraph office open not far from the levee, and she went inside to write out the words on a message blank and pay the man. It would be delivered in the morning, he said.

She rode home again, heavy-hearted that Neil Barnes had proved a turncoat. It was not going to be easy to share the offices with him until Logan returned, but she had to steel herself. It might prove to be very important that Neil not find out he had been spotted. What had convinced him to turn? Money, probably. He might have debts they did not know about . . . or expensive tastes.

She got through the next day, and late in the afternoon

113

a telegram was delivered to her from Pittsburgh. It was from Logan:

> *Arrived safe. Work going smoothly. Got your wire. Be home in month. Logan.*

Home in a month! She read it over and over again, but the words were always the same. Then it occurred to her that since he had sent the wire to the office he might expect that somehow Neil Barnes would read it and be comforted. The thought reassured her, and she left the telegraph blank on the desk as if carelessly, but memorized its exact position.

Barnes was in his office when she went downstairs, and when she returned the telegram had been moved slightly. He had read it.

She left the office before Barnes that day, saying she was tired, and drove home in the swaying carriage, glad to be away. It was a nervous reaction, she was sure, but such game playing was new to her. What would Logan do when he came home? She sighed, thinking she'd be a nervous wreck by the end of the month. Couldn't they renovate the boats more quickly?

Several days later Barnes had a wire from Fraser saying all was well, that the agreements were signed, and that he was on the way back. He would arrive probably a day or two after the letter. Barnes showed it to her. "This's going to put the firm on a new footing, Doris. Now we can really compete with Lily Berlanger."

He went back to his office, and she stared after him. How could he say those kinds of things and be in Howard Paddock's pay?

114

But of course he had to, didn't he? It was all part of the playacting. A deadly game for enormously high stakes. There were times when she wished she'd gone with Logan—then she'd never have found out about Neil. . . .

By the end of the week she was able to talk and even laugh with him without worrying that she was giving herself away. She managed to put it all to the back of her mind, no mean feat, she thought. She did not attempt to spy on him; there was little chance that he'd keep anything incriminating in his desk, and she did not follow him even when he went out of the building during the day.

Kenneth Fraser came in on Saturday morning from La Salle; he arrived barely in time for lunch, stopped in the offices only long enough to say hello to them, and then went to see Stivers.

When she went home that evening Logan was there.

He opened the carriage door when the coach stopped in front of the steps. "Hello, missy—"

She gasped in astonishment. "Logan!" He jumped into the coach and embraced her. She clung to him. "I didn't expect you for weeks!"

"I started back instantly when I got your wire. Where's Kenneth?"

"He came back from Chicago only today—I hardly saw him."

He helped her out of the carriage, and they went up the steps to the door as Murphy slapped the reins. Baxter Ross met them. "Supper'll be ready pretty quick—"

"Thanks, Baxter." She turned so Logan could take her cloak. "What about the boats in Pittsburgh?"

"Ritter has a very good foreman. He'll see the job

115

done, as well as our captains. The plans are all approved. They didn't need me."

She clung to him again, heart beating fast. "I missed you so, darling. But you could have sent a wire here."

"I wanted to surprise you." He looked up to see that no one was near. "And besides, if Neil is in Lily's pay there's no telling who else is."

She let out her breath. "I hope no one else here."

He kissed her. "Let's go have supper."

Mrs. Benson had bought some young pheasants in town that day and served them with a raisin puree. They ate alone, by candlelight, and said nothing at all concerning Neil Barnes. He told her about the trip to Pittsburgh. He'd purchased another small stern-wheeler from John Ritter; he and Fraser had agreed they'd need three boats. It, too, would be renovated to carry cargo, then brought to St. Louis.

"I'm tempted to send a carriage for Kenneth tonight—"

"It can wait till tomorrow," she said. "I'd rather have you to myself."

They had coffee in the study. Logan closed the door, and she told him about seeing Barnes get out of Howard Paddock's carriage.

"You're positive it was Paddock?"

"Yes. You pointed him out to me, remember. Big nose and all."

He nodded. "Neil's sure of himself to meet Paddock that close to the offices."

"He didn't think anyone would see him. What good is Neil to them?"

"Information's the main thing. He can tell them what

116

we've planned, where we'll be, and so on. I wish I knew what Lily was planning."

"Would it be difficult to do the same to her?"

"Probably impossible. From what I hear, Lily takes no one into her confidence." He sipped the coffee, his eyes far away.

She sat by him. "What will you do about Neil?"

"I don't know—" He gazed at her. "You've been able to carry on without shouting at him that he's a traitor?"

Doris laughed. "It was difficult the first few days, yes."

"Then maybe nothing."

"Nothing?"

"Well, I'll talk to Kenneth first, but maybe if we say nothing at all and allow Neil to listen to the kinds of plans we want him to hear—"

"You can't do that for very long."

"No, perhaps not. But he'll do his regular work, and he's quite good at that, you know."

"Can you trust him to do it?"

"Oh yes, I think so. He'll do it very well, matter of fact, so there's no suspicion of his real job." He put the coffee cup aside. "First thing Monday, I'll say in front of him that the yard in Pittsburgh can't complete our boats for another month or more—the reason I came back. Too much delay. We'll feed him as much misinformation as we can."

"Do you think he's got any helpers in the offices?"

Logan frowned. "Well—that's a worry." He leaned over and kissed her. "I'll go see Clarence Yates at once and let him investigate for us."

"He can't investigate everyone, surely!"

"I don't know. Probably key personnel, the ones who have access to the kind of information Lily would want."

"It'll have to be done very quietly."

"That's Clarence's job, and he's expert at it." He rose and pulled her up. "Right now I've something else in mind."

"And what's that, husband?"

"Surely you can guess?"

She kissed him and led the way out of the room.

The next morning Logan and Gualco drove into the city, to the Seven Oaks Hotel, where Fraser was staying, and the two went for a drive along the river with Louis up on the box with Chris Murphy. The meetings in Chicago had gone like clockwork, Fraser reported, not a single hitch. Old Thomas Maxwell, who ran the company, was the kind who preferred to seal agreements with a handshake, but written contracts were being drawn up and would be signed in a fortnight.

The stern-wheelers *Ionia* and *Freedom*, Logan said, would be completed and sent back to St. Louis in three weeks; the third boat would be able to follow in another week or ten days.

Neil Barnes was another matter. Fraser was distressed to hear about his defection. "I suppose it's money—it usually is," he said slowly. "But he always seemed a decent sort—"

"I propose doing nothing about him for the time being. We'll just watch ourselves when he's around."

"He'll catch on to that pretty quick. Neil is no fool."

"Yes, I suppose so. And when he does catch on, I think he'll just leave suddenly, pack up, and get out."

Fraser nodded. "It might be the best way. I certainly don't want to go to the police about him."

"Yes."

"And we'd best be thinking about a replacement."

Logan said, "*You'd* best be thinking about it. That's your department. *I'm* wondering what I should do about Howard Paddock."

"You mean retaliate?"

"I don't know. Any suggestions?"

Fraser sighed. "I hope we don't get into an outright war." He fished out a cheroot and bit off the end. "Is Lily back in town yet?"

"Doris said nothing about it."

"Hmmm. And no attacks on you?"

Logan smiled. "Not recently." He indicated the driver. "Chris and I are both armed, and this coach is partially armored. They must realize we're prepared. Lily can't go about murdering people, do you think?"

"Yes, I do," Fraser said, "and I think you do too. She'll hire it done as she has before. You were attacked by men she hired. Neil Barnes will tell Paddock where you can be found, and they'll send men there. And no way to trace it back to Lily."

Logan grunted. All true, and none of it pleasant to hear. He took out his own case and lighted a cigar on the same match with Fraser. By this time Paddock knew all about their new contracts with Maxwell & Coles, the new steamboats they'd purchased, and indeed all aspects of their business. Was it wise to keep Neil Barnes on, even though they could feed him false information?

Fraser thought the damage was done, and a bit more time could hardly hurt. They drove back to the hotel,

119

where Fraser got out, and Logan drove home again, thinking about the time, years ago, when he'd climbed into Lily's carriage and taken a pistol away from her. If he'd killed her then, none of this would have happened.

But he'd never have found Doris, either.

CHAPTER ELEVEN

Udell Winter was a cautious man, one who thought things through before acting, especially if they concerned money. He was not a suspicious man, as a rule, not at all like Lily, but he had a good many suspicions about Howard Paddock. Paddock was opaque, not the slightest bit open. Some people seemed to be open and nearly transparent, everything being out where it could be examined. Not so Lily, and not so Paddock; and each was opaque in different ways.

Of course, he was used to Lily's foibles and curious habits from his long association with her. She was the most secretive person in the world.

The day after he'd gone with Howard to the Bluebird Club he'd spent an hour reviewing their conversations. What was behind his talk? Surely only one thing. Paddock wanted information from him, information that could implicate Lily—therefore his question about Andrea's death. Of course he'd denied that he knew anything about it, but he knew Paddock didn't believe it.

That had been an exploratory evening, he thought. Paddock had wanted to see how he'd react. Would Paddock follow it up?

And if he did, would he pay for the information? Paddock had a reputation for being cheap. But it all depended on Howard's opinion of him. Did Howard think he would come cheap or dear? If Howard offered enough, what would he do?

He wished there were someone he could discuss it with, but there was no one. There was no point in bringing up the matter to his wife; to begin with, he didn't want her to know, so she could not prattle to her busybody friends. No telling who they might talk to. And, second, she had not the foggiest idea of business or intrigue. Her advice would be worthless.

He would have to figure it out alone and come to his own decisions. Did he know enough about Lily and her affairs to be worth a good deal of money to someone like Paddock? Probably. His observations concerning Lily would fill a book, and if only half of them proved incriminating . . . Old Jacob, for instance, had probably died because of Lily's meddling, and she had certainly paid for Andrea's death.

Howard had made the first move, the sumptuous meal and girly entertainment at the fabulous Bluebird Club, and a little leading conversation. When would he follow it up? Udell was positive, the more he thought about it, that Howard would come to him again. And with that in mind, he left his office and went downstairs to the street, walked around the corner to Whitaker's Bar and Grill, and sat in a rear booth with a stein of beer on the table in front of him.

If Howard Paddock came to him with a solid offer, what would he do?

There was much to think about. He was very satisfied with his present position in the firm and with the money Lily paid him. Since coming to St. Louis he had grown accustomed to a much better style of living. Lily paid him nearly twice as much as anyone else in the firm and gave him Christmas bonuses besides. His wife spent money with both hands.

He thought about his wife. She was a woman with very little to recommend her, physically or mentally, and the expensive clothing didn't help. She had been pretty once, but she'd let herself go over the years, and the simple prettiness had fled like a sunset cloud before the wind. And she'd never been terribly bright. He had married her because of the prettiness a very long time ago and had quickly discovered that she was more shallow than most and given to pouting. How much would he really miss her—if he went away? He thought about a life without her as he drank the beer. It made him smile.

And Lily. She would be furious if she discovered he'd sided with Paddock. Would she be furious enough to send someone after him? Udell shuddered. He knew how her thought processes worked. How vengeful she could be. She was fully capable of sending a man to track him down and do what Edward Taylor had done to Andrea. Murder.

It was something to keep in mind when contemplating a double-cross of Lily.

But it was a big world, and no matter how furious she became, he was sure he could elude her and her long arm. It was possible to cover his tracks, to disappear completely. Especially if he were not burdened with a wife and her many trunks.

Of course, if Lily found out about him, she'd also know about Howard Paddock, and surely the greater part of her rage would be taken out on him. But that was Paddock's problem.

Udell would have to change his name and maybe go

abroad. He'd never been outside the States, and the thought of going was not terribly comforting. He might go to New England, or west to California—no, California was too sparsely settled. Boston, perhaps. Certainly he could easily lose himself in a great city; with a new name and with plenty of money—from Paddock—he could live a life of ease and thumb his nose at Lily.

If things went as they were going, how long would Lily keep him on the payroll? He was sixty-one now, and when he studied the mirror he was sure he could not hide it. Lily knew his age anyway. One day she would decide she needed a younger man, a more active man, and maybe one with more education. He'd never gone beyond grade school. That terrible day could come at any time, and then he'd be cut off without a cent of income. He had heard of pensions, but no one he knew received one. Naturally Lily would laugh at the idea—pay a man after he left her service! Ridiculous. No, she would fire him, and that would be that.

He ordered another beer.

Of course, there were things in his favor now. Lily might *not* fire him at any time soon. He might lay down the law to his wife about spending, saying they must save for their old age as everyone else did. She would whine and cry, but he *could* be firm.

What if he listened to what Paddock had to offer and then related all of it to Lily? Wouldn't she be grateful? She might.

But then Howard Paddock might turn on him and do something dreadful. Udell sighed. He'd best keep his mouth shut, no matter what.

What should he do? Stay as he was or accept a lucrative offer from Paddock? If he accepted, it would

124

change his life.

And if he told Paddock to go jump in the river, how would Paddock react? He might attempt several unpleasant things in revenge. He *was* Lily's partner, after all, a limited partner, but close to Lily. He might persuade her to hire a younger man; Paddock was as capable of that as he was of undermining Lily.

Udell gulped the beer. Out of a job, he'd be shut out of everything. No one would want him—Lily and Paddock both might spread the word, don't hire Udell Winter.

Well, if he changed his name and went far away . . .

And if he stayed as he was, he'd still have his wife.

He pushed the empty stein away and fished for a cigar. What kind of an offer was Paddock likely to make him? Probably half what he was really prepared to pay. Maybe ten thousand dollars. Of course he'd only offer five, at first. Udell puffed on the cigar, closed his eyes, and made mental calculations. Combined with what he already had in the bank, ten thousand would allow him to live the rest of his life, not in luxury, but comfortably, and he still might pick up an odd job here and there.

That meant taking the entire bank account with him. His wife would have to get along on what she had in her purse and what she could realize from the sale of their home. Maybe she had something in the cookie jar.

He ordered another beer.

Maybe he should ask for twenty thousand.

He thought about the girls at the Bluebird Club; they were nubile and smiling and bare-shouldered. He sighed and looked at the glowing end of the cigar, wondering if Paddock hired those kinds of girls for his pleasure. If Paddock did, why couldn't he? He glanced around to see if anyone was watching him. His face felt a little flushed.

125

He hadn't had thoughts like that for years.

Maybe twenty thousand wasn't enough.

Howard Paddock came away from the evening at the Bluebird with no clear picture of what Udell Winter might do if an offer was made to him. He seemed to be the sort of man who would listen. . . . But then what? Paddock liked to know in advance what the outcome would be before he laid down a bet.

He also had an intuitive feeling that if he and Udell could come to terms, it ought to be before Lily returned from Washington. Her very presence might inhibit the bookkeeperish Winter.

He already employed several clerks to pass on information to him concerning policies and changes made by Lily. It was good to keep one's finger on the pulse; no telling when a piece of information might mean the difference between money in the pocket or nothing. Through these clerks he investigated Udell Winter. The man lived with an uncharming wife in a good neighborhood—they had no children—and his wife did not stint herself in the matter of clothes and furnishings. Udell spent very little.

He had seen how Udell ogled the girls at the club. He asked specific questions and learned that Udell laughed easily at jokes concerning unloved wives, never spoke of his own wife—or anyone else's—and apparently never went to brothels. All in all, it told him very little.

It occurred to him that he might set a girl after Udell, to see for himself how Udell reacted, but then dismissed the idea. Udell would become suspicious.

No, he would have to pick his opportunity and make his offer. As simple as that. Udell was basically a simple man, wasn't he? The direct approach might be the best in the long run. At least he'd get a quick answer.

And even if Udell turned him down, he could probably be persuaded to keep his mouth shut. Fear was a powerful weapon.

He braced Udell one Friday evening. Entering the offices when the staff was preparing to go home, he knocked on Udell's door and went in. Udell was behind his desk writing notes on a pad. Seeing Paddock, his brows went up; he smiled briefly and pointed to a chair. "Let me finish this—"

"Take your time," Howard said. He sniffed and fiddled with his watch chain and looked about the office. It was not as large as Lily's, but well furnished, as a general manager's should be. There were pictures on the walls, a second desk where a clerk sat during the day, and a wardrobe closet with open doors; he could see coats and overshoes inside. Two windows looked out over house-tops and stores, and an umbrella stood leaning in one corner.

After a moment Udell stopped writing and laid the pad aside. He intertwined his fingers before him on the desk. "What's on your mind, Howard?"

"Business," Paddock said amiably. "I'd like to do a bit of business with you."

The brows rose again. "In what way?"

"Can we be overheard here?"

Udell shook his head.

Paddock moved his chair closer to the desk. He rubbed his nose and smiled. "We're men of the world, you and I, Udell—"

"No, I'm a simple man, Howard."

"Bosh. Everyone knows that you run the firm, not

Lily. She's only the titular head. You do the real work."

"Well, some of that is true. But Lily makes all the real decisions, you know."

"But you could make them just as well."

"Perhaps." Udell shrugged his thin shoulders. Was this meeting for the purpose of the second move? Paddock was acting like it. He gave the other his full attention, including a small, encouraging smile. "I guess you could make them too, Howard."

Paddock smiled broadly. "Of course, I could." He leaned closer. "Doesn't it sometimes rankle with you to have to take orders from her?"

Udell thought it over. He rubbed his thumbs together and stared over Paddock's head into space. Any man might be expected to feel annoyance at having to do such a thing. "Yes, it does," he admitted.

"Women ought not to be in business."

"Not many of them in it, that's true."

"Business and politics—no place for 'em."

"No, I guess not."

"Have you thought about retiring?"

Udell stared. "Retiring from here?"

"Yes. You must have money saved—"

"Well, I have some, but not enough." He smiled. "I guess no one has enough."

"Maybe you'd like to retire and settle down somewhere peaceful with no one telling you what to do, huh?"

Udell wrinkled his nose. "That sounds good."

"Especially not Lily telling you what to do."

"What're you getting at, Howard?"

"I'm thinking that it'd be nice for all of us if Lily would retire."

Udell almost laughed. "Lily'll never do that."

"No, I think you're right. Not of her own accord. She'd need a little pushing."

"What kind of pushing?"

"Well, just a little help, God willing."

Udell grunted, staring at his guest. "It'd have to be quite a lot of help."

Paddock edged closer, and his voice became more silky. "We all know Lily's done some things she doesn't want known, huh?"

Udell nodded silently.

"Like Andrea, for instance."

Udell licked his lips. "What d'you know about Andrea?"

"I don't *know* anything. But I was the one who found Edward Taylor for you, you remember. You came to me in Cairo—"

"I remember." Udell's chest felt tight. "But I don't know any more than you do." It was true that Paddock had led him to Taylor, a smiling killer. Lily had wanted someone to handle what she called "undercover business." She had employed Taylor, and he knew Taylor had gone to New Orleans, where Andrea had lived with her husband, Logan Jeffries. He knew in his heart that Taylor had killed Andrea. Lily had never breathed a word of it, but anyone who knew the circumstances could put two and two together, especially when Logan had come after Taylor and killed him.

During those days Lily had been damned edgy and irritable. And had gone off with Paige Robinson for an extended vacation. But before she'd gone, she had hired guards who were around her constantly. She feared Logan would kill her also.

And she still had the guards.

"There are other things, too," Paddock said.

The talk was making Udell nervous. He wanted a cigar but was afraid his trembling fingers would be noticed. He glanced at the sideboard on the far side of the room, where he kept a few bottles and glasses. Paddock saw the look and turned his head.

"Have you got a drink there?"

Udell nodded. He got up and went across, opened the cabinet, and took out a brandy bottle and two glasses. He put them on the desk in front of Paddock, who smiled, uncorked the bottle, and poured into both glasses.

Paddock raised his. "Here's to a long life and a happy one. Without Lily."

Udell nodded and drank. Lily was probably a hell of a lot more durable than Paddock thought. A few accusations wouldn't do anything to her. "What's really on your mind, Howard?"

Paddock contemplated his empty glass, smacked his lips, and grinned. "What's on my mind? I'd thought that was obvious. I'm proposing that you and I join forces and get rid of Lily."

"Jesus Christ!" Udell said in a breathy tone.

"I'll make you general manager of the firm—"

"Wait a minute."

"—raise your salary, and—"

"Wait a minute, Howard. It's not that easy." His heart was stuttering, and he felt his chest tighten.

"You're not afraid of Lily, are you?"

"You're damned right I am!"

"Why, isn't it easy? We can let the law take most of the work off our hands. We give them facts and dates. Did she murder old Jacob Berlanger or not?"

Udell had expected no such strong approach, and it

took his breath away. Really getting rid of Lily was something he'd never thought about, and Paddock was saying it was like swatting a fly. And he was bringing up ghosts that were long buried.

Paddock said, "Everyone gossips about it, you know. What do you say?"

Udell shook his head. He indicated the bottle and watched Paddock pour out two more drinks. He gulped his down, and his eyes watered. Team up with Paddock and go after Lily! Jesus Christ! Giving information was one thing, but actively going after her? He didn't want to fight Lily.

Paddock said, "What's the matter?"

"I don't know, Howard—"

"What about old Jacob?"

"I'm not going to get into a battle with Lily, Howard."

"She's only a woman!"

Udell grunted. He got up and tottered to a window and stared out. This meeting hadn't turned out right. Paddock was approaching it all wrong. Paddock didn't know Lily as he did.

"You don't have to fight Lily. You can stay in the background. All I need from you are facts and figures— that kind of thing. It's worth a lot to me."

Udell turned. "I don't have to face her? I'd rather pack up and go."

"All right, fine."

"I'm a bookkeeper, Howard."

"All right. You provide the facts, and I'll do it all myself. Did she kill old Jacob?"

"How much money?"

"What?"

Udell came back to his desk. "You said it's worth a lot

131

to you. How much?"

"Maybe two thousand dollars."

Udell laughed.

"Two thousand and you'll be general manager."

Udell shook his head. "Go away, Howard. Go on away—"

"And a raise in salary!"

Udell went to the wardrobe, took his overcoat off a hook, put on his hat, and walked to the door. Shaking his head, he walked down the hall and pulled on the overcoat.

Paddock hurried after him, caught him at the stairs. "Udell—"

Udell turned, hands in his pockets.

"It wouldn't be wise," Paddock said in a low voice, "to repeat any of our conversation. You understand?"

Udell grunted. He went down the steps, buttoning the coat.

CHAPTER TWELVE

It was not a place she would have chosen for lovemaking, the ungiving seat of a carriage, but Lily did her best to make the occasion a success. Roy Collier would not be denied; aggressive and gentle by turns, she let him take her to fulfillment and gave him her kisses, promising herself that the awkward situation would soon be remedied in her suite—or his.

He made no apologies afterward other than to say, "I simply could not wait, Lily, my love—" He arranged her clothes, with much intimate handling, laced up her bodice, and suggested they share the remaining bottle of wine, to which she agreed.

Then he blew the horn, and after a bit the driver appeared, plodding along the lane from the farmhouse, and they went back to the city.

He held her hand along the way. "I must see you again soon, Lily."

"It cannot be tonight—"

"Then tomorrow. I will send my man for you whenever you say."

"Why not come yourself?"

He smiled. "In an instant, but I fear my face is well known, and I wish to cause you no trouble."

He was right, of course. "Then just before midday. The

same place as today. I will be waiting."

"And I." He kissed her as they came close to the hotel. The driver jumped down and held the door, and she hurried off to the hotel.

Sam Beckhart's messages were tucked under the door, three of them, each gaining in asperity. She ordered a tub at once; then she wrote to Sam saying she had gone shopping and the time had gone by so delightfully that she had not noticed. She sent the message off, and another boy came up with mail. There was a letter from Udell to say that all was well, another from Howard Paddock to ask about progress and to say his "project" was not yet completed and proving more difficult than he'd foreseen. There was also a note from Billy Turnbull inviting her to the theater.

The hotel provided a hairdresser—a short, stout woman in spectacles—and a maid. The maid had clothes laid out for her when she finished with the tub; Lily selected a blue dinner gown with a small bustle—she disliked crinolines—and sat before the mirror while the hairdresser, Mrs. Baggot, combed and modeled her dark hair.

When the maid and Baggot had gone, Lily lighted a cigar and thought about Roy. She would much prefer seeing him, rather than Sam, but to deny Sam would undoubtedly raise a storm. It was annoying to be pulled this way and that, but it would not be for long.

She went to the door at the knock, expecting to see Sam, but it was Miles Broder. He was dressed conservatively, as always; he was a dark, businesslike man who seemed usually to be on the verge of flight, with a hundred things on his mind. He smiled at her and said, "Surprise!"

134

"Come in, Miles. Where's Sam?"

"On his way to a meeting in Baltimore."

She closed the door. "Baltimore! The committee, of course. Why aren't you there?"

"I will be. I'm to escort several important guests. The general meeting is tomorrow. But first Sam sends his apologies. He tried to get in touch with you this afternoon—"

"I was shopping."

"Yes, I saw your note. Sometimes I wish we could slice Sam into several parts and distribute them about the country—be much easier on all of us. He's in enormous demand, you know."

"Of course he is. When will he return?"

"As soon as the meeting's over. That'll be tomorrow night, so he'll be leaving Baltimore the next morning." Miles edged toward the door. "Please forgive us, Lily, but the country needs him."

"Yes, I understand."

He opened the door. "He'll see you the moment he arrives—"

"Thank you, Miles."

He closed the door and was gone. Lily stood with her back to it and smiled.

She sent a message immediately to Roy Collier and waited impatiently for an answer. It came in an hour, a note signed by a servant: "Senator Collier is not in the city. Your letter will be given him as soon as he returns."

Lily stamped her foot and swore. She kicked a chair, then overturned it. Damn him! Of course, he had expected her to be with Sam, but it was a damned annoyance just the same!

Pacing the room, she got her anger under control. She

lighted a cigar and righted the chair, then sat to tell herself to be calm. What should she do? She could hardly go to supper unescorted, and it was unthinkable to allow Dennis Foran to dine with her. She would have to send down for a menu and eat here in the suite. Damn Roy! What was so important that he had to leave the city . . . another woman?

She got up and paced again, puffing furiously.

There was a rap on the door, and she halted, staring at it. She put the cigar in a bowl, crossed the room, and opened the door. A messenger, young and skinny with hair in his eyes, dressed in a blue and ivory uniform that was too big for him, cocked his head at her. "You Miz Berlanger?"

"I am."

He proffered an envelope, and she took it and closed the door.

It was a note from Billy Turnbull. "What about the theater?"

She had completely forgotten his invitation. She ran to open the door and shout at the retreating boy. He turned about and shuffled toward her. "Come in," she said, and left the door open.

Humming under her breath, she quickly wrote out a reply accepting the invitation, signed it, and sealed an envelope. She copied his address from the note, found a dollar, and gave both to the messenger with a smile.

Billy Turnbull arrived in tails and white tie, a black cape over his arm, silk hat on his head. "By George, I never thought you'd stoop so low as to—"

"Oh Billy, you knew I'd go, of course. Sam's out of town—or did you know that too?"

"Of course I knew. That's why I invited you. The play's a new one, I forget the title . . . something about summer. One of the Booths is starring."

He held the cloak for her. "We'll go somewhere afterward—"

She looked at him over her shoulder. "Across the river in Virginia?"

He laughed. "I mean to dine, my dear, to dine."

The theater was crowded, but Billy quickly found an usher who led them upstairs to a box that looked down on the right of the stage. The proscenium was decorated with wreaths and figures in relief, painted white and gold, and the curtain shimmered like satin. Lily gazed down on hundreds of faces, bare shoulders, and moving fans. The room was huge but warm. She glanced at the other boxes, and Billy pointed out the president only yards away, bending over to speak with a gray-haired woman in white.

The play, she saw from the program, was *The Summer House,* a comedy, starring John Wilkes Booth, a rising young actor, brother of the famous Edwin.

An orchestra played as the last arrivals found their seats; then men went along the sides extinguishing lanterns, and the curtain rose. Lily was impressed at the extravagance of the setting; it was much more elegant than the smaller theaters in St. Louis, but she thought the play dull. It was the third night, Billy whispered, and the actors were all stumbling through their lines. She thought Booth a handsome though somewhat stiff actor, and she was positive he looked directly at her several times.

Even Billy noticed it. "He's no fool, that one," he said with a chuckle.

On the way out they met Gilbert Collier.

He was escorting a beautiful younger woman, and was astonished to see them. Billy noticed Collier first. "Well, well, he's got *her* with him!"

"What?"

Billy pointed him out—and at the same time Collier saw them. Billy said, under his breath, "I've seen 'er before. Think she's one of his women."

"You mean a prostitute?"

Billy shrugged.

Collier shouldered his way to them. "This is a pleasure." He looked at Lily. "I was sure you'd be with Sam."

"Sam's in Baltimore," Billy said shortly, staring at the girl.

"Ahhh," Collier said. He drew the girl forward. "Mrs. Berlanger, Senator Turnbull, may I present my niece, Miss Lawson. Lette, this is—"

"Niece!" Billy said loudly. "This lovely girl is your niece?" He reached for her hand and bent over it. Collier winked at Lily over his head.

"How nice to meet you," Lily said. The girl could not be more than seventeen, she thought, a lovely, slim maid wearing pink and white; looking so much younger than anyone in the crowd, she might have been a schoolgirl.

"Lette is in Mrs. Anger's Academy in Alexandria," Collier explained. "I'm very proud of her."

"I'm so pleased to meet you," the girl said softly. "My uncle has been talking about you all evening, Mrs. Berlanger."

"Oh, is that so?" Billy said.

"I've been telling her about steamboats," Collier said,

138

eyeing Billy.

Lily laughed. "If you come to St. Louis, Lette, you may ride our boats as much as you like."

"Thank you, Mrs. Berlanger."

"Well, I must take Lette back," Collier said.

They said good-byes, and Lily watched them move away. So Roy had gone to Alexandria across the river for her. "She's a lovely girl," she said to Billy, expecting him to be slightly chastened.

But Billy was unruffled. "Yes, all of that. His niece, by God. You think he was lying to us?"

She laughed again. "Take me home, Billy."

"But, we're going to eat—"

"I'm not a big hungry."

The streets were crowded as they rode back to the hotel, and Billy was grumpy. When the carriage stopped, she kissed his cheek and got out quickly. She felt very tired; the play had been boring, and Billy's company left much to be desired. Tomorrow when Sam returned it would be different.

He sent a message and came to the hotel in the middle of the afternoon. In her suite he embraced her. "Sorry about Baltimore, Lily, but I had to go. Things are heating up."

She poured him coffee. "When can I go back to St. Louis?"

"I hate to see you go—"

"You know I must."

He sighed and sipped the coffee. "In a few days— maybe even sooner. Our friend Mr. Gil Collier has ceased his attacks, you know."

"He seems a very pleasant man."

He gave her a look. "Well, I don't care why, I'm grateful he's kept his mouth shut." He pushed the cup away. "I'll be tied up in meetings till late tonight, Lily—"

"Can't Miles do some of that?"

"Miles does all he can." He showed her his teeth. "They want old Sam. I'm the candidate, not Miles." He looked at his watch. "I should have news for you today— can I come up later?"

"Before midnight?"

He smiled and shrugged.

"Of course. Sam."

When he arrived he was half-drunk and exhausted, smelled abominably of liquor and tobacco, and could hardly keep his eyes open. She undressed him and put him to bed.

In the morning she had breakfasts sent up, and after a good scrub Sam could function. He apologized for his behavior, saying all he could remember was that he had to get to her room.

He had news. It was not the best: their proposals had been sidetracked in committee—

"What's that mean, Sam?"

"Delay. Only delay. Don't worry your head about it."

"How much delay?"

He shook his head. "Don't know. I'll have to ferret it all out, change minds. But don't you worry, it'll be done."

Sam did not protest when she said she'd return to St. Louis, so there was probably much that he was not telling her. He explained that it was nearly impossible to push members of the Congress into doing anything. They were a headstrong bunch, he growled, some stupid and some

140

blind, and he would have to cajole and sweet-talk them around to his side.

When he had gone, she began to make arrangements to leave the city.

CHAPTER THIRTEEN

Howard Paddock got off the steamboat at Cairo and went immediately to a hotel. He looked up a number of his old cronies and sought out one in particular, Mick Weston. Mick was the owner of two stern-wheelers and did a brisk business along the Ohio, hauling whatever needed to be hauled—at night.

Mick was very happy to see him, because it was to Mick that Paddock had turned over much of his clandestine trade when Paddock had moved to St. Louis. Mick picked him up at the hotel and took him to the Neptune Club. It was an exclusive saloon and grill, patronized only by rivermen, and boasted an excellent kitchen and the finest brothel north of New Orleans.

Mick was graying but still lean and hard, a riverman who now lived ashore and ran his affairs from an office instead of a hurricane deck. "What brings you back to Cairo, Howard?"

They sat in the restaurant, and Paddock watched a waiter pour champagne into two glasses and place one before him. He smiled and raised his glass. "To see my old friends."

Mick grinned. "You never come this far without a damn good reason, Howard. You passin' through to somewhere else?"

"No, I came to see you."

Mick sampled the wine. "What've I got that you want?"

Paddock glanced about, lowered his voice, and sniffed. "I need a good man f'some dangerous work. But I don't want a rouster or a brawler. I need a man who can think and who can do the job, whatever it is."

"Like that, huh? He got to kill somebody?"

"Maybe."

Mick nodded. "All right. Don't tell me no more. I don't want t'know anything about it. Where you need this man, here or in St. Louis?"

"Maybe St. Louis, maybe somewhere along the river." Paddock fiddled with his watch chain. "The job might take a bit of time. God willing."

Mick finished the wine and reached for the bottle. "I know the man you want." He poured into both glasses. "When you want to see 'im?"

"Right away. Does he work for you?"

Mick shook his head. "He don't work for nobody, far's I know. His name's Viktor Kory—leastwise that's the name he was using last. And I don't know if he's in town. I'll have to ask." He picked up a menu. "You want to order?"

The next day before noon Paddock received a note from Mick asking him to come to Mick's office at five o'clock that day. "Someone you want to see will be there."

Mick's office was upstairs, over a row of tawdry stores, only a stone's throw from the levee. Paddock arrived promptly at five in a hired rig and climbed the steps to the second floor. They were dusty and littered with trash, but the hallway on the second was swept and reasonably

143

clean, though it smelled of stale tobacco. Mick Weston's office took up most of the floor; his name was lettered on one of the doors: Weston Freight Co.

Paddock opened the door and was greeted by a skinny, middle-aged man in specs, who occupied a desk piled high with papers. "Who you want, mister?"

"Mick's expecting me."

The man brightened. "Oh, you're Mr. Paddock?" At Paddock's nod he yelled to someone in the next room. "Mr. Paddock's here."

Another clerk came to the door and beckoned. Paddock followed him through two more offices, where boxes and kegs were piled to the ceilings. At the third office the man rapped, put his head inside, said something, and opened the door wide for Paddock to enter. Mick rose and came to shake his hand. "Come on in, Howard—"

A man of medium height, well dressed, rose at his entrance. Mick said, "Howard, this here's Viktor Kory."

"Glad t'meet you, Mr. Kory." Paddock shook a hard hand and looked into a pair of level black eyes. Kory did not smile; he had thick, black brows and a thin mouth.

Mick said, "I can recommend Viktor to do what he says he'll do. But any deal you make with him is between you, and I don't want t'know about it." He went to the door. "You can talk here. When you get through, open the door, all right?"

"All right," Paddock said. Mick went out.

He squinted at Kory. A capable-looking sort, probably tough as sheet metal. "Did Mick tell you what I need?"

"He said you needed a man for an important job." Kory's voice was low and unmodulated. "Whyn't you just tell me about it."

144

"I need somebody dead," Paddock said bluntly. He saw the other's eyes widen slightly. "It might be easy to do, and it might not. It won't be easy if he suspects anything."

"What kind of man is he?"

"He runs a steamship line. He's young and quick and bigger than you."

Kory nodded slowly. "You got a time limit?"

"No, but it ought to be done soon."

"You care how it gets done?"

Paddock shook his head. "I don't care how. But I want proof. There's others involved."

"Proof'll be he don't go home. Where can I get a look at him?"

"St. Louis, if he's available. He works out of St. Louis. I can't afford to have him see me, but I'll have someone point him out to you. That all right?"

"That's fine. Now about the money. I'll want two thousand dollars, half in advance."

Paddock stared. Two thousand!

Kory said, "It's a job with risks. I might have t'hire others to help."

Paddock nodded; it was Lily's money, after all, and she wanted the best. "Come and see me in St. Louis. I'll have the first thousand for you then. I agree about hiring others, because this has got to be done properly and definitely. We don't want any mistakes or excuses."

"There won't be none."

Paddock wrote on a slip of paper and handed it over. "I'm leaving soon's I can get passage. If you come along on the same boat, we don't know each other."

Kory nodded.

Paddock rose and opened the door.

*   *   *

There was another steamboat incident just north of Natchez. A Berlanger-Bryant boat had maneuvered deliberately to cause a collision between a barge and a Jeffries-Fraser boat, the *Monarch*. The damage was not extensive, the captain wired, but annoying because of freight and passenger delays.

The B & B steamboat had been the *Shannon*, and she had blithely gone on her way downstream without any indication of the trouble she'd caused. The barge had apparently not been hurt, because she had also gone downstream after the incident, while *Monarch* limped back to Natchez. Her cargo was put aboard another boat, and the passengers were transferred to a rival line. The captain wired that repairs would probably take another week.

Both the *Ionia* and the *Freedom* had come from Pittsburgh, and Logan had gone north with *Freedom* to La Salle on the Illinois River to pick up the first cargo of the new Maxwell & Coles contract.

He learned about *Monarch*'s trouble when they arrived back in St. Louis for a two-hour stopover. Logan went at once to the offices and sent back word that he would not continue with *Freedom*, which was bound for ports on the Ohio. He had coffee with Doris and Fraser, while Neil Barnes was in the shipping rooms below.

Fraser said, "*Monarch*'s pilot swears it was a deliberate act on the part of the B & B boat, but it might be hard to prove. Matter of opinion."

"I'll go talk to him," Logan replied. "Do we have a boat going south?"

"*Jewel*," Doris said. "She's leaving tomorrow. But why do you have to go? *Monarch* will be in St. Louis in

146

two weeks."

Logan rose and went to the door. There was no one on the stairs. He closed the door. "I think I'll stop in Chadwick and see Dr. Irvine. Maybe I can convince him to testify for us."

"Against Lily!" Fraser shook his head. "I think you're wasting your time."

"Maybe, but it should be tried. Irvine's a rabbit, but he has a conscience. And if he'll do nothing, maybe I can learn something helpful." He wondered if he believed all he said. Irvine's wife would see that nothing was learned, would she not? But he knew he must go there.

He stayed in the office and went home with Doris, listening to her accounts of office happenings. She had seen Clarence Yates several times when Neil Barnes was out, and he had informed her that so far his investigation had turned up no one else involved with Barnes, but that he was not finished.

"He's also keeping a close watch on Howard Paddock, in case Neil goes to see him at night."

"And has he?" Logan asked.

"He didn't say. But Paddock's been out of the city and only returned the day before yesterday."

"What about Lily?"

"She's still away."

Logan smiled. "I like it when she's away."

Mrs. Benson extended herself with supper, serving them stuffed pork chops with a delicious sauce that she said was a secret recipe. Logan complimented her extravagantly, and she almost giggled in delight.

Doris said, "You'll turn her head and make it impossible for the rest of us—"

After supper he walked about the grounds with Baxter

Ross. Ross had very little to report; they took different routes with the carriage each morning and night and had noticed nothing untoward. One of the dogs had barked late at night, several nights running, but he'd been unable to discover a reason, though the fence was loosened in one place on the outside. That had been two days past, and there had been no recurrence.

Doris felt very secure, she said. She never left the offices to go onto the street, and Chris Murphy and Ross were never far away at all other times. Nevertheless, Logan decided to leave Louis Gualco behind. There was no reason to take him along on the river; he would feel better if Doris had the extra protection. He thought Gualco was disappointed, but he said little when Logan told him he would stay.

"I'll only be gone for a short time, Louis."

"You're positive nothing can happen on the river?"

"Not positive, but damned sure."

"I hope you're right."

"No one will know where I am, anyhow," Logan said. "I'll go to the levee early and stay under cover till the boat leaves."

Doris was barely awake when he slid out of bed in the morning. He kissed her, dressed quickly, and hurried out to heat a cup of coffee. He would have breakfast on the steamboat.

Chris Murphy drove him to the levee in the misty morning, halting the coach only yards from the stageplanks of the *Jewel*. Logan walked on board with a valise and waved, and Murphy clattered off.

Several hours later, walking unhurriedly behind a group of chattering people, Viktor Kory crossed the levee and boarded the *Jewel* in company with two young men. He had hired them in Cairo, after making very sure that each was accomplished in the use of knives and pistols.

He had rented an empty office across the street from the Jeffries-Fraser offices, and Paddock had brought Neil Barnes to see him there. Barnes knew Logan's intention to go south on the steamboat *Jewel*. He was also able to point out Logan to Kory.

Howard Paddock was very pleased with the way things were moving. Except with respect to Udell Winter. Since their last conversation, Udell had been grumpy and noncommunicative.

Viktor Kory took a stateroom side by side with his two employees. Their names were Al Slater and Josef Kernig, both drifters who had long and dreary experiences with lawmen. Viktor was not entirely pleased with them, but time did not allow him to search further. Each was a product of large-city slums and an expert at attacking from behind. Viktor had no way to measure their real courage. He discounted everything they said. He had come that road himself.

CHAPTER FOURTEEN

Capt. Ralph McDade of the *Jewel* installed Logan, at his request, in a comfortable cabin in the texas, well away from the other passengers. Logan spent most of his time in the pilothouse, to him the most interesting spot on board. The run to Natchez was uneventful.

When they arrived, the *Monarch*'s repairs were mostly completed. She was tied at the far end of the commercial wharves, and several men were busy painting over the new wood on her bow and side.

Logan transferred his valise to *Monarch* and sat in the captain's cabin to hear the story of the collision. Captain Wilson Rucker was a man of medium height, had white whiskers and goatee, and looked much like a professor. He explained, as if he were in a classroom, how the Berlanger boat had forced them to port in a turn and how the low barge, unseen by the *Monarch*'s pilot, had come out of a mist to sideswipe them. The barge had hardly been splintered and had gone serenely on and was probably in New Orleans by now.

Logan secured the statements from Rucker and the two pilots, sent a wire to the Jeffries-Fraser agent in New Orleans asking him to get a similar statement from the barge captain if possible, and boarded the first steamer north.

As he neared Chadwick, all the old memories crowded in upon him. Andrea and her pony, Benje, riding like the wind through the trees along the river; his father, Dutch; and the midnight, clandestine trips in wagons. How he had hated those trips! But once as a boy he had gone downriver after a man who had cheated his father, old Eli Dietz. He'd confronted Eli, got back the money, then burned the steamboat. The time he told the story to Dutch was one of the few times he'd seen his father smile. Dutch had enjoyed the idea that Eli's boat had burned to the water's edge—with all its cargo.

Dutch. What had happened to him? How had the years treated him? But Dutch was indestructible; he would never change—except for maybe a little more grayness, a few more lines. Dutch had once asked him to take a valuable suitcase to Howard Paddock in Cairo for sale. He had refused, knowing what was in the suitcase and that it was stolen goods. He wondered if Dutch had made the delivery himself. Probably. But Dutch was no letter writer. He had heard nothing from him for a long time.

The Chadwick landing was unchanged, except that the shelter house was new, the old one presumably having fallen down. He was the only passenger to debark, and he had to walk the mile or so into town carrying his valise.

He got a room at the hotel; the building seemed much older, and the entire town looked smaller than the last time he'd seen it; as he walked along the street, he realized it was slowly dying. He saw only a few very young children, many older people, and a half-dozen empty store buildings. At the edge of town he stood for a time staring in the direction of the farm where Dutch lived and where he'd grown up. He would have to see Dutch before he left.

He had a miserable supper in the town's only restaurant, went to bed early, but could not sleep. He got up, smoked a cigar, and sat by the window staring into darkness, thinking of Andrea. He could not put the images from his mind; they crowded in despite him. Things he had not thought of for years came howling out of the forgotten past to haunt him. Long after midnight he fell into a troubled sleep, and a shadowy form that he knew was Lily screamed at him.

In the morning he felt tired.

After an indifferent breakfast, he hired a horse and rig and drove to Dr. Irvine's house, two miles from the town, east, away from the river. It was a once white house, now graying for lack of paint; trees and vines surrounded it, and a rutted drive led to the wide front porch.

On the way he thought about what he would say to Irvine. He would ask for information, if Irvine refused to cooperate with him and the authorities. He would offer to purchase Irvine's medical journals, or a copy of them, covering the Jacob Berlanger period. What good were old books to Irvine? One way or another he would avoid Irvine's wife. Well, he would try.

He got out of the buggy and walked up the steps; the boards of the porch creaked under his weight, and a large, sullen-looking woman was suddenly at the door, staring at him. "Who're you?"

Logan doffed his hat. "I'm looking for Dr. Irvine, ma'am."

"You're not going to find 'im here."

"Oh . . . Doesn't he live here?"

"Not anymore."

Logan persisted. "Then can you tell me where I can find him?"

The woman backed away and started to close the door. "Irvine's dead, mister."

Logan was shocked. He put his hand out. "Wait—"

She paused. "He died six months ago, heart trouble."

"I'm terribly sorry to hear it. Can I talk to you a moment—I assume you're Mrs. Irvine?"

"Yes, I am. What about?"

"I'd like to purchase Dr. Irvine's medical journals—"

"They're burned."

"What?"

"I said they're burned, all of them." She closed the door, and he heard her walking away.

He stared at the rough wood and the iron knocker. Irvine dead! He turned away and went down the steps to the buggy. Lily had won again.

Viktor Kory was not pleased by what he saw of Jeffries. The man was big, as Paddock had said, but there was something about him that was dismaying. Jeffries was wary; he missed nothing about him, and he was like a cat. He had the grace of the born athlete, and when he pointed out the man to his two hirelings, they both whistled, and Al Slater said, "Shit—not him!"

No man could stand up to a bullet, Kory said. "We'll maneuver him into the proper position—" He left the rest unsaid.

He was also not pleased that Jeffries did not take an ordinary stateroom on the cabin deck but instead stayed in the texas. Passengers were allowed on the hurricane deck, but not many bothered to climb up there, and when he did, Kory felt very conspicuous. He was in full sight of anyone in the pilothouse, and he went down immediately, not wanting Jeffries to notice him.

Jeffries came to the main saloon for his meals, usually eating with the captain or one of the pilots, and only invited guests sat at their tables. Kory watched from a distance, frustrated because Jeffries always went back to the pilothouse or into his own cabin.

The doors on the texas cabins were stout. Kory slipped into an unused cabin at night to investigate it. He found a steel bolt inside; probably all the cabins were so constructed. He gave up the idea of attacking Jeffries there. There was nothing to do but wait patiently.

When Jeffries walked off the steamboat at Natchez, with his valise, Kory and his two men followed. When Jeffries bought a ticket on a steamboat headed north, they were not far behind. But Jeffries took Kory by surprise when he debarked at Chadwick. What would Jeffries want in a backwater village? It took him time to get his hirelings alerted and their bags packed. The steamboat was ten miles north of the landing before it put the three ashore.

Then they had to plod through weeds and brush back to the road. When they reached the town, darkness had fallen. Kory quickly discovered that Jeffries was staying in the hotel, and a guarded conversation with the hotel clerk brought him little information. The clerk did not know who Jeffries was or why he was in Chadwick. Kory learned that there was another Jeffries who lived just outside of town, but assumed that since Logan stayed in the hotel, it was only a coincidence of names.

It was annoying as hell that he knew so little about Jeffries. Paddock should have told him more—if he knew.

Kory was surprised when Jeffries hired a horse and rig the next morning and set off on the road out of town. The wooded country around Chadwick would be ideal for an ambush, if only he could have anticipated Jeffries' moves.

He rented horses at the livery stable and followed, keeping well behind. When Jeffries stopped at the white frame house, Kory dispersed his men about it, then was surprised again when Jeffries came out and headed back toward Chadwick. He had supposed the man would keep going.

But this was the best chance. The road was a narrow, one-track trail winding through the wooded area. Kory quickly gave his men instructions. They were to gallop up behind Jeffries, waving as if they intended to go on by, and when they got abreast they were to fire. Three pistols should do the job. When they saw that Jeffries was down, they would halt and drag the body into the brush and cover it, so that no one would find it for days—maybe months.

"Shoot the horse first," Kory said. "That'll stop him. Then the rest will be easy."

Logan heard the horsemen long before he saw them. They were coming at a lope, which caused him some uneasiness. Very few in these parts were ever in that kind of hurry. There was nothing in Chadwick to rush to.

He gave the brown horse its head and turned to face the rear, hand on his pistol. His first sight of the three was not reassuring. They were spurring their horses toward him, coming round a bend in the trail, and he was sure the last man of the three had a revolver in his hand.

He had never seen any of them before, to his best recollection. None looked like farmers, and, as he watched, the leader tugged out a pistol and fired. Logan slapped the reins and yelled at the horse. At the same time he pulled the Navy from his belt and fired back. The three separated instantly and began firing, a fusillade of shots.

Logan concentrated on the leader, fired four times, and saw the horse suddenly stumble and go down with a scream. The rider rolled free, but the horse behind plowed into the first and went down into the woods and brush beside the trail.

Several shots hit the buggy, one of the spokes splintered, and he ducked down. Only one rider was behind him now; the man had emptied a pistol and was reloading as the horse galloped. Logan aimed and fired twice more but could see no effect. The Navy was empty; he swore and shoved it back into his belt. With a little luck he might outrun his pursuer—as far as the town. The man would certainly pull up before they reached it.

Then more shots came. The road ran straight for a short distance, and the rider gained. He could see that Logan was not returning the fire, and he spurred the horse, firing again and again.

One shot slammed into Logan's upper arm on the right side, and another shot struck the horse. The horse swerved off the track and bolted through the trees, and Logan clung to the dash as the reins were torn from his grasp. In another moment the buggy bounced, one wheel struck a stump, and the buggy flew through the air, tearing away a shaft and tumbling Logan out.

He fell into the brush, head over heels, landing in a rain ditch, half-stunned. He had an impression of the rider flashing by—then for a moment everything seemed to stand still.

He came out of it shaking his head. He heard a scream,

156

then a shot, and the scream stopped. Someone had shot his horse.

His arm hurt like fire; a quick look told him the bullet had gone through the flesh of the upper arm near the shoulder, but he could move the arm, so the bone was probably not touched. Gritting his teeth, he crawled from the ditch into the brush and made off at right angles, staying under cover. He still had the pistol.

After fifty feet he halted and surveyed the scene. The horseman was somewhere to his left, to judge from the sounds, probably beating the brush for him. The man probably had not seen him tossed from the buggy and had no idea where he might be. There was no sign of the other two.

Logan pulled the Navy, opened the small leather pouch on his belt, and took out six linen cartrides. He shoved them into the cylinder one by one and tamped them down with the loading lever. He clicked the lever into place, opened a cap box, shook out six copper caps, and put the box away. Carefully he shoved a cap onto each of the six nipples and smiled. Now he was ready for what came.

His arm was bleeding, so he pulled off the coat, tore his shirt to get a strip of cloth, and bound it awkwardly about the wound. As he finished, he could hear the voices of the other two men on the road, calling to the third.

He pulled on the coat again and moved off to the right, away from the voices. Surely they would spread out and search the area, and how could they miss his tracks? But now, he thought, he had an advantage. He knew every inch of this countryside, having played over it as a boy and tramped over it a thousand times while growing up.

But the question that pounded at him was—who were

they? They had appeared suddenly, apparently out of nowhere, and were hunting him down. Were they sent by Lily Berlanger? How did they know where to find him? It was baffling.

He heard a sudden shout and knew they'd discovered the place he'd been thrown. There would be blood also, and they'd know he was hurt or wounded. Now they would come after him like hounds on a fresh scent. Not far off was a creek, a small, winding stream of water that flowed eventually into the Mississippi. Pushing through the brush, he made for it, hearing a horseman not far off. Logan paused to listen; there was only one horseman. The man was moving and stopping, moving and stopping again.

He gained the creek and moved along it, careful to leave as few tracks as possible. When the creek narrowed slightly, he jumped across, using stones that were barely under water. On the far side he took pains to sweep away impressions. He hoped they would think he'd walked in the stream to throw them off and would lose precious time running along the banks looking for tracks.

The far side of the stream was heavily forested, and he plunged into the trees, circling toward Chadwick. He found a deer trail and followed it at a trot, gritting his teeth to the stinging pain.

In half a mile he slowed to a walk, sure he'd lost them. He'd go into town, report what had happened to the sheriff, and let the law take over. Was Lyle Carty still sheriff? If so, Carty would undoubtedly round them up in hours.

He came to a sunny glade—and suddenly the horseman was there, charging him, a pistol spitting fire!

Logan ducked, rolled, and came up with the Navy. The

rider went past at a gallop as he fired. Using both hands to steady the revolver, Logan fired deliberately at the horse, once, twice, three times, and the horse reared, stumbled, and fell. Getting to his feet, Logan ran at the man, who pulled himself up from the downed animal. As the other's pistol came up, Logan fired and saw him whirled about.

When he hurried to the spot, the man was lying face up in the weeds, arms flung out, a red oozing hole in his forehead.

Logan let his breath out and glanced around. The others were probably coming on foot—they'd have heard the shots. He found the man's pistol in the grass and shoved it into his belt. He wished he had time to go through the pockets to find a name, but he'd best hurry.

He crossed the glade and trotted into the woods.

CHAPTER FIFTEEN

Lily sent Dennis Foran to buy the tickets and make the necessary arrangements, and she saw Sam Beckhart for the last time the evening before she left town. He was terribly reluctant to let her go, he said. He would go with her in an instant, and to hell with the campaign.

He loved her, he whispered, as they lolled in her bed; he would never forget her, never stop wanting her. He would come to St. Louis the moment he could get away.

Lily said, "Send me good news, Sam; that's what I want to hear."

"I will, I will, and soon, you'll see. We're ninety-nine percent positive now. It'll only take a breath to make it one hundred."

As he sat up and reached for his clothes, Sam asked her, "Tell me something, Lily—"

"Yes?"

"I've heard some miserable gossip."

"Sam, you know better than to listen to gossip."

"Of course. But—" He sighed.

"But what?"

He glanced at her as he pulled on his pants. "A couple of nasty little voices have told me that you were seen with Gil Collier. Is it true?"

"Collier?"

160

"Gilbert Collier, yes."

She put on a pout. "Of course it isn't true, Sam. Nasty little voices indeed! Why in the world would I—"

"I know, I know."

"I met him with Billy Turnbull at a play . . . he was with some child—"

"Yes, Billy told me." He smiled. "Forget all about it, Lily. It's terrible to be jealous, isn't it? But you're such a beautiful woman, I simply can't help it."

"You're sweet, Sam." She leaned close and kissed his cheek. "I'll get up and make some coffee."

Sam did not come to the train to see her off. He sent a message by Miles, wishing her a safe and speedy journey, and all his love. He was off to New England, Miles said. She would read about him in the papers.

The train was late, and she was impatient to leave; the waiting room was vast and crowded, but somehow the time plodded by. Their baggage was loaded, and she managed to secure several seats at the end of the car by tipping the conductor heavily. When the train finally pulled out of the station she was tired to death.

There was much talk on the train of the new political party composed of men calling themselves Republicans. They were men who had opposed the Kansas-Nebraska Bill and who were pledged to resist the extension of slavery into new territory. In the South they were called "Black Republicans," because the party was opposed to holding black men in bondage.

Lily was annoyed at talk of war. Men like Sam Beckhart would see that the country never drifted that far. She was gratified that many were for Sam, declaring that his was one of the few moderate voices in Congress. They would

161

certainly vote for him.

The journey seemed interminable, and many times she left the train to spend nights in hotels, to get baths, and to strengthen her will for more of the necessary dirt and inconvenience. She swore she would never again travel on anything but steamboats and ships.

But they came at last to the river and went across on a ferry, and the miserable journey was over.

She saw Howard Paddock in the afternoon of the second day of her return. He came to the office, at her request, dressed in a gray suit and white waistcoat with a silver watch chain; he looked like one of the southern senators she'd met in Washington.

"Tell me what you've done about Jeffries," she said with no preamble.

"I trust you had a successful trip."

"It may have been successful, but it certainly was ghastly. What about Jeffries?"

He sniffed. "I've had no report about Jeffries one way or the other. Tell me about Washington."

"Why don't you know about Jeffries?"

Paddock sighed deeply, fingering the watch chain. Lily had a one-track mind, and she was not to be diverted. "I hired a man to deal with Jeffries. He comes highly recommended, and he'll cost you two thousand dollars, half of which I have already advanced to him."

She was astounded. "Two thousand dollars!"

He stared at her. "You tried with a lesser and cheaper man, if you recall. And Edward Taylor failed miserably. Do you want another? You'll litter the land with corpses."

Lily sat and leaned back. Her dark eyes glittered at his

162

witticism. "And where is this paragon now?"

"I'm not exactly sure. He followed Jeffries south. That's why I've had no report. I assume no news is good news."

"Did he go alone?"

"No. He had two men with him."

"What's his name?"

"Viktor Kory."

She nodded. "Washington was inconclusive. Sam swears that we will win what we want, but it'll take more time, and I could not remain there longer."

Paddock frowned. "What do *you* think?"

"I think we'll win but not as we expected. I think it'll come by bits—a bit at a time."

He was silent a moment. "The newspapers say that Sam's campaign is getting under way. Did he devote enough time to this?"

"I think so. Sam wields a great deal of power, and much of the work was done before I got there. Sam wants this as much as we do."

"What's the opposition to it?"

She shrugged. "The usual talk of huge profits. Then Sam has a certain amount of opposition from the other party."

Paddock was silent and Lily waited, telling herself to be patient. He always sniffed and thought about it—whatever it was. She wondered how long it took him to buy a newspaper. Finally he asked, "What's the talk of slavery in the capital?"

"Slavery?"

He fingered the watch chain. "People are beginning to choose sides, you know. Free or slave. What do they say about it in Washington?"

"Sam says slavery will die of its own accord."

"Maybe. How about the others?"

"I didn't talk much about slavery. Why are you so fascinated?"

"Because I think it's going to divide the country if Sam and his friends don't do something about it." Paddock got up and tugged down his waistcoat. He smiled. "But a war would be good for us, wouldn't it?"

"Who's talking war?"

"Lots of people. You don't get out to saloons, Lily. Lots of people."

"Saloons!" She glared at him.

"People say what they really think in saloons." He went to the door. "I'll tell you instantly, soon's I hear anything, God willing." He opened the door and went out.

Lily sat for long minutes, staring at the door. Would a war be good or bad for them? It was difficult to know. The trade along the Ohio and up the Missouri might not be affected, but the Mississippi ran directly through the South. What would happen if the South owned half the river and the North, the other half?

She sighed, rose, and opened the office door to tinkle a small silver bell. Immediately one of the clerks in the next room appeared at the door. "Yes, ma'am?"

"Please ask Mr. Winter to step into my office."

The clerk nodded and ran.

When Udell appeared, he looked tired and drawn, as if under a strain. She asked him to close the door and indicated the chair Paddock had just vacated. "You look peaked, Udell; what's the matter?"

He sat in the chair and sagged. "I'm glad you're back, Lily."

"Thanks. Did you have problems?"

He shook his head.

"Howard gave you no trouble?"

His head jerked up, and she thought he looked very startled. Had she hit a nerve? She said, "He was just here, you know."

"No, I didn't. What'd he say?"

Lily smiled. Udell had something on his mind, no doubt, and it probably concerned Paddock. Udell was not one to dissemble; everything showed on his face, one way or another. It was one of the many reasons he was valuable to her. Men like Paddock, for instance, were different. One never knew what they were thinking—or planning.

"So Paddock *did* upset you. What did he want?"

"I had no real problem with him, I—I mean—you know how he is."

She stared at him, realizing he was very uncomfortable. He did not meet her eyes, and he wriggled in the chair, probably wishing he were somewhere else. What in hell's name had Howard said to him? Her voice was soft. "Something happened while I was away?"

"Nothing *happened*, Lily."

"Tell me."

He looked at her, then looked away. He fidgeted, and the lines in his face seemed to deepen. There was a struggle going on inside him; she could see it clearly, and she waited.

"Nothing happened," he said again, "really nothing."

Lily clasped both hands before her on the desk, gazing at him calmly. What in hell had gone on?

Her silence made him more and more nervous. He licked his lips, looked at the window, and kneaded the hands in his lap. The silence between them grew, and he knew he was no match for her—he'd always known *that*.

"H-Howard came to talk to me," he said at last.

Lily got up and walked about the room idly. Anger was gathering inside her, but she controlled it; mustn't let Udell see how angry she was. She went to the window and gazed out. "Go on."

"He had a—a p-proposition." Now he knew he had to tell it all. Lily would never allow him to get out of the room without his telling every word. He watched her cross to the cabinet, take out a bottle of cognac, and bring it and two glasses to the desk. She twisted out the cork and poured into the glasses, sliding one toward him. That proved she thought this was important. He tasted the brandy and licked his lips.

She asked, "What was the gist of it?"

"Howard wants control of the firm . . . to move you out."

He dropped his eyes as she stared at him. So Howard had made a move toward her! The rage inside her threatened to burst out. With a tremendous effort she got control of herself. She tried to make her voice light. "He thinks big. How did he propose to do that?"

"He said the law would do it, that—"

"The law! What d'you mean?"

He cringed at the menace in her voice, opening and closing his mouth till she said, "Take your time, Udell."

He nodded and swallowed several times, took a breath, and said grimly, "He asked if you'd had Andrea killed."

"What!"

"And Jacob too." He saw how her eyes were glittering—like a snake's—and the sight made him feel faint. Jesus! What would Lily do to him now? Fire him probably—out into the street. He could not stop his hands from shaking, and a tic had developed at the corner of his right eye. Everything he'd worked for was gone, and it was all Howard's fault.

He was surprised when she said softly, "Go on, Udell—I'm not blaming you for any of this."

"H-he came to me, Lily—all I did was listen—"

"I know." She filled his glass again. "What did you tell him?"

"About A-Andrea? I told him to ask you." He didn't remember if he'd said that to Paddock or not, but it satisfied Lily.

"Did he say when he was going to the law?"

He shook his head. "No."

"How many talks have you had with him?"

"Two. Only two."

"He must have offered you something."

"A little money—"

"What else?"

"I would be general manager when you were gone." Udell tried to smile. "—And a raise in pay."

"He is generous with my money. What else did he want from you?"

"All the information I could give him."

She was silent for half a moment, digesting the news. Paddock's position was not that secure; he'd sent her to Edward Taylor, for instance. The law would find that out easily—she would tell them, if it came to it. But Jacob was something else. Paddock must never learn about Jacob. But if he'd asked Udell he must suspect something. It bothered her greatly.

She saw Udell staring at her, and smiled. "You are practically general manager now."

"Well—"

"Do you want the title?"

He gave her a weak smile. "I don't care about that. I have no complaints."

"How much money did he offer you?"

He hesitated. "Two thousand dollars."

She laughed aloud. Draining the glass, she got up and paced the room. "Howard is cheap. Anyone else would have offered you much more." There was contempt in her voice.

"I—I didn't accept, Lily."

"Of course not. What did you tell him?"

"I—I just refused. I merely walked out."

Lily paused, a hand on his shoulder. "Did he threaten you?"

"An implied threat—" Udell cleared his throat. "I would never have anything to do with such a scheme, Lily. I don't know why Howard thought I would."

She squeezed his shoulder reassuringly. "Of course you wouldn't." She resumed pacing. "He misjudged you, Udell." She wondered why he hadn't come to her immediately instead of making her drag it all out of him. Maybe he would have later. . . . Udell was not an intriguer.

"What're going to do about him?"

"I don't know yet. Please keep it under your hat that we've talked." She sat behind the desk again. "Now tell me the conversation from the beginning, as much as you can remember. I want to know everything that was said between you."

When Udell had gone Lily sat for a long time, steeped in thought. She'd been a fool to let Paddock get his foot in the door of Berlanger-Bryant, and yet it had all been very logical. He had the contact with Sam Beckhart.

But logic was often unsatisfactory; it was all right in its place, but it had too many drawbacks. What kind of fate dealt her such annoying hands? She had constantly to modify and augment fate, to push and force it into her own molds.

What was she going to do about Howard?

He was a man who revered money, and she was aware that he had moved mountains to become a limited partner with her . . . because of the riches Sam Beckhart and the government could bring them. Was it sensible that Paddock would expose her or do her public harm when all that was pending?

It was not. Because Paddock knew as well as anyone that it would all collapse if she were.

No, Paddock wanted this information for the future. In a few years, when their pockets were well lined, then he would suddenly "discover" it. He would accuse her and bring the law down, and she would be finished.

What could she do about him?

Now that he'd brought her together with Sam and the project was in the making, Howard Paddock was useless to her. But if she had him killed, wouldn't she again become entangled in logic? The police would surely remember Hiram Bryant's sudden and violent death, and wonder at Paddock's. One of them might pry into her life, into her past, asking difficult questions; they'd find out that her first two husbands had died similar deaths.

No, she had gone to that well too often. Indeed she was in the process of doing away with Logan Jeffries! But Paddock was too closely concerned in that to accuse her.

So she dared not kill Howard, a pity. Death was so

positive. That was its attraction, that never again did the victim rise to confront or annoy her; he was gone forever. Lily sighed deeply, thinking of riding behind Howard's casket to the cemetery. How she would enjoy that journey!

She shook her head to rid herself of the attractive picture. What else could offer that kind of peace and security? Nothing at all? Would geography do it? If she sent him far off? No, he would only return when she least desired to see him, probably to ask for more money. Could she drive him to madness? Oh, if she only could!

What else remained? Buy him off.

She shook her head again and opened the desk to take out a cheroot. Striking a match, she lit it and puffed blue smoke, watching it curl toward the ceiling. It damned well went against the grain to buy off Howard Paddock. He was cheap as dead weeds, but only when *he* paid money out. From her he'd come very dear. And it would cost her for the rest of her life. Blackmail.

No, nothing had the attraction of death.

She stared at the glowing end of the cigar. But Howard didn't have to die as Hiram had. What if his death was "accidental"? If the police were convinced it was accidental, no one would be to blame!

How could it be made to look like an accident?

There must be dozens of ways. Any accomplished gunman—such as one of her own bodyguards—would know. There had been an account of a shooting accident in the newspapers only a day ago, a hunting trip. One man had shot another while crossing a stile.

Of course, Howard didn't hunt. But he could be kidnapped and taken into the woods. . . .

The thought led her into another channel. Howard

could disappear without a trace. Into the blue! Who could the law's finger point at then? What if Paddock announced he was leaving for a trip and then never arrived! He might end up in a lonely unmarked grave somewhere and never be found.

She smiled. That would do very nicely. Maybe better than any of the others.

Then she rose and paced. Of course, Paddock would be cautious and vigilant, guarding against that very thing. He was no fool, and by now he had an idea of her reputation. He might be nearly impossible to maneuver into the right spot.

She swore and kicked the desk. Well, she could wait.

CHAPTER SIXTEEN

Viktor Kory was disgusted. They had followed Jeffries to the stream and discovered he'd crossed it instead of going up it or down, and he'd sent Joe Kernig ahead on the horse to get in front of the quarry.

Kernig had got in front, all right, but now he was dead, a bullet hole in his forehead. And the horse was dead also. Obviously Jeffries had shot the horse and then the man. He'd never hesitated. So both he and Al Slater were afoot—but so was Jeffries, and Kernig's pistol was missing too. Howard Paddock had been exactly right; Jeffries was tough and quick, and a dead shot.

Slater said, "He went that way." He pointed along the deer track. "We going to follow him?"

Kory got up from his examination of Kernig. "Yes. Let's get after him." He took the trail at a trot, pistol ready. If Jeffries reached the town it might get sticky; he'd certainly go to the law. Kory swore under his breath. Joe Kernig had been stupid as hell and got himself shot. He'd been told Jeffries was expert with a pistol. . . .

Forget Kernig. That was all behind him now. He had to concentrate on the job. What would he do if he were Jeffries? Ambush the pursuers? Maybe, but there were two against one. Jeffries would be facing two guns. Would that worry him? Kory didn't know.

The deer track veered off to the left suddenly, almost at right angles. Kory halted. In front was waist-high brush, but not thick. A man might slide through it easily almost anywhere. The trees hid the sun, and he could see only a few rods in any direction. He studied the ground looking for tracks and saw none.

Al Slater was nervously fingering his pistol. "He got away, you think?"

"He's got to be somewhere. And he's hurt."

"Yeh, but how much?"

Kory edged through the brush in the direction of the town. Certainly Jeffries had been going back there in the buggy. Why not assume he'd continue? He beckoned to Slater and moved cautiously, one step after another, watching for movement. After the first hundred feet he began to breathe more easily. Jeffries wasn't going to try an ambush.

He came to an old and weathered rail fence. It ran off in either direction, crooked and half falling down. Slater hissed, and Kory turned to see where Slater pointed, a tiny sliver of new wood on the top rail. Slater said, "He crawled over right here." His fingers lifted the sliver.

Kory slid over the fence. In another hundred yards he could make out the outlines of a roof. Ducking down, he crawled ahead cautiously. It was a barn, the back wall of a barn with a hayrick beside it. Two mules were nuzzling a corral fence nearby. Had Jeffries made for this farm?

Kory sat down and stared at the barn. If Jeffries was badly hurt, he might run to the first house he came to. He could think of no other reason . . . except that Jeffries had visited one particular house. He'd gotten off the steamboat to go there, so he probably knew that person, and maybe others. He wished Paddock had given him

173

more information.

"What you figgerin'?" Slater asked.

"I'm wondering if he went here or went around." Kory got up and moved back into the shelter of the trees. Cautiously he circled, Slater at his heels, until he could see the farmhouse. It was a long, low building, white-washed years past, not far from the barn.

As he stared at the house, a blossom of white smoke erupted suddenly from one of the windows, and a bullet rapped into a tree and spattered him with bark. He heard the report of the rifle as he fell down and scurried behind the tree bole.

Slater said, "They saw us!"

"Somebody saw us. Sonofabitch!" Kory swore. Now what did he do? Was it Jeffries shooting from the house or someone else? He had to assume that Jeffries had reinforcements. No telling who it might be or how many. He motioned Slater back and crawled carefully, keeping trees between himself and the house. No more bullets came seeking them.

Logan left the glade on the run and made straight for his father's house, careless in the first quarter mile about footprints. When the deer trail veered left, he became cautious, brushing out every mark as he continued.

Dutch was in the barn when he walked into the yard and came from the door with a shotgun cradled in his arms. "What you want?"

Logan turned, saw his father's eyes widen in astonishment, and smiled. "I'll take a cup of coffee—"

"Logan! Where the hell you drop from?"

"Off a steamboat." Dutch looked exactly the same, except for white hair about his ears. He had no paunch at

174

all, was stocky and straight as ever, wearing dark pants tucked into boots, a striped shirt, and a slouch hat.

He clapped Logan on the shoulder. "Come on in the house." Then he noticed the blood on Logan's sleeve. "You hurt?"

"A shot. It's not serious—"

"Shot! Who shot you?"

Logan explained what had happened as they walked to the house. Inside he stripped off coat and shirt and sat in a chair while Dutch examined the wound.

"Went right through the flesh. It'll hurt some, that's all." He washed it and put turps on it with a cloth, then bandaged it quickly as Logan gritted his teeth.

Dutch asked, "Who are them fellas?"

"I don't know." Logan put on the shirt again and went to a window. "I don't know if they could track me or not." The window hadn't been washed in quite a time so he pushed the pane down and squinted at the woods beyond the barn. Nothing moved there.

"They didn't get off the steamboat with you?"

"No, but they could have been put ashore right after."

"You got enemies, boy?"

Logan nodded. "Lily Berlanger." He grinned at the expression on Dutch's face. "She never forgets."

"You think it's about Andrea?"

"No, I don't see how. But I don't know anyone else who would hire men like those"—he jerked his thumb toward the woods—"except Lily. She's tried it before—"

There was movement in the trees. He could make out the dark shape of a man, and of another near him. Logan pointed them out to Dutch. "Have you got a rifle handy?"

Dutch grunted. He went into the next room and returned with a long squirrel gun. Logan reached for it, but Dutch said, "I used to this here piece. She shoots a mite to the left." He put the stock to his shoulder, sighted, and fired.

"Shit! Missed 'im. Goddamn punkin-slinger!"

Logan kept watch. There was no return fire, and he could see no further shadows. But now they knew he was in the house, and now they'd probably take up station around it and wait.

Dutch pulled out the ramrod and reloaded the rifle. "Won't be no trick t'go out there after dark and flush 'em out."

"Wonder if they'd tell us who sent them?"

Dutch came close to a grin. "You stick a man's feet in a fire, and he apt to tell you most anything."

"I suppose so. Maybe even some of it the truth."

Dutch built a fire in the stove and made coffee, and an hour before dark there was a halloo from the road. Dutch said, "That's Lyle." He opened the door, and Logan saw Sheriff Carty and five men on horseback. At Dutch's motion he drew back; Dutch went out and closed the door, and there was a long talk.

When Dutch came inside again he showed his teeth. "Somebody found some dead horses and a dead stranger with a bad hole in him. So Lyle and the boys out hunting."

"Did you tell him anything?"

"Said I heard some noises out beyond the barn. They'll chase them strangers into the woods. You hongry?"

There was no telling, Logan thought, where his pursuers had scattered to, and he did not feel like waiting

176

around for Sheriff Carty to run them down. He ate a meal with Dutch, gave him money to pay for the horse and buggy he'd rented, and slept till dawn.

At first light he was up and striding across the fields toward the river. He saw no one and reached the Chadwick landing as the sun streaked the eastern sky with gold and fire. In two hours a steamboat nudged in and he jumped aboard.

Dutch got up when Logan rose and dressed, and they said good-byes at the door. He made a fire and boiled coffee and heated pone and grits, wondering where the two who'd pursued Logan might have gone.

To avoid horsemen, they'd probably faded back into the deep woods or they'd run like foxes to the next county. Well, he'd have a look, and if he found nothing he'd go into town and listen to the gossip.

He slipped out of the house with only a knife and pistol in his belt and went around the barn to the near woods. He quickly found where he'd hit a tree with the squirrel gun; there were tracks plain as the ears on a jug and easy to follow. Two men had crawled back a dozen rods; then they had stood about for a time before heading directly north.

Dutch grunted. The deep woods were that way, easy to see from here. There were tracks of horsemen also, but they seemed to mill about; then they went east. It had been dark when Carty and his men got this far, so they'd missed the tracks and had probably swung around to search along the river. It was likely that men ducking the law would head for the river where they could get clean out of the country fast.

Dutch went north, using his eyes, unable to depend on

177

hearing. A river brawl years ago had left him hard of hearing, an inconvenience he'd sworn about every day since. He moved warily in the first light, though the tracks were easy to follow. They led directly to a wide gully, and when he smelled smoke he halted.

Like a shadow he crawled to the gully and grinned at the sight of two men huddled between dying fires. Both looked to be sleeping, and they had no blankets. Dutch's lip curled. They must be city people; they didn't even know enough to make a lean-to for shelter. He slid silently into the gully, wondering if he could sneak the weapons away from them.

He paused as one of the men moved and then sat up to yawn and lay sticks on the nearest fire.

The fire blazed up, and Dutch saw him clearly. He was a hard-looking man with thick black brows, dressed in a brown suit that was soiled and wrinkled from his night in the woods.

Dutch pulled the pistol from his belt, stood up, and walked into the clearing. The man swung around to stare at him in astonishment. His hand dived inside the coat— then halted as Dutch motioned with the cocked pistol. Dutch said, "What you doing here?"

The other frowned. "I might ask you the same question."

"Except that you trespassin' on my land," Dutch said evenly. He indicated the second man. "Wake 'im up."

Black Brows shoved the other, who growled and then lifted his head to stare into the pistol muzzle. He slowly sat up. "What's this, Viktor?"

"The man says we're trespassing."

Dutch let the hammer down on the pistol. "What's the rest of your name?" He looked at Viktor.

178

"Smith."

Dutch pulled the hammer back, and the muzzle swung to level on Viktor's chest. Viktor saw the expressionless eyes behind the gun, and a little tremor shook him.

"Boller," he said, using a name he'd used before.

The pistol swung toward the other. "Al Slater," Slater said quickly.

"Put your guns on the ground." Dutch indicated the spot. "One at a time. You first, Boller."

"If we're trespassing we'll gladly get off your land. How were we to know? We got lost last night and just decided to—"

"The woods is already full of cow shit," Dutch said. "You just makin' more. Put your guns on the ground like I said."

Viktor sighed deeply and reached inside his coat. Dutch followed the move intently, finger tight around the trigger. Viktor pulled out the pistol with thumb and forefinger and stretched out his arm to place it where Dutch had indicated.

As he did so, Slater moved. He was rattler fast. A pistol appeared in his hand like magic and swung toward Dutch.

Dutch's shot hit him in the throat. Slater fired in one convulsive movement but the shot blasted between Dutch and Viktor. Then he collapsed, and sightless eyes stared at the gray sky.

"Damn fool," Dutch commented.

Viktor had jerked his hand back from the pistol as if it were red hot. Dutch picked it up and put it into a pocket. He moved around and retrieved Slater's pistol, shoving it into his belt. He felt Slater's pulse. There was none.

He asked Viktor, "Who sent you here?"

"Nobody sent us."

"You come here to kill a man. I want t'know why."

"It's something between us."

"No it ain't. You want to tell me nice or do I have to wring it out'n you?"

"It's none of your—"

Dutch's fist knocked him back. Viktor's head hit the ground hard, and he yelped in astonishment and anger.

Dutch said, "They's more where that came from."

Viktor struggled to sit up again, holding his jaw. His eyes were cloudy, and Dutch knew the man would kill him at the slightest opportunity.

"Who sent you here?"

"Nobody sent—"

Dutch hit him again, a swipe alongside the jaw that knocked Viktor flat, face down. He yanked the man back, and his big fist was poised in Viktor's startled face. "Who sent you?"

As Viktor hesitated, Dutch hit him again. This time Viktor was knocked out; he lay still, breathing in shallow gasps. Dutch waited patiently. It took a long time for Viktor to come round. He sat up groggily, shaking his head, glaring at Dutch.

Dutch asked, "Who sent you?"

Viktor opened his mouth, saw Dutch's fist, and took a long breath. "You wouldn't know if I told you."

"You tell me anyway."

"It was a man up in Cairo, a long way from here." His voice was low and throaty. He swallowed several times.

Cairo! Dutch was startled but allowed nothing to show on his face. He drew back his fist, and Viktor cowered.

"His name was Paddock."

"Tell me all his name."

"Howard Paddock."

180

Dutch nodded. "You're right. It don't mean nothing to me." Christ! Howard Paddock after Logan! Or had he sent these men after him! No, they had followed Logan. He motioned Viktor. "Get up. We going into town."

"What for?"

"I takin' you to the sheriff." Dutch rose and uncocked the pistol. He stepped back, looking at the two small fires. He was about to order Viktor to cover them with dirt when Viktor moved. He grasped two handfuls of dirt and ashes as he gained his feet and flung them both into Dutch's face. In the next second he broke for the woods.

Dutch fired, but the shot went high. He was blinded, and as he fought the dirt he heard the crackling of brush as Viktor ran. When he could see again, the man was gone. Swearing, he followed, but knew he'd never catch up. Viktor was a much younger, more agile man.

He gave up the chase in the first quarter mile and went back to extinguish the fires.

Howard Paddock—after all these years! Why the hell did Howard want to kill Logan? He scraped dirt over the coals; then he went into town to send a telegram.

CHAPTER SEVENTEEN

Howard Paddock sent for one of his clerks, Harry Alquist, and sat him down in the office with a cigar. Harry was a youngish man, not an athlete but a bookkeeper, and a man with an inquiring turn of mind. His clothes were indifferent; he was not imposing, just the sort of man to blend into a crowd.

"I need a job of work," Paddock began, "and you may be the man for me. D'you object to a bit of travel?"

"I'm not married, Mr. Paddock. No—what kind of travel?"

"I want you to go down to Arkansas, a little town there."

"To work on books?"

"No books. I need to find out a few things. I want you t'be a sort of detective."

Harry's eyes grew round. "A detective? I've never done anything like that, Mr. Paddock."

"It won't be that hard. There's no danger at all. I just want you to ask some questions. You're a smart lad. You can do that, huh?"

"Oh, yes, I can do that, sir." Harry fiddled with the cigar. "What kind of questions?"

"I've got a list for you. First there's something else. Secrecy."

"Secrecy? This is all secret?"

"Yes it is." Paddock leaned forward. "A great deal depends on you doing this right, Harry, and there's a good bonus in it f'you if you do, God willing." Paddock lowered his voice. "You got a girl?"

Harry nodded.

"I don't want you to tell her a thing. Not a thing. You understand?"

"Yes, sir. Not a thing."

"You're not to tell anyone else either. You're to tell your girl that you're going on a short trip, a business matter, and you'll be back shortly."

"She'll ask what kind of business. She knows what I do."

Paddock rubbed his chin. "It's a real-estate matter. You're going along with a gentleman to act as his secretary—"

"But I'm not? I'm going alone?"

"Yes, you're going alone. But tell her it's about real estate and that's all you know. When you get back I'll have a story prepared for you." Paddock smiled. "We don't want to get you into trouble with your girl."

"No sir."

"Can you leave today?"

Harry blinked at the cigar. "You mean this afternoon?"

"Yes."

Harry blinked again. "Yes, I guess so—yes."

"All right. Go home and pack a valise and come back here. I'll have your money, and we'll discuss what I want you to ask. Then we'll put you on a steamboat."

Harry got up and went to the door. Paddock said, "Remember, not a word to anyone."

183

One of Paddock's assistants went with him to the levee, put him on a B & B steamboat, the *Locust*, and left as a steward took Harry to his stateroom. Harry had lived all his life in St. Louis and had never been on a steamboat before. It was a grand feeling as he walked out into the main saloon. He had been inside several large hotels, such as the St. George, but they did not compare to this huge room. He gaped at the intricately carved archway colonnades that ran the length of the saloon—on each side—at the huge white and gilt chandeliers, at the plush furniture and the overhead clerestory windows. There were huge mirrors that reflected his almost shabby clothes, and the thick, figured carpet was finer than anything he'd ever seen.

He went out to the promenade to watch the boat back from the levee and start downstream. What a lucky man he was! Mr. Paddock was footing the bill and paying him besides!

He took out the list of questions and read it over. Who the hell were these people? Paddock had given him only the barest idea. He knew the name Lily Berlanger, but the others meant nothing to him. He put the paper away and smiled at the distant shore. He was on a secret mission! Yesterday he had been only one of a number of bookkeepers in a dusty room. Today he was on a grand steamboat on a secret mission!

When the steamboat put him ashore at the Chadwick landing, he was disappointed. There was only the landing, a few boats tied to the bank, a shelter house, and nothing else. The road led into the distance, across a low field, and he thought he could see rooftops there. He took his valise and set out.

Mr. Paddock had carefully rehearsed him in a story he

must tell when he got to Chadwick. He was a cousin of Lily Berlanger's, come to see her. He would pretend surprise that she no longer lived in the town; it would give him a chance to ask all the questions he could think of. Mr. Paddock wanted to know as much about Lily and her ex-husband, Jacob, as he could find out. He especially wanted to know about Jacob's death.

"Write it all down when you're alone," Paddock had told him. "I don't want you to forget anything."

Paddock also wanted to know about someone called Logan Jeffries, who had once lived in the town. His father still lived there. Had there been any relationship between Jeffries and Lily in their early days? Anything at all?

However, he was cautioned against seeing the elder Jeffries, who was known to be a brawler. Paddock said, "Stay away from him."

There was only one hotel in town—a small, seedy town, Harry thought—and he was given a room overlooking the main street. The clerk was a very old man with a limp, and when Harry told him he was a cousin of Mrs. Berlanger's, the man looked astonished.

"They moved up North years ago! Didn't they write to you?"

"No," Harry said, "the last letter we got was from here."

"Hell, Miz Lily moved when old Jacob died. Did you know he was dead?" The old man peered at him.

"No. What'd he die of?"

The old man squinted his eyes. "Folks say lots of things 'bout old Jacob. Too bad you didn't git here b'fore Doc Irvine passed away. Doc took care of Jacob, you know."

"You mean there was something about his death?"

Harry leaned in conspiratorially. "What was it?"

"Hell, I dunno a goddamn thing."

"Well, what do folks say?"

The old man made a face. "Some thinks he was hanted—they was a spell on him."

"Did you know Jacob?"

"Well, I knowed him, but not well. I knowed him before Lily married him. After that things changed. Jacob didn't git around like he did, but folks mostly liked him. He was a fair man, y'know."

"Who put the spell on him?"

The old man made another face. Then he grinned. "Folks says that Lily did. Who else, huh?"

Later, when he introduced himself in one of the two saloons in town as Lily Berlanger's cousin, he met a certain amount of hostility. The Berlanger woman had not been well liked, he discovered, and had been cordially hated by some who had worked for her and been laid off without warning. She had not played fair with them, they said. They were very willing to tell him that Lily had killed old Jacob. Nobody could say how.

Harry wrote it all down as Paddock had ordered, including the names of those he could remember.

The next day he talked to Sheriff Lyle Carty. Carty was a skinny old-timer with hollow cheeks and scraggly hair. He knew every man, woman, and child in the county, he said, and had known Lily and Jacob as well as anybody, but never liked Lily much.

"Lily would as soon stick a knife in you and turn it as look at you, but Jacob—he was a good man. Too bad he had to marry up with her."

Harry said, "Folks say she killed him."

"Yeh, I know they do. Most of it's just talk, 'cause they wasn't there." Carty put his feet up on the desk and rolled a brown cigarette. "I seen old Jacob die all right. Took him a sight of time. Doc Irvine thought it was his stomach or his insides somewheres. But Doc couldn't cure him."

"Did you ask Irvine what Jacob died of?"

"Yes, I did. He said it was a stomach disorder." He winked at Harry. "I tole Doc one time that I'd like to dig 'im up and see if they was arsenic in 'im."

"Arsenic!"

"Yeh. Doc just looked at me like I was turnin' green—real astonished, you know. Then he just went out and got in his buggy without sayin' a word."

"Did anybody ever dig him up?"

"Nope. Got to go to the law f'that, of course." Carty lit the cigarette and puffed. "I guess it's jus' as well to let Jacob lie in peace."

"What about Logan Jeffries? Did you know him?"

Carty laughed. "Hell yeh. I knowed him and his pa. Still see Dutch couple times a week. He lives right over there—" He jerked his thumb. "Logan's a big man in the steamboat business nowadays."

"Oh, izzat so? Were Logan and Mrs. Berlanger good friends?"

Carty roared with laughter. "Friends? Hellsfire! They hated each other. Lily hated all them Jeffries worse'n poison."

"But didn't Logan marry her daughter, Andrea?"

"Oh, a long time afterward. And Andrea was her *stepdaughter*. Yeh, guess she hated Logan for that too. Andrea died down in New Orleans after they

187

was married—"

"Did Lily have anything to do with that?"

Carty stared at him, then shrugged. "Why'd Lily want to kill her own daughter?"

"Yeh," Harry said, "that don't make sense. Where'd she come from, Lily?"

"New Orleans. I seen her the day she got off'n the steamboat. Pretty godddamn woman. Never could see what she saw in old Jacob—except his money. Had a French name—"

"Lily had a French name?"

"Yeh. Lemper—Lemper-something. I seen it on her suitcases. Lempereau, that was it!"

Harry carefully wrote it down when he got back to the hotel. When he looked over his notes, it seemed to him that he'd about wrung out the town. What else could they tell him? He made a full report to Mr. Paddock, including every scrap of information he'd discovered, and mailed it to him. He also sent a wire to say that he'd mailed the letter and was returning on the next boat.

He was surprised to get a wire in return, telling him to stay until the letter was read.

Harry had never had a paid vacation before, so he enjoyed it—as much as possible. Too bad the town was so small. But on the second day he met Rena Hedges, a girl who had once worked for Lily Berlanger as maid and cook's helper. Rena was working in the hotel as a maid and general scrub. She came into Harry's room to do the bed while he was working on his notes, and they talked as she worked.

He was surprised to learn she'd known Lily well. She

188

told him innumerable stories of Lily's home life and of Andrea. She and Andrea had been friends—as much as Lily would permit.

Yes, Andrea and Logan had been in love since their school days and had often met secretly along the river. Andrea had a pony and rode much as she pleased in the woods. Rena didn't think Lily knew much about *that*. Lily had hated Logan, yes, but she'd hated Dutch more. Dutch and his brother had stolen furs from Lily's warehouses—at least Lily said they had.

Then Harry asked, "Did Lily speak French?"

"No, never heard her, why?"

"She had a French name."

"Oh that. She was married before, in New Orleans. I heard her say so once. Usually she didn't tell nobody; but I overheard it."

That afternoon Harry sent another wire to Mr. Paddock explaining about Lily's French name. The return wire was immediate. Harry was to go at once to New Orleans and investigate the first husband, Lempereau. Additional money would be sent to him when he arrived. There was also the short sentence "You're doing good work."

Harry was very pleased. He had begun to entertain a notion of going into detective work full-time. It was enormous fun poking into other people's lives. He packed his bag and took the next steamboat south and strode the decks, staring about him, peering at faces, noting how people dressed and what they did. Detectives observed things, according to the dime novels he'd read; so he began to train himself to observe.

He was startled, as he sat in the main saloon sipping

coffee, to observe a pretty young lady go into her stateroom, followed five or six minutes later by a well-dressed man. Not long before, Harry had seen the man in the company of an older woman he assumed was the man's wife. What was he doing in that stateroom? Harry ordered more coffee and waited. When the man came out at last, he was very furtive about it, and his hair was awry as if whipped by the wind. An assignation!

When the girl reappeared, composed and groomed, Harry studied her. He kept an eye on her and saw her go into the stateroom again, followed by a different man. She was a prostitute!

How fascinating what one could learn if one kept one's eyes open! Harry watched her with four different men during the day and began to feel very sophisticated; he had discovered something that no one else knew, and all because he was a detective. He was a man of the world.

After supper he met the girl on the shadowy deck, and she had become so familiar to him by this time that unconsciously he tipped his hat and spoke to her. She came to him immediately, with a smile. "How do you do—my name is Mandy."

Harry stumbled in getting his name out. She was a pretty girl and wore strong perfume. It tickled his nose. When she suggested they walk along the deck and took his arm, he went eagerly, listening to the babble of his own voice when she asked him where he was bound.

But in the deep shadow of the wheelhouse, he felt her move close to him, and her voice was like a caress, asking him if he liked her. "Of c-course," Harry said—and felt her fingers suddenly close about his private parts.

He jumped, yelping in surprise, and she instantly whirled about and walked away from him. Harry leaned against a bulkheard, watching her go, all his sophistication draining away.

He made inquiries in New Orleans and put up at a cheap hotel—force of habit—and sent Mr. Paddock a wire to say he'd arrived and where he was staying.

More inquiries directed him to public records, and he soon discovered that Lily Berlanger had been Mrs. Jacques Lempereau, and before that Lily Kupper. Kupper was her maiden name. Hours of poring over records got him the information that Lempereau had died of an internal malady and had been buried in St. Luke's Cemetery. He went there at once.

There was a gravestone with Lempereau's name on it, all right. But the cemetery was not an imposing one. Lily had put her beloved first husband in a seedy plot, and the gravestone itself was not large. It was rather cheap, in fact, Harry thought. The cemetery was weedy and uncared for, and the solitary gatekeeper told him that he was the only one on duty, that the gates were locked at night. "Who'd want t'git in, hey?"

Harry agreed with him and went away.

He sent Mr. Paddock a long wire, detailing what he'd learned. Why Mr. Paddock wanted all the rather boring details, Harry could not imagine. Who cared what Lily's maiden name had been, or where her husband was buried?

He was astonished, therefore, to receive a wire from Paddock telling him to remain where he was until a letter arrived. Paddock also wired him money and seemed very pleased.

Then a second wire arrived to say that Mr. Paddock was coming to New Orleans himself! It closed with the curt statement "Remember your instructions." That meant he was to keep his mouth shut. Holy Christ! If Mr. Paddock was coming south himself, he must be onto something!

CHAPTER EIGHTEEN

It was during the midst of her worries about Howard Paddock that Lily received a letter from Paige Robinson, and her heart soared. He was coming to St. Louis and, if all went well, would arrive within a week after the letter reached her.

One of his own steamboats, the *City of Bayou Tel*, had just completed repairs, and he had booked passage on her. In the last year his firm had purchased three steamboats for the Natchez-to-New Orleans trade, but now and then one came upriver to St. Louis. Paige was taking advantage of this charter. He was impatient to see her.

Lily pushed the worries out of her mind and went into a flurry of preparation. She ordered the house cleaned from top to bottom, the garden weeded, fences painted, and even her three carriages painted and polished. She had not seen a hairdresser since returning from Washington, and she immediately engaged the best she could find and sat patiently while the woman washed, combed, and tugged, snipping and shaping. . . .

It had been an eternity since she'd seen Paige and held him. He was the one man in the world she really loved, and yet they lived apart—and always had. How many times had they talked of marriage! His wife had run off with another man, and he had obtained a divorce and had once promised to marry her when it became final. But the year had passed. . . .

Maybe now he was coming to propose to her!

That must be it. It would be like him to say nothing and then to suggest it as they were quietly dining somewhere with the lights very low. . . .

Everyone in the office noticed the change; it was whispered throughout the building, and most wondered what magic had transformed her. Everyone breathed easier, praying the magic would continue. Udell Winter was the only one who knew the truth, and he had been sworn to silence. Lily was even secretive about happiness.

It was her custom each morning to read the several newspapers that were placed on her desk before her arrival. She would peruse them with her morning cup of coffee and occasionally call Udell in to discuss some interesting item.

Three days after she had received Paige's letter, she saw the lead story in the *Democrat*. It caused her to scream in terror.

The *City of Bayou Tel* had blown up in midstream and sunk with nearly all aboard.

Udell and several clerks rushed into her office at the scream and found her staring at the newspaper as if it were a live cobra about to strike. Wordless, she pointed to the headline, and Udell read it with a sinking feeling: The steamboat's boilers had exploded as she was nearing Cairo. The explosion had been witnessed by several other boats, which had immediately rushed to gather up survivors. Paige Robinson's name was not among those listed.

Udell quickly sent a messenger for a physician; then he gave Lily brandy and convinced her to stretch out on a couch until the doctor arrived. She seemed to be in a fog, unwilling to talk, to listen. . . .

The doctor gave her a sedative, which was all he could do, and advised rest and calm. Lily roused herself once and swore at him, and he hurried out, astounded and indignant. Udell got rid of him.

After she went home, she stayed in bed all the next day, unable to eat, uncaring about anything. Paige was dead—God! Paige was gone! It drummed through her head: she would never see him again, never feel his arms about her . . .

She was away from the office for more than a week.

And when she returned, she was moody and often irritable. Udell urged her to go away, rest, lose herself in other surroundings, and, all in all, it was good advice, she thought. But to travel on the river would bring back memories of Paige, and she would not board another train unless it was a matter of life or death. So she stayed in St. Louis.

And three weeks after Paige's death Roy Collier showed up.

He sent her an engraved card from his suite at the St. George Hotel: Gilbert Collier, United States Senator. On the back he had written, "I must see you. Roy."

His arrival cheered her up. She sent the messenger back at once saying she was delighted and suggesting they dine at the hotel that evening.

Howard Paddock was disgusted with Udell Winter, but he had no recourse. His friends among Lily's office staff all told him the same thing. Lily trusted Udell and

195

probably would not replace him, no matter what Paddock or anyone else said.

He saw Udell once after their last secret conversation in Udell's office; they met on the stairs and Paddock stopped him.

"You've said nothing?"

Udell shook his head. "What should I say? You know her temper."

"Nothing occurred between us."

"Yes, exactly. So that's where it stands." Udell felt himself remarkably in hand. He had expected to see and talk with Paddock and had steeled himself. He would simply deny everything. What could Howard do? Nothing. He stood silent as Paddock glared at him; then he nodded and went on up to his office. Paddock stared after him and went down to his carriage.

Udell had said nothing to Lily, he was sure. Else Lily would have sent for him, raging.

But the matter didn't end there. One day he would sit where Lily sat; he felt it was his destiny. And from the beginning he had felt safe from Lily's wrath—since the death of Hiram Bryant. Lily had had *him* killed, but she could not kill another partner, could she?

He was encouraged to get the wire from Harry Alquist in Chadwick and waited impatiently for the letter. He sent a wire telling Harry to wait; Harry wasn't costing him much, and there might be something in the letter that needed more investigation. He was delighted to get another wire about Lily's first husband, and he ordered Harry to New Orleans at once.

Harry's news about Lempereau was very interesting, especially the report that he had died of an internal malady! Was it possible that Lily had done away with

196

him too?

The more Paddock thought about it, the more he convinced himself that it was not only possible, but probably true. He wired Harry to stay put, that he was coming on the next steamboat.

He packed a bag, sent Lily a note that he was urgently needed in Cairo on personal business, and rushed to board a southbound boat.

On the trip south he had plenty of time to make plans. His first order of business was proof. If the body of Lempereau contained poison, and if the body of Jacob Berlanger contained the same poison, then any court would convict Lily of murder. He was positive she was trapped. *If.*

And it was possible that his knowledge of the murders could be the lever that ousted Lily; he might never have to go to the law at all. He would prefer not to; he and the law had little in common. He might be able to make some accommodation, move Lily out of the company, but allow her compensation—he could be generous.

If Lily could read the handwriting on the wall. She would scream and rage, deadly as a tigress, but he had the big club, knowledge of the two murders. He might even bring in the murder of Hiram Bryant. Lily would, of course, shrill to the law that he, Paddock, had provided the murderer, Edward Taylor. But even the law would be able to see that *he* had not employed Taylor. How could he know what Lily wanted of the man?

And the clincher was that Lily, and not he, had profited by Bryant's death. She had assumed control over the entire company after buying out Bryant's son, Alfred.

Yes, he was free and clear of Bryant's murder.

And if Lily was sensible she would allow him to buy her out at a reasonable figure, and the law would never enter the matter at all. It was very neat and tidy—as long as he had the club over her head. He would say to her, sell or go to jail—and maybe hang by the neck until dead.

And one more thing. He would show her a copy of the letter kept in his lawyer's safe and to be opened in case of his death. It would delineate all of Lily's crimes and point to her as his killer because of his knowledge of them.

It would insure his future. Paddock laughed. He had Lily now. *If* Lempereau and Jacob had been poisoned.

Viktor Kory ran like a deer, bent over to make himself a smaller target. The shot that Dutch fired at him went wide, and in another moment he was out of range.

He headed for the river, running across fields, through woods and brush. He quickly left his pursuer behind. When he stopped to get his breath he was completely alone. The big, burly man had not been able to keep up, but he had mentioned the sheriff. He was probably a close friend; didn't all small-towners know each other?

He would be smart not to go back to the hotel. He had nothing of value in his suitcase anyway.

It was too bad about Slater and Kernig, but the one had been stupid and the other, slow. He dismissed them from his mind and concentrated on his next move. He had to get away from this section of the country, because if he stayed the sheriff would probably gather him in with ease, and then there'd be the horses to pay for and the bodies to explain. . . . A small-town judge might not be able to see his side of it, and Kory shuddered to think of work gangs, or worse.

He could be sure that Jeffries had gotten away clean,

and there was no telling where he'd gone. But first he'd get away, then he'd worry about Jeffries. A man had to save his own skin, for without it nothing else mattered.

When he came to the river, he sat on the bank and watched it flow, a murky, brown tide with streaks of deep green far out and sunlight dancing on bits of yellow-green brush. A breeze swept downstream, seeming to hurry the river on, and birds darted here and there in the trees around him. He'd have to go back to St. Louis and face Paddock; no way out of it. He could waste months trying to seek out Jeffries by himself. Paddock could provide the means of pinpointing him. Jeffries had to surface somewhere, had to live somewhere—maybe even had a wife, though Paddock had said nothing about that. He had failed in his first attempt and had alerted Jeffries, but it never occurred to Viktor Kory to give up. He had a vast confidence in his ability, and temporary setbacks could be expected now and then. He would have to convince Paddock of this truth, though Paddock would be understandably annoyed.

Kory watched a small skiff glide past on the far side of the river, swift as a shooting star, and then he got up. The easiest thing would be to go downstream. He could probably make some kind of raft. He glanced around seeking fallen branches; then he began to think about how he'd tie them together. He had nothing—unless he tore up his shirt. Glancing back toward the town, he thought about waiting for dark. He might slip back and steal one of the rowboats tied by the landing.

But he hated to wait that long, and, besides, he was no woodsman. He might have enormous trouble getting back to the landing in the dark. It was bad enough pushing through brush and trees in daylight.

He started walking south, keeping the river close on his left. He'd never in his life been on a raft, anyway, and had only stepped into a small boat once or twice. However, one sat in a boat and used oars. Not so bad. The river would take him, too, if he got the boat into the stream.

How far was the next town? He would get a steamboat there.

He saw half a dozen steamboats as he walked, but all were far out, and though he yelled and waved several times they did not stop or seem to hear him.

By noon he was tired and hungry. He'd seen no farms, nothing but woods and grass. The river made great loops that were miles across, and he knew he was tramping maybe ten miles to go one mile south. Just the idea of it was tiring, but he was afraid to try cutting across a loop because it might not prove to be a loop and then he'd be miles from the river, and maybe lost. Once, he climbed a tree to see ahead, but could make out nothing but the tops of trees. It was discouraging; all he could do was follow the damned river.

Late in the afternoon he came to plowed land lying fallow, surrounded in part by a rail fence. In the distance was a group of gray-brown houses, from which barely visible tendrils of smoke rose. A man walked beside a mule not far off, and Kory slid behind a tree to watch for a moment. The man was walking away from him, toward the houses.

When he continued, he quickly came to a path that led to the water, and in a tiny cove he found two crudely-made rowboats tied to the bank. Grinning at his luck, Kory untied one and stepped in gingerly. There were two heavy, short oars in the bottom, and the boat smelled of fish. Obviously people from the distant houses used it for fishing in the river. He shoved out of the cove into an eddy that spun him around. It took several moments to get the boat under control; the clumsy oars were hard to manage, and he'd never rowed before, but he pulled through the eddy into the stream, and the river caught the boat. In another moment he was moving rapidly.

An hour after dark he came to a town.

He glided past it, rowed to the bank, and left the boat half-pulled out of the water. He walked into the town to discover that all the stores, five or six in all, were closed and that there was no hotel. But there was a stable with a light inside; its door was half open. Kory went in. There were horses in all but two of the stalls, and from the back he heard sounds; someone was singing off-key but enthusiastically.

The singer was a heavy, bearded man wearing boots, ragged pants, and an undershirt. Suspenders hung down behind him almost to the floor, and he was frying meat in a skillet that sat on a belly stove.

Kory stopped in the doorway of the back room and said hello.

The bearded man swung around in astonishment, mouth open. "How'd you git in here?"

"The door was open." Kory jerked a thumb over his shoulder.

"That goddamn door. Can't keep 'er shut." He looked Kory up and down. "What you want?"

The meat smelled good; his stomach had been rumbling for an hour or more. Kory said, "I just got in town and there's no place to stay."

"We don't get many folks that wants to stay. You know somebody here?"

"Not a soul. I'm looking to get on a steamboat soon's I can."

The bearded man nodded. "You gimme a dollar, and you c'n sleep in one of them stalls . . . and I throw in some shank meat." He indicated the skillet.

Kory handed over the money.

CHAPTER NINETEEN

When Logan returned to St. Louis, he found that Neil Barnes had, as Fraser had predicted, suddenly emptied his desk and departed without a word to anyone. Fraser was relieved, he said, and promoted one of his office clerks to take Barnes' job, a bookish-looking young man named Marvin Rodda.

Neil Barnes had been living in an upper-class boarding house within walking distance of the office, but he had checked out when Louis Gualco went there to inquire. No one knew where he had gone.

There was a telegram signed by Dutch waiting for Logan. It was rather artfully worded—for Dutch, Logan thought—and he smiled at the idea of his father so carefully choosing his words. But what Dutch had to say was startling:

> *Saw two men. One still here, one left fast.*
> *Named Viktor Kory. Sent by H. Paddock.*

He showed the telegram to Fraser. "'One still here' probably means he's dead," Logan said. "Dutch must have squeezed the information out of him."

"Howard Paddock?"

"Well, I'd expect that Paddock hired the men for Lily.

She wouldn't want her name mentioned. They probably didn't know they were working for her."

"Yes, of course. That's probably it." Fraser rubbed his chin, studying the slip of paper. "Does your father know Paddock?"

"Very well. They did considerable business together a long time ago."

"This man Kory . . . do you think he'll come back here?"

"Yes, to report to Paddock why the attempt failed. Paddock knows by now it failed—"

"I don't like this at all, Logan."

"Neither do I." Logan shrugged. "We don't know the details of why Kory was hired, but I think I'll ask Clarence Yates to keep a man on Paddock. The more we know the more we can guess."

"Why don't you wire Dutch and ask what Kory looks like?"

"A very good idea."

The three remodeled stern-wheelers were busy hauling munitions, Fraser said, so far without a single hitch to mar the industry. He was happy with the profit-and-loss statements that Doris prepared. But he was extremely uneasy and concerned as Logan detailed his trip to Natchez and Chadwick. They sat in Fraser's office with the door closed, and Fraser asked a hundred questions and examined Logan's wound. A doctor traveling on the steamboat, Logan said, had treated and rebandaged it, saying the wound would heal with no trouble.

Fraser was philosophic on hearing that Dr. Irvine had died and his records been destroyed. All the luck seemed to be on Lily's side.

In the afternoon Logan and Louis Gualco went to

Yates' office, where Logan arranged for surveillance to continue round the clock on Paddock. He received Yates' report that, so far as he could discover, Neil Barnes had worked alone, that there was no accomplice among the Jeffries-Fraser employees. Yates was sure Barnes had left town for an unknown destination.

"I am told that Barnes came from Cincinnati, and he may have gone back there."

"Let him go," Logan said. "He's unimportant to us now."

Doris knew nothing of his wound until he told her that evening after supper. They were preparing for bed, and when he took off his shirt she was horrified to see the bandage. "What happened to you?"

"It's hardly anything." He did his best to make light of it, but she demanded details.

He explained how he'd gone to Irvine's house, talked to his snarly widow, and left. The horsemen had come along the road suddenly. "They were shooting at my horse, to halt the buggy. This was only a stray—"

"A stray! You mean a stray *bullet!* It might have killed you! There's no difference between bullets!"

"But it didn't."

Doris leaned against him, eyes closed. He put his arms about her, trying to think of the proper words.

She said, "You didn't tell me there'd be danger."

"I had no reason to suspect any."

"You should have taken Louis along."

Logan nodded. "I know. I—I underestimated Lily again. But I promise—from now on Louis will be in my back pocket."

Doris sighed and said no more, but as they got into bed

205

she slid her arms about him. "When will this come to an end?"

"You mean with Lily?"

"You know very well that I mean Lily. I met you while you were escaping assassins—" She sighed. "I sometimes feel I should take a pistol and march into Lily's office myself."

He chuckled. "I believe you would."

"If it would end all this worry. We have to go about with guards! We live in an armed camp!"

"I think Lily does the same—"

"That doesn't make it any better, Logan Jeffries."

"Lily deals in homicide. She's a violent person. Kenneth and I are trying to live within the law as well as we can and protect ourselves."

"The law! It's doing nothing for you—or us."

He kissed her cheek. "That's a continuing problem of the law-abiding citizen. The law ignores him until something tragic happens. We're at the mercy of people like Lily—but we *are* protecting ourselves, and it will come to an end one day."

She snuggled close to him, pulling his arms about her. "I knew all this when I married you—" She touched his bandaged arm. "But I thought then I'd be able to control the worry better. But I can't."

He held her tightly. There was nothing he could promise her except caution and vigilance. So much depended on Lily. He could not tell Doris how surprised he'd been at the attack in Chadwick, because it seemed to signify a vicious renewal of Lily's vendetta against him. All that would depress Doris even more.

But he was very disturbed at Lily's persistence. Was it because she feared that one day he'd kill her on account

206

of Andrea?

He could think of no other reason.

Logan received another report from Clarence Yates about Paddock. Yates' man had managed to talk with one of Paddock's household staff. Paddock had left the city to go south, possibly to New Orleans. The man was positive he'd heard Paddock say to the woman who lived with him that he'd be in New Orleans for a few days and then return. He knew nothing more, except that Paddock had gone alone.

Fraser suggested it was a business trip. "Why else would he go there? If it was a pleasure trip, wouldn't he have taken the woman, whoever she is?"

"God knows about Paddock."

But there seemed no reason for the expense of shadowing Paddock so far away. What mischief could he be up to in Louisiana?

Yates also had a weekly report on Lily, and when they looked over the reports for several weeks it revealed an unexpected fact. Yates said, "Paddock no longer goes to Lily's home. He used to go there often."

"That's curious," Logan said.

"Lily has hosted several small gatherings in her home since she came back from Washington," Yates said. "Businessmen and politicians, but no Paddock. Is that interesting to you?"

Fraser said, "It means he wasn't invited. Maybe they've had a falling out."

"And," Yates continued, "Paddock hasn't attended any of the civic functions Lily appeared at."

"But he hires men to kill Logan," Fraser said darkly. "For her or for him?"

"For her," Logan said with assurance.

Yates said, "I'd like to be able to look into Lily's brain for a minute. I'll bet it's a seething mass—"

"No bet," Logan agreed.

Two days after Howard Paddock had left St. Louis to go south, Yates had another report. A late-night visitor had gone to Paddock's door and been admitted for a short time. Yates' man described him as medium sized but could say little else because of the dark. He had not followed the visitor.

Yates' question: Was this Viktor Kory?

Dutch's second wire had described Kory as being of medium size and height, dark, with heavy brows, well dressed and having a Northern accent.

Logan was positive it was Kory and asked Yates to have him followed if he showed up again.

Viktor Kory had gone at once to Paddock's home on arriving in the city; he had prepared a story that Jeffries had detected him and his men and had laid an ambush, killing the two henchmen. Kory had escaped with his life—and much of it was Paddock's fault for not giving him enough information on Jeffries. Why, for instance, had Jeffries gone to Chadwick?

But Paddock was not home and was not expected back for several weeks. No one was at liberty to say where their employer had gone.

Annoyed, Kory left and went to a hotel near the waterfront to consider. But it was not a difficult problem. He needed the promised thousand dollars, the remaining half of the fee. All he had to do was kill Logan Jeffries. And now the man was alerted.

But a thousand was a great deal of money, and he knew

of no other way—aside from a bank job perhaps—to get so much.

This time he would know more. The next morning he set about collecting information about Jeffries, starting with his office. The Jeffries-Fraser offices were not nearly as large as those of Berlanger-Bryant, but just as crowded during business hours, and he was able to move freely through the lower floor. A few casual questions to employees brought him the information that Mr. Jeffries was not often on the premises and that Mr. Kenneth Fraser was in charge.

He took up station opposite the main door of the establishment, hoping to see and follow Jeffries—he was sure he would recognize him again—but Jeffries did not show up. He hung around for two days, with no luck.

Then a casual conversation, overheard in a restaurant nearby, told him that the company officials came and went by way of the shipping yard where their carriages were kept. Kory entered the yard that afternoon pretending to be a shipper from another city inquiring about a cargo; he struck up a conversation with a clerk and came away with the information that Jeffries' wife worked in the offices and that she often came and went with her husband. "In that carriage over there." The clerk pointed it out, saying that sometimes the driver spent an hour or two in the city during the day making household purchases.

But the clerk did not know where Jeffries lived. Kory thought the man looked at him oddly when the question came up, and he changed the subject.

At the end of the day he was watching when the carriage rolled from the yard, but he was unable to see inside it. He followed on horseback for a mile or so, but when the driver turned around and stared at him, Kory gave up the chase.

He had taken up residence in the Nestande Hotel, which had a tap room and catered to drummers, sporting women, actors, and petty gamblers. He spent nearly thirty dollars on women the first week he lived there. One suggested he rent a house and let her move in with him, but he explained he was only in the city a short time and was due back in Pittsburgh when his work was finished. He was vague about the work.

Then, as he sipped a beer at a tap-room table, Kory recalled Jeffries' trip to investigate the steamboat *Monarch*, which was undergoing repairs at Natchez. Did Jeffries investigate all such accidents? Maybe Jeffries handled outside affairs for the company and the other one, Fraser, ran the offices.

Was that the way to get Jeffries to a little out-of-the-way spot along the river? He'd disable a steamboat and Jeffries would show up. The more he thought about it, the better it sounded. If he could get Jeffries into the open, he might cut him down with a rifle—he might. The man was sure to be more careless far away from a city.

But how to disable a steamboat?

There would have to be extensive damage, or the boat captain would have it repaired quickly and Jeffries would not need to investigate. Possibly the best way would be fire. Of course, he'd have to be on board, under an assumed name, and he'd have to make sure the fire didn't destroy *him* as well as the boat. A controlled fire? Not very damned likely. He might set a fire in a stateroom while the boat stopped somewhere for wood; he would then walk ashore. But if detected early the fire would be easily doused.

What about blasting powder? It might be planted somewhere aboard, with a long fuse. He could carry the powder on board in a suitcase and then take his time about deciding where to place it. If he put it in a stateroom during a wooding-up, then walked ashore and watched the boat blow—

There was one flaw in all these plans. If he damaged a boat in an out-of-the-way spot all the passengers would be put onto another boat long before Jeffries arrived. And if *he* did not answer the roll call, they'd know who had done it. Damn. People were sure to remember him, even if he stayed in his cabin. He had to eat, and it would cause plenty of comment if he took his meals in a tiny little cabin. . . .

It was not an easy problem. And he'd get the rope for certain if he caused the deaths of passengers—and if he was caught.

But wait—there were plenty of times when steamboats were tied up with no one on board but a watchman. Even in St. Louis he might shoot Jeffries on the levee. There were rooms to let along the waterfront, and he could fire from a window while Jeffries crossed the levee. He ought to be able to evade one watchman late at night, set a stateroom fire, and get out.

Kory smiled at the idea. He'd set about immediately watching the steamboats along the levee late at night to perfect his plans.

But it had to be a Jeffries-Fraser boat.

He left the tap room and walked to the Jeffries-Fraser offices on Third Street. With no trouble he obtained a flyer listing all the company's steamboats. He studied it in the Osage Saloon on Front Street, where there was a bulletin board listing steamboat arrivals and departures.

The saloon was a regular haunt of steamboat men, and he struck up an acquaintance with one, a rough-talking, middle-aged man who swore he'd been a mate and discharged because of petty jealousy—but from the manner in which he soaked up whiskey, Kory was sure there was another reason. He bought the man drinks and in this manner learned that Jeffries-Fraser also owned three small stern-wheelers that were not mentioned in the flyer.

"Because they handle special cargoes," the man said with a wink.

"What's that?"

"They secret."

"Why?"

The ex-mate leaned across the table with another wink. "Munitions," he said. "Gunpowder and that sort."

It was fascinating knowledge, but was Jeffries on board any of them? The man did not know. The boats did not keep schedules either. He learned their names, *Ionia*, *Freedom* and *Lucy Flint*, and he saw *Freedom*, tied at the levee several days later. He saw that it was patrolled by armed men who eyed him as he strolled past.

Jeffries was a harder nut to crack than he'd at first supposed. What if he staked out his victim's house? He'd think about that next. He hung around the Jeffries-Fraser offices but never caught sight of Jeffries; of course, the man was wary now and wasn't showing himself at all.

Paddock had really given him a sonofabitch of a job.

And then one morning, when he entered the Osage Saloon, he noticed the gaudy-colored poster tacked up on a wall. The St. Louis Rivermen's Fraternal Association was giving a fancy-dress ball at the Armory Hall in eight days. All rivermen were invited to attend, on payment, of course, of the door fee.

Kory stared at the poster; this would solve his problem, all in one blow! Logan Jeffries was sure to be there, out in the open.

CHAPTER TWENTY

Howard Paddock arrived in New Orleans on a blustery day that promised rain but then withheld it. He put up at the New Francis Hotel and sent for Harry Alquist. Harry arrived two hours later, having been out, walking the levee, he said.

Paddock fussed that they'd wasted half a day, but he had to admit that Harry had no idea when he'd arrive. They took a hired rig to St. Luke's Cemetery, and Howard stood with hands clasped behind him, staring at Lempereau's grave. He was no more impressed by the surroundings than Harry had been, but he was far more pleased.

"You know what we have to do now?"

Harry shook his head.

"We have to dig up the body and have it examined for arsenic."

"Dig it up?" Harry was startled.

Paddock glanced around. The driver was a hundred feet away, fiddling with his harness; there was no one else near. "If you don't have the stomach for this, Harry—"

"Oh—well, of course, I didn't expect—"

Paddock added a bit of sugar. "You've done well up to now, Harry, and I want to keep you on the payroll."

"Of course, Mr. Paddock. It's just that I—"

"You didn't expect this. All right. But it has to be done, you understand, God willing." Paddock sniffed and rubbed his nose. "Has to be done." He stepped closer and lowered his voice. "This is between us, Harry. All right?"

"Y-yes sir?" Harry looked confused.

Paddock glanced around again. "I believe this man"—he indicated the gravestone—"was murdered. If we find arsenic then it'll be positive."

Harry had grasped everything. "Then the man in Chadwick—Jacob Berlanger—you think the gossip is true? He was murdered too?"

"Yes, of course."

"And you're going to open the grave in Chadwick also?"

"Has to be done, Harry." Paddock sniffed. "It has to be done. Now, the first thing is to find a physician to help us. He'll make the tests to prove or disprove arsenic."

Harry cleared his throat. "But will the authorities allow you to do that, sir?"

"Dig up the grave?"

Harry nodded.

"Oh, I expect not. We'll have to do it when there's no one around, Harry. I don't want the world to know. Who's in charge of this cemetery?"

Harry pointed. "The caretaker stays in that house, but he locks up at night and goes home."

"I see, good. He's an agile young man is he?"

"No sir. He's a real old fellow, can hardly get around."

Paddock smiled. "Even better." He fished out a cigar, bit off the end, and struck a match. "What we need is a wagon and one horse, a couple of gravediggers and the physician. Can you arrange for the wagon and the diggers? Men who can keep their mouths shut."

"Of course, sir."

"All right, I'll find the physician. We'll dig up the casket, take it to the doctor's shop, and let him make the tests. Then we'll have to bring the remains back and plant them again. I may need them later."

"What for?" Harry asked.

"If I have to go to court." Paddock walked to the carriage. "When we go back to the gate, I want you to hop down and take a good look at the lock. Can you pick a lock, Harry?"

Harry shrugged. "I can get a jimmy to break it open."

It took Howard Paddock another day to find a physician who would do. He made a number of inquiries, pretending to search for a doctor he vaguely described, a man who'd been on the skids because of drink, and he learned about three.

The first was feeble and no longer in practice, the second was quarrelsome and probably too talkative, but the third was a man named Rosso Cowart, who had a neighborhood practice in a shabby district, a middle-aged, shifty-eyed, bald man who looked undernourished and who obviously needed money. He lived in a run-down house, half of which was given over to his consultation and operating rooms, was unmarried, and, Paddock thought, perfect for his plans.

He went to see the doctor with a pretended complaint, in order to talk to him in private, and was pleased by the man's easy disregard for ethics. Cowart would, he thought, do almost anything for money short of murder, and he had a laboratory sufficient for his needs.

On his second visit Paddock introduced himself as an agent for a large company. He had been hired, he said, to track down a certain person, and he had done so but had discovered the person in question had died and was buried nearby. Now his company demanded to know how the person had died. "No autopsy had been performed," he told Cowart. "My assistant checked the records and found no such entry."

"Such a thing is rare," Cowart agreed, "unless foul play is suspected."

"It was not then, but is now." Paddock played his important card. "But my investigation must be done in secret."

Cowart stared at him. "In secret?"

"I will pay well, Doctor. In cash, on demand."

Cowart licked his lips. "Can the body be brought here?"

"Yes, certainly. I have arranged everything."

"You will take the body away afterward?"

"Yes, of course. It will be reburied . . . in case the law requires an official grave opening, much later."

Cowart took a long breath. "Five hundred dollars."

Paddock's eyes widened. "I had thought two hundred would be sufficient."

"The risk is great—to me! My practice—"

"Three hundred."

"Please, four hundred."

Paddock shook his head sadly and went to the door. "Three hundred is the best I can do, sir. Perhaps another—"

"Very well," Cowart said with a sigh. "When do you wish to do this?"

Paddock smiled. "Within the next two or three days. I will send you word. I imagine midnight or later would be best?"

It was a cold, clear, moonlit night when the two gravediggers recruited by Harry began their task. Harry stood by the growing pile of sandy dirt, while Paddock walked up and down between the headstones, smoking a cigar. This kind of affair was not to his liking, but he did not dare leave it to Harry.

He had told Harry that it would be necessary to dig up Jacob Berlanger's tomb also, but how could he go to Chadwick? He had no wish to see Dutch again, and it would probably be impossible to set foot in the county without Dutch finding out. He had once sent a man to kill Dutch for the gold he knew Dutch had buried, but Dutch had not died, and the man had not returned. He was very sure Dutch had no suspicions about who had sent the man, but he could not bring himself to go there, just the same. Let sleeping dogs lie.

If Lempereau's remains contained poison it was enough. He would tell Lily, if he had to, that he'd dug up Jacob too. She would believe it. Hell, she was guilty! Of course, she would believe it.

It took almost three hours to dig up the casket and put it on the wagon. Then he paid off the gravediggers— Harry would have to fill in the grave later himself—and they set off; Harry drove the patient horse. It was slightly after midnight when they arrived at Dr. Cowart's office. The three of them carried the heavy casket into the house and into the laboratory, and they left the doctor to his work.

Paddock had brought along a flask of brandy, more than half-empty now, which he finished off. He and Harry smoked cigars, and Harry read newspapers by a glowing lamp. Paddock was too nervous. He paced the room, puffing like a locomotive, wondering what the scene would be like the day he faced Lily with his knowledge. He'd have to work it all out beforehand, to know exactly what he wanted and how far he would go in being generous with her. Lily would not take defeat gracefully.

That day was still perhaps a year away. He'd have to wait until Berlanger-Bryant was rich from government business, until *he* was so rich that it did not matter if the scandal terminated the company's government connections. Then, when he bought Lily out, he might well sell the rest of the company, retire, and enjoy his wealth. He'd always wanted to see Europe. . . .

It seemed to take forever for Dr. Cowart to complete his examination, and when he came into the room he brought a terrible smell with him. He said pompously to Paddock, "I found sufficient evidences of arsenic poisoning to justify an unassailable verdict of death by that means."

"You're absolutely positive?"

"Of course. I was deputy coroner in the city of Jackson for five years. I have seen this before, sir. My opinion will stand."

"Then there's nothing else to say," Paddock said. He handed over an envelope with the promised cash. "If you will close the casket, sir, we'll put it back on the wagon."

It was a wearing night, though Harry did all the work. He filled in the dirt, smoothed it over by moonlight, and scattered bits of grass and twigs on it before Paddock finally announced himself satisfied. Grave robbing as an avocation was long in the past, he told Harry; no one would suspect that Lempereau's rest had been disturbed.

They drove back to the city, and Paddock stumbled upstairs to his hotel room while Harry returned the horse and wagon to the livery. Having locked the door, Paddock sat on the edge of the bed and poured himself a nightcap. It had been time well spent; Lily Berlanger was in the palm of his hand. He could prove she was a murderess. He looked at himself in the mirror and grinned. From this night forward his fortune was made! He sniffed and giggled and gulped another brandy. He was not a poor man now, but when he gained control of Berlanger-Bryant he would quickly become rich!

But not for a year at least. The company was prospering now, but in a year's time it would be wallowing in government dollars. If he removed Lily too soon, it would upset the apple cart. He would bide his time and then play the trump cards. Everything in good time.

He slept till late afternoon, and when he rose he considered taking Harry to supper, but then decided against it. Harry was too much of a bumpkin; there was no sense in listening to that kind of prattle for very long. He consulted a bellboy and handed over several bills, and in a short while a young lady rapped on his door.

She was of an odd coloring, having dark eyes and brows and reddish hair with black roots. She wore a silky shirtwaist that was tied with colored strings in front, very loosely tied, and a blue cloak over the shirt and full skirt. Paddock smiled, thinking how garish she looked—but she was young and that covered a multitude of shortcomings.

He invited her in, and she immediately began to take her clothes off. "Hello, my name is Salli, what's yours?"

"You may call me Robert. But—er—don't undress—"

She stared at him. "Yeh? Why not?"

"We're going to supper."

"Oh." She smiled. "You want to eat first, huh?"

"Yes." He held the cloak for her, and they went downstairs. He decided against the hotel dining room; everyone would stare at him, knowing exactly what she was. He called a cab, and they drove to a coffeehouse. It was a place with low ceilings, colored lamps, mysterious shadows, and layers of tobacco smoke. They were seated near a profusion of plants in a room filled with gilt-framed pictures and black statuary. Salli had been here many times, she said. Many of her gentlemen friends preferred the place.

When she was seated, Salli said, "You must be from up North?"

"I'm from Cincinnati, yes."

"I never been there. Izzat in Missouri?"

"A little east of there."

"I've got cousins in Missouri. What kind of business you in, Robert?"

"I'm in land development." Paddock beckoned a waiter and ordered for them. He poured wine, and she sipped it hesitantly, as if she'd never had it before. She usually drank gin, she told him, but the wine was nice. But it didn't have any kick to it.

The waiter brought them *filets de poisson en soufflé*, which she had never had either.

After brandy and coffee he took her back to the hotel and locked the door. "Now, my dear, you may undress."

That was something she knew about.

*   *   *

221

The next day he and Harry left for St. Louis on the *City of Madelon*, a fairly new packet that boasted a five-piece orchestra that played in the saloon for several hours each day at suppertime.

Paddock was in an expansive mood. Everything was going well. *His* affairs were going well. He'd heard no word at all from Viktor Kory, but presumably the man had done his job and returned to the city; why not assume the best?

He walked the promenade several times each day, enjoying the good weather and the ever changing river views; he played cards in the saloon and actually won a few dollars; and he met Beatrix.

He was introduced to her one afternoon as he was enjoying coffee in the saloon, reading one of the newspapers the stewards had bought at the last landing. A skinny, wizened man came along and asked if he and his "friend" might sit at the table, and Paddock graciously offered to let them. Beatrix was dark and had unfathomable eyes and an easy smile. The man's name was Walter, he said, and he soon left them to go to his stateroom for a nap.

Beatrix then asked if he would buy her a drink, and he called a steward. When the drink was before her, Paddock asked, "You're doing business on the boat?"

She smiled. "Only when the whim strikes. We're going to Pittsburgh, Walt and me."

"You have a house there?"

"Walt and his Missis have. They got nine girls, counting me. You want to have some fun?"

"I'm in Indiana. Come along when you finish your drink. I'll leave the door ajar." He rose.

Beatrix smiled and nodded.

She increased his expansive mood, and he was sorry to see her disembark at Cairo in order to take another boat up the Ohio. But when he retired there would be lots of girls like Beatrix.

CHAPTER TWENTY-ONE

Lily dressed carefully for her supper engagement with Roy Collier. She wore an underskirt of gray and white foulard, a short blue overskirt, looped up by means of lapels, a silken scarf tied in front, and a cashmere paletot. The effect, she thought as she examined herself critically, was very satisfactory. But when she came close to the mirror, she firmed her mouth to see the tiny lines that no amount of massaging could erase.

Beauty was a fleeting thing, the doggerel poets said, and she sighed deeply, turning her head this way and that. She was still beautiful. They would sit in soft lantern light, and Roy would never notice the tiny lines.

She went downstairs pulling on her gloves. In a note Roy had asked her to allow him to come to the house for her, but she had begged off, preferring to ride in her own armored carriage, with Tony Burke beside the driver. She would meet him at the St. George.

She had cast off the somber mood, she thought, and she hoped that Roy's good looks would not remind her too much of Paige. . . . But, in any case, she could no longer allow herself to dwell on the past. It was unhealthy, if nothing else.

When she went out to the steps it was very dark. The lanterns beside the door cast a soft, yellow glow over the dark carriage. The driver was tugging at the harness, talking to his team, and Tony Burke had let down the iron steps and pulled the door open for her. She nodded to him and got in. "You know where to go?"

"St. George," he said and climbed to the box.

She sighed, thinking he would never learn manners. The driver had shoveled coals into the foot brazier, and she put her feet onto the scrolled iron and sank back into the plush cushions. This was her first outing, except for trips to the office, since Paige had gone. He should have listened to her—should have married her—but now it was too late. Always too late. Paige had been impossible in many ways. He'd had a thousand excuses why this or that could not be done—or had to be done. She'd never been able to fathom him, and maybe that was part of his charm for her—or was it charm? It was partly annoyance, she was sure. No other man had ever denied her as he had. No other man had infuriated her—and then with a smile made it all right again.

Roy Collier was really nothing like him, except for a vague physical resemblance. Roy was predictable—or she thought he was; he had been thus far.

She glanced out when they reached the city streets. A fog had drifted in from the river and was creating pretty rings about the street lamps. She heard a newsboy shout and then a teamster curse, as the carriage blocked his way for a moment. It was street German, probably something dreadful; the city was filling up with Germans. Then the carriage slowed and rolled to a stop. Tony Burke's boots clattered as he dropped down from the seat. He opened the door.

She stepped out and a voice said, "Lily! There you are—and more beautiful than ever!"

It was Roy, come to the street to greet her. Not so predictable after all!

They had supper in his suite. "I don't want to share you with anyone," he said. He looked bigger than he had, perhaps a bit more refreshed since he was away from Washington. He pulled her into his arms as soon as the door was closed, and she went willingly.

A small table had been laid with a centerpiece of roses and ferns, and Roy pulled a cork and poured champagne into iced glasses. "To us," he said and clinked glasses with her.

She smiled at him over the glass. "What in the world are you doing in St. Louis?"

"I came to see you." He indicated a settee and took the bottle; they sat side by side. "I'm going back to Alabama and thought I'd make a side trip. Aren't you glad to see me?"

"Delighted. Of course I am. Especially without Billy Turnbull to translate everything for me."

He laughed and refilled her glass. "Billy can be a pain in the—"

"Ass," she said, and he laughed again.

"There's no one like you, Lily." He rose at a knock on the door. "That'll be our supper." He opened the door, and a youngish, dark man rolled in a cart, quickly served the first course, and left. "Bring your glass," Roy said. "There's another bottle."

He seated her, leaned down, and kissed her cheek and sat opposite.

She tasted the soup and raised her brows. He said, "It's something the chef recommended. *Crème de*—I forget the

226

French. *Potiron*, I think."

"Pumpkin?"

"Yes, pumpkin and shrimp. What's shrimp, *crevettes?*"

"I believe so. Cream of pumpkin and shrimp! How exotic." She glanced at the cart with its gleaming covers. "You've been conspiring with the chef? What bizarre dishes have you selected?"

"Not bizarre at all, I fear. But I won't spoil the surprise. You must finish your soup."

"Very well. What have you heard of Sam's campaign?"

He shrugged. "It's going well, I believe. He debated the Republican, General Fremont, and Fremont came off second-best, according to the newspapers. The pundits say that Fremont won't carry a dozen states."

"Will Sam make a good president?"

Collier laughed. "It all depends on where you're standing. As good as any, I suppose. Have you finished?"

She put her spoon down. He rose and took both dishes, before lifting the larger cover. "Young pheasant with raisin puree!"

Lily clapped her hands. "Perfect! I was hoping for pheasant."

"Of course you were." He served her and poured the last of the champagne. "Is business pressing, Lily?"

"No—not terribly."

He sat and sipped the wine. "Come with me to Alabama for a vacation."

She looked into her plate. God! He sounded so much like Paige! It was precisely the kind of thing Paige might have said.

He asked, "What's the matter?"

227

"Nothing—nothing at all. I was thinking about it."

"It'll be summer soon. Let's go before that. Surely you've managers who can—"

She shook her head. "I couldn't possibly, Roy. Not at this time."

"But—"

"Please don't press me."

He nodded and got up to get the second bottle of champagne. "I hope you're not in love with Sam—"

"No, I'm not." She watched him open the bottle and pour. "Has he picked out a wife yet?"

"I believe so. The gossip says so. How did you know it?"

"Sam told me he might have to—for political expediency."

"Ahhhh. Well, you should never marry a politician anyway, Lily. Their standards are different."

She smiled. "Aren't you a politician?"

"Yes, but not for long. I'm not going to run for national office again. I'm going to retire to my farm and put all that behind me. Are you ready for dessert?"

"In a moment. Why are you retiring?"

"Because of lack of faith, I guess."

"I don't understand."

"Congress will not face the hard facts. The members know terrible trouble is coming, and they refuse to shoulder their responsibilities. I believe it will go on this way."

"What are you really saying?"

He looked at her and shook his head. "War."

Lily pressed her lips together tightly. War would be marvelous for business. "Surely not—"

228

"*I* see it coming and so do a few others."

"Does Sam?"

He shook his head again. "I doubt it. Sam doesn't want to think about it. He hides his head in the sand . . . as do most in Congress."

She sipped the wine. War could not come for two or three years at the earliest, and that would give her time to buy or build a factory, as Howard Paddock had once suggested. Armies ate up enormous quantities of material, and someone had to supply it. . . .

He said, "But I didn't come here to depress you. Let's not talk about war."

"How long will you be in town?"

"Only a few days." He glanced at the cart. "There's cake and strawberries."

She held the glass out. "I couldn't eat another thing." He poured into the glass and met her eyes. He got up and came round the table to kiss her.

"I missed you terribly, Lily—"

"I've thought about you often too, Roy, and that lovely picnic we had in the woods."

"That's my best memory of you." He slipped his arms under her and rose, lifting her easily. She laughed, still holding the glass, and offered it to him. He sipped, then turned about and went into the bedroom.

She kicked her shoes off, and he put her on the bed, sitting beside her as she drank the rest of the wine and put the glass aside. She sighed when his arms went about her, and she lay full length beside him and thought she imagined the words as he whispered, "I love you, Lily—"

She pressed against him, and her mouth sought his. He rolled half on top of her; then his fingers were busy at her

229

hooks, tugging them open. His eyes were dark pools of unfathomable shadow in the gloom of the chamber, and his flesh was hot to her touch, as her arms slid inside his coat. He sat up again suddenly and stripped the gown from her shoulders, murmuring words she did not catch. She was mildly surprised at the ease with which he slid the dress from her body and peeled the chemise away.

Then he rose and undressed quickly, smiling down at her nakedness. Lily stretched languidly, like a cat, and watched him. This reunion was so much more satisfying than the one in the carriage in the woods had been. And she welcomed it particularly because of Paige; she must not allow his memory to overwhelm her.

He crawled onto the bed, a bronze shadow in the meager light of the sitting room. His lips closed over her breast, and she sucked in her breath and writhed. Then in a moment his knee came between hers, and he lowered his body as she reached for him. He said again softly, "I love you, Lily—"

She closed her eyes and smiled in the darkness, and the words she'd never said before were only a breath and not quite uttered: "I love you too, Paige—"

Her agent in New Orleans, Mr. Haig Kelley, sent her, along with a sheaf of regular reports and opinions, a short note that surprised her greatly. Howard Paddock was in New Orleans, obviously not on company business; he had not made a courtesy call. Was he still part of the firm?

Lily sat in her office and frowned at the note. Howard had said he was going to Cairo, had he not? What was he doing in New Orleans?

She sent off a wire to Kelley asking him to investigate quietly and report only to her.

It was entirely possible, of course, that Howard's personal business had taken him first to Cairo and then on to New Orleans, but she could no longer trust him after what Udell Winter had said. It was annoying, too, that she had no contact with Viktor Kory. She ought to remedy that when he had finished with Jeffries. He might well be able to arrange Howard's permanent disappearance . . . on just such a journey.

Kelley's return wire said that Paddock had left New Orleans, but that he would canvas the hotels and see what could be turned up.

It was eight days before she received a letter from Kelley. Howard Paddock had stayed at the New Francis Hotel and had had only one visitor, a young man portrayed by the hotel staff as nondescript, but having a northern accent. They did not know his name.

Paddock had spoken to no one in the hotel concerning his business, but there had been one interesting event. According to a night clerk, Paddock had stayed out until nearly dawn one night, and when he returned his boots were filthy with a peculiar, yellowish mud. He had given them to a boy to clean.

Kelley had made several attempts to discover where the mud had come from, but so far had no luck. He had obtained specimens of the mud from the boy, who had scraped the boots in an alley beside the hotel.

Lily wired him to keep trying. What ever Paddock did was of interest to her.

Two days later a wire came from Kelley saying Paddock had come back to the hotel that dawn riding on a wagon driven by a young man. Kelley was trying to locate the young man.

Lily paced the office. What in hell was Paddock doing on a wagon at night?

CHAPTER TWENTY-TWO

Dutch sent off the telegram to Logan and went back home to think about it. He had gone upriver once before to sell Howard Paddock a suitcase full of items, and it had been a long, hard trip. But it was spring, and the rains were about over; and the more he thought about it, the more angry he got. This time he had nothing to sell to Paddock. This time he had revenge on his mind.

He had never been fond of Paddock, not even in the years when he traded with him often. Paddock had cheated Karp more than once, outwitted him more than anything else, but that was to be expected. Karp did not possess a quick mind, which largely explained why he was now languishing in prison.

It was not because of what Paddock had done to Karp. Dutch smouldered because Paddock had sent men to kill Logan. Dutch had been reared in a hard school, according to which a man fought his own battles and never sent another in his place. Dutch could admit to himself that there was little love generated between himself and his son, but Logan *was* his own flesh and blood. There was one last thing he could do for him to make up for a life of neglect.

Paddock had broken the unwritten law, and so he, Dutch, could do the same. He could put an end to Paddock.

He made his preparations, cleaned and oiled two pistols and a rifle, cooked a packet of meat and wrapped it in oiled paper, packed bread and a bit of fruit, a bottle of whiskey, a few utensils, and a ground sheet, and locked the house and barn. He left a note for Lyle Carty and set off across the fields, heading north, riding a gray, the best horse he owned.

He would much have preferred to go by steamboat, but he didn't dare. Dutch was a superstitious man; he knew, if he boarded a steamboat again, he would die. Old Jake Darcy's curse was clear in his mind. Jake had said that Dutch would die under the paddles of a steamboat, and since that time Dutch had never gone on the river again . . . on a steamboat.

But Jake Darcy and the curse did not concern him as he rode. Paddock was in Cairo. He would go into the office and confront the schemer and watch him sniff and wriggle and shout that he knew nothing about it. Dutch had never killed a man in absolutely cold blood, but it would be the height of stupidity to give Paddock a chance to defend himself. He'd have to shoot, get out, and evade pursuers. He had no intention of dying because of Howard Paddock. Let Paddock do *that*.

It was his only plan, based on the facts as he knew them.

The St. Louis Rivermen's Fraternal Association hired the Armory Hall, and more than five thousand tickets were sold. Many of these were purchased by people who wanted to show support but had no intention of attending, since they lived as far away as Natchez.

Kenneth Fraser bought twenty tickets and passed them out to Logan, Marvin Rodda, and other members of the firm. It was to be a gala night. There would be prizes, dances, speeches during and after the dinner, and a great deal of drinking. At a time when drinking to excess was almost an accepted thing, the association's meetings never failed to set new records—mostly for the number of members who ended up in jail.

The association had three distinct divisions: owners, operators, and employees. The operators included pilots, captains, and certain others of management and crews. The employees were everyone else, whether based on land or on the river. Almost all who wound up in the city's drunk tanks were employees. The police therefore planned to surround the Armory Hall in force, their black carryall wagons ready.

Viktor Kory frequented the hall as it was being prepared; he found it a simple matter to obtain one of the hundreds of badges given out to officials and other officers, so that he might come and go without question. The hall was large enough to contain a thousand persons without crowding. It had three floors and a small maintenance area on the roof, as well as a basement. The second floor, mostly comprising offices, would be closed to the public, except for the mezzanine, which was colonnaded and open to the view of anyone on the main floor. The ceiling of the main floor was therefore very high, but flat, and was being decorated with bunting and strips of twisted, colored paper and flags. Around the railing of the mezzanine were tables and chairs; nowhere was there a place for a rifleman to stand without being observed by hundreds of people.

The inside of the hall looked austere, as befitted such a building; it had very few nooks and crannies. The immense roof was held up by metal columns painted to look like marble; they marched in two rows about the center and were hung with bunting.

Absolutely nowhere inside the huge building could one hide with a rifle until use could be made of it. It was frustrating.

The outside of the building was quite another story. Though an element of austerity remained, there were numerous nooks along the front of the building at the sides of the broad steps that led to the massive front doors. However, it would be dark when the crowds would begin to gather, and those hiding places might well be useless to him.

His getaway after the deed was another consideration. The area about the hall was parklike, largely grass and hard-packed dirt, and surrounded by a five-foot-high decorative wooden fence. The fence would present no problem; a child could scramble over it anywhere. All this open space about the hall would, on the night of the gala, be filled with coaches, buggies, various carriages, horses, and hundreds of drivers and footmen.

But it would be dark.

Kory walked about the grounds. Workmen had put up a hundred or more poles with metal crosspieces, on which lanterns would be strung. But they would, for all their numbers, dispel only a small portion of the gloom. It would still be dark, and in between the carriages, darker still. Kory smiled. This was where he must meet Jeffries and dispatch him. A single well-placed shot, or one true thrust with a blade, and he would be off like a shadow, and no one would ever come near. With the tiniest bit of luck, no one would even witness the deed.

But the plan had one flaw. He would have a very limited amount of time to accomplish his purpose; it would have to be done as Jeffries entered the hall or left it. Jeffries would get by him, if he were not in exactly the right place at the proper time.

He would not face Jeffries; he would let the man go by him; then he would step out and aim for the middle of his back as Jeffries passed near one of the lanterns. If there were people with Jeffries, the chances were good that no one would get a glimpse of the killer.

In that respect the plan was excellent. Kory went away rubbing his hands together. Jeffries was as good as dead.

When the Rivermen's Association event was announced, and when Fraser purchased the tickets, Louis Gualco was disturbed. This was something he had not foreseen. He discussed it with Logan as they had lunch together in a restaurant near the offices.

"I don't suppose I can talk you out of going?"

Logan smiled. "You should be talking to Doris. She's bought a new gown—"

"All right." Louis shook his head. "But if I were this Viktor Kory, this is the kind of affair I'd use to attack you."

Logan frowned. "How do you think he'll do it?"

"I haven't yet seen the building, but there must be ways. A bullet in the back maybe, while you're dancing."

"Damned inconvenient."

"It's no laughing matter, Logan. I'm serious. This is one time you'll be out in public, rubbin' elbows with all kinds. It gives me the shivers."

"What kind of precautions can we take?"

"I don't know yet. Let me think about it. With your permission I'll go look at the building first. How long will the party last?"

Logan shrugged. "Near midnight, I'd guess."

"But you could leave at any time?"

"Any time after the speeches and introductions, yes. If Doris doesn't scream and kick her feet."

Louis smiled.

He went that afternoon to look at the Armory Hall, inside and out. The inside pleased him greatly; it was all open and provided no hiding places, but as he stood on the steps in front of the building and surveyed the vast level area where carriages and horses would be placed, he frowned. He was looking for a weak link, and this was it. He could visualize the throngs coming in all directions, converging on these steps, moving up them slowly. Could he spirit Logan and Doris in through another door—and out the same way?

It could be the answer.

It took hours of searching for the proper authority, and he found it at last in the person of Major General C. H. Larson, a pudgy bewhiskered man of seventy, long since retired from active duty, but the administrative head of the Central Department of Missouri.

"Unlock the other doors?" Larson asked. "I have already informed the committee that—"

"It may mean a man's life, General."

"Bosh! A man's life. What are you telling me, sir? That a man in great danger of his life will risk it for this affair?"

"But it's practically compulsory, sir."

The general's brown, glassy eyes stared at his visitor. He shook his white head. "You would cost me the salary

238

of a watchman, sir. No, I will not unlock the doors. The committee has already agreed that the front doors are sufficient for their purposes. The following day, when the clean-up crews enter, then the rear doors will be available to them."

"But sir—"

"No buts." The general waggled his finger. "This building houses many thousands of dollars of government property, and I cannot go beyond my standing orders, young sir. If this man is in the danger you mention, let him stay in safety somewhere else."

"But, General—"

"I have given you all the time I can, sir." The general stood up.

Louis went back to the offices and had a talk with Fraser, telling him what he'd found out. "The general refuses to cooperate, so I think my best chance of guarding Logan is to hire more men. I want to surround him."

"You're convinced of the danger?"

"Yes, I sure am. This is Kory's best chance to get Logan out in the open. If we could've used a rear door, I'm sure I'd have been able to slip him in and out so fast that Kory wouldn't have had a chance to get at 'im."

"You think surrounding him will do it?"

"It's the best thing I can think of. Oh—there's one other thing—"

"What is it?"

"Can you use your influence to see they each go alone?"

"What!"

"I want Logan to go alone."

Fraser made a face. "I'm not sure either of them will

239

like that."

"I think Doris will. It's Logan's best chance of staying alive. If he's by himself, he won't be worrying about her. If he has to run, he can run."

"I see what you mean." Fraser nodded. "All right. I'll talk to Doris within the hour. Matter of fact, I'll escort her myself."

Louis smiled. "Good. I suggest you go to Logan's house and leave with her from there."

"So Kory will think I'm Logan, is that it?" Fraser gave him a look. "Very ingenious, Louis. I'm delighted Logan hired you."

Louis laughed. "Don't worry. Kory will see in an instant that you're not Logan."

"Before or after he pulls the trigger?"

"He's not going to snipe at you from a distance in the dark. He'll have to get close. That's why I want to surround Logan."

"All right. I'll see what I can do. Why don't you insist Logan wear a breastplate?"

Louis rubbed his chin. "I wonder if he'd do it?"

He would not. Logan protested going to the affair alone, but Doris had already heard Fraser's explanation and agreed. It was wise to do as Louis suggested.

"We'll be together all evening long, darling. It's only going and coming we'll be apart. What's the harm?"

"Very well—"

She slid her arms about his neck and rubbed her nose on his. "You will do what Louis asks, won't you?"

"For your sake. We won't go at all if you'd rather."

"No, I want to go. It isn't right that some one person can direct our lives. I want to go, but I also want to take

240

all the proper precautions." She could feel the pistol under his coat. "And I want you to wear this."

"I will. I'm never without it."

"Yes, you are. Take it off now, and take me to bed."

CHAPTER TWENTY-THREE

When Howard Paddock returned to St. Louis with Harry Alquist, on the *City of Madelon*, he sent Harry home with a stern admonition: "Keep your mouth closed tight, Harry. Perhaps you and I can do a bit of business another time."

He had no intention of ever seeing Harry again, but the boy did not know that. Harry practically pulled his forelock and hurried away across the levee. It had probably been the adventure of his life, Paddock thought, amused. But sterner things were in the offing; Lily was sure to question him concerning his progress, and he thought about it on the drive home. He sent for Viktor Kory at once and waited impatiently until the man arrived.

Kory was prompt, to Paddock's surprise, and outlined his plans for the association gala. "It's the best time to do it. A perfect time."

Paddock sniffed and nodded. "And when Jeffries is dead, where will you go?"

"Probably up the Ohio to Cincinnati." Kory showed his teeth. "Maybe Pittsburgh—where I have certain friends." He outlined a woman's shape with his hands and Paddock smiled.

"Good to go far off."

"I'll get the boat that night while the coppers are still chasing their tails. On the way I'll stop here to see you."

Paddock nodded again. The money. "I'll get it from the others and have it ready. You don't need more men?"

"What others are you talking about?"

Paddock sniffed and waggled a finger. "That's not necessary. They don't want to be known anyway. You deal with me."

"What if something happens to you?"

"Nothing's going to happen to me, God willing. You do the job good and proper and the money'll be ready—in cash. But after it's done and you're safe out of town, let Mick Weston know where you are. I may have another job for you."

"Why not now?"

Paddock fingered the watch chain and rubbed his nose. "Time, my lad. Time. A bit of time must pass between one thing and another. Half a year maybe."

"That's a hell of a long time, half a year."

"What about more men?"

"For this job? No. Other men would just be in the way," Kory grinned. "This'll be a rapier thrust, not an infantry charge."

"By God, that's almost poetry, Viktor. I didn't know you had a soul."

Kory half closed his eyes. "As much as the next, I reckon. I've never been much for religion."

"Yes, weighs a man down—"

"Hard on his innards, Mr. Paddock, religion. Anything else you want to say?"

"No, I leave the plans to you. All I want is results. We're depending on you heavily, Viktor. This is damned important to all of us. Damned important."

"It'll be done, never you worry." Kory rose and went to the door. "All I care about is the money. No tricks about it, Mr. Paddock. You have it ready on the night."

"My promise," Paddock said, and watched him go out and close the door carefully. Paddock rubbed his hands together, got up, and poured out a dollop of cognac.

He saw Lily the next morning and, as he had expected, her first words were of Kory. "What has he done, Howard?"

Paddock made himself comfortable in one of her easy chairs and repeated some of what Kory had told him about the events along the river, but left out all the significant ones. In this new version Kory had come to Natchez as Logan had left it, and there had been no confrontation.

She said with asperity, "You mean then that nothing's happened?" Her face was severe. "He didn't follow orders?"

"Now, now—you know Logan. He's not so easy to anticipate. Give Kory a chance to observe him. I've impressed upon him that it has to be done right—the first time."

"Well, he's not been very effective. Are you sure you've picked the right man for the job?"

"I am sure." Her tone was sarcastic, and Paddock squirmed a bit, wanting to snap back at her, but he managed a smile. "Believe me, Lily, he will do the job, but we must leave him to do it his own way."

"And in his own time." She snarled the words. "Time is important to me, Howard. So far he's done damned little for his money."

Paddock sniffed. "Logan is not an easy man to kill. He's his father's son, you know. You should remember

Dutch very well—"

She half rose, and her face grew red, and Paddock stared at the rage in her shouted words, "Of course I remember Dutch. But it's not Dutch we're after! Logan is not immortal, damn you, Howard!"

"Calm yourself. . . . There's no need to shout at me."

Lily glared at him, drumming her fingers on the desk top.

He said, "Are you going to the association ball?"

"I'll put in an appearance, yes. Is there anything else we have to discuss?"

"Are you dismissing me?" He sniffed and rubbed his nose.

She sat back, staring at him, recalling Udell's remarks. How she would love to pry into his mind! What was he up to? With an effort she smoothed out her expression so nothing showed on her face. She made her voice even. "Was there something else, Howard?"

He rose at once, grunting and tugging at his waistcoat. "No, I s'pose not. Nothing else, God willing. I'll get along—" He went to the door, turned to glance at her, and went out.

For several moments she sat still, thinking over their conversation. Kory had done almost nothing, according to Howard; it was not reassuring. Was Howard taking her money and doing nothing? She pursed her lips wondering if a thousand dollars was that important to him. She had to assume it was not. But if he did not report any progress soon, she'd do something about it.

Maybe ask for the money back.

She plunged into the business at hand, held a short meeting with Udell and her department heads, wrote several letters, and sent them to be copied. Just before noon the mail clerk came into her office.

There was a letter from Kelley, the New Orleans agent. He had made progress. He'd put on half a dozen men and scoured the city to find the yellow mud. Lily caught her breath as she read on.

Kelley had found it at St. Luke's Cemetery!

St. Luke's!

That was where she'd put Jacques! She swore, and the letter almost dropped from nerveless fingers. How in God's name had Howard tracked down that grave? She forced her eyes back to the sheet of paper. The source of the mud, Kelley wrote, was one of three graves, which Kelley thought peculiar. Two were newly dug and the funerals had not yet taken place. The third was an older grave which apparently had been recently opened, though pains had been taken to hide the fact.

Kelley went on to say he'd interviewed the caretaker, who could shed no light on the matter. No grave had been opened to his knowledge, and certainly there had been no authorization. Kelley had been thorough and examined the records.

Lily sat, staring into space. It had to be Jacques's grave. Paddock would be interested in no other. Haig Kelley had known nothing about Jacques, of course; he hadn't mentioned the name on the gravestone, but it *had* to be. *It had to be.*

So Howard had discovered her great secret.

He had gone to New Orleans and dug up the casket — why else dig it up except to examine what was inside? Lily closed her eyes, her body icy. She felt sluggish and breath came hard for a moment. As she reread the letter, a brief flurry of panic came over her. The police would arrive with their wagons and clanging bells; they would troop up the stairs and into the office; they would carry her off, and everything she owned would be forfeit!

Howard Paddock would do this to her without a qualm; he would do it with a smile and set up the drinks afterward. As Udell had told her, he coveted what she had, and here was proof. She had no greater enemy.

The panic gave way to anger. Tight-lipped, she opened a desk drawer, fished in the depths, and drew out a revolver. With her thumb she pulled the hammer to half cock, turned the cylinder, and looked at the shiny copper caps. They were all in place. She rose and, still holding the pistol, walked to the center of the room. She ought to go immediately to Paddock's office and kill him.

If she did it would cause a storm, but not as great a one as faced her otherwise. And Howard would be dead—and unable to profit from anything ever again.

A clever lawyer would save her. A hundred excuses could be found and sworn to. . . .

She looked at the door, her mind almost made up.

Then someone rapped. She was startled, and her hands began to shake. The pistol dropped to the floor, and she instantly stepped forward to stand over it; her long skirts covered it completely.

"Yes?"

A clerk put his head round the door. "Senator Collier to see you, ma'am."

Lily took a long breath. "G-give me five minutes, then tell him to come in."

"Yus ma'am." The door closed.

She scooped up the pistol and tottered to her desk to sit. God! Howard had almost faced his Maker! Thrusting the gun into the drawer again, she got up and went to the mirror to pat her hair. That was not the end of it for

Howard. Had he also gone to Chadwick to dig up Jacob?

The thought made her feel faint for a moment, and she leaned against the wall. The room seemed to close in upon her, and her head throbbed in sudden pain. She turned. Howard had sat there, in that chair, and smiled at her this very morning, knowing what he knew. Anger took the place of cold fear, and she gritted her teeth. She drummed both fists on the wall in frustration.

As an echo, someone rapped on the door and Lily swung round.

Roy Collier opened it and smiled at her. "Good morning, Lily."

She forced a smile. "Come in, Roy." She crossed to him and tilted her face up for a kiss.

He said, "You look pale . . . is anything the matter?"

"No, nothing—but business. A few annoyances this morning. They will pass."

"Let me take you for a drive."

She hesitated, then smiled. "Yes, why not?" God, she needed a breath of air! She went close and kissed him again. "You look surprised."

"I didn't think you'd accept."

"Is the offer withdrawn?"

"No, no, no—come along! I'm delighted!" He took her cloak from a hat tree and held it for her. "It's a fine, fresh day with hardly a cloud in the sky. The best time of the year, they tell me."

They went out to the hall, and Lily said, "Excuse me a minute, Roy." She went into the chief clerk's office. "Have Tony Burke meet me on the street right away."

"Yes, ma'am." The clerk pointed to a boy. "You heard? Go get Burke." The boy ran.

She went down the steps with Collier, and they waited

in the doorway until Burke showed up. She gave him instructions, and he hurried away. Roy handed her into his coach, and she set back gratefully. "Tony will follow us on horseback if you don't mind, Roy—"

"Is he necessary?" He patted his side. "I am armed, you know."

"He won't be in the way."

"Is your life really that endangered? I wouldn't have thought so."

She smiled at him. "I have enemies. One can never tell how desperate they are, can one? I think it's foolish not to take every precaution."

"Enemies! You astonish me. What enemies?"

"Business mostly. But remember, my darling from the civilized East, we are on the edge of wilderness here. To the west are savages and outlaws aplenty."

"I've heard they call St. Louis the gateway to the West—"

"Long ago when the fur trappers and traders were active; St. Louis was the center, yes. But that's long past."

They waited till Burke appeared on a horse, hunched over, a rifle in a scabbard under his leg. He looked more like a ruffian than ever, she thought. But he moved in behind them as the carriage rolled away and followed dutifully, several rods behind.

She said, "I really know very little about you. You're a planter's son, you said, and you went to school at Harvard—"

"You don't want all the nasty details, do you? I was almost thrown out for a prank. They called me a high-spirited boy, and my father intervened so I was allowed to finish school."

"You became a lawyer, but you went to Europe first."

"You do remember! I'm astonished. Yes, I knocked about England, France, and Germany, but I liked England best. I ran out of money, and my father refused to send me more, so I came home and took an office in Montgomery." He slid his hand under hers and squeezed it. "It was a dull existence; I think that's why I entered politics, to get away from my father and uninteresting cases."

"Is your father still living?"

"No, not for nearly fifteen years."

"Tell me about your wife."

He smiled. "It was not a happy marriage, I'm afraid. It was partly arranged—at least we were thrown together, so I'm sure that was the case, though it was never stated. As a dutiful son I did what was expected of me, and the girl said yes."

"What was her name?"

"Paula." His face changed, and he brushed back the hair from the side of his head. "We never quite got on properly. Quarreled, you know. She became a picky woman, always at me to do something different from what I wanted." He glanced at her. "Marriage is a damned difficult undertaking, isn't it?"

"My marriages were happy—"

"Then you're lucky. Well, I became lucky after a while. Paula ran off with a man, and I got some peace at last." He smiled and kissed her hand. "I don't think my father ever forgave me for it either."

"Why not? She was the one who ran off."

"Well, that sort of thing isn't done. Not done in my father's circles anyway. And of course he blamed me for it. He'd been blaming me for years—" Roy laughed. "When I look back on those years now it almost seems they happened to someone else."

"But you're going back to Montgomery. And you're giving up politics."

"I'm giving up the Senate," he corrected, "not necessarily politics. I find politics more interesting than practicing law. As far as Montgomery is concerned, I'll look around. I've many friends in Richmond—"

"And will you marry again?"

"I don't know. Will you?"

She shook her head, thinking of Paige. They were driving north, not far from the river, which gleamed like old brass in the sunlight. The wheels of the carriage rattled over pebbles and rasped on the sand; its swaying moved her against him, and after a bit he slid his arm about her shoulders. She laid her cheek against the rough tweed of his coat; it was very pleasant being held by him.

He said softly, "I wish I could stay—"

"Why can't you?"

"Certain promises to my family. Duty, you know."

"Can't you postpone for a week?"

He hesitated, thinking it over. "I might," he said at last, as if doubtfully.

"There's the Rivermen's Association ball very soon," she said. "I want you to come with me as my guest. It'll be a very fancy affair. I know you don't care about that, but I'd be proud to show you off."

He laughed. "When Sam Beckhart hears about it, you'll have explaining to do."

"Leave Sam to me. I'll tell him you came to St. Louis and made it impossible for me not to invite you—you're a senator, after all. And by this time Sam must be actively courting his chosen bride. Or will it be a business marriage?"

"I have no idea."

A rounded thumb of land jutted into the brown river; it was dotted with trees and nearly level—was it the same place she'd paused at once with Sam so long ago? She pointed it out to Roy, and he asked the driver to stop there. The team swerved off the road, and the wheels bounced over tiny ridges and gullies and came to rest in thick grass.

Roy opened the door and jumped out to help her down. Tony Burke was sitting on his horse at the edge of the road, not looking at them. He seemed to be engrossed by something on the far shore, one leg up over the pommel of the saddle.

She said, "Let's walk down by the river. Are you in the mood for walking?"

"Of course. With you, anywhere. Your father was a lawyer, wasn't he?"

"Yes."

"You were close to your parents?"

"Oh yes, very. I had a happy home life as a child. We weren't rich, but not poor at all. I don't remember my mother ever saying a cross word." None of that was true, but Roy would never know. She'd had a miserable life during her school days, but Roy didn't want to hear about sadness.

"I'm still astonished that you ended up in charge of a great company." He took her arm, and they walked slowly. The ground was grassy and uneven; the sun's warmth was welcome on their shoulders.

"It wasn't planned. It just happened, and I wish

252

sometimes that it hadn't. My husband, Jacob, was in business in a small town and doing very well when he died. I merely continued the business. Nothing remarkable about it at all."

He looked at her shrewdly. "Would he have had the wisdom and foresight you've shown?"

"Of course he would. Jacob was a fine man and just as shrewd as any. Unfortunately his long sickness made it impossible for him to carry out all his plans. I did it for him."

"I see. And then you took a partner—Mr. Bryant."

"Yes, Hiram Bryant was a jewel, a positive jewel. I nearly went to pieces when he was murdered. What a terrible period!" Lily shook her head. "I pray I'll never see its like again."

"You never talked marriage to Bryant?"

"I? Never. He was much older, you know. He had a grown son."

"Ah, I didn't know that." He squeezed her arm. "It seems to me you've had more than your share of personal tragedy. Two husbands and a partner have died. . . . It is really astonishing."

She glanced at him with sudden suspicion, but his face held no hint of mockery or anything but compassion. "It has been hard," she said, wondering if others thought the same. Probably some did.

They came close to the water; the bank shelved steeply to the swirling flow, and he held her tightly lest she slip.

"The Father of Waters," he said. "I have not seen it before. It's a mighty river—but so muddy!"

"We're only a few miles from the confluence. The Missouri is the muddy one. People call it the Big Muddy."

"Yes, I'd forgotten." He still held her warmly, both arms about her. Lily glanced over his shoulder; the trees hid them from the carriage and Tony Burke. She lifted her lips to his, and they clung together for long moments. He relinquished her with a deep sigh. "I rather wish we'd come alone."

"Will you stay another week?"

He smiled down at her. "You make it very difficult to refuse."

"Then you mustn't."

"And what is my reward if I stay?"

"Come to my house tonight. There'll be no interruptions, I promise."

He nodded and drew her close.

CHAPTER TWENTY-FOUR

Logan went to Clarence Yates' office, accompanied by Louis Gualco, and received several reports. Howard Paddock had been visited again, late at night, by a man of medium height. Yates' agent thought he was the same man who had visited before, and he followed him to the Nestande Hotel. The man was registered there as James Boller. A separate watch was being kept on him.

"I think there's little doubt he's Viktor Kory," Yates said with considerable satisfaction. "We can stop him in his tracks by turning him over to the police."

"Not yet," Logan said. "I want to know what he's up to."

Yates shrugged and shook his head. It was obvious he disapproved. He took another paper from a file. "I've been able to get a young man into Berlanger-Bryant as office help. The gossip so far has been of no value. Do you want me to keep him on?"

"What do you expect to gain from him?"

"Some hint of Lily's movements perhaps. Something to follow up on."

"All right. Keep him there for a few more days."

Yates nodded. "It's been in the papers about the rivermen's affair. I suppose you're going?"

"Yes, certainly."

"I advise against it."

Logan smiled and caught Louis Gualco's eyes. "Have you two been talking? That's exactly what Louis tells me."

"Louis is right. You should listen to him."

Louis said, "I suggested he and Mrs. Jeffries go separately. Kory isn't after her, and this way we can surround Logan."

"You could put me in a basket and carry me in," Logan said sourly.

Louis agreed. "I would if I could."

"We'll take all precautions," Logan said, "but I'm not going to live in a barrel—"

"Then let me turn Kory over to the police."

"No."

"Why not?"

"Because we know now who he is and where he is. If we turn him over, Lily will get someone else, and we'll have to start all over again . . . and maybe not be so lucky."

Yates grunted. "But this way Kory has the advantage. He may evade us. He may do any one of a hundred things that we can't stop him from doing—"

"I know it's a chance," Logan said reasonably, "but give it another week."

"Till after the ball."

"Yes."

Yates sighed. "Very well, Logan. I'll keep you informed." He pointed his finger. "But you stay away from the Hotel Nestande."

Logan's brows rose. "It never occurred to me to go there."

"Fine. Do you think Kory got a good look at you in Chadwick?"

"I don't know."

"Good enough to pick you out of a crowd easily?"

Logan said, "An interestin' point."

"Yes. It means Kory will have to get close to make sure. Why don't you change your appearance as much as you can, Logan?"

"You mean limp on one foot?"

"Not a bad idea. Slouch your shoulders and comb your hair differently." Yates clasped both hands on the desk. "We have to assume Kory will recognize you, so make it as hard for him as possible."

"All right." Logan looked at Louis and found him grinning. "Both of you are convinced that Kory will try to kill me on the night of the ball, is that it?"

"How could he overlook such an opportunity?" Yates asked. "He tried once and failed, and now he's got to make good."

"Have you been able to learn anything about him?"

Yates shook his head. "I'm positive Kory is just the name he's using now. He may change it every month, for all we know. It might take a year to run him down, and we can't wait that long. I think you're making a mistake, Logan, by not stopping him while we have the chance."

"Keep your man on him." Logan got up and went to the door. "Maybe he's formed some habits, or maybe he'll lead you to someone else." He smiled. "And the day before the ball you can do whatever you want."

"You mean the police?"

"Yes. He's all yours."

Yates rubbed his hands. "Now you're getting smart. I

was afraid you were losing your gray matter altogether."

Dutch rode steadily, walking the gray for the most part because of the rutted path he followed, but the miles fell away, and the weather remained fair. Several times he drew on a poncho and hunched over as rain squalls spattered the countryside, but they soon passed and the sun came out.

He kept to himself, making small purchases in the hamlets he rode through, only now and again asking directions or questioning the road ahead. He did his best to attract little attention, but he no longer feared recognition from passersby. It had been a long time since he was famous; there might be a few in the river towns who would remember him, but not in the ordinary farm community. To them he was just an old man making his way from one place to another, a man who obviously had little . . . except the gray horses and the rifle. He concealed the pistols under his coat.

At night he camped under the trees, off the trail, made his fires in hollows and always did his cooking before nightfall, so that no one could spot the glow from a distance. He made small fires, barely enough for heating coffee and broiling meat, so that the smoke mingled with the overhead leaves of a clump of trees. After eating he moved on to find a place to sleep. He left nothing to chance.

But he could not control the actions of others, and despite all his care, they came into conflict.

It was just past midday when he came over the brow of a grassy hill and saw before him the neat fields of a farm in a long valley that stretched off to his right. Halfway down the slope of the hill he reined in and put both hands to his ears. Was that shooting? He cursed the fact that his hearing was poor and nudged the gray forward, staring toward the small group of buildings a quarter of a mile distant. There was a farmhouse, a barn and outbuildings, surrounded by trees and fences; it looked to be better cared for than many.

And as he looked, a horseman galloped around the house, firing a pistol into the windows. Seconds later another followed, and Dutch reined in again and leaned on the pommel. He had heard of raids on prosperous folk, done by fast-riding, wild gangs, and it looked as if he had stumbled onto one. Someone was firing from the house, and for a moment it sounded like a battle. A bullet rapped into a tree not far away from Dutch, and twigs rained down. He nudged the gray forward and halted in the shelter of several thick oaks. Two men dismounted and rushed the door, disappearing inside. He heard half a dozen shots; then it was quiet.

Dutch surveyed the fields. He would have to go around, make a detour of probably half a mile, to stay in the trees. It was none of his business what happened at the farmhouse; let them take care of themselves. He reined the gray to the left and began to move along the slope, when several shots caused him to halt. A man had come from the house and was shooting at the weather vane atop the roof. Two others appeared lugging a small trunk. They set it down, and a woman ran from the house. Even at that distance, Dutch could hear her screams. One of the men knocked her down. She got up, wildly swinging her arms, and ran at him. The man pushed her away and ripped at her clothes; in a moment she was nearly naked.

Two men then converged on her and pulled her down into the weeds. Dutch swore and turned the gray; he had never liked to see women beaten and raped and had fought many a vicious fight on that account.

A fourth man came from the house, paused a moment on the stoop, then pointed. The others looked around.

Dutch halted, realizing that he was out in the open and that they had seen him. Without hesitation he kicked the gray and went down the slope at a gallop. He knew they would come after him. They wanted no witness to the raid.

He saw them all run to their horses, and he pulled the rifle from the scabbard and leveled it at them, as the gray ran flat out. His shot went wide, and he set about reloading, annoyed that after all his precautions he'd become involved in this crime. He let the horse have its head, cutting diagonally across the newly seeded fields toward the distant woods, and looked back at them. There were four men; they appeared young and roughly dressed, but rode good horseflesh and were probably well armed. A few shots came seeking him out, but he knew it would take an enormously lucky shot to hit him.

They would try to reach him as quickly as possible, finish him, maybe bury the body in a hasty grave, then return to the farm to finish their looting.

Dutch turned in the saddle, aimed as carefully as he could, and fired the rifle—again with no apparent result. His pursuers were beginning to separate, as the man on the fastest horse gradually pulled away from the others. He was a man in a brown leather coat and black slouch hat; he was too far away for Dutch to make out his features. He emptied a pistol at Dutch, firing six shots slowly. Two cracked very close, and Dutch reloaded and fired the rifle once more.

He entered the woods, and it took all his attention to pick a path in the straightest line possible; any turn to right or left would bring the pursuers that much closer. There was no path, and all at once the river shimmered through the trees, off to his right, half a mile away. Dutch began to edge toward the left. If he could lose one or two of them, it would bring the odds down. He glanced back quickly; the man in the brown coat was beginning to gain on him.

The woods were thinned by glades and small grassy areas bright with sun; there were occasional windrows of brush piled up in gullies by run-off water, and now and then a fallen tree blocked his path, brown and leafless. Dutch swerved the gray around one of these, reined in suddenly with a pistol in each hand, and blasted at the brown coat as he came galloping into range.

The pursuer had no chance to evade. Dutch saw three or four of his bullets slash into the man's chest. The brown coat fell sideways, and the horse ran off through the trees to the west. Dutch turned the gray and dug in his heels; the man was dead before he hit the ground.

One fewer. He ran the gray for a mile; then he eased up and examined his back trail. The hoofprints were plain as printing on the damp earth; even a city-bred blind man could follow them, by touch alone, if nothing else. He swore and went on, wondering how far they would follow him. Now that he'd killed one of them, it was serious.

He did not detect them for more than an hour, then it seemed they were on his tail very suddenly, so suddenly that he began to suspect there might be something ahead that they knew about, a place in which to corner him. He

261

kept close watch behind, and when he was out of sight of them, he turned off to the west and galloped the gray as hard as he could make the horse go. In less than a mile he saw the river—it must be the L'Amguille—and realized they wanted to come on him as he was trying to swim the gray across. They'd have had him dead in their sights.

The river ran roughly north, and he followed it, keeping it close on his right. Now and then a rifle shot came seeking him out, but only a few of the bullets came close. They seemed content to stay on his tail, or were they unable to close the distance?

Possibly they were waiting for nightfall.

The gray was a good, willing animal, only three years old, and had stamina, which is why he had selected it. They went mile after mile, walking, loping, and galloping, and the pursuers did not gain again. Dutch was content to let them follow, and in fact he welcomed the dark; he was willing to put his woodsmanship against theirs, and as the day wore on they seemed to sense his confidence.

They made one more attempt to close in on him. As he was moving up a long slope, they came on fast, spread out, and began firing as they came into range. Dutch was riding with the rifle across his thighs. He halted the gray, turned, and aimed carefully from a standstill. When he fired, the man in the center whirled about and fell from the saddle. Dutch rammed his heels in, and the gray jumped forward. Shots cracked around him, and the men yelled in rage. But they pulled up.

At the top of the slope Dutch reined in and got down to examine the gray. None of the bullets had touched them. He took a few swallows from the whiskey bottle, allowed the gray to crop grass for a dozen minutes while he watched the back trail, and reloaded the rifle. Were they bothering to bury the man? He hoped so.

He could imagine their anger now that two had been shot. If they had any sense, they'd call off the vendetta, but he was positive they would not. They would convince themselves that he'd been lucky and that the luck had changed in favor of the odds. Dutch had dealt with their kind many times before; they dreamed of revenge and tortured their enemies in those dreams, over and over again. He knew the kind of fate that awaited him should these two manage to take him alive—or even half alive.

He looked at the caps on his revolvers and went on, walking the horse through the trees and leaving a plain trail. The ground was soft from recent rains, and there was no chance to outwit them by erasing the marks. So he ignored them.

Then the land began to change and became more hilly and gullied by run-off storm water. The gray had to pick a trail very carefully, wending in and out, around outcrops and up steep banks. Dutch began to look for a good ambush spot. They would be instantly wary, of course, as soon as they saw the uneven terrain, but they had no choice if they wanted to reach him. They'd have to follow.

But they'd be very slow about it. They'd seen him shoot.

He found a likely spot, tied the gray in a hollow, and waited, the rifle poked between two clumps of grass. The light was beginning to wane, and he was in shadow, but the trail was not. He waited an hour and was beginning to wonder if they had decided to circle around, fearing the ambush he'd set. But as he pondered it, he decided they could not know where he was, and even if they did, it might take them hours to crawl up on him from behind, and by then it would be dark.

They came on foot, leading the horses, eyes busy, searching out every nook and clump ahead of them. Dutch drew a bead on the leading man, but as he fired the man moved quickly aside, and the bullet richocheted off a slab of rock near him.

Dutch swore and crawled back to the horse, mounted, and rode on in annoyance. He grinned as he heard shots explore the grass clumps where he'd been. He was happy to have them waste ammunition.

The ground became slightly less uneven, and as he came close to the river he saw that it was a much smaller stream than previously. He began to wonder if he could swim the gray across in the dark. If he could get far enough ahead, he might try it, especially when it was too dark to track him. He'd be free of them then. He studied the sky and decided it would be dark in about two hours.

As he rode, he opened his food sack, cut strips of cooked meat, and chewed them methodically.

He came to a section of level land, furrowed by plows and neatly edged by a road. He loped the gray along the fields, as long shadows rippled beside him. There were houses in the distance, and he passed several men trudging from the river, fishing poles over their shoulders. He waved, and they waved back, and one raised a catch of fish as if in triumph.

Then he plunged into woods again, and there was only a worn path dipping and curving, diving through sudden freshets and nearly losing itself as the woods became thick and as darkness fell like a blanket. He halted on a rise of ground from which he could see the trail behind for a quarter of a mile and allowed the gray to crop grass. The sun had gone, but a twilight remained, sufficient for him to see the two riders, and as he watched them approach, Dutch felt anger inside him that he should have to run farther.

He looked at the caps on the pistols again and began to walk down the rise, a pistol in each hand. Why not settle it here?

He was in shadow, and the riders did not see him until they were close. They rode barely a hand's reach apart, side by side, and Dutch brought up the pistols, thumbs drawing back the hammers. That was the quick move they caught sight of, and for an instant both men were frozen. Dutch's first shot hit the man on the left and spun him around. The man on the right gave a cry and spurred his horse. The animal reared and jumped, and though Dutch aimed deliberately at the horse's belly, the shots missed. In the next seconds the man was galloping the animal back the way he'd come. He disappeared into the shadows, though Dutch could hear the hoofbeats for half a minute.

The man he'd hit was on the ground, motionless.

Dutch circled him, ready to fire again. He was a young one, probably not yet twenty, wearing shabby clothes, worn boots, and a striped shirt. He was on his belly, and when Dutch turned him over the shirt was bloody. Dutch's shot had gone in at the base of the neck; he examined it in the dusk, wondering why he'd aimed high. But the bullet had done the job. He'd aimed very quickly, and the target had been moving. . . .

He searched the body and found very little, a short knife, not worth much, tobacco, flint and steel, and four dollars. A thrifty man, he pocketed the money, found the man's pistol, a Navy in good condition, and shoved it into his belt. He also found a cap box and bullet pouch and put

265

them into a pocket. The horse, a skinny sorrel, seemed skittish, eyeing Dutch and moving off when Dutch approached. He gave up after a minute and went back up the rise to the gray. Someone would find the body soon.

He didn't care one way or the other.

CHAPTER TWENTY-FIVE

There were a dozen things that required her decisions about the house, and Lily kept busy most of the morning with Dossey at her heels. She discussed moving furniture, buying various articles and crockery, rearranging the layout of the garden, whitewashing sheds, and repairing the drive. She had a session with the cook and sent her driver into the city with a list of supplies. He was to bring back shrimp, oysters, squab, and beef from Mr. McWhorter's store near the levee. McWhorter had sent a note saying he'd received fresh shipments from the gulf.

Then she luxuriated in a tub and smoked a cheroot while she soaked. It was possible to put Howard Paddock out of her mind when she kept busy, but now thoughts of him crept back to gnaw at her.

She got out of the tub and sat while Ulise combed and fussed with her hair. The situation with Howard was intolerable, and yet she felt almost powerless to change it, lest she arouse curiosity where it would least serve her. Even Roy Collier had remarked on the personal tragedies that had dogged her, and he was unaware of Andrea.

What *was* possible against Howard?

She could not sit idly by while he planned and

267

schemed—what was he planning? Howard was no fool; he would not upset the golden apple cart, surely, just to further his ambitions of the moment. He would wait till the company was far along the path to riches.

Yes, Howard would wait, but lay his plans, too— prepare the quicksand that would close over her head one day. Proof of that was his clandestine investigation of Jacques's grave.

Lily sighed deeply. She must also plan for the future— a future that did not include Howard—but must never let him know. She must move him out of the company in some manner, and yet that might be difficult as a permanent solution, of the kind that had served her so well in the past.

It made her ill at ease that Howard was the one who'd hired Viktor Kory to rid them of Jeffries. Because he might also employ Kory to do away with her. It was annoying as hell to think she might have paid for it! She watched Ulise's deft hands in the mirror, but of course her mind worked that way, and maybe Howard's did not. He did not seem to her to be a man like Jeffries, for instance. Howard was strong only when propped up. He might try to use his terrible knowledge in a more distant manner, such as going to the law with it.

No, he might not go that far, but he might *threaten* her with the law. What was Howard's opinion of her? That was important.

And if he did, what would she do then?

She was going round in circles with her thoughts. And it all came down to the question, what was she eventually going to do about Howard Paddock?

Lily closed her eyes. In the beginning it had all been so easy. Jacques had never suspected what was happening to him, nor had Jacob. Of course Jacob had protested and objected and fought the inevitable, but in the end had succumbed. Even Hiram Bryant's death had been accomplished in such a way that it was impossible for any guilt to be brought home to her.

How marvelous if Howard would go in the same way.

But she knew he would not. Howard was suspicious and wily, and he quite possibly knew more tricks than she. And he had a murderer on his string.

But wait a moment—wasn't there something that Howard had not considered? Upon Jeffries' death she owed Viktor Kory one thousand dollars. *She* owed it, not Howard. And in that case she could make certain conditions, such as paying him personally. The idea made her brighten, and she smiled as Ulise tugged and combed. If she could woo Kory away from Paddock . . . Why not? She stared at herself in the mirror; she was still beautiful, desirable to men. What might Kory do for a night with her? Lily smiled again and Ulise glanced at her, startled at the sudden change.

She had once promised Paddock a reward, and the next day Hiram Bryant had been found dead. Could not the same thing happen again?

Of course it could.

Ulise confided to cook later in the kitchen. "She's a spooky one, Miz Berlanger. You should've seen her, grinnin' like a tiger cat and not even lookin' at what I'm doin'."

"Oh, she's got a gennelman friend coming this evening, that's why. They ain't anything spooky about her."

"Yeh? Maybe not, but you didn't see 'er face."

*   *   *

Roy Collier arrived just before eight o'clock, and Dossey showed him into the study where Lily was waiting. She rose, and he kissed her warmly as she stretched to run her arms about his neck. He was so big and broad.

He held out his hands to the fire, while she poured wine with a grace that charmed him. She wore a pearl gray robe and fine linen decorated with gold, worn with a pale yellow underskirt with the same designs in rich embroidery; it had no collar and was scalloped, and he thought the effect, with her glimmering pearls and dark hair, was exquisite.

"You take a man's breath away, Lily—"

She brought the wine to him and tilted her head for a kiss. "You say exactly the right things, Roy. Come, sit by me here." She sat and patted the love seat near the fire. He was tall and maybe a bit broader than Paige and had just a hint of Paige's profile and manner.

Paige. An involuntary shudder moved her shoulders, and Roy took her hand. "What is it?"

"It's nothing."

"You can't be cold."

"No. I was—thinking of a—friend. Someone who went down on a boat recently. A boiler explosion."

"Ahhh. I read of them in the papers."

"They happen too frequently."

"Yes, far too often I'd say. I'd think something could be done. Don't you employ engineers?"

"Dozens." She sipped. "Their reports flood my desk. But it's difficult." She took a long breath and smiled at him. "I'm sorry I brought it up. Let's talk about pleasanter things. Are you hungry?"

He laughed and kissed her cheek. "Hungry for you."

270

"Well, first things first. Cook has gone to enormous pains on your behalf, and I wouldn't dare delay going to the table. Tell me what you expect to do in Montgomery—or wherever you decide to set up home."

"First I'll think about where to settle. As I said, I have many friends in Richmond, and I may go there. It's a center of things in the South, you know. New Orleans is a bit too sultry for my taste, though I love the city. If I find a home in Richmond, I'll rent out the farm, or sell it, and take up my profession again."

"And go into local politics?"

"Probably." He smiled. "An old fire horse, you know, eager to smell smoke again."

"And you think there will be war?"

Roy sighed. "I wish I could say I didn't think so, and maybe a miracle will happen. If it comes, what will you do, Lily?"

"Stay here in St. Louis and wait for it to end, I expect. There's nothing else I can do." She glanced around at a discreet rap at the door. Dossey stood there.

"Dinner is served, ma'am."

"Thank you, Dossey. We're coming."

Cook had outdone herself with grenadine of beef, oysters, potato puffs, and asparagus. There was a centerpiece of red, gleaming apples and lacy, green stalks she did not recognize, two candles, and wine. Roy sat opposite her as Dossey poured and retreated.

Roy raised his glass. "To the most beautiful woman I know."

Lily giggled and simpered. "You're too generous, darling."

"Not a bit."

She thought of the lovely young girl she'd seen him

with at the theater in Washington. Well, perhaps girls did not count. Or relatives. The soup was cream of carrot, which Roy exclaimed over. "This woman is a jewel! She could make her fortune in Washington."

"Please don't say that in front of her," Lily begged. "Cooks are even more difficult people than politicians."

Roy chuckled and shook his head. "Oh, no, not a bit of it. Politicians are the worst, mostly because they're not at all bright. They have small minds and enormous egos, and if they were not allowed to have people who did the actual work, nothing at all would get done. The entire process of government would float away, out to sea."

"You sound as bitter as Sam!"

Roy pulled at an ear. "I try not to be. Please excuse my lapse. When is the rivermen's ball?"

"In a few days, on Saturday night."

"Fancy dress?"

"Yes."

Dossey came and took away the soup plates. He served the beef and refilled their glasses. She said, "I will come to the St. George—it might be best that way, if you don't mind. I like to have Tony Burke about."

He shrugged. "Of course. I'll be ready when you say. Who will be there?"

"The governor and local officials, and, of course, leading steamboat owners and their staffs—" She thought of Logan then, wondering if he intended to be present. Probably. Wouldn't it be odd to come upon him suddenly, face to face? She might do well to surround herself; Logan was such a violent person. He might do anything.

She stared at Roy. His face was turning red, and his hands suddenly clawed at his mouth! She was startled—

thinking instantly of poison. No, he seemed to be choking! He made gagging sounds, pointed to his mouth and rose, nearly upsetting the table. Glasses spilled, and silverware clattered to the floor.

Lily shouted, "Dossey! Dossey!"

Roy staggered about the room and fell to his knees; she ran to him, pounding his back. Dossey was suddenly there, pushing her aside, pounding hard. Roy made retching sounds, his face blue.

Then the old man reached into Roy's mouth, and all at once Roy collapsed on the floor, and Dossey turned to her, nodding and panting. "It come out, Missy." He showed her a bit of half-chewed meat.

"Thank God," she said, going to her knees beside him. Dossey gave him a towel, and he patted his face, glanced at her wanly and gasped, getting his breath back. The color came into his face once more, and in a moment he rose and slumped on a chair as Dossey stood over him.

Roy thanked the old man. "I never had that happen to me before! I'm so sorry, Lily—"

"Don't be sorry! *I'm* sorry it happened—are you all right?"

"Yes, yes." He smiled at her, embarrassed. "But I'm afraid I don't feel like eating—"

"Never mind. Of course not. Come along, we'll go into the study." She took the wine glasses and a bottle. The incident had shaken her, and she went ahead of him to put the glasses and bottle down before he noticed her trembling hands. Roy had actually been near death for a minute—in her house! What a storm that would cause. There had been several sly remarks in the newspapers when Hiram Bryant had been murdered in his own bed. They had gossiped about Jacob, and one of the writers

273

had mentioned in passing that it was curious how many persons near to Lily Berlanger had suffered violent deaths. Her lawyer had sent a stiffly worded note to the newspaper, threatening suit, and the paper had printed a retraction.

Thank God, Roy was all right. She asked him to pour the wine, and they sipped it together as he watched the dancing flames in the fireplace.

Then she sent the servants to bed and took Roy into her own chamber. He had recovered completely, he said, though he still seemed pale to her. It had undoubtedly shocked him, too; he spoke of it once as a "brush with death" and she hushed him immediately, saying it was not so. "You're going to live to a ripe old age. Tomorrow we'll laugh about this."

"I certainly hope you do, Lily. I've spoiled the supper—"

She slid her arms about his neck. "No more talk about it. Take me to bed." She kissed him and backed away. "Are you sure you want to?"

"Of course I want to!"

She turned about. "Then unfasten me."

Roy stayed the night and the next morning until noon. They lunched together on crusty, baked fish fillets with French white wine; then they drove into town together in her carriage—he had sent the hired rig back the night before.

He said, as they neared the hotel, "Each time I'm forced to leave you I feel a touch of panic. Do you suppose I'm in love?"

Lily pressed his hand. "You mustn't speak of love, then go hurrying off to Alabama. It isn't seemly."

"Maybe not, but I want to be with you every moment."
He sighed deeply. "I've asked you to come along with
me."

"Roy darling, I have affairs to tend to—"

"Yes, I've never known a business woman before." He
smiled. "There can't be many."

"There aren't."

"Why don't you give up the business? Surely you have
money enough and more to see you through the rest of
your days."

It surprised her. Give up business! "Do you have any
idea what you're asking? It's my life!"

"Surely life is more than that."

She gazed at him curiously, wondering if he would
really want her to give up all she'd worked for so many
years. She allowed herself a quick peep into a future
without the company; she saw herself sitting on a stoop
somewhere, knitting perhaps. It was stifling. "I will
never give it up," she said slowly.

Roy nodded. "I didn't think you would." He leaned
toward her and kissed her cheek. "When will I see you
next?"

"Tomorrow . . . Yes, tomorrow." She looked up as the
carriage slowed. The hotel doorman was reaching for the
handle.

She was closeted with Udell Winter for a short time
before lunch; they went over routine matters. The
Jeffries-Fraser suit was expected to come up in a month
or so, and the company lawyer was confident it would be
thrown out; Udell had a number of letters informing him
that the federal government was asking for bids on
considerable cargoes to be transported from Pittsburgh

275

to several cities along the lower Mississippi. There was also a wire from Sen. Sam Beckhart's office telling them to expect the queries.

Udell commented, "Your Washington trip is paying off, Lily. I'll get answers in the mail as soon as possible."

"Who else is bidding?"

He shrugged. "There's no way of knowing."

Maybe Sam had seen to it that only her company was bidding. He might have that much power. . . . But even so, it was progress; she should not doubt Sam when he said that it would all come as they planned, if only little by little.

"What about Howard Paddock?"

Udell scratched his chin and made a face. "I've seen him only once, and he warned me to keep my mouth shut."

"I see. No new offers from him?"

"Of course not, Lily. And if there were, I'd report to you immediately."

She thought he was a little stuffy about it and smiled. "Of course you would, Udell. I have no doubts. Are you going to the ball?"

"I rather doubt it. My wife is ill—"

"Oh? Too bad. Please give her my best."

She had a lunch sent in and ate it alone in her office, thinking about Roy. He would never take Paige's place in her heart, but he came close. There was something about him that made him more attractive to her than anyone else she'd met—including Sam Beckhart—and she wondered how definitely he'd made up his mind to return to Alabama.

She smoked a cigar with coffee, her office door locked, and turned her thoughts to Howard. There had to be a way to rid herself of him, without buying him off.

She knew he was thinking the same of her.

Having finished the cigar, she opened a window, went out to the hall, and summoned one of the clerks. "Go find Tony Burke and bring him to me."

"Yes, mum." The man hurried off.

He was back in about twenty minutes and stood in front of her desk shaking his head. "I looked everywhere for 'im, mum. Nobody's seen 'im."

"He's not in the building?"

"If he is, mum, he's hidin' himself. I looked ever'where."

"In the yards as well?"

"Ever'where, mum."

She dismissed him and swore, thinking of Howard. Had he approached her bodyguard, as well? Would Burke stop the carriage on the way home tonight and empty a shotgun into her?

CHAPTER TWENTY-SIX

After leaving the hill where the last fight took place, Dutch rode hard for half a day, unwilling to be found by the local law and charged with the man's death. He well knew how local lawmen functioned. He took pains to mingle his tracks with others, and after five or six hours he felt at ease.

He holed up in a pleasant, deserted valley, rested the gray, and slept. The running fight had set his blood to coursing in a manner that had been foreign to him for a decade. He was getting too old to brawl, but he enjoyed it; it was too bad such exciting encounters were illegal. He could remember a time when the law went its own way and did not get involved when a few men decided to settle matters with fists, knives, or pistols.

Of course, everyone was much more civilized now. The old days were gone forever. Except that a few old timers like himself were still around with their ancient ideas—ideas of settling wrongs without bothering about the law.

The next morning he was on the road again. He went through several tiny hamlets; none had a telegraph wire, and news arrived slowly; he had none to tell them.

In four more days he came to Cairo.

It lay across the river, and he took the ferry with much

trepidation. The ferryman assured him he'd never had an accident in five years and didn't expect one now. Dutch was relieved when the man was right. They went across the river with no incident to mar the journey, and Dutch hurried ashore and mounted the gray, trying not to think that he had to make the return trip very soon.

He went at once to the street where Howard Paddock's store had been and was dismayed to discover it had a new name. Paddock's was painted out, and the name Wolfe & Son was lettered in its place.

When he tied the gray and went inside, a tobacco-chewing clerk told him that Paddock had sold out "a long time ago and gone up to St. Louis." He thought Paddock was in the steamboat business now, but he'd never known Paddock personally, and it was only a guess based on what others had said.

Dutch went out and leaned on the hitch rack, wondering if Paddock would be in St. Louis. There was no way to find out, except by going there.

He swore and got on the gray.

Viktor Kory had solved all his problems concerning the Armory Hall ambush—except for one thing. He had seen Logan Jeffries only twice, both times from something of a distance, and the more he thought about it, the more he realized it was the weak link in his chain.

And there was one other fact he had not considered before. All the men would be dressed in similar attire. It was a fancy-dress ball, after all.

He went back to the Jeffries-Fraser building and hung around for several days, becoming acquainted with a clerk in the shipping department. He bought the man drinks and fed him a story about being a plainclothes government agent—he had a badge, purchased in a pawn shop, that looked authentic—on the lookout for certain felons thought to be in the city. On the second day he got lucky when Logan Jeffries was pointed out to him. Jeffries was on the stairs, about seventy feet away, and he got only one good look, but it was the face he remembered. Jeffries was tall, broad shouldered, and dark. He would know him when he saw him again in the Armory Hall yard.

He had a second bit of luck also. A small rainstorm swept across the city from the river very late in the afternoon, as he waited near the loading docks behind the building. Jeffries and his wife came out of the building and went across the yard with two other men, one a driver. They got into a carriage and rolled out of the yard. Kory followed.

This time he was able to tail them all the way home; the driver was concerned with trying to keep dry and did not bother to glance around. Kory marked the house and nearly rubbed his hands in satisfaction as he passed by. Now he'd be able to follow Jeffries to the Hall and not make any mistakes.

That night he went to Paddock's home again to request an advance on his money, but Paddock was not in an agreeable mood. "You've spent the entire thousand already?"

"I have to live."

"You're living high on the hog!"

"I don't think so."

"What about Jeffries?"

"I have plans for him. It's all worked out. I know where he lives, and I know his carriage. I'll have him cold."

Paddock sniffed and nodded, pulling at his watch chain. "God willing," he said. "You didn't do so well in Chadwick. My friends were very disappointed."

"What about the money?"

"Are you going after Jeffries alone?"

"Yes, I plan to."

"Isn't that a mistake? You had three men before and—"

"It's not a mistake. Besides, I have to consider getting away afterward. I can't afford to get caught. Let me have three hundred dollars."

Paddock stared at him. "I think it's a grave mistake. We discussed a crew of men, and you haven't done it."

Kory began to get angry. "I'm the one putting my neck out, Mr. Paddock. I know what I'm doing."

"I certainly hope so." Paddock sniffed. "In any case, I haven't got the money. I—"

"You promised me!"

"Jesus! I promised I'd have it when the job was done, not now, two days before! You must keep your word, sir."

Kory walked to the door and back, the anger smouldering in him. It was true that Paddock hadn't expected his demand, but Paddock was a rich man. He looked about him at the obvious opulence. "You must have money in the house!"

"I'm sorry, Kory, I have no money to give you. Not today."

"You must have! Give me fifty dollars then."

Paddock blew out his breath, frowning. It was annoying, but perhaps it was the best way. "All right." He turned, and said over his shoulder, "Wait here. Have a chair." He went out and closed the door.

281

Kory was pacing the room when he returned. He was a caged leopard very nearly showing his claws. Paddock handed him the money, and he took it without counting and thrust it into his pocket. "Thank you." He went to the door and slammed out.

Paddock sighed. There would be a time when he did not have to deal with such creatures. It could not come too soon.

He went to Udell Winter the next day and requested a thousand dollars in cash on Lily's account. Udell was astonished. "If Lily wants the money, why are you requesting it?"

Paddock was very patient. "Please go and ask her to sign whatever you need." He sat in a chair near Udell's desk and took out a cigar. Udell stared at him for a moment; then he got up and went to see Lily. When he returned, he had a small black metal box, put it on his desk, and counted out a thousand in bills; he handed them over without a word.

Paddock thanked him politely, put the money in an inside coat pocket, and went out trailing blue smoke.

Clarence Yates came to the office next morning and took Logan aside. "My man on Viktor Kory reports that he followed you and Doris yesterday evening when you went home."

"He followed us! Damn!"

"And afterward he went to see Howard Paddock at home, late at night. He came out in a bit of a snit and spent the rest of the night with a girl at his hotel."

"He quarreled with Paddock?"

Yates shrugged. "No telling. I don't like it that he tailed you. What plans have you made for the ball?"

"Kenneth is going to escort Doris. We'll go separately."

"That's good. I'm sure Louis will handle it well." Yates smiled. "And tomorrow my men will corral Mr. Kory and take him entirely out of circulation. It'll be a worry off my mind."

Doris took several afternoons off and visited a well-known dressmaker, Mrs. Frances Laymon, a widow whose husband had been killed in the beast house of the local zoo. Mrs. Laymon made for her a lovely, low-cut evening gown of blue-black velvet, over which she would wear a bretelle of blond velvet. The bretelle was made with velvet ribbon and lace and had a body and elbow-length sleeves. Looking at herself in the full length mirror, Doris thought she had never owned such a beautiful creation.

She was also appalled at the price—two hundred dollars! But Logan merely shrugged and smiled, kissing her cheek. "I will not have you going to the ball looking like a washerwoman."

"Logan! Is that what you think I—"

"Of course not. It's just that the most beautiful woman in the hall must be dressed accordingly."

"I never know when you're serious."

"I am certainly serious at this moment. And I believe I can call in witnesses to support my position."

"Your position about what?"

He laughed. "That you are a beautiful woman!"

She went to him quickly and put her cheek against his. "I must learn never to argue with you. By the way, what did Clarence Yates have to say today? I saw him take you into the hall."

"Very little. He gives me a daily report on our enemies. Today he reported that Kory went to see Paddock late at night. But there's no way to know what they talked about."

"You probably."

"Maybe."

At the first opportunity he met Chris Murphy and Baxter Ross in the stable, informing them that Viktor Kory had tailed them to the house and asking them to keep an especially good lookout for the next several days. In the morning he packed the clothes he would wear to the ball and took them to the office, where he would change.

Louis Gualco had worked out a plan; he would drive a closed buggy to within a quarter of a mile of the rear of Logan's house. Logan, in old clothes, would slip out the rear, over the fence, and meet the buggy and be driven to the office. Unless Kory had half a dozen sharp-eyed men spread around the house, Louis said, they would never suspect.

Later on, Kenneth Fraser and Doris would drive to the ball in the usual carriage, accompanied by both Ross and Murphy on horseback.

To Logan it was an annoying necessity, and he submitted to it only because of Doris' fears for his safety. He itched to come face to face with Kory again. Though when he said so, Louis rolled his eyes.

A series of small incidents kept him on the levee for the next day, Louis Gualco close beside him. Two Jeffries-Fraser steamboats had sustained damage while tied up and though their first thoughts were on Berlanger-Bryant, nothing could be proved. It was possible, the engineer of one boat said, that the damage to his boat's firebox had been done by a disgruntled fireman on his own. It was being repaired, and the firemen were all questioned at length. Two were discharged because of discrepancies in their stories.

The second steamboat was damaged astern by a floating log, and though a small boat had been noticed nearby at the time, it might have been coincidence.

The guards aboard all Jeffries-Fraser boats were told to be alert, especially at night, and Logan made several inspection rounds, doing his best to discover a weak point in their system, but he could not. Even Louis grudgingly gave his approval but pointed out that if a man wanted to seriously damage a boat, it might be an easy matter to swim in the dark to the stern and do his deed there. Logan gave orders that lamps were to be placed so as to illuminate the after parts of each boat and the surrounding water, thus eliminating that danger.

While on the boat, he was told, to his annoyance, that it was common knowledge that Jeffries-Fraser was locked in a life-and-death feud with Berlanger-Bryant, which was the reason behind the recent spate of damages, beginning with the disabling of the *Jewel*.

The officers, and even the captain, believed the same . . . else why were these things happening? And though he did his best to refute them, he could see that he was not believed. Everybody seemed sure that Lily Berlanger would cheerfully stick his head on a pike.

Logan returned to the office; he had done all he could to safeguard the boat and to halt the rumors, but he was positive the same rumors were strong on Berlanger boats. There was no evidence that Lily was trying to stop them.

As he was preparing to leave the office in the evening with Doris, Clarence Yates appeared.

"Bad news, Logan."

"What is it?"

"I'm afraid I've let you down."

"What in God's name is it?"

Yates sighed. "Viktor Kory has eluded our watch. He's got away, and we haven't a clue about where he is."

CHAPTER TWENTY-SEVEN

Lily had steaming hot water brought upstairs and a tub filled. Dossey brought a bottle of her favorite red wine, which she sipped as she undressed. She put the bottle and glass on a chair beside the tub, lighted a cigar, and stepped in, sinking down slowly till the water was up to her neck. How luxurious. She stretched, keeping one hand dry for the cigar, and sipped the wine, soaking till the water began to seem cool to her.

Then she got out, dried herself, and called in Ulise to do her hair. She finished the wine, sitting patiently as Ulise combed and curled, arranged the hair perfectly, and tied a thin towel about it. "I will finish when you are dressed, Miz Lily."

"All right." She doffed the robe and drew on drawers, a chemise, and petticoats, allowing Ulise to fasten them firmly in the back. After the ball she would bring Roy back with her, and they would spend the end of the week together. There was an inn not far upriver where they could go for absolute privacy and a marvelous view— perhaps ride horseback along the trails, if the weather held. He was sure to ask her again to come to the South with him, and perhaps she would go. She had business acquaintances in Richmond.

She had bought an evening dress for the occasion, a

dark, midnight-blue velvet, over which she wore a pearl canezou of French silk with flat bows of delicate Mantua ribbon in front. Inlaid fans of coral, ivory, or mother-of-pearl were the height of fashion; hers was ivory, with lacy points. Ulise took off the towel and continued arranging her hair, enclosing it partly with a net fringed with pearls. The effect, Lily thought, was imperial.

"You will turn all eyes, Miz Lily," Ulise said, stepping back to cock her head critically.

"Bring my cloak, please." Lily went out and down the stairs to speak to Dossey. The carriage had been brought around earlier and was waiting, as Tony Burke lounged beside it, talking to the driver.

Ulise held the cloak and draped it over her shoulders, and Lily went out quickly and entered the coach.

When they arrived at the hotel, Roy was waiting, standing just inside the door. He recognized the carriage and came out as the driver jumped down to hold the door. Roy was hatless, wearing a black suit and white ruffled shirt with a white cravat and a pearl stickpin. He slid in beside her. "You are a vision! Each time I see you I wonder how you keep getting more beautiful!"

"You must never leave politics, Roy."

He laughed and kissed her cheek. "Are you suggesting I am not telling the exact truth?"

"Certainly not."

"I am stating my opinion, and on that I rest my case." He held her hand tightly. "Do not call on me tonight for a speech. I have nothing prepared, and I'm far out of my district."

"Have the newspapers found you?"

"Oh yes. But we came to an agreement. I promised to

make no news in St. Louis, if they would say nothing in the columns about my being here. I must say they were not ecstatic, but they eventually came round."

"I'm sure your name will be noted as attending tonight—"

Roy shrugged. "I bow to the inevitable. At least I will be with you." He kissed her hand. "Have you thought again about coming south with me?"

"Yes, I've thought about it—"

"Do I detect a note of possibility?"

She smiled. "I would love to go, but I will not suffer those damned trains again. When will you be in Richmond d'you think?"

"Probably very soon. You can go the entire way by steamboat and ship. Do you know Richmond?"

"No, not at all."

"Then I will arrange everything. Wire me when you start, and I will receive you as a princess. We will declare a holiday and—"

She laughed. It was fun being with him. "I rather prefer going quietly. I've never been in a parade, you know. I'm sure it's something like a zoo."

"Well then we won't put you on exhibit, but I insist on introducing you to the local society. Surely you won't object to that—as a matter of fact, I met you at such an affair, you recall."

"Yes. I will put myself into your hands."

"Ahhh, that is something I look forward to." He glanced through the window. "We seem to be approaching the hall."

Carriage and buggies crowded the street, and a line of men dressed in red-and-white coats slowly got the rigs

289

into a double file, waving them on into the huge yard. Hundreds of small flags greeted them, and dozens of colored lanterns brightened the evening.

It took an eternity to move up the broad roadway to the canopied entrance, but at last the carriage halted, a red-coated attendant opened the door, and Roy climbed down to hand out Lily. The coach door slammed, and the carriage rolled away as the next moved up. The drivers would congregate about the door later and bring the rigs back for their owners.

The Armory Hall was decorated like a huge palace, with a myriad colored lanterns about the entrance way and a painted sign that proclaimed: The Rivermen's Fraternal Ball. Lily took Roy's arm, and they moved along a broad walkway, perhaps a hundred paces to the wide, stone steps, in company with hundreds of others, chattering and laughing in anticipation.

There was a huge foyer, where outer clothes were checked, and a heavily patronized bar. A lead-glass wall with rounded doors led into the main hall, which held hundreds of tables and chairs in three tiers and in which there was a dance floor in the far center, near the orchestra that occupied the wide dais. To Lily's critical eye it looked very well organized. Her tickets were examined by uniformed men at the glass doors, and they were bowed in; another uniformed young man led them to draped seats on the upper tier. These were the select seats, the owners' tier, and as they were seated another young man brought them a beverage list and waited patiently as they made choices.

"I'll have the red wine," Lily said. She pressed back into the plush, listening to the chatter about her, wondering if Logan Jeffries was nearby. She set the velvet reticule beside her and slid her hand over it, feeling the comforting hardness of a small pistol through the cloth.

Roy selected champagne, and the waiter went away. He asked, "Do you know many of these people?"

"Very few," she said. "My managers deal with them when necessary." She glanced around as the orchestra began to play.

Roy said, "Would you like to dance?"

She hesitated, and he smiled. "I believe you danced with me once—"

"Yes, but—" She sighed.

"You'd rather not?"

She closed her hand over his. "If you want the truth, I detest it." She did not tell him it was not the dancing she minded, but the music. Music made no sense to her; the sounds were confused and sometimes maddening.

"Of course," he said, "it doesn't matter in the least."

Several politicians came by, talking in low tones, and she recognized the governor and one or two of the state officers and spread the ivory fan to hide her features. She was positive the governor would come to her table if he noticed her or Roy, but he passed by. In the next draped booth was a man named Newton, owner of a small packet line; she had met him once somewhere, and as their eyes met he smiled and inclined his head. She smiled back. His wife craned round, a fat-faced woman with too much rouge on her cheeks, and smiled. Lily nodded and looked away.

On the dance floor a hundred people were moving in a stately waltz, and the waiter came with bottles and glasses. He placed a silver ice bucket next to Roy, opened the red wine, and poured; then he opened the champagne. He left them a decorative menu and departed silently.

On the other side were five younger people and an older man with a white beard and hair. She recognized him from his pictures in the newspapers: it was Elmer Hatfield, an early pilot who had won several exciting races with his famous steamboat, the *Flying Eagle*. He was recounting stories to his group with theatrical expressions and gestures. He had them laughing and hanging on his every word. She wondered if they were his relatives, though none looked like him in the slightest.

She did not see Logan Jeffries anywhere.

She sipped the wine and watched the dancers and the busy throng. The people were never still; they moved constantly from table to table, chatting and laughing, clinking glasses. Roy kept her attention with a repertoire of stories concerning officeholders; several well-known pilots came by and nodded to her or spoke a few words, and she smiled at them pleasantly. One stayed on good terms with pilots. She saw several of her captains and officers in the second tier and pretended not to notice when they pointed her out to friends.

This was one of the very few large gatherings she attended during the year. Ordinarily she preferred small, intimate groups of her own choosing, but attendancy at the rivermen's ball was almost *de rigueur*, especially for an owner. An absence would be noted by the newspapers and commented on, even if the person was ill or out of the city.

But there were compensations; she could sit quietly by, watching but not joining in, being seen but yet distant. She had informed the committee firmly that she would not speak, that she would not allow herself to be introduced, and that she would leave early.

They had of course acceded to her demands. Lily Berlanger was far too important to cross.

Viktor Kory dressed carefully at the hotel; his attire included a black suit, a white tie, a black beaver hat, and a black overcoat—because it had pockets. For several reasons he had decided not to go to Jeffries' house or to follow him to the hall. The most important was that Jeffries was sure to attend, so it would be a waste of time. He hired a rig to drive him, but when he walked into the grounds he found himself eyed by the dozens of attendants clad in red and white. It had not occurred to him that they would be present in such numbers.

He went quickly into the hall and sat in the bar sipping a mixed drink, the invention of one of the bartenders, and thought about his task. It was probably not possible to shoot Jeffries at the beginning of the evening when hundreds were going in. He would have to wait till later, when the guests would begin to leave in small groups.

If he was lucky and Jeffries stayed till very late, then nearly all the attendants would be gone too. He had not liked the look of them; most were young and probably very agile. If they saw him shoot Jeffries, they might be able to run him down.

There were a good many policemen about also, but Kory was not concerned with them. He knew they were present to haul away obnoxious drunks; they had carryall wagons parked alongside the building. There were probably a few plainclothes men present also, to guard against pickpockets, but they would not be out in the yard.

And though he had expected hundreds of carriages, the reality was quite something else again. As they began to arrive in numbers, the yard was a crawling mass of horses and rigs, and hundreds of people moved through. Jeffries might be anywhere.

He walked completely around the hall, discovering that the front entrance was the only door being used. That was a bit of good luck. He discovered, too, by talking to one of the young attendants, that all the owners' carriages were being taken to a special area, one closer to the entrance. When he prowled through it, he found Jeffries' carriage; the big, burly driver he recalled was sitting inside smoking a cigar with a second man.

He went back to the hall and entered, showing his ticket, and walked slowly around the second tier, looking for his quarry. Jeffries was on the upper circle, near the end, sitting with his wife and another couple. He recognized Mrs. Jeffries first, and had to look hard at the big man next to her. The light was poor on the upper tier, and Jeffries was sitting so that his features were not easy to make out.

Kory found a table on the second tier from which he could keep Jeffries in view, ordered whiskey, and watched the dancing. After an hour the orchestra stopped playing, and the musicians left their instruments and filed out. Waiters appeared with carts and began to serve supper. He had a choice of beef or ham, the waiter said; he chose beef and received a plate with beef slices, potatoes, and peas. The beef was not too tough, but halfway through the meal a group of men walked out onto the dance floor, and the speeches began. There were seemingly interminable introductions and long-winded oratory.

Twice Jeffries got up and disappeared from his view, and each time Kory scurried toward the door, but Jeffries did not go outside.

Kory hardly listened to the speeches; all his attention was on his victim. When he finished the beef, it occurred to him he might be much better off waiting in the foyer than suddenly getting up to chase Jeffries out—he might be remembered that way. So as one speech came to an end, he rose during the polite applause and made his way out.

But he could not hang around the foyer, either. The uniformed attendants stared at him, so he stepped outside and lit a thin cigar. Standing on the steps, he could view the park, a jungle of parked carriages and waiting horses. Off to his right were several drivers, standing around a metal tin in which a fire had been built; he saw them passing a bottle back and forth.

The steps were much too public.

He walked down to the broad drive and along it to the entrance-way road. It was deserted now, and the colorfully clad attendants were nowhere in sight. That was better. It was dark here, too. In a deep shadow he drew the revolver he planned to use, a .36 caliber Starr, and examined the caps out of habit. Perfect.

It was so dark in the road that he feared for his aim. He ought to get very close—and yet he did not want to approach Jeffries *too* close. The man had an awesome reputation for quickness and strength. Paddock had warned him.

He strolled back toward the owners' carriage park and

turned as several people walked down the steps of the hall. Drawing back into the shadows, he watched them come into the park. These people were leaving early and in a few minutes they went out, the wheels of their carriages rattling on the hard ground.

As he waited, a dozen others came out and rode off one by one, probably bored by the long speeches. The giving of prizes was still to come.

He took a turn through the yard, eyes on the front doors, and came close each time a big man appeared, but these apparitions were rare. He did not count them, but probably a hundred people left the hall by twos and threes, before Jeffries finally materialized.

Kory was surprised that he was alone. The big man came to the door with a woman, left her there, and walked down the steps toward the owners' section. He was undoubtedly going for the carriage and would bring it to the steps, where his wife would enter. This was better than he'd hoped for. Kory drew the Starr pistol and moved into the deep shadows, holding the firearm down by his side so that no glint of light could reach it and give his position away.

It had to be Jeffries. The man was tall and broad-shouldered, had dark hair, and was not wearing a hat, cloak, or overcoat; he had a long stride, with authority in every inch. Kory watched with narrowed eyes, gritting his teeth tight. Since the light was behind Jeffries, he stood motionless; tonight he would earn his thousand dollars, and in the morning would be far away.

He held his breath as Jeffries came past him, now only a shadow in the gloom. Kory stepped out silently and raised the pistol.

He called out, "Jeffries!"

The man halted and turned. Kory fired, and his victim staggered back. He fired again and again, and all the shots went true. He was too close to miss. Jeffries was dead before he collapsed on the ground. Kory ran to the body and fired one more shot through the back of the head.

As he ran for the fence, he heard shouts.

CHAPTER TWENTY-EIGHT

It was probably a bit over a hundred miles, as the crow flew, from Cairo to St. Louis, but Dutch knew he'd travel twice that distance by horseback. He set out, grumpy as a bear, heading north. It might be all in vain. Paddock might be in New Orleans for all he knew—or in Europe.

The weather remained fair, cool at night but sunnier each day. It was getting on toward summer. He avoided towns and houses as much as possible, wanting no repetition of the recent chase. He had been aware for years that he seemed to attract trouble wherever he went; he did not consciously look for it, but he didn't avoid it either. He knew he had an air of confidence that rubbed some men the wrong way, but that was their problem, not his. He was too old to change.

But he did make a definite effort to avoid people. Several times he got off the trail to allow a rider or a wagon to pass without seeing him, even though it galled him to do so.

He came to an area of farmland; the countryside was cleared of trees for as far as he could see, and he could not avoid the town that squatted in the middle. He might have gone around it in the dark, but he did not feel like waiting for hours. He stopped at the store, as most travelers would, and bought cheese and tobacco and asked about the road ahead.

The proprietor, a white-haired man with rheumy eyes, looked over his specs. "You alone?"

"Yes."

"Advise you t'wait for some others."

"Why?"

"Because they was a killing up in Jackson County few days ago. Man come in just like you doing now. Had him a lead horse, and they took it'n ever'thing he had."

"Who took it?"

The man shrugged. "Nobody knows, course. It was all in the weekly. Man name of Leffit or Leggit—something like that."

Dutch grunted. "I'd wait here a week f'some others."

"Yeh, you could. But it'd be safer."

Dutch thanked the man and went out to his horse. Hell, there had been murders and robberies along the Mississippi for decades. Maybe there always would be. It was so easy for a determined hard case to murder or rob and get away downstream or across the river into another sheriff's jurisdiction. But if he let that possibility stop him, he'd never see Paddock again.

He rode most of the day before the farmland was behind him. The trail led into a region of low hills and forest, and long before sundown he rode off the trail and found a sheltered spot where he could make a small fire under thick trees. He broiled meat and made coffee and put the fire out before dark. Then he walked, leading the gray, and bedded down a mile from where he'd made the fire. He selected a spot where no one would stumble upon him in the night and went to sleep.

Shortly before midday the next morning he came upon the woman.

She was lying in the grass and weeds not far off the trail, and at first he thought she was dead; she was motionless, and there was dried blood on her clothes. Dutch approached her warily, making sure she was not bait for some hidden rifleman. He made a wide circle and came back to her, turned her over and discovered she was still breathing.

The wound was in her side, just below the left armpit; the bullet had gone through, leaving a deep furrow. She had lost blood, but not enough to cause serious danger; she sipped water from his canteen and stared at him blearily. He thought she was very frightened.

"It's all right," he told her. "Who shot you?"

She shook her head, wincing. "I don't know."

She was a handsome woman, about forty, he reckoned, but dressed in cheap clothes, an old, brown coat and shoes of poor quality. She seemed worn out. Dutch said, "I got to bandage that wound so it don't bleed no more." He sat her up. "Let's take off this here coat."

She helped and laid the coat over her knees. It looked to him as if the bullet had gone in the back, and she confirmed that it had hit her as she was running away.

"Running away from what?"

She took a long breath and pointed toward the east. "My husband and I were coming toward the river, when the shooting began. I never did see them, but there must have been at least two. My horse bolted, and when I got hit I grabbed his mane but fell off here, I guess."

"What happened to your husband?"

"I don't know. I heard him yell at me once, but the horse carried me away—"

"All right. I'll go have a looksee." He examined the wound. "We got to take this here dress off your shoulder

300

so's I can bind up the hurt. You think we c'n tear up some strips from your underskirt?"

It was very painful to slip the dress off her shoulder, and he was as gentle as he could be. The dress buttoned in front, and it was necessary to undress her almost to the waist to get at the ugly wound. It had been a long time since Dutch had seen a woman's bare breasts, and he gritted his teeth, turning her half away. The wound was still bleeding slightly. He used the strips of white cloth to bind the edges of the wound in its own blood and tied them firmly. Then he helped her dress again.

She had suffered the entire operation in near silence, and when it was finished she was pale and shaking. He eased her to the grass and folded one of his blankets under her head and put the other over her.

It occurred to him only then that he hadn't asked her name.

"Julia Brown," she said. "You think my husband might still be alive?"

"I'll go take a look." He got up, thinking to leave her a pistol, but she was in no condition to fire one anyway. He tied the gray near her and set off with the rifle in one hand and a pistol in the other. Her tracks were easy to follow, leading generally east, as she had said.

He came upon the body of a man after about a half mile.

The man had been shot four times, twice in the back; he had been robbed, and there was no sign of his horse. The body was at the foot of a low bluff that ran eastward for several hundred yards. Dutch quickly found the place where several men had waited atop the bluff. Apparently they had seen the travelers approach and had got ahead of them and fired as they passed.

It was lucky for her, he thought, that the bushwhackers had decided not to follow her. They figured the man would have what money and weapons the couple owned. They may not have known she was wounded.

He went back to the body, pondering his next move. He could not leave it for animals to find; the woman would protest such treatment, and he could not tote it to the next town for burial. He had no idea how far the next town was, and anyway rigor would set in.

He looked at the bluff, walked along it, and selected a spot. Then he dragged the body to the place and, with much effort, caved in the bank. It took more than an hour to bury it and tamp down the dirt. He carried stones to cover the spot, and when he was satisfied, he marked it with a pole stripped from a nearby tree. It would have to do.

When he rode back to the woman and described the man he'd found, she began crying. They had been married ten years, she said, and he'd been good to her. It was terrible to think he'd gone that way.

"He went quick," Dutch said. "That's better'n sufferin'."

It did not cheer her up, he saw, but it helped some.

She said she felt stronger, now that it was all over, but he insisted she remain under the blanket. "I'll go see if I c'n find your horse."

He rode the gray along a slope, heading toward the river; the runaway horse would probably follow a line of least resistance, downhill. He was right. He found the animal less than a mile away, contentedly cropping grass. It was a sorrel mare.

When he brought the horse back, the woman was sitting up. She didn't want to be a burden to him, she said; could he see her to the next town?

"What you going to use for money?"

She had none. "I can sell the horse."

"Then what? You going to walk back east? Where you come from?"

"We came from a town near Odelia. You know where that is?"

Dutch shook his head.

"My husband wanted to go to St. Louis. He thought he might get work there. He was a good carpenter."

"Can you stand?"

"I think so." She tried to get up, and he helped her, liking the feel of her on his hands. She stood erect but she was dizzy.

"We ought t'get off the trail, then I'll fix you something to eat. You need t'get your strength back."

"I don't want you to—"

"You do what I say," Dutch said. "Now come along. Lean on me." They moved off toward the dense woods. He found a spot in a hollow, surrounded by thick-boled trees, and insisted she lay down wrapped in a blanket. He went back for the horse and did his best to cover all evidences of their passing. It was unlikely, he thought, that the bandits would return, but it was as well to take no chances.

He made a small fire and broiled meat, giving her as much as she would eat, along with a few biscuits that he toasted over coals. Since he had only one cup, he gave her coffee first, and when he was sipping his, she asked him if he'd buried her husband.

"I buried him," Dutch said and was gratified that she asked no more. Before dark he put the fire out, explaining that it could be seen for long distances at night. She was

303

asleep almost as soon as she lay down again. Dutch made a circle about the camp, saw and heard nothing, and went back to curl up near her.

She was a very good-looking woman, who had light brown hair, brown eyes, and a well-shaped face. Her breasts were firm, not large, but well formed, and he thought of them as he drifted off to sleep. It had been so long. . . .

In the morning she felt stiff and uncomfortable. Dutch examined the bandage; it was slightly bloody, but no worse than he'd expected. She would have to put up with it for a few days; then, he thought, the pain would ease. He offered her the whiskey bottle, but she refused it.

They ate meat and cheese for breakfast and drank coffee by turns, and he saddled both horses. She had been riding astride, she told him, because it was the easiest way. There were few to see her.

He helped her into the saddle; she could not use her left arm as well as she wished. The wound pained her less when she kept the arm still. The dizziness had gone, she said, but he could see she was suffering from the loss of her husband. Several times when he looked at her closely that morning he saw that her eyes were tearful.

They came to a tiny hamlet late in the afternoon, but it had no doctor and no hotel. There was a doctor in Gering, the storekeeper told Dutch, but that was fifty miles east, and there was no telling if he'd be in his office or making his rounds, which might take days. They went on and camped in the woods.

When for half a day they again took the trail, it came close to the river and hugged the bank where the land was level. A dozen steamboats passed, going both ways, roiling black smoke that followed them for miles. What wouldn't he give to be able to ride a steamboat again!

Julia had never seen a steamboat before and gazed at them wide-eyed. When one came close, following an invisible channel, she exclaimed over its ornate wood-work and hugeness as it pushed upstream. People on the decks waved at them, and she waved back in excitement. It was a Berlanger-Bryant boat, Dutch saw, the *Locust*, and he spat in the water after it, wondering if Howard Paddock might be aboard.

How easily Paddock could get away from him—if he knew enough to do it.

Then the trail curled away from the river, into rolling hills, and they camped that evening in a rocky cul-de-sac, surrounded by towering trees that served as sentinels. Julia was tired from the journey, but she was definitely feeling stronger. The wound pained her, but not as much as it had; she could feel it healing.

They were better friends now, too. She had become used to Dutch's taciturn ways and to his abruptness and cold manner, and he had softened toward her. She was obviously doing her best to overcome the hurt and to do her share. She insisted on taking over the chores of cooking, which she handled better than he.

Also, she had repaired her appearance, by combing her hair, wiping away the tears, and washing the blood from her dress. Dutch gazed at her often and occasionally allowed himself to think about her in the little house at Chadwick. But she was a good ten years younger than he. . . . And she had relatives in Ohio, she said; she would undoubtedly go back there after they got to St. Louis.

What would happen when they arrived? He thought about it frequently and once or twice thought he saw her looking at him pensively. She owned nothing but the horse and the well-worn clothes she had on, and she was hundreds of miles from her relatives and lacked the means for the trip. Of course she might get work, but it would pay her probably so little that she would be unable to save enough for a very long time. He might offer to lend her money.

A dozen times the question was on the tip of his tongue, and he suppressed it. It might be better to wait and see what developed when they got to St. Louis. He had told her he was on a matter of business but had not said what kind.

"I live in a little town near the river in Arkansas," he said in reply to her question.

"I've lived in a small town all my life."

"I moved there when I left the river—"

"You mean you worked on steamboats?"

"Yes, here and there, all kinds of boats. I always been close to the river."

"And what do you do now?"

"They's farming," Dutch said vaguely, "Tradin' horses and such." He couldn't tell her what his real avocation was. "You got any children?"

"Two boys. They're both married now. Are you married?"

Dutch shook his head. "M'wife died a few years ago. I got one grown boy, too."

"Then you live alone."

"Yes."

That night he told her they would probably reach St. Louis sometime the next day, and she seemed to digest it slowly; he knew she was thinking about what she would do then. Of course, she was a stranger, only someone

306

he'd met on the trail, and her problems were really not his business. Maybe he was growing soft, but could he just walk away from her?

As they prepared to roll up in the blankets on either side of the circle of rocks that had held the fire, she said haltingly, "I owe you so much, Dutch. . . . I don't know what I would have done if—"

"You don't owe me nothing," he said harshly.

"I owe you my life."

"I d'want you talking that way. Now go to sleep."

He heard her sigh, and she turned over. After a long while she said softly, "Dutch?—"

He feigned sleep, and she said nothing more.

In the morning she seemed preoccupied. They had breakfast and went on; in the middle of the morning they came to a line of stores facing the river. One had a bold blue-and-white sign: Dry Goods.

Dutch reined in and helped her down. She could dismount by herself, but it was better not to tear the wound open. He indicated the store. "I want you t'go in here and buy yourself another dress. This'n's all stained and—"

"Dutch, I—"

He put several bills into her hand and folded her fingers around them. "Don't gi' me no sass. Just do like I say."

"But Dutch, I can't take your—"

"You can do like I tell you, and I don't want you cryin'. It ain't anything to cry about, buying a dress. You hear me?" He glanced around quickly as she dabbed at her cheeks with the back of her hand.

He said, "I'm going in the store there, get me some 'bacco." He turned about and left her standing by the horses. When he got to the door of the grocery, he saw that she was slowly walking toward the dry-goods store. She was a damned good woman, all right.

He decided then, as he watched her enter the store, that he wasn't going to let her get away easily. She needed someone. She needed him.

And he needed her.

CHAPTER TWENTY-NINE

Doris stepped out of the tub, dried quickly, and folded a robe about her; then Logan came in. He was dressed in old pants and a wool sweater, and carried a dark coat over his arm. He said, "It's almost time. It's a damned nuisance, but I'll see you at the ball."

She kissed him. "It's better to be safe. Stop complaining."

"I'm a born complainer."

"You certainly are not! Is Kenneth downstairs?"

"Yes, he came in almost an hour ago." He hugged her tightly, stepped back, gave her a grin, and hurried out. Downstairs Kenneth Fraser walked with him to the rear of the house, asking if he were armed. Logan showed him the Navy pistol and opened the kitchen door. It was dark outside. He shook Fraser's hand and stepped into the enclosed porch, eased open the outside door, and went down the steps to the ground. It was a dark, moonless night with a misty overcast. He walked slowly through the large yard, avoiding trees and the strings about cook's vegetable garden. At the rear fence he halted, listening. No sounds except distant ones. He slid over the board fence and dropped into weeds.

Three minutes later he stepped out of the shadows to greet Louis Gualco.

Louis had a small buggy whose side curtains were tacked down. Logan got in with Louis, and they rolled away as the horse trotted easily. Louis said, "I've had a good look around and damned if I can see him anywhere. I don't think he's watchin' the house."

Logan smiled. "It's kind of disappointing that we've gone to all this trouble and he didn't."

"He'll be waiting at the hall."

"You're sure?"

Louis grunted. "If he's been paid to kill you, he'll be waiting."

Logan changed into dress clothes at the office, wondering about the *if*. Maybe Kory had been fired after the missed chance at Chadwick. Maybe another assassin had been hired. Maybe Lily had given up, deciding he was too difficult a target. If so, she might wait a year or so before trying again, in order to lull him into a false sense of security. It would be like Lily, wouldn't it?

Why did she want him dead? Because of Andrea?

Louis drove to the Armory Hall, and they arrived late, though dozens of carriages were still jamming the drive. Louis went around to the far street, halting the buggy by the decorative wooden fence. It was very dark so far from the lights.

"They'll meet us here."

The two men he'd hired were leaning against the fence; they moved to the buggy, as one of them called out Louis's name. Logan got out and nodded to them; he saw two square-jawed men, plain faces, and dark suits that stretched over heavy shoulders. They were off-duty policemen, Louis had told him, glad to get the extra money he offered.

They slid over the fence and walked through the yard

toward the hall, Louis in front, the others behind. At the owners' lot they picked up Baxter Ross and Chris Murphy, and all six walked quickly into the hall's foyer without incident.

"He wasn't waiting," Logan said.

"You didn't see him," corrected Louis. "We'll be here when you come out."

An attendant looked at Logan's ticket and opened the door.

The speeches were nearly over, when Lily finished the wine and pushed her glass away. Roy smiled. "Had enough?"

She nodded, gathering up her reticule; the speeches were dull, as she'd expected, and she cared nothing for the awarding of prizes later. She got up and, as Roy followed her, strode quickly toward the foyer. There were men in the bar, talking and laughing; someone was playing a piano.

She said, "Burke should be here."

"He's probably outside and didn't expect us so soon."

"He needs discipline, that one."

Roy squeezed her hand. "I'll go out and get the carriage. Stay here where it's warm." He opened the door.

She watched him go down the steps and along the drive to the road. He crossed it and disappeared into the gloom where the carriages were parked.

Only seconds after he disappeared from her view, she heard shots. Three or four in quick succession, followed by one more. An icy hand gripped her heart, and she opened the door and flew down the steps. Others were running too. A policeman shouted, and half a dozen

311

uniformed men hurried toward the road, several with lanterns.

Lily had a terrible premonition. She drew the cloak tightly about her and halted suddenly when she saw that the men were grouped about something on the ground. Then lanterns were brought, and she saw it was a figure, a man, sprawled in the roadway. Slowly she approached, and suddenly Tony Burke was at her elbow, asking if she was all right. She paid no attention, pushed him away, and went on.

A policeman asked her to stop, but she cursed him and shouldered her way into the group. Someone raised a lantern high as they turned the body over.

It was Roy.

Tony Burke took her arm, led her to the carriage, and put her inside. She felt she was dreamwalking—it was all happening to someone else, certainly not to her. Roy dead on the ground? How could that be? He'd been laughing and chatting with her only a moment before.

Paige was gone, too.

She felt alone. She lay back on the soft seat and closed her eyes, rocked by the swaying carriage. Who had shot Roy?

Who else but Logan Jeffries. He was her only enemy—aside from Paddock, but Paddock hadn't the guts for a thing like that . . . and anyway he wouldn't attack Roy.

But then, why would Jeffries attack him?

She shook her head in frustration. It might have been a robber, someone desperate enough to hold up his victim almost within reach of the police. She should have asked if Roy had been robbed. She would ask tomorrow.

During the long ride home she thought about Paige

312

the way he'd laughed with her and teased her at times, and the memories of him began to merge with the closer memories of Roy; they had been so alike in many ways. She ached with the pain of his absence; she reached out her hand in the coach, but he who had been there such a short time ago was not there now. The terrible picture of the shadowy group of men standing about his fallen body brought tears to her eyes. God! Why had he been shot? If only she had gone with him to the carriage! Maybe it would have been different.

She lost all feeling for time and was surprised when the coach halted and she heard Burke clamber down and open the door. "We here, ma'am."

Grimly she crawled out, leaning on Burke's arm, and went up the steps and into the house. She heard Dossey's voice but ignored him and went upstairs at once, dropped her cloak on the floor, and crossed to the cabinet she kept in the bedchamber. Pouring out a stiff dollop of brandy, she sipped it standing at the window. Paige and now Roy. It was too much. No one should be expected to weather such storms. Was the Almighty toying with her, displeased because of what she'd done to Jacques and Jacob? And to Andrea, too?

No, that was foolishness. She must not allow herself to think in such terms. She finished the brandy and went to pour more.

Someone rapped lightly on the door. "Miz Lily." It was Dossey.

"What is it?"

"They a policeman here, Miz Lily."

She shouted, "Tell him to go away!"

Dossey left, but in moments he returned. "He say just let 'im ask a couple questions, Miz Lily."

313

She threw a cosmetic jar at the door and screamed. "Get him out of my house! I won't see anyone. And don't knock on that damned door again!"

Dossey did not return.

She sat in a chair by the window and drank a third of the bottle, her mind filled with the things she and Paige had shared . . . the trips, the lovemaking, and the quiet suppers in out-of-the-way cafes in New Orleans. The being with him—*just being with him*—that was what had mattered; none of the rest was important, not even the lovemaking. But having him near was everything. It had been life.

Toward dawn she fell into a troubled sleep in a chair and woke stiff and exhausted, her head woozy and thick. Getting up, she tottered to the bed and fell across it to sleep again.

Dossey did not dare wake her, and she slept till dark.

When she finally dressed and went downstairs, drawn and pale, Dossey was apologetic. There had been two policemen in the house most of the day, he said, waiting to question her. They had finally gone away but promised to see her the next day.

He showed her the newspapers. They'd had a field day. United States Senator Murdered! Assailant Unknown Shot five times!

She put them down and drank the coffee he brough her. When she finished the coffee, she read the newspaper columns. The police had no leads and no idea who had done the murder; the body had not been robbed and no one had seen the assailant. He had made good his escape and might now be anywhere.

So Roy had not been robbed.

The paper mentioned that he had escorted the famou

314

Mrs. Lily Berlanger to the rivermen's ball, but that Mrs. Berlanger had been unavailable for comment. The newspaper described her as being "overcome by grief." Gilbert Collier and she had been very close friends.

Where did they get their information? She called Dossey and warned him that she would not tolerate any of the staff talking to reporters. Dossey confessed that half a dozen reporters had sat on the steps for hours, but he swore none of the servants had told them a thing.

But the next day she had to face the police. It was either an interview in her own parlor or a trip to the police station, a lieutenant said. He was firm and stated he would bring a wagon and see that she was placed aboard.

She consented to see him, a Lieutenant Combs; he was very polite and properly dressed, a man of perhaps forty, with hard, brown eyes and lank, black hair. He sat on the edge of the chair she indicated and opened a small notebook. He wrote down her answers. Yes, she and Senator Collier had been friends since her recent trip to Washington. He had come to St. Louis to visit, for only a few days, before going on to his home in Alabama. No, they were nothing more than friends, but his death had been a terrible blow to her; it was so unexpected.

Combs said, "There is persistent talk, Mrs. Berlanger, that you and the senator were considering marriage."

Lily rose, face convulsed. "I did not know the police were interested in gossip. If that is all, sir, I will have my man show you out."

"Please, Mrs. Berlanger, I have to get at the truth."

"The truth is that he is dead." Her tone was acid. "I suppose you know that much?"

"It is necessary to try every avenue when we have so

315

few clues. I'm sure you want the murderer brought to justice as much as we do."

Lily managed to suppress her anger. "Yes, of course. But I think it unnecessary to go about it in a detestable manner."

"I apologize, Mrs. Berlanger. Have you any idea why he was shot?"

She resumed her seat reluctantly. "No, of course not. If I had, I would have notified the police instantly."

"The senator never spoke to you of enemies?"

"Never. I believe he had none."

"Not even political ones?"

She shrugged, fixing the policeman with a cold eye. "It was well known that he was leaving national politics. He had announced that he would not run again for his seat in the Senate. Why should a political adversary kill him?"

"Revenge, perhaps, for something in the past—"

"Are you suggesting that someone would follow him west to St. Louis for that purpose? It sounds idiotic."

Lieutenant Combs' face flushed, but he was dogged. "What was his attitude, his manner, the evening he was shot?"

"Happy—alive." Tears came to her eyes, and she dabbed at them almost with annoyance and glared as if daring Combs to return to his early questions.

He ignored the tears. "Did he speak to anyone in your presence—or greet anyone that you didn't know?"

"No. No one."

"His manner was untroubled?"

"Completely."

"No signs of brooding, for instance?"

"No, of course not!" She rose again. "Is all this

necessary, Lieutenant? I know nothing at all to tell you."

He sighed. "Very well, thank you, Mrs. Berlanger, for your help. When we learn anything further, you will be notified." He bowed and walked to the door and let himself out.

At the office she sent for Howard Paddock, but he was unavailable, a clerk told her. The clerk did not know where he was. She sent a messenger to his home, but the man returned empty-handed. His household staff had not seen him either.

She did not believe that for an instant, and it set her to thinking. Why was he avoiding her? Had he anything at all to do with Roy's death? Would he gain anything by it? She worried the thought like a terrier with a bone.

Viktor Kory fled through the ranks of dark carriages and shuffling teams. He gained the wooden fence and slid over it in one bound. In the deep shadow he halted and listened. The outcry in the yard gained volume with each passing moment. There were shouts and orders—but all were distant. No one came his way; he had accomplished his mission; he was now away free, and much richer—or would be, as soon as he picked up his money from Paddock.

He paused to reload the Starr pistol and thrust it into his belt. Then he set out on foot for Paddock's house. He had come in a rented rig, but he dared not even try to find one now. He turned his overcoat collar up, to conceal the formal dress, and walked quickly. It took half an hour to get to the house.

When he arrived, Paddock was not home. He was at the rivermen's ball, the housekeeper told him. Everyone was there.

"He'll be back soon," Kory told her. "Let me wait inside for him." She was reluctant, but finally opened the door when he pressed her.

He paced the parlor, smoking cheroots, one after the other, and was eager to get away. He had no real fear that the police would track him down; what clues could they possibly have? But the death of a well-known steamboat man like Jeffries would make a splash. The police would run around in circles making noise; they'd probably haul in dozens of suspects for questioning, just to put on a show of industriousness. He wanted to be far out of reach.

Paddock did not arrive for another hour.

When he came in, he glared at Kory and sent the servants to bed. Kory was surprised that he was apparently in a foul temper; he watched Paddock lock the doors to insure their privacy. What the hell was the matter with him?

"You—for God's sake!" Paddock almost yelled. "You've caused a stink, you have!"

"What d'you mean? I did what I was supposed—"

"You did no such thing!" Paddock's rage boiled over. "You shot the wrong goddamn man! You shot a United States senator!"

Kory was astounded. He stood, mouth agape, staring at the other. "I—I shot Jeffries!"

Paddock dropped into a chair and mopped his face. He closed his eyes, then glared at Kory. "You shot Sen. Gilbert Collier. There will be hell to pay tomorrow, I promise you. If I were you I'd get my worthless carcass out of the state—out of the damned country!"

"I don't believe it!"

"Go on," Paddock said, waving his hand toward the door. "Get out—get away as fast as you can—and keep your mouth shut."

"But—I know who I shot!"

Paddock shook his head. "How could you? And do what you did?"

"But the man turned when I called his name!"

"He turned?" Paddock sighed wearily. "Of course he turned. Anyone would turn, hearing someone call out behind him in the dark."

"But I saw him!"

"You *wanted* to see him! Collier and Jeffries are about of a size; both wore the same kind of clothes. You *wanted* to see Jeffries, and you did. You killed the wrong man, Kory." He waved toward the door. "Get out. Get out as fast as you can."

"But the money!"

Paddock grunted. "Money for what? You've been given a thousand dollars. Be happy you got that."

Kory drew the Starr. "You not going to cheat me—"

"Don't be a fool!" Paddock glowered at the revolver. "Put that thing away. Do you think I'm an idiot? This is all down in black and white—in an envelope in my lawyer's safe. Your name, description, and so on. It'll be burned when you're safely away." He pointed his finger. "I'll tell my friends I didn't see you. Now get away tonight."

Kory stared at him. No thousand dollars. He put the pistol in his belt and moved toward the door. He'd shot the wrong man? How was it possible? And yet Paddock wouldn't dare tell him so if it were a lie. A United States senator? He opened the door and went out into the cold night. Everything had suddenly turned to ashes. Was

Paddock right, that he'd seen what he wanted to see? A man who looked like Jeffries and answered to his name? He swore and started walking fast along the street.

CHAPTER THIRTY

They halted a few miles from the city at Julia's request. She couldn't go into town riding astride the sorrel, she said; people would snicker at her. It might be all right for a young girl.

Dutch said, "You ain't got a sidesaddle. How you going to stay on?"

"I'll stay on." She pulled her leg over with a swirl of skirts and tightened her knee about the pommel. "I'll stay on as long as we walk the horses."

Dutch grunted, watching her closely. To him women riding sidesaddle were ridiculous. God never intended a woman to sit on a horse like that. But then a lot of things about women were over his head—their clothes, for instance. But Julia did look fine in her new dress. He'd insisted she throw the old one away and start fresh. She had even bought a scarf for her head, and it looked rather stylish, he thought.

The first thing to do was to find a place to stay. He had never been in St. Louis before, but he knew there were plenty of hotels; it was a center of travel, after all. People came and went all the time. But he didn't care much for hotel living. It was bare and lifeless, providing only hard necessities, and a woman like Julia, he thought, would find it confining.

On the other hand, he couldn't take her to a boarding-house and register as man and wife, sleep together in the same room, and all. It would sit hard with her. She might not complain, because he'd be paying the bills, but it would hurt her inside.

They'd have to go to a boarding house as friends, and get separate accommodations. It would cost more, but there was no avoiding it. If she'd been any other woman, it wouldn't make a difference, but in Julia's case, it had to be done. He wanted her to think well of him, and he wondered how he could tell her the things he was thinking. He was not good at that.

The first houses to appear were little more than shacks, sheds, and tents, and off to the left were people camping near the river; they had built lean-tos and looked cosy. The road widened after a bit and took on the semblance of a street, and the houses along it got better. Dutch had read somewhere that St. Louis comprised ten or fifteen thousand souls, a lot of people congregated in one place.

He told her what he was thinking, that they'd have to go to a boardinghouse, and she only nodded. He could see she hadn't thought it through, but after a moment she looked at him thoughtfully and he wondered what she would say. But she did not speak. He recalled what she had said—that she owed him a great deal. She was willing to repay him then.

But that would be taking advantage of her, and he didn't want that kind of a beginning. According to his morals, he was an honorable man.

He stopped and bought a newspaper, the *Democrat*, at a grocery store and looked through it for ads. There were dozens, including a column of boardinghouse ads, all of which sounded fine. Most seemed to be run by women, and he selected Mrs. Stokes' house, because it sounded average.

The house was on Dicker Street, and Mrs. Stokes was a tall, gray-haired woman with wise eyes and veined hands. She was surprised to hear that they were not married, but only traveling together.

"Because we has to," Dutch said. "Give us separate rooms." He knew Julia was also surprised at his words, for a different reason.

He met Mrs. Stokes' terms, put the horses in the stable behind the house, and took his gear to the small room assigned him. It was on the second floor and contained a thin carpet, a bed, a washstand, and two chairs with tapestried bottoms and rung backs.

As he sat down to smoke a cigar, he began to think about Howard Paddock. What would it take to find him?

The newspaper he'd bought was full of the rivermen's fraternal ball and the murder that had taken place outside its door. A United States senator had been shot by a person or persons unknown, and a state-wide search was underway. Dutch smiled at the state-wide; it was a favorite term of lawmen, because it implied hundreds of diligent men leaving no stones unturned when, in fact, it usually involved no more than a few telegrams.

But his attention was riveted by mention of Lily Berlanger's name. The dead senator had escorted her to the ball!

It was another death close to Lily. Had she anything to do with it? He read the entire paper from front to back. The murder had taken place days ago, and it was old news and not very detailed, because it had all been said before. No one had been arrested; in fact the police had no clues.

Lily Berlanger, when questioned, could shed no light at all on the murder and stated the senator had no enemies.

Old Jacob Berlanger hadn't had any enemies, either.

Dutch grunted and stared through the grimy pane of the window, wondering how Lily would profit by this death. He wished he'd known about the annual ball, because Howard Paddock had undoubtedly attended. He might have accosted Paddock in the parking area and . . . He looked at the paper again. That was exactly how the senator had died. Someone had accosted him in the carriage parking area.

He'd be willing to be a pretty penny that Lily had had it done.

Logan had told him that Paddock worked for Lily now, so he went to the Berlanger-Bryant offices and asked a few questions. Yes, Mr. Paddock was part of the firm, but no one he asked could tell him anything else. No one was sure what he did.

But a gray-haired Negro man who worked on the loading docks told him that Mr. Paddock kept his carriage under a long shed, as did the other company officers; but he did not know which one it was.

The weather had turned warm; the evenings were cool but had none of the icy edge of the preceding month. When Julia suggested they go for a walk on the first day they were at the boardinghouse, Dutch was glad to go. She took his arm, and they set out, walking in the street, because there were no walkways. He knew she had something on her mind, and he could guess what it was.

She wanted to get a job to support herself.

He asked, "What can you do?" He patted her hand. "I mean b'sides housework?"

"Washing and cleaning is honest work."

324

"Maybe it is, but it's hard, too, and nobody wants to pay much f'it. What else d'you know?"

"Well, before I was married I was a governess."

"What's that?"

"It's like a teacher. I took care of seven- or eight-year-old girls for a time. There was a girl's school near our house, and I worked there for almost a year. I took the girls on outings, for instance."

"Could you do that here?"

"Well—" She was doubtful. "I suppose so."

"Why not?"

"Well, Dutch . . . it was different then. I lived at home and—"

"What you gettin' at?"

She shook her head. "Nothing. Let's just walk."

"Seems t'me that's better than washin' and cleaning. Usin' your head 'stead of your back is—"

"What about *you*, Dutch? Did you find out what you came here for?"

"Not yet."

They walked in silence for a time. She was a proud woman, of course, and probably hated to be in the position she found herself, forced to take charity from him. He knew it was immensely important to her to find work.

There was a solution at the back of his head, but he was afraid to present it to her. If they married—just for convenience—it would make a difference, a legal difference. He wondered how she would feel about it; would she still consider it charity? She might.

He ought to tell her how he felt about her. They had only known each other a short time, but they'd been through some trying moments. She was a damned

325

good woman.

But she was much younger than he. If he told her how he was thinking, she might feel sorry for him. He couldn't stand that.

So he said nothing.

They returned from the walk, each with his own thoughts, and after she went inside, he sat on the porch with a cigar, ignoring the attempts at conversation of several other boarders. He was aware that they glared at him, but he cared nothing for them or how they felt. His thoughts were of Julia. A marriage of convenience would solve everything. Well, it would solve some of the problems, maybe not all of them. The main thing would be to keep them together. He could not let her get away from him. He could not.

The next day he took up a vigil outside the Berlanger-Bryant shipping yard, but he had no luck. If Paddock went in and out, he did not see him. And a nearby shopkeeper, nervous because of the big, rough-looking man hanging about the street, called a policeman, who asked Dutch to keep moving.

Julia went out soon after Dutch and quickly found a job in a hand laundry. She spent the day ironing and returned to the boardinghouse after dark, exhausted, almost too tired to eat.

Dutch was very angry. "I won't have you doin' that! Tomorrow you draw what's comin' to you and quit."

Tired as she was, Julia smiled. "I have to do this, Dutch."

"No, you don't. Long's I got money in my pocket you don't."

As gently as she could, she told him that it was really not his concern if she worked and that it was her intent to

326

pay him back every cent he'd put out for her, but this made him more annoyed.

"I don't give a goddamn about the money! I d'want you workin' like that, and you going to stop it."

He was astonished when she burst into tears.

Clumsily he tried to comfort her and was surprised when she clung to him, still sobbing. She had to do it, she said, she *had* to. But Dutch was adamant. She would not work in that goddamned laundry another day. He would not have her so exhausted that she could hardly lift her head. And for the moment she gave in.

The next morning she felt fresh again; after breakfast she was determined to go back. Dutch said, "I going with you. You draw your pay f'yesterday and that's that. Hear?"

Julia sighed. "Yes, Dutch."

"Then come along." He walked with her to the laundry and waited outside, smoking a cigar.

In five minutes Julia came out, her face flushed.

He said, "What is it?"

"They won't pay me."

"What! Why not?"

"They said I must work a week or nothing."

Dutch smiled. "Well, ain't that something. They got rules—" He opened the door.

"Dutch! What're you doing?"

He glanced at her and went inside. He was in a narrow, gray hallway that was broken by doors. Julia had come in behind him and he turned. "Which one?"

She pointed silently, biting her lip. The door had black lettering: Gabriel Rothmuller, Mgr. Dutch turned the knob and went in. Two men, seated at desks, looked at him. One was obviously Rothmuller, a big, black-haired

327

man with bushy sideburns and small eyes encased in bags. The other looked like a bookkeeper, slim and sallow.

Rothmuller said, "Who're you?"

Dutch gave him the shadow of a smile. "I come in t'get Julia's wages f'yesterday. I'll take 'em in cash."

"Are you talking about the woman who was just in here?"

"Yes." Dutch leaned on the desk.

"She's got nothing coming. We require our employees to—"

Dutch grabbed the man by the tie and shirtfront and lifted him from the chair as he yelped. "Maybe you did'n hear me."

Rothmuller swung an arm, and it connected on the side of Dutch's face. Instantly Dutch slammed the big man against the wall. Rothmuller's head hit with a loud thwack, and he slid down the wall, mouth hanging slack, eyes glazing. The bookkeeper jumped up, and Dutch moved in front of the door. He pointed to the chair the man had just vacated. The other hurried to sit.

Dutch said, "How much she got coming?"

"Dollar'n a half," the man said, staring at Rothmuller, who was breathing in gasps.

"Get it," Dutch said.

The bookkeeper pulled at a drawer, took out a box, and opened it. Inside were coins and a few bills. He counted out a dollar and a half and pushed the money toward Dutch.

Dutch shook his head. "They's a collectin' fee. 'Nother dollar and a half."

As the bookkeeper counted it out, a man came into the room with a sheaf of papers. He stared at Rothmuller, sitting on the floor. "What the hell—"

The bookkeeper said, "This man hit Gabe!" He slid out of his chair, out of Dutch's reach. "He's in here robbing us!"

The newcomer, a husky young man, dropped the papers on the desk and charged Dutch. Dutch ducked a wild punch and hit the other a solid blow in the midsection. He caught the man and lowered him to the floor. Then he picked up the money, shoved it into his pocket, and moved toward the bookkeeper, who yelled at him to keep away.

Dutch pinned him against the wall and said softly, "I come in here f'what's right, not to rob nobody. You hear that?"

The bookkeeper nodded quickly.

"And if you go callin' the police, I come back and swat you. Hear?"

"Yessir—"

Dutch looked at him hard. "Maybe I swat you anyhow." He raised his big fist, and the bookkeeper's eyes rolled up and his face turned pale. Dutch let him slip to the floor. He stepped over the man and went out to the hall.

Julia was waiting with eyes like saucers. "Are you all right?" She rushed to him, looking him over.

"Course I'm all right." He slid an arm about her, and they went out to the street.

"Did you get the money?"

He nodded. "They seen to do what was right, soon's I explained it to them."

She was astonished. "Rothmuller did?"

"He was the first to agree."

She stopped and faced him. "Did you hit him?"

329

"Naw—I just pushed him a little." He grinned and took her hand. "You got to talk to these folks right is all." He gave her the money.

"But there's three dollars here!"

"Well, that's for the trouble of collectin' it. They seen that too."

She shook her head, not believing him, but she stepped close and laid her cheek against his. "What would I do without you, Dutch?"

He glanced around to see if anyone had noticed. He took her arm and hurried her along the street.

CHAPTER THIRTY-ONE

The death of Roy Collier was a hard blow, and Lily stayed home several days, feeling weary and drawn out. The police did not return, but Dossey told her that newspaper reporters hung about asking questions of anyone who would talk to them. Lily told him to go for the police and have them cleared out.

She read the newspapers diligently, but the police made no arrests and apparently had no hope of making one. It was frustrating.

The *why* of his death was the most frustrating of all. If the motive had not been robbery, then what had it been? Was it possible the culprit had intended robbery and had not had time? But he could have held up Roy without killing him—and more silently.

She sent for Paddock again and was informed he was out of the city. "Where is he?"

Her messenger did not have that information. She shouted at him to go and get it.

When he returned, he said, "No one knows where he is, Miss Lily."

"Someone has to know." She sent him to Paddock's home with instructions to find out. "Or don't come back."

This time he returned to say Mr. Paddock's household

staff believed him to be in Cairo, Illinois. But he had not told anyone why he was going there or who he would see. Lily dismissed the man and threw a pencil across the room.

Paddock did return in a week and was informed as soon as he set foot inside his house that Lily had sent for him every day of that week. He sighed, accepting a drink from Josine; he would have to face her, no way out of it, but at least he had blunted her anger by staying out of her reach.

The next morning he went to her office, with a bland expression and raised brows. She wanted to see him?

Lily controlled her temper. "Sit down, Howard. Yes, I want to talk to you. What do you know about Roy's death?"

"Roy?" he said in surprise. "Who is Roy?"

"I mean Gilbert Collier. Senator Collier."

He shook his head. "Really, Lily, how in the hell—I mean, how in God's name should I know anything about *that?*"

She stared at him. He was the picture of innocence. But he was probably right. He didn't even know Roy.

He said, "Is that all you wanted?"

"No, of course not. I've had not one single report from this man—what's his name?—Kory. What has happened?"

Paddock spread his hands. "I don't know myself, Lily."

"You don't know!" Her voice was on the rise. "I paid him a thousand dollars! What have I got for my money?"

"I wish I could tell you, but I can't. He hasn't reported to me, nor sent me a note—nothing. I was in Cairo inquiring about him and found out nothing. It appears he uses a variety of names—" He looked troubled. "I fear we've been swindled, Lily."

"*We've* been swindled!" She rose, glaring at him. "*I've* been robbed, not you, and by your advice. I was a fool to think you could carry out a—"

"Now wait a minute, Lily. This could happen to anyone. When you deal with crooks you must expect it. And we had to hire his type to do the job you wanted. No one else would, you know."

She sat again, feeling defeated. She glared at him as he fiddled with his watch chain, until he looked away, sniffing. How much of what he told her could she believe? It sounded all right, but wouldn't it be like Paddock to split her thousand dollars with Kory and have no intention of doing the job? Would he stoop to chicanery for five hundred dollars? Maybe he'd never hired Kory at all.

At last she said, "So I'm out the money and the job is not done."

"It's not a pleasant thing to face, no."

"And where is Kory?"

"I don't know. As I said, I've been trying to track him down and have gotten nowhere. None of his friends have seen him. They say he's probably changed his name and gone off somewhere." He spread his hands. "I wouldn't know where to start looking."

"Maybe in New Orleans," she said nastily.

"New Orleans?" His brows climbed. "I've no idea, but it's a large city. Where would I start?" He knew in that instant that she'd found out about his nocturnal doings at St. Luke's Cemetery, and he smiled inwardly. It was bothering her, was it? Good.

But how in hell had she found out?

*   *   *

"James Boller, alias Viktor Kory, never returned to the Nestande Hotel after the rivermen's ball," Clarence Yates said. He sat in Fraser's office with a small notebook. "I think he got out of the city either before the ball or just after it."

Fraser asked, "D'you think he had anything to do with Senator Collier's shooting?"

"That thought has occurred to me of course, and I've been trying to run it down, but so far no luck."

"Why would he shoot Collier?" Logan asked.

"I've talked to the police at length," Yates said. "As you know, I have friends on the force—was one of them once. They have more facilities than I have, and they say there's no evidence to believe it was a political assassination, and the body was not robbed. For one thing, Collier had already announced he would not run for his Senate seat again, and his term was up in months." Yates shrugged. "So why kill him? As far as Kory is concerned, how could he know Collier?"

Logan nodded. "But it's curious that Kory disappeared at the same time. Is it only a coincidence?"

Yates shrugged again. "A fact is a fact. He disappeared the day before the ball and hasn't turned up."

Fraser said, "What other facts do we know? He tried to kill Logan in Chadwick, so we assume he was here in town to finish the job."

Logan brushed the hair alongside his head with a hand. "Is it possible, Clarence, that in the dark of the carriage yard he shot Collier instead of me?"

"Jesus!" Fraser said loudly. "I never thought of that!"

Yates hadn't either, obviously. His eyes widened and he swore. "You're both about the same size—damn it,

334

that *could* be the answer! Remember—I wondered how good a look he got at you in Chadwick!"

"And so," Fraser continued, "having shot the wrong man, he gets out of town fast."

"But finds out the next day that he's shot a senator and not Logan," Yates said. "What does he do then?" He looked from one to the other. "Does he keep going or does he return to finish the job?"

"I wish I knew," Fraser said, staring at Logan. "But I've got an idea for you. Go on a vacation. *You* get out of town."

"It's just a theory," Logan said. "It may be dead wrong."

"It's a hell of a good theory," Yates closed his notebook. "It fits all the known facts. I'm inclined to accept it." He shook his head. "The poor bastard, in the right place at the wrong time."

Fraser grinned. "He was with Lily Berlanger too. I wonder if she knows the man she employed to shoot Logan, shot Collier?"

"Maybe that's why he got out of town fast," Yates said. "Does anyone mind if I share this theory with the police?"

"Why?" Fraser said.

"I can't see that it'll hurt Logan, and it'll keep my stock up with them. Got to keep my fences repaired."

"Go ahead," Logan said. He went out to have lunch with Doris.

She had an office of her own, a smallish cubbyhole, but Fraser had promised her a larger one soon. They had food sent up from a restaurant, and he told her his theory concerning Senator Collier.

She nodded in surprise. "I think you're probably right.

335

There's no other plausible explanation, is there?"

"I haven't heard one."

"But it isn't over yet, is it?"

"Yates thinks Kory has left town."

"But he doesn't *know* it. How could he?"

"Experience, I suppose. No, he doesn't know it."

She sighed. "So we go on as we have been, living with this hanging over us."

"Kenneth wants us to go on a vacation."

She sighed again and patted his hand. "That's only putting it off. When we get back—"

"*If* we go." He smiled. "I'm not eager to be chased out of town. I'm for staying and facing whatever has to be faced. That's the only way to end it."

Doris curled her fingers around his. "I pray you've chased him out of town for good."

He was silent, staring at her.

She said, "What're you thinking about?"

"Lily," he said. "No one's chased Lily anywhere."

Lily paced the office after Howard Paddock had gone. His explanations seemed reasonable and plausible, but certainly he'd known what she would demand of him and had been prepared for it. That he would lie about Kory did not make sense; certainly he wanted Logan Jeffries out of the way nearly as much as she did. There was an old grudge to settle—he'd told her so several times. So, he did not lie. Kory *had* disappeared. Perhaps he'd decided to take half the money and forget the rest. As Paddock had said, he was a criminal, after all.

She called for her carriage and left the office early, feeling restless. All her dreams of being with Roy on a glorious vacation were gone up in smoke. It was doubly hard to bear, because it had been such a short time ago that Paige had been taken. The Almighty was toying with her for some obscure purpose of His own . . . If there was an Almighty.

Dossey and the household staff tiptoed around her. Cook had bought some brook trout in town and poached them in butter for her supper; then he served her strawberries and brandy. But after supper she was restless again and paced the parlor, wondering why a man would run from a thousand dollars. No one could be *that* difficult to kill! The man must be erratic.

She thought of ordering her carriage and driving into the city, but instead she sat in the study before the fire and drank more brandy. Howard Paddock had failed her miserably. And not only that, he was plotting against her. How in the world had he stumbled onto Jacques's grave in New Orleans? She had put him into a small, rundown, out-of-the-way cemetery where no one but indigents ever went. If Paddock could ferret out Jacques, why couldn't he find Kory?

In the morning, she read the newspapers, as usual, at her office desk over coffee. And was astonished to read that the police had a new theory concerning the death of Sen. Gilbert Collier! They thought it possible that the killer had shot the wrong man!

Lily stared at the paper, anger rising inside her. Had Kory killed Roy, thinking him to be Jeffries?

She screamed for Paddock.

A clerk ran to get him, and when Paddock appeared he came into the room hesitantly, frowning at her. "What is it, Lily?"

"Shut the door."

He closed it and approached her. She shook the

337

newspaper at him. "Have you read this?"

"No. What's the matter?"

"The police say that Senator Collier was probably shot by mistake. So Viktor Kory *did* shoot him!"

"I can't believe it!" He took the paper from her, scanning it hurriedly. Lily was terribly agitated, flushed and angry—more so than he'd ever seen her. He found the item and read it, cursing inwardly.

"It's only a guess, Lily."

She shouted. "But it's the truth, isn't it!"

"How do I know that?"

"I think you know! I think you know a great deal more than you've told me." She threw the newspaper at him. "The police say it's the only theory that fits the facts. And it does, doesn't it, Howard? Roy Collier was about Jeffries' size—and your man Kory made a mistake. Admit it!"

He hesitated, backing away. "Of course not—I don't know a damned thing about it." He rubbed his nose, glaring at her.

"So, in effect, you killed him!"

"That's ridiculous!"

"When was the last time you saw Kory?"

"I—I don't remember—a month ago."

She screamed at him, "Have you ever told me the truth, Howard? You take my money—you lie to me— you work behind my back—"

"Lily, be reasonable!"

She sat suddenly, hair streaming over her face, and tugged open a drawer. Paddock saw the pistol as she yanked it out and ran for the door. The first bullet smashed the panel over his head. The second rapped into the wall, as he somehow got the door open and scuttled out. Two more bullets cracked past him as he fled down the hall and down the steps to the street.

He halted at the foot of the steps, sweating and cursing. Jesus! She'd tried to kill him! His hands were shaking. He mopped his face with a handkerchief, listening to the hubbub from the top of the stairs. Voices. People wondering about the shots and milling about. He put the handkerchief away and walked along the street. He had to get away from her, that was sure. Lily was a killer, and, given time, she'd shoot him dead.

He went around the block to the alley and ordered his carriage readied. Lighting a cigar with shaking fingers, he sat in it while they hitched up the team. Part of her rage had to do with Jacques Lempereau, he was sure. How she knew that he'd dug up the body was a mystery, but she knew. It was making her unstable.

The smartest thing he could do would be to stay as far away from her as he could. God only knew what she'd do next!

CHAPTER THIRTY-TWO

She had missed him. Swearing, she threw the pistol into the drawer and went around the desk to slam the door. In a moment someone rapped on it, and she shouted, "What d'you want?"

Udell Winter put his head in. "Are you all right, Lily? What happened?"

"Come in, Udell." She saw faces in the hall. "Get back to work—all of you!" He closed the door, motioning them away.

He stared at the bullet holes. "What happened, Lily?"

"It was an argument." She sat behind the desk. "What am I going to do about Howard?"

"An argument?"

"Yes, an argument. That man has never told me the truth. I should never have taken him into the company. He is a liar and probably a thief—"

"Buy him out."

"I doubt if he'd sell. I wouldn't."

"Then send him away."

She stared at him and nodded. "Yes, I suppose so. I can't stand the sight of him. Transfer him somewhere—don't care—as far away as you can. And if he objects—send him to me."

Udell risked a smile. "I doubt if he'd come."

"Get rid of him."

"What shall I say about the shooting?"

She slumped in the chair and glowered over his head at the neat round holes. "I don't care—but see that they shut up about it. I don't want the police here."

"All right."

"Howard threatened me, you know. The things he said! I was afraid for my life!"

Udell stared. "Howard threatened you?"

"He accused me of terrible things—and he just flared up! If I hadn't had the pistol handy, I don't know what would have happened. I wanted to frighten him off, that's all."

"I see—"

"I want you to tell me the instant he comes back into the building."

"Yes, Lily."

She waved her hand toward the door. "Have that fixed after I leave tonight."

"Yes, I'll send for a man."

She nodded.

When he had left she took the pistol out and reloaded it slowly. How bleak the future looked! But of course, her mood was angry now, as black thoughts roiled in her head. Paddock had been astounded when she had pulled the gun from the drawer! He had gone white, stumbled to the door, and fled in abject fear. Lily laughed aloud, recalling his fright.

But damn it, she'd been too angry to aim straight. She'd lost a marvelous chance, just when he'd shouted and threatened her—no one could blame her for protecting herself.

But maybe it was for the best. The police would be so

damned difficult; they asked so many questions, poking and snooping. But God, if she'd killed Howard, all her problems would be solved, and he'd never be able to refute a word—and Jacques's grave would be safe. She ought to practice with the gun. Tony Burke would show her.

One thing was certain. Now Paddock was an open enemy, no longer one skulking behind gravestones. She rose and crossed the room to the cabinet and poured out half a glass of cognac. Her hand was steady—she held it out and found that her fingers scarcely trembled. She sipped the brandy and frowned at herself in the dressing mirror beside the armoire. The lines were deeper about her eyes and at the corners of her mouth; there was a strand of gray here and there in her dark hair; and there were obvious wrinkles in her forehead. How many were put there by Howard Paddock?

She returned to the desk, feeling cold. She could hear a distant chatter from the offices; probably everyone was gossiping about what had happened, like a swarm of buzzing insects. Couldn't Udell control them? She started to rise, then dropped back again. Let them get it out of their systems, the fools. It was probably the most exciting thing that had happened to any of them, and they *had* to talk. They had each other to chatter to—and she had no one.

Everyone she cared about was gone.

It was lonely; there was no one to think about, nothing to look forward to. Her world had suddenly become colorless. Even though Paige had been far off, in New Orleans, she'd known he was there, and she had been able to go to him. And he had written often—she'd saved every one of his letters. Maybe she should burn hem. . . . But she knew she would not.

Then Roy had come into her life and made her feel like a woman again, and for a time it had been wonderful.

God, how she needed a change!

At the window she stared at the river, a huge, complacent, brown highway leading south. It waited for her, ready to take her away when she asked. Long ago, when she'd lived with Jacob in Chadwick, she had many times come to the point when she could not stand another day! Not another hour! She'd packed in a rush and fled to the river.

Jacob had never understood, had probably been incapable of understanding, because the quiet little town determined his way of life. He had been amazed when she'd told him the first time that she was going to Memphis. "What in the world for?"

But Jacob must have had an inkling; he had kept silent and never once asked embarrassing questions. But his eyes . . . Lily sighed, thinking of his silent protestations, his silent accusations. He must have known that there was only a shadow of business to transact in Memphis, that it was an excuse. Jacob hadn't wanted to lose her. If he'd screamed, she might not have come back.

Mr. Rector's club was in Memphis.

She'd discovered it by talking to certain persons on her several steamboat trips to New Orleans. Rector's was a place where a girl could meet men discreetly, no last names and no ties. Only the present.

She could not remember all the names they gave, it was probably a different one each time. And they were content with what she told them. Could she do it again? She went back to the mirror and studied herself, touching the lines. She wasn't too old, too unattractive.

Many of the women at Rector's had been much older.

But then she'd been a nobody, a woman from nowhere, come to town with money to spend, and she'd disappeared as she'd arrived.

But now she was Lily Berlanger. Her pictures had been widely circulated in periodicals and newspapers, and some of the drawings were quite good—recognizable. Thousands would know her at sight, and she made news wherever she went. Her agent at Memphis would call the press and announce her presence. No, he damned well would not! Not if he wanted to keep his job. She'd travel incognito.

What had happened to Lucien? Of course, it was not his right name, but he'd been European; his accent had not been faked. He had been a man like Paige, tall and broad shouldered, with a twinkle in his dark eye; he'd teased her as Paige did, deftly peeled off her clothes as Paige did, and gathered her up in strong arms, naked and wonderfully wild. . . .

Could she do it again?

Why not? She desperately needed a change and all it entailed. But did she dare go to Memphis alone? She would take Tony Burke along, of course, but not when she went to Rector's. Was it possible for her to slip outside her cocoon of guards and be an ordinary woman again, just for a night? Was there still time?

Finishing the cognac, she looked at the bottle and sighed as she put it away. Everything had changed since those distant days. Now she was rich and powerful, but her life was not exactly as she had envisioned it; it was lonelier, and she had not foreseen that a man like Howard Paddock would undermine her like a slimy mole, digging into moldering graves for evidence to use against her.

And it seemed that every countermove she considered would put her into someone else's hands. Maybe someone as ruthless and greedy as Paddock. And yet she *had* to counter him.

If Paddock had opened Jacques's grave to examine the body, she might act quickly and have the casket moved to another burial spot—or even have another body put in Jacques's place. Lily smiled. That would be the most damaging to Howard—if he ever got a court order to exhume Jacques's body. There would be no trace of poison, and Howard's case would fall apart. It would also banish all the gossip about how poor Jacques had died.

But it would mean someone had to know.

The someone would probably have to be Haig Kelley, and she'd never met him, never even seen him. Udell had hired him as the best prospect from a list of applicants, and Udell had never met him, either. She would be placing herself into the hands of a stranger, which was an invitation to blackmail. He might easily turn out to be worse than Paddock.

No, that was unlikely. No one was as greedy as Howard, except perhaps the nearest politician. Even Sam had been greedy.

There were times when she regretted being a woman. She had to depend on men for so many things she might do herself . . . And men were difficult and changeable and all the things that Howard was.

She looked at the empty glass in her hand and decided she needed another sip. Every move she made for protection seemed to divide and divide again, extending her culpability or guilt in a dozen directions. Someone would have to go to New Orleans either to tell Kelley what to do or to do it himself. He'd need helpers; he'd

345

have to bribe people or somehow hush mouths. Could such a thing be done in absolute secrecy? Probably not—Howard had tried it and failed, because she'd found him out. Who would find her out?

She poured the cognac. *How many people knew now?* Udell, of course, or he strongly suspected, and Howard knew. How many had he employed to dig up the grave and have the body examined? Four? Maybe five?

Too many already.

Sighing, she drank off the brandy in a single gulp, wincing as the fiery liquor burned her throat. There were days when everything seemed to close in on her. But that was a foolish way to think, wasn't it? All in her own mind. She was still powerful, still had enough money to buy whomever she chose, to hire and fire and change lives. She went again to the mirror. She *was* a beautiful woman; anyone could see it, despite the few little lines.

She would send Haig Kelley a letter with money enclosed. She'd order him to move the body in secret, using as few people as possible, cover his tracks completely, and report back to her. She'd tell him only that it was a matter of business, out of the ordinary to be sure, but business. It involved a lawsuit. He would believe that; Kelley was an intelligent man and would know that sometimes business took curious turns. If he asked for any other explanation, she would stick to the story.

But what would Kelley do if Howard Paddock raised a stink that got to the newspapers? If Howard accused her publicly and the court exhumed the grave of Jacques Lempereau, what then? Would Kelley keep his mouth shut, or would he come to her for more money?

If he did, she'd give it to him. It was the easiest way

It made her feel better.

But what about Howard? Had he noticed her angry reference to New Orleans when they'd talked. And if so, had he put two and two together?

More important, would he think to move the body himself for safekeeping?

Probably not. New Orleans was a long way off, after all. And though he might be aware that she knew he'd been there, he probably would not suspect how *much* she knew.

She put the bottle away and went to the window. That was what she'd do, write to Kelley and order the thing done. But she'd sleep on it first—see how she felt in the morning. It might be a good idea to ask Udell for Kelley's correspondence to get an iea of what kind of man he was.

She turned from the window with a smile.

With the next morning's mail she got a rude shock, a letter from the chief clerk for Lenz and Jarnoux. The very thing she feared had happened! The clerk wrote asking her to fill out a stupid form! A routine examination, he said, had failed to turn it up. Would she please comply?

Lily swore aloud and pounded the desk in frustration. t was a form that testified that monies owed to Andrea ad been paid to her.

Jarnoux had long ago assured her that all papers elating to her, to Jacob, and to Andrea were in a onfidential file and would at no time be disturbed by ffice personnel. And yet here was a letter.

Her first inclination was to fire off a telegram, ordering he file closed and the officious clerk dismissed.

But wouldn't that draw unwanted attention to the file? It might be best to do as she was asked—then take the first boat south and beard Jarnoux in his office to demand that the file be turned over to her. She had seen Jarnoux once before, a long time ago, and he had refused the same request. But this time she would couch it in very certain terms, and stating the obvious fact that Lenz and Jarnoux could not guarantee confidentiality. . . .

She called for a clerk and had him make steamboat reservations at once. He informed her quickly that *Shannon* was leaving for New Orleans in the morning. Would that do? It would. She ordered accommodations for herself and for Tony Burke, who would go along as bodyguard.

When the clerk had gone, she leaned back, closing her eyes. If she had to go to Memphis, might it not be easy to go on to New Orleans to see Kelley herself?

Or would that matter be handled better by letter? Well, she did not have to make up her mind this moment. She'd decide as she went downriver on *Shannon*. There had been a change recently, and Bush was now captain of *Shannon*, was he not? She looked up the list. Yes, Thornton Bush. She wondered what he looked like.

She informed Udell of her decision to go downriver, conferred for an hour with him and several others, then called for her carriage.

Wasn't it interesting that Lenz and Jarnoux were in Memphis? She had been thinking of that pleasant city only yesterday, and of the good times she'd had there. Maybe, when her business was finished. . . .

She smoked a cigar in the carriage on the way home the first time she'd done that. Thinking about good times in Memphis caused a certain excitement inside her. It had been a long time since she'd wholly enjoyed herself for any prolonged period—not really since she'd gone away with Paige, and that had been eons ago.

God, how she missed Paige!

She was absolutely alone in the world. Both parents were dead, and she had no other relatives that she knew about; there might be some cousins, but they were strangers whose names she didn't even know. Once she'd heard her mother speak of distant cousins but she'd never seen them, and since they'd never come to her for money, they probably weren't aware of the relationship. So she was alone, and she had no will.

It was the first time she'd thought about a will for herself. Whom should she leave her property to? It was a devastating thought. She must discuss it with a lawyer. Logan Jeffries must never get it.

When the carriage stopped in the drive, she got out and went up the steps deep in thought, barely nodding to Dossey as he opened the door. It was not a good thing to be alone, but as she considered the people around her, her tiny circle of friends—who were they really?—there was no one. God, the closest person to her in all the world was Udell Winter!

She dropped onto a chair in the den and stared at the dancing flames in the fireplace. Dossey coughed, could he bring her something? She asked for brandy, and he crossed to the sideboard and brought back a bottle and a glass, filled the glass, and went out silently.

It was incredible that Udell should be her sole friend—and yet he was not really a friend, because she didn't know him except at the office. She didn't know a single one of his likes or dislikes; for too many years he'd been just a shadow, a voice, someone to handle the various tasks that plagued her. Undoubtedly he had long ago guessed what she'd done to Andrea, but had never said a

349

word. No, he was not really a friend; he was just the closest person to her.

When she thought about it, she had to conclude that she had no real friends.

Everyone she knew—everyone who came close to her—wanted something. Except Paige and Roy. Howard Paddock had been a friend, and even a lover, for a short time. But he wanted more from her than anyone else. Udell, at least, had never really asked for anything; he accepted what she gave him, of course, but no one could blame him for that.

Why was it that she had no friends? Probably because she was the head of a huge shipping company whom people were reluctant to approach. There were undoubtedly thousands who would happily bring her into their inner circles if she would go. For a long time she had followed a policy of refusing invitations to dinners and large gatherings, mostly because they bored her. It might be wise to change that. For her own sake, she needed a social life—Paige had said so many times. She thought about the wonderful intimate evenings they'd spent together, dining in coffeehouses, driving about the city, lying in each other's arms. . . .

Would she ever find anyone else like Paige?

Not unless she made an effort. Well, in the morning she would go downriver to Memphis; then, when her business was concluded, she'd try to slip again into another skin—what was the name she'd used so many years ago?—Greta! She'd called herself Greta, a name from a storybook. She'd become Greta again, just for a night or two.

It was an exciting thought. She poured more brandy and sipped it languidly, staring into the flames. How different her life had become—how different from her early visions of what it would be! Reality was always harsher than dreams, in sharper focus, bringing more pain with it. Once she'd dreamed of the future, of herself at the center of a vast, admiring audience, moving grandly among people and riding out in an open carriage under a canopy of blue as in a parade—fleeting images that betokened power and respect. But she had not become an empress; she had power, but she was not loved for it, something she did not always understand. But, of course, many were ungrateful and many harbored resentments, because she was something they were not. She knew those things, could plainly see the feelings of those around her on their faces. Only Udell masked his distaste from her—he knew about Andrea and said nothing, for instance. Other emotions he could not conceal.

But she must accept what she could not change.

What should she do about Howard Paddock? For the immediate future she would write to Kelley in New Orleans.

She must do what she had to do.

CHAPTER THIRTY-THREE

Two policemen came to the house looking for Dutch. He was sitting along on the porch, smoking a cigar, when they came along the street examining the numbers. He watched them decide this was the house, open the gate, and approach, staring hard at him. Dutch nodded politely.

He knew instantly they were after him, but he also knew they'd never seen him before and had only a description.

They tramped up the steps and one rapped importantly on the door. The other frowned at Dutch. "What's your name?"

"John Thomas Larch." So Rothmuller had signed a complaint over a dollar and a half. He ought to go back and throw the man against the wall again.

Mrs. Stokes came to the door. "Yes?" She did not seem surprised to see uniformed policemen; apparently she had dealt with them before, and not always to her advantage to judge by her manner.

The larger policeman said, "We looking for a Mr. Brown."

Mrs. Stokes glanced beyond them to Dutch. "You want Mrs. Brown or Mr. Brown?"

"I told you. *Mr.* Brown."

Stokes closed the door part way, and the policeman shoved his foot in. She said, "There ain't any Mr. Brown here. I got nobody named Mr. Brown."

The two policemen looked at each other. One said, "You got a Mrs. Brown?"

Mrs. Stokes nodded.

"She ain't married?"

"I dunno. But she lives by herself." Mrs. Stokes glowered at the man with his foot in the door. "What you want him for?"

"It's an assault charge. You're positive there ain't no Mr. Brown? This's the right house."

"Course I'm positive, it's my house ain't it? You want to see m'book?"

The policemen muttered between themselves and decided they had best look at it; they went inside.

Dutch did not stir. They were back in five minutes, grumbling. They went down the steps without a glance at Dutch and walked away.

Mrs. Stokes came out to the porch. "What they want you for?"

"Collectin' a little pay, that's all." Dutch rose. "Guess we going to move out."

"Yes, maybe you better. They be back."

Dutch went upstairs and knocked on Julia's door, telling her what had occurred. "Dutch! Now I've gotten you in trouble!"

He chuckled. "Hellsfire, I been in trouble all m'life. This ain't no bother. Get your things t'gether. We going to move to another place is all."

Julia had told Rothmuller where she lived. "But I told him I was a widow," she said. "Maybe he didn't believe me."

353

"No, he didn't." Dutch gathered up his possessions, paid Mrs. Stokes, and went out back to the stable. He was saddling the horses when Julia appeared. Mrs. Stokes had detailed what had happened, and she was frightened that Dutch would be arrested and put into jail.

"They got to catch me first," Dutch said reassuringly. He helped her up on the sorrel's back and mounted the gray. They walked the horses to the street, taking the direction leading away from the policemen.

In less than an hour they were signed in at Mrs. Rose Swann's boardinghouse, as Mrs. Smithers and Mr. Miller. They had come across the river that day, Dutch told Mrs. Swann, having traveled from Holbrook, a town in Illinois. They would probably stay a few days and go on to Kansas City either together or separately. Mrs. Swann was hugely uninterested in the tale.

Mrs. Swann's house rules did not allow the guests to visit one another in the rooms; she did not allow smoking in the house in any room, including the parlor—if guests wished to smoke, they could go outside. She also did not allow spirits, snuff, or chewing tobacco. But rules were nothing to Dutch. He went at once to Julia's room, and they talked quietly, away from the door.

He did not know how long it would take for him to conclude his business, but he asked her not to look for household employment, a request to which she objected. "I have to work, Dutch."

"It ain't the work I care about, it's the kind of work."

She reached for him, to touch him gently. "You're better to me than anyone ever was, but—"

"No buts. It'll be like that laundry all over again. Coppers going to be chasin' me all over the country."

"Maybe I can get a job teaching."

"That's better."

He went out and bought a newspaper, and they studied the ads together. There were two ads for teachers, and Julia carefully cut them both out.

In the morning she went to answer them, and Dutch went back to the Berlanger-Bryant building to watch for Paddock. He hung about the shipping yard where the carriages were kept, but Paddock did not appear.

Toward midday a man in a slouch hat and rough clothes sought him out. "You hangin' around lookin' for work?"

Dutch nodded. If he said no, they'd probably ask him to leave.

The man offered him a job, and he accepted quickly. What better way to watch for Paddock? He spent the afternoon loading and unloading wagons with a work crew.

Toward evening, as he was waistdeep in kegs on the back of a wagon, Howard Paddock came out with another man, strode to a chaise that had drawn up, waited for them, and drove off.

Dutch was pleased. At least now he knew Paddock was in town.

Julia was astonished to hear that he'd taken a job, though he explained it was only a matter of convenience. The business he had come to conclude was dragging on. . . . He asked what she had done.

She had gone to answer both ads, and the first wanted a male teacher and the second a teacher of higher mathematics, positions for which she had no qualifications. However, she had been offered a post as assistant to a nursery school teacher and had accepted. She did not yet know what would be required of her, but whatever it was, it would probably be easier than ironing.

Dutch was delighted, and they went out to a small restaurant to celebrate; they ate steak and beef, and later plum pudding, and to Dutch it was like being young again to sit opposite her. It was the first time in more than twenty years that he had gone to a restaurant with a woman, and he was reluctant, when it came time to leave, to go out into the night.

But it was a fine evening, and they did not go back to the boardinghouse immediately; Julia suggested they walk a bit. She held onto his arm and they talked. She wanted to know everything about him, she said, and he told her what he could, leaving out the violence and the midnight journeys. In his story he became an ordinary riverman and then a farmer whose wife had died years ago. If she was curious why an ordinary farmer should have pressing business in St. Louis, she did not ask, for which he was thankful, since he had no ready answer. But at the same time he felt a measure of guilt—for perhaps the first time in his life—that he was deceiving someone.

One day, if it became possible, he would gradually tell her the truth; it had to be gradually, lest she pack up and run off in horror at the enormity of his crimes.

He was thinking more and more of taking her back to Chadwick. He would remodel the house, paint it, and add another room—even fix the floor and perhaps buy a carpet. The roof was stout, and the general structure was sound. But a hundred other things had to be done, too, such as repairing and whitewashing fences, pruning some of the fruit trees, and weeding the garden. The place would look run-down to her, he was sure, though he had no idea of what she was used to. Probably not the very best, since her husband had not appeared overly prosperous: he'd worn poor and mended clothes, for instance.

But she deserved better. And he was not a poor man, not like many of his neighbors; he could give her better things. There was enough buried in the garden now to last them for a while, and he could easily support them by farming and a bit of hunting. It wouldn't even be necessary to go on another midnight raid for the rest of his life. Lyle Carty was retiring anyway.

She said, "Where is your mind, Dutch? A thousand miles off?"

"What?"

"Here I am, chattering away, and you're not listening to a word."

"What did you say?"

"You see?"

"I was thinkin' about going home t'Chadwick, that's all."

She was silent then, and they walked several minutes without speaking, the sounds of their footsteps loud in the quiet street.

Abruptly he said, "You could come back with me—" He took a breath. He'd said it at last, the thing deeply on his mind. He was a man who'd seldom been afraid of anything in his life, and now he suddenly feared her answer.

Her steps slowed; then she halted and looked at him. She was nearly as tall as he, but much more slender, and her eyes seemed enormous in the night. "Tell me what you mean, Dutch."

He took another breath, muscles tight. He wished for a fight in which he could explode some of the tension inside him. His voice sounded gruff and harsh. "I want to marry you, Julia."

He saw her eyes close, then she seemed to lean forward and was suddenly in his arms. In the next moment he realized she was crying.

"What you doin' that for?"

"I—I don't know, Dutch—I'm sorry. I'm just a silly, foolish woman."

"No, you ain't—" The tension had gone out of him, and a curious joy was taking its place. Was she accepting him? Else why was she in his arms? He said, "What you think, Julia?"

She pushed back and looked at him, eyes brimming. "I'm very happy, Dutch. Of course I'll marry you!"

"Sonofabitch!" Dutch said. "Sonofabitch!"

The next morning, at work on the shipping dock, Dutch watched Howard Paddock arrive, climb out of his carriage, and stride away without a glance around. He noted the rig and where it was parked after the horses were unhitched. Paddock traveled in style, with a matched pair of bays.

In the evening it was no trick at all to follow Paddock across town to his home.

Julia was his good luck charm; everything was suddenly falling into place. Paddock had evaded him for a long time, but no more. Unless a miracle intervened, this night would see the job finished.

He sat with Julia only a short time, then she had to prepare for the next day's work. She had only one dress, and it must be sponged and ironed, with an iron borrowed from Mrs. Swann; her hair must be put up.

Dutch went to his room, took off his boots, and lay

down on the bed fully clothed. He dozed off, waiting for midnight, and when it came he methodically put the boots on again, examined a pistol and slid it into his belt, shrugged into a heavy coat meant to protect him against the night air, and let himself out.

No one was on the unlighted streets. Used to the dark, he walked with long strides and arrived at Paddock's house in slightly more than half an hour. It, too, was dark.

It was a large, handsome building with a stablehouse in the rear; Dutch went along the side, feeling at windows. When he found one that gave to his touch, he shoved it up and clambered inside. The house smelled of tobacco and food—he was in a dining room, he discovered by opening a door that led to the kitchen.

He padded through the downstairs rooms, then went up the stairway silently. At the top he could hear voices; there was a light under one door, and when he laid his ear against it, he could hear someone giggling. A girl's voice, then Paddock's heavy tones. This must be the bedchamber. Dutch smiled in the gloom. The servants were all outside, above the stablehouse, and Paddock and the girl were alone. The girl was an unexpected obstacle, but she would probably faint when he appeared.

He took several minutes to look into the other rooms on the floor; one was obviously the girl's chamber, for it smelled of powder and perfumes that almost made him sneeze. There was no one in the others.

But on the way back in the dark hall, his foot caught a heavy tripod pedestal, on top of which was a potted plant. In an instant the plant smashed to the floor with a horrendous racket.

Dutch froze as the sound echoed through the house.

There was silence in Paddock's room, then the door suddenly burst open and light flooded out. Paddock, in a loose dressing gown, stood in the doorway, a heavy pistol in his hand. Behind him, Dutch could see the girl, naked as sin, sitting on the bed, chewing her lip.

Paddock saw him instantly, took a hesitant step forward, peering incredulously. "Dutch! Is that you, Dutch?"

They were fifteen feet apart, and the pistol was pointed at him. Dutch said, "It's me." He wondered if he could get the revolver out of his belt before Paddock could fire.

Paddock was wrapped in astonishment. "What the hell you doing here, Dutch?" He looked at the stairs. "How'd you get in?"

Dutch took a step forward. "In a window." He thought about jumping at Paddock full length—but what if Paddock moved back? Then he'd really be at Paddock's mercy.

An awareness then seemed to come over Paddock, and his face changed. He suddenly *knew*. He raised the pistol and fired.

Dutch ducked, scooping up some of the dirt and shards of the broken pot. He flung them at Paddock. The first bullet smashed into the wall behind him, the second rapped into the wall at his side. He saw Paddock twist away from the shower of dirt and pottery and fire again. The bullet missed; Paddock was jerking the trigger in his excitement. He fired twice more as Dutch rushed him, and both bullets went wide. He gave a little cry as the pistol clicked empty.

Dutch's fist hit him in the throat.

The girl screamed as Paddock was hurled across the room and fell in a heap on the carpet. Dutch was on him like a wolf, both fists flailing for a few seconds. Then he stopped and lifted Paddock's head. The man was dead. The fist in the throat had done it. Dutch had seen this before. He let the head drop and looked at the girl. She was still screaming. He got up and slapped her hard, and she collapsed on the bed, not even trying to cover herself.

Dutch kicked the pistol under the bed and went out the door and down the stairs. He felt a little shaken by the fusillade that had greeted him; it was worse now than when it had happened, and he told himself to ignore it. Paddock had been too excited and frightened to shoot straight, but he'd made a lot of noise. Someone was working at the rear door—the servants probably. They'd be all over the house in another minute.

He went to the front and let himself out as voices filled the house—the girl was screaming again.

He hurried along the dark street, glancing over his shoulder to see the lights coming on in Paddock's house. He was glad he hadn't been forced to shoot the man in cold blood. It hadn't occurred to him he might have to face a hail of bullets, but now it was over, and he'd evened the score. And Logan was free of danger from Paddock.

But the girl had heard his name. She'd be able to tell the police that the killer had been a man named Dutch. How many could there be? She might not be able to describe him, in her hysterical state, but surely she'd remember the name. He had to assume she would.

He and Julia had better get out of town immediately. Maybe even tonight.

He made sure he met no one on the return trip, let himself in the front door, and padded upstairs to Julia's room. She was astonished at his knocking and opened the door sleepy-eyed to gape at him.

He said urgently. "Something's happened, Julia. I got to git in a hurry."

"What's happened?"

"There ain't time to tell it now. You want to come?"

She didn't hesitate. "Of course. Let me get dressed—"

The took the road south, out of town. It was pitch-black under the trees, and they had gone no more than a mile when Dutch drew rein. There were lanterns up ahead.

Julia said, "What is it?"

"Prob'ly the police. They sure Johnny-on-the-job t'night."

"What'd you do, Dutch?"

"We better go back and figger a bit." He turned the gray and waited for her. "They watching all the roads. I didn't spose they'd get there so fast." He hurried her along, not giving her a chance to speak. Apparently, Paddock had been important enough for the police to hustle to round up his killer. Maybe Lily Berlanger was shoving them hard, too.

He thought about the levee and gritted his teeth. He damned well didn't want to board a steamboat.

But they had to go back into the city. It would be impossible to stay on horseback with Julia outside of the city, because the first copper who saw them would haul them in. In the city there were people about, especially along the levee. Maybe they could get a boat across the river.

A half-dozen steamboats were loading or unloading, gangs of men sweated by the light of torches, and lanterns swung from wires. Dutch stared at them, wondering which ones were Jeffries-Fraser boats.

If he knew where Logan lived, he and Julia could probably get sanctuary . . . just for the time being. He had to think about her now, more than about himself.

More than about himself.

If he was caught, what would she do? She'd be at the mercy of men like Rothmuller. They'd grind work out of her and turn her out. It was an idea he couldn't stand; he put it out of his mind and frowned at the busy line of steamboats. There were dozens, lined along the levee. Most of them were dark and had watchmen sitting on the decks, probably half asleep. The ones loading were in the bright lights—and in those lights he saw the police. Men came along the levee in twos, staring at everyone.

Dutch pulled back into the shadows, and his eye was caught by the hanging sign: Swenson Hotel. He dismounted and pulled Julia off the sorrel to her surprise. He indicated the hotel. "We'll put up there for the night and take a steamboat in the morning."

She nodded and watched him tie the horses and enter the hotel. Then he took her hand. The man behind the desk was dozing. Dutch reached across the counter and shook him awake. "We need a room."

The man, fat and pink-faced, blinked rapidly and glanced at the clock on the wall. "Sure, mister—"

Dutch said, "We just come across the river on a flattie. You got a stable?"

The clerk gave him a pen and turned a worn register. "They's a stable round the block, Dortmund's. He'll take 'em." He jerked his thumb.

Julia edged close to Dutch and read what he had written: Mr. and Mrs. J. Martin. Dutch took the key from the clerk and handed it to her. "You go on up to the room. I put the horses away."

She very nearly called him Dutch, but managed to smile and nod. Dutch went out quickly, and as she mounted the wooden stairs, she saw the clerk make himself comfortable again. Evidently, late arrivals were commonplace along a busy levee. It relieved her somewhat. She had never before avoided the police.

Dutch was gone nearly an hour, and she was pacing the floor when he returned. She ran to him, "I was so afraid they'd caught you!"

"Naw. I was selling the horses. Took some time."

"Selling the horses!" She hadn't expected it.

"We don't need 'em."

"No—of course not." Dutch was so direct and decisive. She hadn't even thought about them, all her worries were for him.

It was a small room with a single bed, a washstand, and a lamp; there was also a rickety chair, a threadbare carpet on the floor, and flimsy curtains over the one small window, which looked into an air shaft. Dutch glanced at the bed. "You get some sleep. I'll sit up here." He pulled the chair out.

"You'll do no such thing! You need your rest, too."

"It ain't fit—"

"Dutch—we've both been married. Let's not act like children. Come to bed and sleep."

She was right, of course. He undressed quickly, turned the lamp down, and blew it out. The bed was barely wide enough for both of them. It was impossible not to touch her, so he put his arm out and pulled her close. She sighed in contentment and after a bit whispered "Dutch—"

"Yes?"

"I wouldn't want the good Lord to think the wrong

thing, but I'm so happy we met, even if it was in a terrible way."

"Me too. Sometimes things turns out for the best."

"This will."

He held her close and stared into the darkness, hearing the muted sounds from the levee. He was sure of it.

CHAPTER THIRTY-FOUR

The journey south on the *Shannon* was uneventful. Lily stayed in her cabin except for an occasional walk on the promenade, coat collars turned up. Once or twice she went up to the texas and had drinks with Captain Bush and listened to him talk about the river. But it was only to break the monotony; river lore did not fascinate her.

They came into the Memphis levee after dark. Her bags were carried off and put into a carriage for hire, and she drove to the Seadon Hotel with Tony Burke, who sat on the box with the driver. Burke seemed more and more sullen, she thought, but perhaps he hadn't enough to do. In must be boring for an active man to do nothing but follow her about.

At the hotel she engaged a small room for him on another floor and took for herself a suite facing the river.

The reply to her message to Jarnoux seemed to express surprise, but he wrote that he was happy to hear she was in the city and would see her at her convenience. She would go at once.

Lenz and Jarnoux had offices in an ancient, red-brick building that smelled musty when she entered the large and drafty foyer; it was a smell of age and snuff that persisted as she climbed the creaky stairs to the third floor and as Burke flopped on a chair at their foot. A male clerk took her name and disappeared behind a varnished door and returned immediately, followed by a bent, white-haired man.

The man bowed to her. "I am Marvin Jarnoux, Mrs. Berlanger—"

She hadn't recognized him, he was so changed. It had been years since she'd seen him, but he looked decades older. She rose and smiled. "Yes, of course, Mr. Jarnoux. How lovely to see you again."

"Please come this way." He shuffled off through the door and all the way down the hall. "Mr. Lenz is no longer with us, you know. Passed away last year—"

"I'm sorry to hear it."

"In here—have a chair please, Mrs. Berlanger." He closed the door and dropped gratefully into his leather chair behind the desk. It was a large, square office, as stuffy as the rest of the building, windows grimed and brown curtains half pulled. "What can I do for you?"

She pushed the clerk's letter across the desk, and he picked it up carefully and squinted his eyes behind the spectacles to read. She reminded him that the file had been promised confidential handling and told him she'd been unhappy at receiving the letter.

He nodded and smoothed it on the desk, blinking at her over the specs. "This is signed by my chief clerk, Mrs. Berlanger. You may be assured all matters pertaining to you are confidential. This form is exactly as he says—"

"I wish to have all the files in my possession, Mr. Jarnoux."

"But that is impossible, Mrs. Berlanger!"

"I don't agree. They pertain to me, and I can no longer est confident that their contents will remain secret."

"But you can!"

She tapped the letter. "This is proof, Mr. Jarnoux, that I cannot."

Jarnoux hunched over the desk, looking suddenly like a white-haired gopher, she thought, claws extended and mouth fixed in a grimace. "The provisions of Mr. Berlanger's will—"

"I don't care a damn for Jacob's provisions! He's gone and I'm here. Have you more respect for the dead than the living?"

"It isn't a case of either, my dear Mrs. Berlanger. I must respect the law above all."

"The law isn't interested in this! The law has better things to do, Mr. Jarnoux, than push its fingers into my affairs—affairs like this one that are ages old!"

The old man waggled a finger at her. "Where would we all be if those sentiments were carried out universally? I am an officer of the court, madam. I must abide by the law, and I will."

Her voice rose. "Then you refuse me?"

"I'm afraid I must, my dear Mrs.—"

"I will pay you for the files then."

"But don't you see that I—"

Angrily she brought down her fist onto the desk. "No, I don't see! The first thing I know you'll be giving my confidential papers to the press!" She rose, glaring at him. "You have not heard the last of me, Mr. Jarnoux." She stalked out of the room slamming the door behind her.

The clerks stared as she swept out and went down the stairs. Tony Burke looked at her hard and said nothing. He hurried out and opened the carriage door.

There was little she could do to force Jarnoux; he

probably had the law on his side, and being a lawyer and in his own territory he might easily outmaneuver her if she took him to court. It was doubly hard to swallow the pill, because she had been sure a face-to-face meeting would change his mind. He was a little, old-fashioned country bigot with a mind like a turtle's.

She went to the hotel, changed, and had supper alone in the restaurant. Despite her statement that he had not heard the last of her, she knew she must withdraw. To hammer at him would only draw attention to the Berlanger files. Apparently Jarnoux did not even realize that Andrea was dead.

When she bought an evening newspaper and took it upstairs to her suite, she was astounded to read of Howard Paddock's death. He had been killed by an intruder, according to the woman who had been with Paddock at the time. She had not been able to describe the killer, except to say that he was a big man and not young. The intruder had taken nothing from the house, and police speculated that he had not expected to find the woman there and had escaped as quickly as he could when she screamed.

Lily read the item over and over again, hardly able to believe her good fortune! Paddock was out of the way forever! Some blessed thief had done her an enormous good turn. The column said that Paddock had emptied a pistol at the assailant without hitting him—there had been no blood found at the scene. The girl, a Miss Josine Pike, stated that the intruder struck Paddock a single blow and then left the house.

It reminded her of Dutch. It could not be, of course, but the description and the single blow.

It changed her outlook. Now she would not have to

write to Kelley in New Orleans, nor move the body, nor worry about Paddock's shadowy manipulations. She ordered brandy and tipped the waiter extravagantly when he brought it, lit a cigar, sipped the liquor, and suddenly felt much younger.

Now all she had to worry about was Logan Jeffries.

It had been years since she'd enjoyed one of the city's private clubs, and she had no one to introduce her, but money should do the trick. It always did.

In the middle of the evening she donned a cloak and went downstairs and out to the street. There were a half-dozen rigs waiting for fares, and she stepped into the first, asking if Mr. Rector's club was still in existence.

"Oh no, Mum," the driver said. "Not for a year'r two. But I c'n take you to Gloria's."

"Is the clientele the same?"

"What's that?"

"Do the same people go there?"

"Oh yes, mum. Was you meetin' someone there?" He grinned. "At Rector's I mean? 'Cause he'd be at Gloria's then."

"Take me to Gloria's," Lily said. She was annoyed at the man's forwardness but reflected, as the chaise rolled through the streets, that other women obviously sought the services of gigolos. It was good, in the interests of anonymity, to be only one of a number, and she must remember to simper and act as if the evening's adventure were all that could be on her mind.

Gloria's Club was housed in a once-lovely mansion, set back from the street and at some distance from its neighbors. There was a tangle of shrubbery about the entrance of the drive that she thought looked rather uncared for; then came trees, shadowy and mysterious, that marched to the wide steps where two torches leaped and sent sparks flying. The rig halted between the torches, and the driver accepted his fare with a touch of his cap; she stepped down, and instantly the rig was off in a clatter. A man in evening dress moved forward, bowed, and said, "Welcome to Gloria's, madam. Will you come this way?"

She followed him into a foyer, lit with candle lanterns and hung with lush draperies, where another man took her cloak. She could hear the inevitable sounds of musicians playing; feeling someone touch her arm, she glanced around. A third man smiled and said, "If madame will follow me, please—"

They went into a hallway, arched and dim, its walls lined with plants in huge Grecian vases. The man stopped. "Does madame wish to dance?"

"No," Lily said.

"Ahh." He smiled and indicated a wide door. "Shall we go this way then?" He opened the door and bowed her inside.

She was in a large room with low ceilings and hangings on every wall but no windows at all. There were small tables amid potted plants, and a constant hum of chatter and conversation arose from every side. The room seemed filled with couples and occasional foursomes, and the sounds of music were less apparent. The man led her to a table in the center of the room and held a chair for her, and she sat down, wondering what sort of a club she had blundered into. All about her people were talking and drinking, a few got up and disappeared, while others came to sit—where were they going and coming from?

A waiter appeared, asking if she would like wine and

she nodded. "Red, please." He wrote something on a pad and went away.

In a moment he was back with a note on a tray and handed it to her gravely. She took it with surprise. The note read, "I am René. May I join you?"

She looked at the waiter. He indicated a young man standing between two tables; he smiled at her, and she smiled back. He came forward and sat opposite her, as the waiter disappeared once more. "Thank you, madame," René said. "You are very beautiful."

He was young and suave, had long, black hair, a small neat moustache, and olive skin; he might be French, Italian, or Slav, though his English was unaccented. He might also be a farm boy with training and a new name. She gave him her best smile and did not pull away when he fondled her hand.

He said, "I have not seen you before at Gloria's."

Lily did her best to simper. "I've never been here."

"Ahh, that accounts for it. Do you live in Memphis?"

"No, New Orleans. I came here quite by chance."

He gave her a dazzling smile. "I hope it will not be your last, madame. Ah, what may I call you?"

"Greta."

"A beautiful name." He kissed her hand. "Would you care to order something?"

"I've ordered red wine. Please tell me, what is customary here?"

"In what way?"

Lily hid her exasperation. "Why do people come here to Gloria's?"

"Ahh, I see." He leaned forward conspiratorily. "They come to find love."

She blinked at him. This was a huge, ornate brothel

He said, "Women come here, madame—er—Greta, to seek lovers." His brows went up. "Am I being too blunt?"

"No, not at all." She glanced at the next table. A man very like René was whispering in an older woman's ear as she giggled. So it was a brothel for women. This was not at all like Rector's Club, and she realized the cabbie had been paid to deliver her—and any other unescorted woman—to this place. Gloria, whoever she was, was a keen businesswoman.

The waiter appeared with a bottle and two glasses. René said, "May I order something, Greta?"

She nodded and heard him order Château La Tour Blanche; he smiled at her as the waiter walked away. Leaning close he said, "The wine can be sent to a private room if you wish, Greta."

She saw the couple at the next table rise and thread their way out. In a moment a middle-aged woman came in and sat down, glancing about her as if she were looking for acquaintances.

René poured for her, and she sipped the red wine and gazed at him over the rim. "What are your charges, René?"

His brows rose, then he smiled again. "Five hundred dollars for the night, Greta."

"Plus the wine."

He shrugged. "Of course."

"Do you have an hourly rate?"

She thought he glanced at her sharply. "One hundred dollars."

She continued to sip, wondering if he was worth it. She had never paid a man for love, and the idea was somewhat shocking to her, but it was also provocative. René was a handsome devil, no doubt of it, and probably had an excellent opinion of himself. She wondered then if she might refuse him and find someone else. Probably. It would mean very little to him, but the next gigolo would be of the same stripe.

He answered her unspoken question. "If you prefer someone else—"

"No," she said very near to sarcasm, "one man is very like another."

"Oh, I assure you not!"

"And you will please me?"

He grasped her hand. "I will please you beyond measure, I promise! I will take you to heights—"

"Finish your wine," she said, unmoved. She would much have preferred the very different atmosphere of Rector's. This plush house was very businesslike, only a scratch under the varnished surface. It occurred to her to stand and leave at once; what René spoke of as love was really only raw sex with a stranger, performed under rigid rules and within specific times. One hundred dollars for an hour! What an enormous fee! Would any man pay that for the most beautiful courtesan in the world! Probably not.

But the older woman at the next table had surely been here many times before; she was even now conferring with a handsome young man who caressed her hand.

Lily filled her glass with the last of the bottle. If she left now, would she regret it when she returned to St. Louis? She might. She bent her head listening to René's whispers about the pleasures in store for her, and, despite herself, she found them provocative.

When she arose, it was to follow René as he made his way around the tables and to an open door at the far side

the room. There was a curving stairway, and he took
r hand as they moved up it together, then along a hall
a door slightly ajar. He pushed it open, and she entered
find herself in a bedchamber. A four-poster with pink
>unces and gauzy, tied-back material occupied the
ntral position; the carpet was thick, and the two
ndows were heavily draped.

At her elbow René said, "What is your wish, my
ve?"

She thought his expression dulled as she said, "I have
ne for only an hour."

"Then may I have the money now?"

She counted out a hundred dollars and put it into his
nd. She'd heard it said that men, too, usually paid in
lvance. She suddenly wondered if there was a Gloria.
aybe Gloria was a man late of the bordello trade and ran
is house as he had run all the others.

René asked if he might undress her, and she smiled.
)f course."

He was very slick, never asking where this hook was, or
at. He had done this many times before, she thought.
e slid the gown over her head, untied her chemise and
tticoats, then stripped her naked with an intake of
eath.

"My God, you are beautiful!"

She pirouetted for him, arms above her head, smiling
the expression that crossed his handsome face. Then
tore at his own clothes with more, she was sure, than
s usual ardor. She slid onto the bed, feeling nothing but
riosity; this was a diverting game with only pleasure as
s end result, something she had paid for.

There were colts and stallions, as she had seen many
mes in the field, and René was a stallion of surprising

proportions. He crawled onto the bed beside her, kissed her lingeringly, hands sliding into her dark hair, tangling it. His lips moved down her neck as she twisted; he kissed her nipples one by one and Lily laughed aloud, delighted with her bargain. He moved down to her toes and back up again, sending her into paroxysms of ecstasy as he tarried at the joining of her thighs. When he entered her, she arched her back and clung to him almost in desperation. What a marvelous bargain she had made!

And the hour was over too soon. She writhed on the bed, looked at him with eyes heavy-lidded as he quickly dressed and then came to smile down at her. "Goodbye, Greta—"

She stared at the ceiling when he was gone, feeling more alone than ever.

God, how alone!

CHAPTER THIRTY-FIVE

As Logan entered his office, Fraser said, "Sit down, sit down. I was about to have you paged."

"Anything serious?"

"I don't know. Something interesting, though. I've just had a wire from Arni Geber in Memphis. He's an energetic young man as you know probably better than I." Fraser shook a telegraph form. "He says Lily Berlanger is in town."

Arni Geber was their agent in Memphis. Logan shrugged. "What's interesting about that?"

"She's registered at a hotel under another name."

"Ahhh, that *is* interesting." Logan took the form and frowned at it. "He's positive, I suppose?"

"He knows her very well. At any rate he'd never wire us unless he was positive."

"Yes. What have you done about it?"

"I've wired him to look into it—with discretion. I'm curious about anything that Lily does."

"I agree. Do you want Clarence to go down there?"

"Let's see what Arni turns up first. She may be visiting her cousin Maybelle, for all we know."

"And dodging newspapermen."

"Yes, maybe." Fraser clipped a cigar and sat behind his desk; he pulled out a lower drawer and propped his foot up. "The police apparently have nothing new to tell us about Howard Paddock's death—"

Logan sat. "I've been thinking about it. *That* may have been self-defense. According to the newspapers, they dug six bullets out of the walls. Not one hit his attacker."

"Excitement."

"Yes. And the single witness is not very credible. Did she know Viktor Kory by sight?"

"I asked the police that question. Yes, she did."

Logan brushed at his hair absently. "I can't help wondering if Lily had anything to do with it. For the second time one of her partners has died—violently."

"The police are aware of that, I can assure you." He lit the cigar and puffed furiously. "It *is* suspicious that Paddock is killed just when Lily's out of town."

"Yes, and if Kory didn't do it, who did?"

Fraser grinned. "A good samaritan. Howard Paddock is going to burn in hell for a long time, in a brighter flame than some—but when Lily gets there she'll outdo him."

"Amen," Logan said.

It was a good bet, Fraser thought, that Viktor Kory had got well out of the area after the Collier shooting. Clarence Yates had supplied the police with a theory and a description of Kory, along with his Nestande Hotel address. Yates stated that Kory would be stupid to remain in St. Louis.

But, of course, he could not be sure that Lily had not hired someone else to deal with Logan.

However, there were no signs that she had. Logan went about his duties—with Louis Gualco close by—and the days passed quietly.

A week after Paddock's death there was a problem with *Freedom*; a paddle bucket had gotten smashed in a slight collision with a wharf boat as the steamboat was wooding north of St. Louis, and Logan hurried to oversee the situation, since *Freedom* was carrying explosives.

The incident was not serious, except that a fire had been started by the work crew and disaster narrowly averted by the prompt action of the boat's captain, who organized a bucket brigade and flooded the deck, ruining several barrels of gunpowder, a small price to pay.

When the bucket was repaired, Logan went on to St. Louis with *Freedom*; there some of the cargo was unloaded and sent by wagon train west toward Springfield and Fort Smith. Several dozen crates of shovels were to take its place. But the crates had not arrived on the levee, and *Freedom* was forced to remain an extra day.

It was the fourth such accident that *Freedom* had sustained, and, as Logan had coffee with several of the crew, he learned she was considered by some to be a hoodoo and a jinx.

"That's old wives' talk," said Captain Trotter when Logan mentioned it to him. "You know how rivermen go on about superstition. There's nothing wrong with *Freedom*. She's sound as a round rock."

"You don't believe in luck?"

"Oh, I believe in good luck all right. Luck's nice 'have, but I don't believe in jinx talk."

Logan busied himself along the levee during the day, talking to several of their captains; none had any trouble with Berlanger-Bryant to report. The wagons loaded with the crates of shovels arrived late in the day and were hauled aboard *Freedom* and placed along the main deck. *Freedom* was carrying knapsacks, kitchen utensils, canteens, lanterns, kerosene, a small number of kegs of gunpowder, along with a hundred crates of uniforms.

379

Most of the steamboat's crew was ashore, and when the work was finished, Captain Trotter dismissed the rest, saying they would get up steam in the morning. Rounding up the others would probably take half the night anyway. A guard was stationed and lanterns were hung along the sides and the stern, and Trotter himself went ashore to see his wife.

Logan went to the office to find that Doris had already left for home and that Fraser was preparing to go. "I've a wire from Geber in Memphis. He's got an interesting tale to tell. Lily evidently went there to see a firm of lawyers."

"Lawyers?"

Fraser consulted the telegraph form. "Lenz and Jarnoux. Ever hear of them?"

Logan shook his head. "Maybe something to do with a delayed shipment. She's being sued?"

"Yes, that's possible. But why would Lily go there herself?"

"Did she go alone?"

"No, a man named Burke was with her, but he was definitely not a lawyer. More like a bodyguard, Geber says. She put up at a hotel under another name, went to see this Lenz and Jarnoux, then spent a night at a private club that caters to women."

"What d'you mean caters to women?"

Fraser grinned. "It's a female cathouse. Very expensive."

"I'll be damned. She spent the night?"

"Well, most of it. The next day she stayed in the hotel and the day after she boarded a steamboat north. So if she's coming here she'll arrive tonight or tomorrow."

Logan was silent, wondering why Lily would consult lawyers in another city when she had her own staff

380

Ordinary legal affairs would be handled by the staff. What was so important that Lily made the trip herself? Was it because of the brothel?

He said, "Do you think Geber can find out from Lenz and Jarnoux what the connection with Lily is?"

"I doubt it. You know how lawyers are."

"Yes, I suppose so. What about a little bribery?"

Fraser smiled. "The enemy's tactics, eh? Do you think it might prove to be important to us?"

"God knows. But it is curious as hell. There's got to be a reason."

"All right. I'll get off a wire to Geber in the morning and tell him to do what he can. Any trouble with *Freedom?*"

"No, the shipment arrived, and she'll go downriver tomorrow."

"But you're worried about her?"

Logan shrugged. "Just some talk of a jinx." He smiled at Fraser's expression. "I'll go to the levee and have another look on the way home."

"Jinx," Fraser muttered, shrugging into his coat. "That's all we need."

Lily boarded the B & B steamboat *Belle Chasse* and was shown immediately to a suite. Supper was sent up to her, along with red wine, and she dined alone as the boat slowed upriver in the gathering darkness.

Jarnoux's refusal rankled—she was not used to refusals of any sort—but perhaps her presence and demand would have some effect. He might clamp a tighter control on the previous papers. She should have pursued another course with him. He might have been more amenable to womanly wiles. . . .

And she should have talked with him about his own firm. What would happen to the papers at his death, for instance? Who was heir to his company? She had no idea.

But perhaps she could insure complete privacy—it was an idea worth pursuing. She'd write to him, asking that all papers relating to her or her family be destroyed if the firm of Lenz and Jarnoux passed out of control. Such an order could be placed in the file, if he agreed.

After all, if he was dead what did he care?

CHAPTER THIRTY-SIX

Dutch woke before dawn, slid out of bed, and dressed, while Julia was struggling with the idea of awakening. He went downstairs and out to Front Street, wary of policemen. But he saw none. They certainly would be looking for a man traveling alone; by this time they would surely have an excellent description of him, and no doubt his name.

He bought a newspaper and took it back to the hotel. Paddock's murder was one of several mentioned; a stagecoach bandit had killed two men north of the city and robbed several prominent citizens, and a drunken Indian had shot a storekeeper. Dutch read the accounts with satisfaction; the events would spread out the police force, not a numerous organization in the quietest of times.

But most interesting of all, the account of Howard Paddock's murder did not mention a description of the attacker, nor the name Paddock had uttered—Dutch. Was it possible that the naked girl he'd seen had been so shocked that she had not remembered? Yes, it was possible.

Julia was dressed and ready to depart when he returned. They paid the bill and went down the street to the restaurant the clerk recommended. Breakfast over, they went to the nearest steamboat office and waited till it opened for business. Dutch bought two tickets on the *City of Ponca*, a packet boat bound for New Orleans, and they crossed the levee looking for her name.

Dutch found himself sweating, though the morning was cool. He was about to board a steamboat for the first time in more than twenty-five years. Old Jake's curse was in the front of his mind, but he could not turn back now. He had Julia to think about. She was more important than any old riverman's curse—deadly though it might be.

He thought she noticed his nervousness from her anxious glances, but she probably attributed it to worry about the police; he let her think so.

He saw several policemen strolling along Front Street, but they did not appear interested in him and Julia, and he hurried her along. The *City of Ponca* was tied up far down the levee; rousters were loading wooden crates from two wains drawn up by the stageplanks. A boat's officer examined their tickets and called for a boy, who took them to a stateroom.

How would old Jake's curse happen? He could not chase it from his mind. He would die under the paddle wheels, Jake had screamed at him. That meant he would fall overboard at some point, and the heavy paddles would pound him to pulp. When he went on deck with Julia, he stared at the massive bulk of the wheelhouse. He damned well did not want to die under those paddles!

And he would not if he ran ashore now—

Maybe if he stayed in the cabin the entire time; how would the curse get him out and over the side? Maybe by putting Julia in danger. He had to stay with Julia, not let her out of his sight. And if the curse happened, it damn

384

well happened. But he would fight it to the end. He would fight it with his last breath.

He would fight it for Julia.

That thought made him feel a little better. Having something important to fight for had always won him battles in the past, and this one was not going to be any different—except that his opponent was something unseen.

The *City of Ponca* was getting up steam; they would depart in an hour, one of the stewards told him. Julia was like a child, exclaiming over the pearl-handled cutlery in the main saloon, the Brussels carpeting, and the gilded chandeliers. She had never been near a steamboat before, and it was all new to her and tremendously exciting to think they would be pushing out into the huge river and chugging downstream very soon. She hugged Dutch's arm, asking endless questions, seldom waiting for answers. Someone began playing the grand piano, and a group gathered to sing; a waiter brought them coffee and cakes, and a glass of whiskey for Dutch . . . which Julia sipped.

Then the police arrived. Two men stationed themselves at the stageplanks, and two more sought out the chief clerk and demanded his passenger list.

Julia dropped against Dutch, face pale and hands trembling. He said, "Don't act like you going to own up. They don't know you from Adam's ox."

"I'm so scared, Dutch."

He patted her hand. "Act like you don't care."

"Tell me about where we're going. What's the name of t—?"

"Chadwick."

"Yes. What's our house like?"

385

He got out a cigar. "It ain't all that much right now, but I going to fix it up a mite. It got a good roof and it's built good, but it needs paint, a little work on the floor, probably some curtains—"

"And a barn?"

"Got a good barn. Two corrals, some cribs and sheds, four damn good mules and five horses, a few chickens—"

The police came into the saloon and looked around, two big men with billy clubs stuck in their belts. The chief clerk was a big stooped man with an eyeshade and a pipe. He followed the police as they walked the length of the saloon, staring at everyone.

They stopped at Dutch's table and frowned at him. One said, "What's your name, mister?"

"Miller," Dutch said. "Enos Miller." He got out his glasses, put them on and squinted at the officers. "Oh, you policemen!"

Both men grunted. They moved on, and Dutch turned to Julia, "What's policemen doin' here?"

Julia mumbled an answer, and Dutch gripped her hand hard. He took off the glasses, winked at her, and sipped the whiskey. Julia stifled a giggle.

The steamboat backed into the stream, reversed engines as bells clanged, and started downriver. Dutch walked the promenade with Julia and watched the city recede, keeping one eye on the wheelhouse.

They had made it. The police were ashore and all danger was past—but for the curse.

Julia said, "Dutch, you're still edgy—"

"I didn't know it showed."

"Do you think they'll wire ahead?"

He shook his head. "No, we got past 'em all right. They

386

won't bother us no more."

She waited till they had walked to the foredeck, when no one was near. "You want to tell me what happened, Dutch? Why were the police looking for us? It wasn't just because of Rothmuller, was it?"

He didn't meet her eyes. "No, it wasn't."

She waited without speaking.

He looked at her, and after a moment he thrust both hands into his pockets. "It was because of a man named Howard Paddock."

That astonished her. "Didn't I read about him in the newspaper?"

He nodded. "I went to his house. He shot at me, and I killed him."

She stared, one hand to her cheek. "Did you know him?"

"Long time. He was a thief."

"The papers said he was a partner—"

"I know what the papers say. But he was a thief all right, and he set a man on Logan one time. Tried t'kill him. No tellin' if he'd do it again. That's why I went t'see him."

"To kill him?"

Dutch took a breath. She would be digging up damned big potatoes in a minute. "I had it in mind, yes." He looked at her. "But I dunno if I would or not when I got there. Except that Paddock pulled a pistol when he seen me and started shooting. I only hit 'em once."

She was silent, biting her lip.

He said, "You do a lot of things when a man starts shootin' at you."

"I don't blame you, Dutch! Not for that."

"For what then?"

She moved into his arms. "Not for anything." She took several long breaths. "You did what you had to do—"

He squeezed her and kissed her cheek. "It's all over now."

"But won't they keep looking for you?"

He chuckled. "Let 'em look. We going to be a far piece in a day'r two. They ain't going to come snooping by every farm in three states. Not for Howard Paddock's killer."

They had supper, walked the deck again, and retired to the stateroom. They were in bed before Julia asked, "Dutch, how did you come to know a man like Mr. Paddock?"

"It's a long story."

"We've got time."

"You a damn persistent woman, ain't you?"

She snuggled close to him. "Curious, I guess. Was it when you were on the river?"

"Yes. Paddock wasn't always a big, important man. He usta be just a trader. I traded him stuff."

"What kind of stuff?"

He sighed. "I usta buy goods lower down on the river and sell 'em to him in Cairo, that's all."

"Why couldn't he buy the goods himself in the first place?"

He patted her rump. "He did. But I brung him stuff too, so he bought it. You know cotton sells for different prices up and down the river, huh?"

"Oh. You sold him cotton?"

"Very seldom," he said. "Go to sleep."

She was quiet for a long time. In a very low voice she said, "Dutch—?"

"What?"

"You weren't just a riverman, were you?"

"Yes, I was. Just an ordinary riverman."

"I don't think so."

"Why not?"

"I don't think you were an *ordinary* anything."

"Go to sleep."

She was silent for a moment. "There's more, isn't there?"

He grunted.

"Will you tell me sometime?"

"One of these days."

"Promise?"

"Go to sleep."

"Promise?"

He sighed again. "I promise."

By the time the steamboat nudged into the Chadwick landing, Dutch had talked himself into a fatalistic state. He had slept very little during the trip, and though he kept his nerves under tight control, he was easily irritated and constantly watchful.

His preoccupation was something new to Julia; she did not understand it, and she could not draw it out of him. She became certain after a while that it concerned Chadwick. The closer they got, the more edgy Dutch seemed to become. Perhaps there was someone in the town—or something about the town—that he feared, even though she could not imagine Dutch afraid of anything. It was an enigma. It was something she had to put up with for the time being. When they reached Chadwick she would see what it was.

As the boat's prow pushed into the mud at the bank,

the planks were hauled out and Dutch stood on the main deck, staring at the paddle wheels that still turned slowly, churning up the brown water. The mate shouted at him to get moving. "You all the only passengers gettin' off, mister."

Dutch turned and looked at him, curled his fists and smiled. He took a step, then halted. Let the man yell, what did he care?

Julia said, "What is it, Dutch?"

Dutch picked up their bags and walked across the planks to solid ground. The mate swore at him and ordered the planks in, and the *City of Ponca* backed, paddles threshing.

He stared at them. Old Jake's curse hadn't happened! The old blowhard's words had been empty, no more important than a child's! He'd been a fool to believe! All the years he'd stayed ashore—and the curse was nothing. He watched the steamboat move into the channel and glide away, gray smoke trailing from the twin chimneys. All these years he'd stayed off the river. He looked at Julia and smiled; she had a peculiar expression on her face, he thought. He wondered suddenly, if he'd stayed on the river, would he have lived? His life then had been violent, and so many of his cronies and the men he'd known had died, one way or another, in fights or accidents or drunken orgies. He might have gone that way . . . Maybe old Jake had done him a great favor, after all.

Because now he had Julia.

She said, "That's the first time I've seen you smile since St. Louis."

"Steamboats make me nervous."

She looked after it, almost gone now around the far

390

bend. "So it was the steamboat!"

"The damn things keep blowin' up," Dutch said. He took her arm, "Come on. They ain't any rigs out here. We got to walk into town."

CHAPTER THIRTY-SEVEN

Lily was in an excellent mood when the steamboat reached St. Louis. She sat in her suite, a bottle of red wine on the table, along with the remains of a meal; she was planning for the future. Now that Howard Paddock was gone, she had no partners, was entirely free to act as she pleased. Of course, there was Sam Beckhart, who would expect his cut of the government business he generated, but that was of no importance; his fees would only be added to the costs.

She would now truly become queen of the river. In the next year she would come into her own, the most important figure in the region, the single richest, most powerful owner along the entire Mississippi!

Despite the gradually increasing talk of a war between the states, the future looked very bright. Even if the Mississippi were blocked, half Northern and half Southern, there was still the upper river, as well as the Missouri and the Ohio. According to the experts, the Ohio would never be obstructed by war, but would become a great highway by means of which she would amass further riches. Let war come. What a boon it would be!

She was finishing the wine, as a steward came to the door to announce that St. Louis was in sight. She gave him orders to find her a carriage when they came in and donned a cloak to go out to the promenade.

It was a balmy night and a round, pale moon was high in the dark sky. She loosened the cloak and clutched the guards as the boat trembled with reduced speed. The beat of the huge paddles changed its tune, and the boat curved in toward the far-off levee. She gazed at the city, a jungle of glimmering lights and columns of foggy smoke rising and layering. As they came close, she saw the line of steamboats, the familiar levee scene, and the sounds came across the water, men shouting and wheels grating on the stones. A hundred lanterns flickered, spreading their tiny pools of yellow glow through which men and wagons moved.

The steamboat slowed to a crawl, inching its way in, waves slapped the sides, and it began to roll slightly, the forward way gone. It eased into a berth between two other boats and shuddered as the prow rode up on the levee, and men jumped ashore to fasten the lines.

A hubbub quickly arose as roustabouts hauled out the planks and swarmed aboard to attack the cargo; passengers fled down the main companionway with boxes and valises, shouting to those on shore, but Lily stood silent, watching. She felt disdain for the frantic ants, hurrying with their bandboxes and choked suitcases, each rushing to beat the other to a hired rig. The steward would come to her stateroom in a bit to announce that her carriage was waiting below, and she would go out sedately, as befitted someone of her station, a boy following with her bags.

She turned to go back inside, when she heard the jingle of engine bells and glanced at the next boat. It was moving slowly, backing bells clanging, pushing out into the stream. She paused to watch as rousters cheered from the main deck and a parting cannon boomed.

The boat swung into the river, paused and reversed engines, then came moving ponderously past, paddles clunking and churning the dark water.

Every steamboat leaving for its destination enriched somebody; this was not a Berlanger-Bryant boat—she must buy more boats—and she glanced across the empty space to the next boat. It was strung with lanterns, almost as bright as day, and she frowned as she stared at the pilothouse. What did that name mean to her? She'd heard it recently in some connection—

A man came along the hurricane deck and paused to look over the guards to the water. He was a big, well-dressed man, wearing a beaver hat.

Lily gasped and clutched the rail with both hands. The man was Logan Jeffries! There could be no doubt. It was he!

She stared at him, then turned and went inside to the stateroom and grabbed up her small reticule. Clutching the cloak tight about her, she ran the length of the saloon, down the companionway, and across the stage-planks to the levee. Someone called her name, but she ignored the voice.

She hurried along the levee to the stern-wheeler and went across the single plank to the main deck. A man materialized from the dark, "Here, you—" He saw the form was a woman and halted, "What you want, Miss?"

"Mr. Jeffries," she said. She half ran to the companionway, and the man said nothing. At the top she looked back and saw him staring up at her.

It was a small boat, its crates and boxes stacked neatly, taking up every available inch of space. There were boxes on the boiler desk, lashed down and painted with names and numbers. She halted, dug into her reticule, and pulled out the pearl-handled revolver she practiced with.

Where was Logan?

The deck was shadowy, despite the many lanterns that were hung along the sides. She had seen him on the hurricane deck, and there was a ladder. She ran to it and climbed up. She had one enemy in the world, and he was here, close by. With Logan gone she would have no other fears; she would hold sway over the river. . . . There was no one on the hurricane deck.

The boat had no texas, and there was no one in the dark pilothouse.

She looked over the side, as she had seen Logan do. A moving shadow on the main deck caught her eye. Running to the ladder, she went down—and saw him.

He saw her at almost the same instant. She heard him say, "Lily!"

She pointed the revolver and fired.

Logan was annoyed that Captain Trotter had allowed the crew and officers to go ashore; it would have been better had an officer slept aboard, since *Freedom* was talked of as a jinx boat. Only two watchmen were aboard as guards, and one was asleep when he came from the office after talking to Fraser.

"They ain't any danger, Mr. Jeffries," the watchman said, "we carrying damn little gunpowder and nothin' else that'll explode."

"Show me the powder."

The man picked up a bull's-eye lantern and led the way aft. The dozen kegs of powder were carefully stacked between crates of uniforms near the after rail, far from the fireboxes. There was no chance that a spark could reach them, and he nodded with satisfaction as the man held the lantern high.

"All right, Fred. Go back to your post."

"Yes sir."

Logan moved along the stern, gazing out over the river. A steamboat was coming in to the levee just to his left, one boat over, lights blazing on the cabin deck. He would have to speak to Captain Trotter before *Freedom* left for downriver. Even though the danger was at a minimum, it was not a good idea to allow laxness.

The steamboat to his immediate left was getting ready to shove off, and he watched the passengers waving and visitors hurrying ashore as the boys yelled. He climbed to the hurricane deck to take one last look around. For some reason he felt a curious restlessness that could not be explained . . . a feeling of portentous events. Maybe he was missing something in his tour; maybe Fred had not told him everything about the cargo. After all, Fred was only putting in hours for a pay envelope. It might be a good idea to go back and take another look at the gunpowder barrels.

But topside everything was in order; his closest inspection could turn up nothing out of place. He took a minute to watch the newly arrived boat slowly creep in to the levee and make fast. As he walked forward, he saw Louis Gualco move the buggy along the levee in order to stay clear of the debarking passengers and of the half-dozen wagons that were congregating to load cargo. The usual controlled uproar began to take place. Teamsters clamored for attention, the mate bawled, and passengers scuttled off across the levee in different directions.

The boat next to *Freedom* fired a parting cannon and

396

moved out into the stream.

Logan strolled aft on the far side of the boat, making sure all the lanterns were lit and made fast and the pilothouse closed tight. He climbed down to the main deck to have another look at the fireboxes. He was being an old woman, wasn't he? The idea of a jinx had probably got under his ribs, and he wanted to prove to himself there was nothing to it. His uneasy feelings were upsetting him unnecessarily.

The gunpowder barrels seemed . . . He looked up as a shadow moved on the far side of the deck. Someone had just climbed down from the hurricane deck. Damned curious!

It was a woman!

He thought at first it must be Doris come to look for him. It astounded him that Doris would—it was not Doris!

The woman stepped toward him, and he saw her clearly in the mealy lantern light. It was Lily!

It was Lily, and she had a pistol!

Astonished, he said, "Lily!"

She raised the pistol and fired. All in one quick motion.

He heard the shot crack past and strike a lantern, shattering it to bits. He grabbed at the Navy in his belt and half drew it—but how could he shoot her? He turned and ran aft.

She fired three times, as fast as she could work the hammer, and the bullets sprayed, one shattering another lantern. He heard her angry scream—and a whoosh of flame sprang up beside him. The hot lantern oil spattered over the uniform crates and several caught fire!

Lily shouted something and fired again. The bullet

smashed wood nearby, and he heard the sounds of her feet running along the deck toward him. She fired again, smashing a stern lantern.

She was screaming his name, and he glanced back to see that her white face had become a mask of rage. Then the flames came between them. He saw with horror that they were enveloping the kegs of powder. One would set off the next—

He ran to the stern and dived into the dark water.

With powerful strokes he swam away from the boat. His clothes seemed as heavy as lead, and he appeared to make scant progress. Then suddenly he was at the stern of another boat, grabbing at the rudderpost. He pulled himself to the surface and looked back.

He was aware of wild sounds, clanging bells, shouts, and the roar of flames.

At that instant *Freedom* exploded.

Logan ducked under the water and up again. The explosion was deafening. The entire boat lifted from the water and broke in two; the after half disintegrated! A rumbling sound filled the air—then the shock wave hit him and slammed him against the boat. He managed to cushion his head. The water heaved him up, a huge wave rocked the steamboat, and he grabbed the bottom rail of the after guard and pulled himself onto the deck.

When he looked around, most of *Freedom* had gone. The foredecks were down in the water, blazing fiercely but the place where he and Lily had stood was only heaving water, cluttered with bits and pieces of debris, more of which rained down. A huge column of black smoke roiled and tumbled, spreading out over the river, obliterating the round moon.

The fire had lighted the gunpowder. Steamboat and

Lily were blasted into nothingness.

Logan lay flat on the deck, breathing hard, the stench of smoke in his nostrils. He thought of Andrea. She had been avenged.

EPILOGUE

Logan received a letter from Memphis, from the law firm of Lenz and Jarnoux; it was signed by Mr. Jarnoux himself.

Mr. Jarnoux had learned from the newspapers of Mrs. Berlanger's tragic death, and his own investigation had proved the story to be true. He had also discovered that Mr. Jeffries' wife, Andrea, had died.

> *I apologize for not writing you sooner, Mr. Jeffries, but I was led to believe that Andrea was alive. However, this is to inform you that as Andrea's husband you will inherit her share of the Berlanger estate, which I am informed is considerable.*

It was indeed very considerable.